SOLSTICE

Also by David Hewson

Semana Santa
Epiphany

SOLSTICE

DAVID HEWSON

WARNER BOOKS

A Time Warner Company

Warner Books, Inc., 1271 Avenue of the Americas,
New York, NY 10020
Visit our Web site at http://warnerbooks.com

W A Time Warner Company

Printed in the United States of America
First Printing: July 1999
10 9 8 7 6 5 4 3 2 1

Library of Congress Cataloging-in-Publication Data

Hewson, David.
    Solstice / David Hewson.
        p.   cm.
      ISBN 0-446-52449-2
      I. Title.
    PS3558.E844S55   1999
    813'.54—dc21   98-47240
                                                              CIP

This is the excellent foppery of the world: that when we are sick in fortune—often the surfeit of our own behaviour—we make guilty of our disasters the sun, the moon, and stars, as if we were villains by necessity, fools by heavenly compulsion, knaves, thieves, and treachers by spherical predominance, drunkards, liars, and adulterers by an enforced obedience of planetary influence . . . an admirable evasion of whoremaster man, to lay his goatish disposition on the charge of a star!

EDMUND, *KING LEAR*, ACT 1, SCENE 2

SOLSTICE

DAY ONE

JUNE 19

CATCH A FALLING STAR

1
Blood

Central Siberia, 37,000 feet, 0417 UTC

British Pacific Flight 172 had left Tokyo for London Heathrow right on schedule, every one of its 332 seats occupied, every ounce of weight, every moment of balance accurately calculated. The route was standard these days: no more long, circuitous detours to avoid the Soviet Union, no more boring stopovers in Anchorage. Just a sharp hook to the west after takeoff, on to Vladivostok, and then a dead straight line along the great circle, coming down over Finland into Britain over the North Sea.

This was a two-man operation: one captain, one first officer, both watching the LCD screens of the new all-digital flight panel and relying, for the most part, on the autopilot to guide the plane's movements.

Ian Seabright didn't like to admit it to anyone, particularly the company's inquisitive human resources staff, but these days flying just plain bored him. It had been different when he first got into the game, straight from the RAF, in the seventies. Then you used your brain, sometimes your muscle, too. Today you just minded the computer, watching the dials flash and alter on some screen, making sure the silicon pilot didn't do anything wrong.

He was fifty-three, in reasonable health, a little overweight from all those long-haul stops in hotels where the food was free

and there was precious little else to do. The first officer was
Jimmy Mulligan, a bright, red-haired Irishman who'd worked
his way onto the flight deck the hard way, through a private
pilot's license and then a low-paying gig as a flight instructor in
the States. Seabright liked Mulligan. The man was smart, polite, hardworking. And yet, at just pushing thirty, he was already starting to look bored. Seabright, only two years from
retirement, didn't envy him—with nothing to look forward to
but this tedious round of routine. The idea of all those wasted
hours in the cockpit appalled him.

Seabright looked at the moving map on the GPS. They were
nine hours out now, cruising in still air at 37,000 feet in the
middle of nowhere with the weather looking fine and sunny all
the way, every inch of the route in daylight, straight into
Heathrow. Out of the window some godforsaken part of Russia
passed by slowly, even with a ground speed of 530 knots. A
piece of nothingness in western Siberia, he guessed.

"You going to marry that girl, Jimmy?"

The Irishman smiled. "You mean Ali?"

"I believe that was the young lady you seemed to be proposing to last night."

Mulligan thought about it. "You think she took it that way?"

Seabright closed his eyes and thought: They can fill these
damn things with all the computers they want, but this little
ritual won't ever go away. You just coop up a crew in some foreign hotel, leave them there for three days, and see what happens.

"She's sweet, all right," Mulligan said. "A guy could do a lot
worse."

"A *lot* worse," Seabright agreed.

"Which makes a guy think, well, maybe he could do a lot
better?"

Seabright stared at Mulligan and wondered why this short,
meaningless exchange sparked a little flame of anger inside
him. It all just comes around, he thought. There are things you
can never tell another man. You just have to wait, let him discover it all for himself, then look him in the eye and say: Yes,

me too. The casual drift from bed-hopping first officer to married (happily or otherwise) captain was one such journey.

"Looks like we've got company," Mulligan said, staring out over the starboard wing. Seabright followed his gaze. A good ten miles off, on a parallel course tracking the same flight level, was a white 747 with imperceptible markings on the side. He dialed up the inflight frequency and put out a call. There was no reply.

"Bastards," Mulligan muttered, reaching for a pair of pocket binoculars in the seat pocket. Then he focused on the distant shape and let out a low, sweeping whistle.

"Jimmy?"

The first officer took away the glasses from his face. "Sir, wasn't there something in the paper about a summit in Tokyo? Lots of VIPs expected to be flying out?"

"Why do you think we're packing them into every square inch we've got right now? There was a world summit. Ended yesterday."

"Well," Mulligan replied, passing over the binoculars, "it looks like we've got the American President himself on our wing. Can't expect those chaps to talk to the likes of us, now, can you?"

Seabright looked at the long white shape of Air Force One through the glasses. This was a new one for the book.

"I think you're right there. . . ."

Then he snatched the instrument away from his face in a rapid involuntary physical jerk, feeling, for a moment, as if his upper torso were in spasm. The pain was sudden, sharp, and intense. And he wasn't alone. Next to him Mulligan was moaning. He had his hand to his forehead, eyes closed.

"You okay, Jimmy?" This was unlike him. Mulligan never swore, never complained about anything. The first officer rubbed his head for a moment or two, then unclenched his eyes and looked at Seabright. His eyes were more than a little pink, unfocused, watery too.

"Damn headache," Mulligan complained. "Came straight on me like that. Just my turn to get one, I guess."

"Sure."

Seabright knew he had the makings of one himself. And the tension of the sudden muscle spasm had not gone away entirely either. His gaze shifted to the display panel. "Looks like you've got an amber alert light on the main gear, Jimmy. Nothing to worry about, I'm sure, but take a look."

"Sir . . . ow!"

And the strange thing was, Seabright felt it too. A sharp, stabbing pain in the right temple, so hard it made him wince, just like Mulligan. Then it went away as quickly as it came, leaving a dull throb behind.

"What the hell was that?"

Seabright wiped his forehead, felt the sweat there, scanned the panel as he ran through the possibilities.

"You check the cabin pressure too, Jimmy. I got that pain as well and I don't think we're both imagining it."

They scrutinized the dials, went through the routines they knew by heart, and confirmed the pressure, stable at the equivalent of 6,000 feet.

"You think it could have dropped, just momentarily, without us noticing it?"

Mulligan's face was close to the color of his hair, and Ian Seabright felt, deep in his gut, something hard and cold and angry start to knot there and wait for him to recognize it.

"No," he replied. "That's just not possible."

"I can pull out a record of the pressure if you like. See if it took a sudden drop."

Seabright nodded, just for something to do, knowing this really wasn't the cause of it, knowing the pressurization system was behaving just as it should.

Mulligan punched away at the control deck, watched the displays shift and change on the color LCD screen. When he finished, he only looked more baffled. "Maybe it was one of those things," he said, wanting to take back the words the moment he said them.

Seabright nodded and neither of them needed to say it, the phrases just passed unspoken between them, the old pilot's doggerel they drilled into you year after year. All those half-smart, half-true little maxims ran through both men's heads at that moment . . . that there really is no limit to how bad things can get, and how you shouldn't believe in miracles, you should *rely* on them. And, in particular this one: When in doubt, predict that the trend will continue.

They sat in silence, in trepidation, and then they heard the security key turn in the cabin door and saw Ali Fitzgerald walk through, her face white and pale. The very appearance of her made the knot in Seabright's stomach turn on itself once more until this tangle of pain in his gut was rock-hard, icy and immobile.

"We've got a medical out there," she said, and Seabright could see how close she was to real panic. "It's a bad one, sir, and I already asked. There's not a doctor on the plane."

Seabright stared hard at his first officer, checked the panel and made sure nothing else was blinking there except the one errant amber light on the main gear.

"You okay on your own, Jimmy? Don't just say yes. Think about this. I don't want more than one emergency on my ship."

Mulligan thought before he answered; he knew the old man would demand that.

"I'll be fine. Best leave the door unlocked anyway."

"Yes," Seabright said, then unstrapped the shoulder harness, pulled himself out of the left-hand seat, and followed the stewardess to the door, held it half-closed, not letting her through.

"Sir?" She looked into his face, not understanding, not far from the edge, he thought, not far at all.

"Ali," he said, as quietly, as gently as he could "Your shirt. You need to change it. You need to put a jacket on. Something. You can't go back through the cabin like that."

She looked at herself, at the broad red bloodstain that marked the entire front of her white blouse, down onto her skirt, marked her skin too, around her neck, where she'd held the man's head, trying to do something, trying to do anything.

"No, sir," she said, then waited for him to open the door, stepped behind the bulkhead that separated them from the first-class cabin, and pulled out a clothes carrier. It happened so quickly he scarcely had time to tear his eyes away. She tore off the blouse, then the skirt, washed her neck and forearms rapidly with a damp Kleenex and a bottle of Malvern water, and put on the dirty uniform she was carrying back from the outward journey.

"He's in business, sir. We've got the medical kit."

"Good," Seabright answered, and watched her step in front of him, turn in to the first-class cabin, smooth down her dress, start to do her job.

He followed her down the aisle, felt the eyes on him, the tension in the seats, and thought to himself that Jimmy Mulligan could do a lot worse. A hell of a lot worse if he wanted to.

2
Sunrise

La Finca, 0308 UTC

It was pushing four in the morning in the white-walled bed-room-cum-office on the first floor of the Mallorcan mansion. Somewhere else in the great airy country house people were beginning to stir. The computer screen burned a luminescent gray. The whispery haze of dawn came in through the window. It was a little cold just then, but the latent heat of the previous day, so hot it left him thinking he had never escaped Morocco, made the room smell damp.

"Michael?"

Sara Wong looked at Lieberman from the screen, her picture jerking a little with the slow frame rate, but not so much that he couldn't see something was going on there, something to do with concern and affection and other emotions he preferred not to think about too directly.

For a while, there had been little in his thoughts except this serene Chinese face gazing back at him from the other side of the world. Then the great domestic earthquake had struck, and the walls came tumbling down around their lives.

"We ought to get on with this," she said, her voice a little tinny down the line. "NASA or somebody else is paying a fortune for this direct satellite uplink. They may get a little cross if they find we're just staring at each other like a couple of tongue-tied kids."

"Yeah," Lieberman said, grinning. "This is a hell of a long way to come to find your ex-wife staring back at you from the PC."

"Strange for me too," she said. "Now we've got that out of the way, can we get on to something real?"

Lieberman lazily ran his fingers over his head, twisting his thick black curly hair.

"I told you," Sara said from the screen. "So many times. One day it will just fall out."

He blinked, uncomprehending, then jerked his hand away from his scalp like a guilty kid. Sara had a way of mothering you, even after all these years separated.

"So what time is it in Lone Wolf?" he asked.

She looked really nice tonight. Just a plain white shirt, two buttons open at the neck, and her skin a pleasant shade of brown on the screen.

"You can count, Michael. You know what time it is."

"Let me guess. Nine hours back from this bustling corner of civilization makes it . . . six fifty-two in California."

She leaned forward, touched something on the keyboard that was out of sight of the camera perched on top of her monitor, and two analog clocks appeared on his screen, one marked Lone Wolf Observatory, Los Altos, Northern California, the other Mallorca, off the northeastern Mediterranean coast of Spain, the first with the hands at 6:54 P.M., the second nine hours later.

"So." She smiled. "Tell me about the people. How are they?"

"Okay. Not that we've talked much."

"You know anyone?"

He shook his head, and six thousand miles away in Lone Wolf Observatory, Sara Wong watched the intelligent tanned face move in the faint gray light of the monitor. Michael had always reminded her of some myopic bird of prey, trying to focus on the horizon, wondering whether to stretch his wings and fly or just stay motionless on the tree, doubtful if he could make the kill if he found it.

"Only one, and that's by reputation alone. The show's being run by that Cambridge guy, Bennett."

"Simon Bennett?" She looked excited. "He did the paper on planetary tides and . . . what was it? Heliocentric syzygies."

"Yeah. I'd do that too if I thought I could pronounce it after a few drinks."

Sara frowned. "That's an educated attitude."

"Sorry." He did his best to look contrite.

"And the rest?" she asked.

"They seem friendly enough."

"Work on it, Michael. You could use some contacts."

"Thanks. I'll bear that in mind. Your tan looks great."

He meant that. He really did.

"Yours too. Not that sunbathing is recommended these days."

He stopped for a moment, wondered whether to say it, did anyway. "It's still that hot there, huh?"

She nodded, and, for once, he couldn't read her expression.

"Been pushing a hundred for three weeks now. You need to keep out of it. There's people getting burned, talk of a skin cancer scare. The TV people say maybe it's El Niño, or just some kind of new level of instability in the weather system. Or maybe this little galactic ballet that's on the way. I don't know. The *National Enquirer* certainly seems to be making hay with it. Myself, I think we should be taking it more seriously."

"Yeah."

"And there?"

He really didn't know how to answer that one. "Be fair. I only just turned up."

"Right," she said, and he could almost imagine there was something hard and grim in her voice, a wisp of anger because of the way he was avoiding the question. "But what's it like *now*, Michael?"

"It falls at night. You'd expect that. But from the little I've seen and what people tell me, during the day it's hot, dry, and sunny with no letup. I don't smoke anymore, you'll be glad to hear that. But if I did I wouldn't dream of lighting up around here. One match out that window and this whole damn island would be on fire. It's like walking on tinder. Just dry grass, dead trees, people wondering when the rain's going to come and clear the dust from their throats. There are pictures of this place when it was a farm. It should be green and fertile. Instead, it's just dry and desiccated."

They were both silent for a while, letting NASA clock up some expensive dead time on the satellite uplink.

"You're going out tonight," he said, wanting to lighten this a little. "You've got that nice clean look about you I recognize. It says, 'The hell with all this, I'm going to go out, I'm going to get taken to some nice, expensive restaurant somewhere and order lobster tails and Chardonnay.' Am I right?"

She smiled a little; that was enough.

"Okay. You're right."

"With him?"

"Him?"

"You know. Do we need the water torture right now? Do I have to spit out the syllables?"

"You mean 'him' as in 'my husband'?"

"Present husband. I have to correct you there."

"Present and only husband."

"Yeah. Some guy."

She wasn't interested in this, she never was. Her mind was elsewhere. It was so obvious in her round, open face, and the way those big almond-shaped eyes kept staring at him—with some sadness, some worry he didn't want to see.

"Michael, talk to me. Please. We lost the satellite links through to Kyoto twice this afternoon. The solar flares got really bad and they just went down with all the damn electromagnetic activity. Not for long. Just a few seconds."

"How bad?" he sighed.

"It put out some entire power systems, complete domestic and industrial grids down. Some suburbs in Tokyo. Australia a couple of places. Some telecommunications links went out too. Shut the Tokyo Stock Exchange for forty minutes, killed most of the high-speed data lines between some of the main Asian hubs and the West Coast. Plus they closed the airport in Hong Kong for three hours because they had no air-traffic control.

Some big magnetic wipeout, they think, but my guess is they
don't really know. People are too busy fixing things to find out
what really happened. I guess that's understandable. And people are mad too. It got close to a full-scale riot in Tokyo when
they closed down the Nikkei. On the TV there are these guys
in shirtsleeves in the street screaming at each other like they
could kill someone."

He could picture this. He could see this angry scene in his
head, and match it against all the others he'd seen since this
particular heat wave began. This was the age of the frayed temper. Sometimes it felt as if the heat were just peeling off some
outside layer of humanity from your body and letting the sky
take a long look at the beast that lived underneath.

"People get mad in cities these days, Sara," he said, and
hoped he sounded convincing. "Hell, they always did. What's
new? How long did the burst last?"

"Peaked at nine seconds or so. That's all, and look what it
did. You believe that?"

The day was getting brighter by the second. It beckoned him.

"We're scientists, Sara. It's our job to accept anything that
happens provided there's some proof it exists. Are these emissions just magnetic or are you seeing X-ray activity too?"

She stared at him, looking a little blank. "Search me,
Michael. We're still waiting on the data. Like I said, most of the
links were down and these things don't just come back up
again like a dog begging for a bone, not after they get hit that
bad. Once we get it, once it's been through analysis, we'll post
it. You take a look. See if it makes sense to you."

"Yeah. You bet. Some coincidence, huh? You and me getting
lumped together on the same job like this? I'm really glad it
happened."

Sara was scared, he thought, and even if he didn't have the
words to chase away the demons, he could just try a little old-
fashioned courtesy.

"I guess this is our field, Michael, and it's a pretty specialized
one. Who else are they going to drum up?"

Sara felt flushed, wondered if he was going to embarrass
them both. But when she looked he was back running his fin-

gers through his hair again, not thinking about her at all, or even noticing the impatient way she was watching him from the monitor.

"True," he said. "It's nice to be wanted. Why don't you go eat, Wong girl? You look hungry. Jesus, you look starving."

Her face came back at him from the monitor, so open, so truthful, and she didn't need to point out how very wrong he was.

"You think anyone knows what's going on here, Michael? All this climate change, all this unpredictability. Why don't these things fit the way they should? Why are we going through this stuff now? Not in two years' time when this solar cycle is supposed to peak? What the hell's happening?"

"Sara," he said, and wished his voice didn't sound so grown-up, "nature's happening, and we're just baffled because we're too dumb to understand it. There's no evidence this is anything other than the usual chaos we have to deal with the more we understand what's going on around us. What bugs us is that it's out of our control. This isn't global warming. We don't just persuade Gillette to take CFCs out of their shaving cream, pay the Chinese to burn gas, and then wait for the ozone hole to close. All that kind of stuff is just a kid's game here. We're dealing with the sun, and whatever it's planning to do, it will do. I know some people find it hard to believe there can be anything in this universe that human beings don't control, but the sun is one of them. We don't write these rules, we never did, and if something out there feels like changing them from time to time, then that's its business."

Mistake, he thought immediately, as soon as he saw the heightened fear in her face.

"B-but don't get me wrong," he stuttered. "There's nothing here that suggests we're seeing more than a few climate changes that have been going on unnoticed for centuries. The thing that's changed is that we can kid ourselves we understand a little more this time around. Welcome to the circus."

"Yeah, I guess you're right," she said, not sounding convinced. "Take care, Michael," she added, sighing. She blew him a kiss down the screen, her big almond eyes examining him in a way he didn't even begin to want to think about.

"You too, Sara." He watched the video panel collapse back into the monitor, leave a soft gray blankness in its wake.

Lieberman got up from the desk and walked over to the window. Out to the east dawn was marching in, good and yellow, none of the pretty colors associated with smog and pollution, just plain old sunlight, which was (he guessed; no one had actually said as much) one of the reasons the project had chosen La Finca in the first place. All this isolation helped when you wanted to measure the stuff that poured from the heavens: There was no pollution, no radio interference, no ground lighting to ruin the night sky. Just pure data, and whatever else the heavens wanted to rain down on you.

Nice, he thought, and wished to God he could shake that last picture of Sara out of his head. She looked unhappy, scared, which wasn't like her. It wasn't like anyone who worked in Lone Wolf, which—until he got fired for taking a drunken poke at Sam Smith, the director, at that Christmas party three short years before—had been as close to paradise as he was ever likely to find.

"Work," Michael Lieberman said quietly into the room. Then he buried himself in the pile of reports sitting on the computer.

3

Turbulence

Central Siberia, 0421 UTC

The man was about his own age, Seabright reckoned, and probably out of condition. He was marginally overweight, with a round, flabby face, receding hairline, and bright blue staring eyes. They'd reclined the seat in business as much as they could, let him lie back, bleeding all the time. It was everywhere, on his jacket, on the seat, and, most of all, on his face. The scarlet gore was still pumping out of his nose, fast and furious, big sticky bubbles of it, coming through his fingers whenever they took away the wet paper towels to let him snatch some extra air.

Seabright didn't let anything show, not on the outside, just noted inwardly, in a little wrenched portion of his stomach, that this man thought he was dying. It was in his eyes. They stared back at him, pleading: *Why me? Why me?*

Seabright gave him a thin-lipped smile, then took Ali by the arm, led her to the window by the central bulkhead, and ran through the possibilities.

"What's his name?"

"Weber. German businessman. Traveling on his own."

"Does he have any previous medical history?"

She shook her head. "He says not. My guess is maybe high blood pressure—when he got on he had a florid complexion, was puffing and wheezing. But then we all were. It was hot."

"There's no evidence of heart failure?"

"I'm a flight attendant, Captain," she answered quickly, then cursed herself for letting it come out like that. "Sorry. What I meant to say was, all I know is what I got from the training courses. I don't think there's any evidence of that. On the other hand, I've never seen anything like this before. One minute he was fine, a little red in the face, the next he's complaining of a headache, right out of the blue, pushing the button and asking for an aspirin. Before I could get it to him, this happens. It was just pouring."

"Yes." He could see that for himself. "But it's slowing down now, isn't it?"

"Not much. He's been bleeding for thirty minutes now. I let it go on for a while without bothering you. But you saw the state he's in. He's lost a lot of blood. And he's still losing it. There's nothing . . ." She looked furious with herself. "There's nothing I know how to do. Or anyone else we have on board, for that matter."

"No."

She looked at him and he knew what she was thinking: This was why you had a captain.

He ran through the options. His calmness, his reassurance, was as important to her as to the sick man behind him.

"I'll see if there's a diversion we can make. We're not exactly within spitting distance of a great hospital out here. Moscow might be the best bet, and that's maybe two hours out or more."

"He can't go on like that for two hours."

"This is a nosebleed, Ali. It has to stop sometime."

She said nothing for a moment, just stared at him with an expression he found infuriating, as if there were something here he ought to understand better.

"Yes, sir. Just a nosebleed."

Seabright wanted to get away from this, wanted to get back to the closed, secure cockpit and not look at the agony in her face.

"Is there something else?"

She didn't answer.

"Ali?"

"It's stupid. It's crazy."

He could get bored by this, he thought. And he could get angry too. His forehead was throbbing. His temper was bubbling beneath the surface.

"If you've got something to say, say it."

She hesitated, not wanting to appear foolish. "He's not the only one."

"What?"

"When he started ringing for the aspirin he wasn't the only one. I've got three back in economy with nosebleeds. Not so bad as this. But bad enough, enough to scare them. Scare me. And more than I can count screaming about headaches. What's going on, sir?"

Seabright couldn't take this in. It made no sense.

"It's the crowd thing," he said. "They see one person doing it, they just follow." Even as he said it, he knew it was feeble.

"No." She wasn't just scared, she was angry too, and somehow this seemed to be directed at him.

"When it started, some of these people couldn't even see each other, sir. And it happened all at the same time. As if someone pressed a button or something and we all started hurting. And the blood too. Hell, *I've* got a headache."

She gazed straight into his face. "Haven't you? Sir?"

"I have now," Seabright lied quietly. Then thought about all the things he'd read and never really absorbed, about how an individual received more radiation in a three-hour plane journey at 37,000 feet than during an entire month working inside a nuclear power station. The German's face came back to him: big red gouts of blood, clotting, full of mucus, pouring down his face. But there was nothing in the records about a spontaneous event like this. Nothing he could remember.

He felt a sudden need to be back up front. "You know what to do, Ali. Keep me posted."

Then he marched back to the cockpit, not too quickly, not showing anything that any of the people in business or first, most of them looking a little more grim than usual today, could even begin to think of as panic.

You can't see inside a person's head, he thought, and added, as a postscript: Thank God for that. Because right then he was seeing exactly what would be waiting for him once he opened the security door.

He smiled at the front-row passengers in first, two sleek-looking Japanese moguls in dark silk suits, sipping their champagne, picking at little plates of caviar, both sweating uncomfortably. Then he pushed open the door, closed it quickly behind him, and stared at Jimmy Mulligan.

The little Irishman was slumped up against the yoke, just conscious, aware enough to look back at him with the same scared eyes he'd seen two minutes before. His face was red with blood, still pumping down onto his white short-sleeved officer's shirt, a steady liquid stream, thick and livid.

"Couldn't move," Mulligan mumbled, his voice a drunken slur. "Sorry, sir."

Seabright stepped back through the door, picked up a half-full champagne bucket and a couple of cloth napkins, returned, and placed them in Mulligan's lap, then leaped into the left-hand seat and strapped on the shoulder harness.

"Clean yourself up, Jimmy. Get some water on your face."

Seabright punched up the moving map display. He'd give it fifteen more minutes before making a decision, and if there was time, then Moscow it would be. But just in case, he pulled up the database of local airports, a string of names he didn't recognize. In a little under forty minutes they could be down somewhere that was supposed to have the facilities to handle this kind of emergency. If he was willing to take the risk on a backwoods airfield and a medical system that was probably primitive even by Russian standards.

He stared ahead, out of the wide-view screen of the cockpit, watching the empty land roll slowly underneath them, not a city, not even a small town in sight anywhere. And not a cloud either. It was so sunny and clear he felt he could see straight off the edge of the earth.

"Sir?"

Seabright had let his mind go blank, and mentally chided himself for the slip. Too much to do, too much to think about.

He knew all the symptoms of the cockpit malaise that let your head drift off into nowhere just when the going got tough.

To his relief, Mulligan looked better. He wasn't slumped in his seat anymore, his hands seemed steady. The bleeding was stopping. He'd be okay. Maybe the same thing was happening with the stricken German back in business.

"There was a call," Mulligan said, and his eyes were still scared. Seabright wondered why he'd not seen that. "Air Force One put out a Mayday. I got half of it, then I must have blacked out."

"Shit."

Seabright dialed the frequency and tried to listen through the white noise screaming through the speakers. There was half a voice there, then it stopped. From what little he heard, he could detect a low note of growing terror in the pilot's voice. They weren't the only ones trapped in this invisible storm in the sky.

"Air Force One," Seabright yelled, "we have your Mayday and will relay. What's the problem?"

The white noise diminished a little.

"Damned if I know," said a shaky voice through the din. "But we're losing systems here, we're losing everything, and . . ."

The sea of electronic screams came back.

"Sir!"

He'd almost forgotten about Mulligan. This situation was so bizarre.

"The lights . . ."

Seabright glowered at the LCD panels and what he saw there made his heart freeze over. It wasn't just the main gear anymore. There were sinister little yellow and red lights flashing in places he'd never seen before, not even in training, warnings about pressurization, control servos, heating, and fuel flow, digital screams for help from systems that had nothing to do with each other, could not be connected by anything except their presence in the great electronic nervous system of the machine.

He punched the emergency button on the moving map, located the closest airfield, mentally registered that it was pretty much close to dead ahead, but 130 nautical miles away. He keyed the radio to the distress frequency and started to read out something he had committed to heart many years ago, in a two-seat tandem Chipmunk trainer, learning to fly in an RAF base in the Highlands of Scotland.

"Mayday, Mayday, Mayday, Dragon 92 . . ."

And when it was over he really didn't know if he'd reached the end of the message or not. There wasn't sufficient space left by the pain for that kind of thought. Somewhere through the routine little chant a hole had opened in his head, and into it had flowed white-hot molten metal, the color of the center of the sun, and it had roared and raged through every neural quarter it could find, screaming all the time, in his voice, in Jimmy Mulligan's too, with a deafening loudness that shook this small enclosed world, flying 37,000 feet above the earth, rattled it so hard he felt his body straining against the straps of the shoulder harness, so hard he thought it would shake everything, the aircraft, his mind, his being, into pieces.

It was impossible to gauge how long this lasted, or the amount of time, after it was over, it took him to come back to some form of consciousness. The aftermath was almost as painful as the experience. His head felt as if it had been hit with an iron bar. There was blood in his mouth, and he felt it streaming hot and sticky from his nose. He turned his neck—such agony there too—and strained to look at Mulligan. The first officer was awake, conscious, not the slumped, dead form he'd expected to see. He could move. Pretty soon, he thought, the man might speak.

The aircraft had settled down too. After the worst moment of clear-air turbulence he'd ever encountered, they were safe, they were flying, held in place by the checks and balances of the autopilot that kept them on course and never stopped for headaches, sudden hemorrhages, or any other frailties of the human species.

Out of nowhere, the pressurization circuits popped. There was a slight bang—one he knew from all those hours running through the drill—and the oxygen masks dropped down from the overhead panel.

This was where the training came in. This was where you acted first, thought later, and these instincts never left you, always clicked into place, sent you scrabbling for the mask, got it firmly in your hand, pulled the clear plastic mouthpiece around your face, adjusted the elastic retaining straps around the back of your head, stayed calm, stayed cool, then, when everything was okay, got your breathing back to normal, let your pulse rate slow down somewhere into the lower reaches of anxiety.

The air tasted stale and metallic, but he could live with it. In a moment or two he'd try taking the mask off anyway. This was another trick of the lights, an errant circuit going haywire, not some massive depressurization of the aircraft. He looked at Mulligan. The first officer had his mask on too, the mouthpiece stained by blood. He was breathing with a regular rhythm. There was no need for worry there. Aft, the stewardesses would be earning their pay ten times over, fighting to keep the cabin calm, making sure the masks had dropped on schedule, were on and working. This had happened to him once before and Seabright remembered it well. No great depressurization then either, just some hot turbulence rolling off the Karako-rams.

He reached for the transmit button to resend the Mayday message, then stopped, found he could hardly bring himself to take a breath of the stale, tinny oxygen coming through the mask, could hardly dare to look at this sight, so strange, so terrifying in front of him.

Every tiny cell of every LCD panel on the display was now alight, screaming furiously for attention in ways that couldn't be true, couldn't make sense, cycling madly from green through amber to red and back again, beating to some internal rhythm that just got faster, more manic as he watched.

Then reached some kind of climax, some form of satisfaction, and stopped.

Seabright listened to the sound of the aircraft dying, listened to the engines winding down, the fans and circuits growing cold, saw everything electrical on board cease to function, stared at the dead dull face of the display panels, and knew this was impossible, knew that no conjunction of events could kill every circuit in the machine, every backup with it.

The aircraft now stayed aloft through momentum and the locked aerodynamic form of its ailerons and elevators alone, buoyed in the current of air 37,000 feet above central Asia, no noise in the cockpit, nothing but the slow, insistent rush of air past the fuselage. It would be different behind them, behind the closed door, back in the passenger section. The two men couldn't hear the screaming there. They didn't need to. It was bad enough in their imaginations.

Even without power the cockpit was bright. The sun streamed in through the wide, clear windows, illuminated the electronic deadness that surrounded them, made plain their relentless, uncontrolled passage through the air.

Seabright stared ahead, out the window, watched the way the horizon was now starting to slip imperceptibly upward as the aircraft settled into a slow descent, and tried to guess the rate they were falling, tried to work out how long it would take them to sink from the sky to the ground.

4

Annie and Mo

La Finca, 0649 UTC

Michael Lieberman wandered downstairs for breakfast just before seven, drank the best part of a pint of fresh orange juice and three strong coffees, and wondered what he'd got himself into.

In Lone Wolf, and many other little hubs around the world where the serious solar astronomers gathered, Lieberman was the "sunspot man." His early career as a designer of solar-powered satellite systems was largely forgotten, though not by him. Now he was the one they turned to when they needed a map of that big burning orb in the sky. Not the expert with the longest list of qualifications after his name. Not the one with more papers in the library than you could fit into a lifetime of reading. It went deeper than that; it relied as much on informed hunches and some subterranean intuitive guesswork even he felt hard-pressed to rationalize. He had a feel for this area, could look at the data, the flow of the solar tide, the jerky rhythm of the X-ray charts, and, most of all, that restless pattern of blemishes on the face of the sun that he'd made his own. He could read the way the umbras and penumbras shifted and moved constantly, then pretty much guess where they might go next. And just now, with the spot cycle coming unexpectedly to a peak two years before it should, when anyone could buy a filter to stop that big yellow ball of glass from burning out your retina, then just stare at the sun and see the spots with the naked eye, that was a talent to nurture.

La Finca was like no science project he'd ever seen, not in two decades of professional research. There was no one else down for breakfast, no gossip and hopeful flirting across the tables. The place was occupied, however. He'd seen as much when he came in the previous evening, walked from the helipad, across the yellowing, lifeless grass in heat that was still unbearable, and met Simon Bennett, who'd politely, if distantly, shaken his hand on the doorstep before making an excuse and disappearing into a big, barnlike building set next to the main mansion where everyone seemed to be staying.

Lieberman had eaten a solitary dinner, sinking a couple of beers until his head felt dull, and trying to stop from wondering where the next infusion of money would come from after this little enterprise ran its course. Academic tenure was something he'd learned to despise (particularly since he no longer had it). But there were times, when the bills came through the door of his small rented apartment in San Francisco like confetti, that it had its attractions. At least he and Sara never had kids in the three jumbled years they'd been married. That was one consolation, he thought, then cursed himself for his dumbness. If there *had* been kids the marriage never would have gone sour in the first place. The tough and delightful business of raising a family would have swallowed them up. But you couldn't control your genes, couldn't order up kids like a pizza from Domino's.

He wasted time in the dining room counting off the long minutes to the eight A.M. meeting Bennett had promised. Finally, with almost half an hour to go, the door opened and a woman walked in, hand in hand with a child who looked about nine years old. Lieberman smiled at them and got back a nice grin from the kid, something a little less warm from the woman. The mother was thin to the point of angularity, with a pretty, narrow face and long chestnut hair flowing down her back. She wore a loose cotton flowered shift, and her face and exposed arms were the color of walnut, that overtanned look that was so unfashionable these days, when the dread phrase "skin cancer" seemed to be on everyone's lips, all the more so now that the climate seemed to have turned so hot and wild. She looked like a hippie, he thought, one of the kids who populated Berkeley when he'd matriculated there at the end of the seventies. Like them, she looked a little lost.

But not the daughter, who, in snatched glances, grinned curiously at him, full of life, bright blue eyes shining, fair hair, long like her mother's, dressed in jeans with a cheap cheese-cloth top. Not much money there, he thought, and maybe that got to the mother, but it certainly didn't bother the kid.

The girl went over to the buffet and picked up a huge circular pastry, like a snail shell, and started to unravel the end, tearing off chunks, stuffing it into her mouth, staring at him all the time.

"They *pay* you to eat that stuff?" Lieberman asked finally.

She gazed at him and Lieberman was aware of being judged, in that swift merciless way that he recognized as a particular childhood trait. Then the kid looked at her mother, saw the gap in her concentration, picked up another pastry off the table, put it on a plate, and brought it over to him.

"You should try it, they're great," she said. Lieberman heard the mother sigh—she didn't need this, or want it, he thought—and took a big bite. The kid was right. It was delicious.

"These things have a name?" he said, staring at the girl, aware of the mother hovering behind him.

"Ensaimadas. You only get them on Mallorca. They're made of flour and lard. That's pork fat. Do you say 'lard' in America? I can't remember."

Lieberman put the ensaimada back on the plate and said, "Lard will do, lard will do just fine. Sit down if you like. My name's Michael Lieberman."

The girl smiled, and her mother just looked, but with the kid in the lead they joined him.

"Annie Sinclair," she said. "This is my mom. Mo."

Lieberman bent down, hooded his eyes, and whispered, "Does she speak?"

"When I get half the chance," Mo Sinclair replied coldly, a trace of something that sounded faintly Scottish in her voice, then drew up a chair. "Annie can talk the hind leg off a donkey. It sometimes makes me superfluous."

"Ah," he said, and let his hands flutter in a small wave of surrender. No man in sight, except this failed one who'd picked them up at breakfast. It was so obvious. They had a compact closeness between them that didn't let much light through, even on a shining, golden day like this.

"You work here?"

Mo Sinclair smiled wanly, and he was aware of being examined for a second time, evaluated in a more clinical, icy way. "I am tech support for the network. When your PC goes haywire, call for Mo. Most times I can fix it. It's a small talent but it gets me work."

"You two been here long?"

"A few months. We were just traveling on the island and I saw an ad. It's just a temporary thing."

"And school?" he asked, looking at Annie, whose eyes went straight to the floor.

"Like I said," Mo Sinclair added quickly, a note of nervousness in her voice, "we're just here temporarily. There's time for school later."

"Yeah," he said. "Sure."

And couldn't miss the way Annie darted a sly glance at him.

"I wish I traveled more when I was a kid," he said, nodding.

"You *do*?"

"Yeah. When I was your age an outing to Woolworth's was a big thing. You don't know how lucky you are, Annie."

The mother was looking at him frankly and he felt vaguely offended. He was just trying to claw back a little of the situation, nothing more.

"What do you do?" Annie asked.

"Oh," Lieberman replied in a flash, "I'm a professor. Don't take that wrong—I mean, I'm not the pompous type. Some people paint. Some people fix computers. I professor. Professoring is a full-time thing with me."

Her eyebrows were halfway up her head.

"But what kind of—"

"Oh, I get it. Just being a professor isn't enough, huh? You want the grim details? Okay. Well, I used to design the things that turned sunlight into energy out in space. But that sort of fell out of fashion. Now I'm the sunspot guy. You know, those freckles on the face of the sun that everyone seems so excited about just now? If you want to know something about them—how big they are, what they're planning to do next—I'm the person to ask."

"Oh," she said, looking a little disappointed.

"I also launch my own personal space rockets and communicate with aliens in other galaxies. I'd love to tell you more about it, but then I'd have to kill you."

Annie Sinclair giggled and stuffed half a pastry in her mouth. "Bullshi—"

"Annie!" Mo Sinclair interrupted quickly, stifling a laugh. "Mind your manners."

Lieberman just grinned. Then looked at his watch. "Well, it was cool meeting you but I have to transport out of this particular dimension. A meeting. Maybe someone's going to tell me why I'm here."

"You don't know?" Mo asked.

"Nope. They send the contract, I do the job. Got any ideas?"

She shrugged, in a halfhearted way that made him think there just had to be a little more to it than this.

"Don't tell me," he said. "You just fix computers."

"That's right. I don't think it's a big secret, but there's no reason to clue us in."

"Right."

"But *you* can tell us later."

"I can?"

"We can buy you lunch!" Annie broke in.

"Oh, your mom's probably got things to do," Lieberman said, offering Mo an out.

"No . . . I'd—we'd like that," the mother said. "We'll show you around. Go into town. Pollensa's beautiful."

"I bet. But I have to run now. You know where this briefing room is?"

"Outside. In the old stable block. That's where the offices are."

Lieberman smiled, felt a little uncomfortable with the weight of their stares, made his excuses, and went out the door.

It was bright, the heat already building in the air. The layout of the site was pretty easy to grasp. The big mansion was used for accommodations. The work took place in a vast single-story barn sprouting antennae on its roof, set a hundred yards from the house out toward the clifftop. It wasn't much of a walk but it stole the air from inside him, even this early in the morning. The weather was on some strange, vicious bent, a searing cycle of heat that seemed to be tightening on itself. The grass crackled underfoot, dead, dry, and yellow. The heat bore down from the cloudless sky. The only sound came from the waves roaring against rock just a couple of hundred yards below the cliffline ahead. He walked to the edge and leaned on the perimeter wall. A couple of helicopters were parked, silent, sleeping fifty yards away. Behind the mansion, a massive four-square shape of gleaming stone the color of the dead grass, stood a line of bare mountains that stretched beyond his line of vision, harsh and inhospitable. At their foot was the bright blue Mediterranean running to a white line of foam where it met the impassable rock. When they said Mallorca, he thought he was coming to some holiday island. This felt more like being stranded in some reclusive millionaire's hideout in the Galapagos. It was hard to think of anywhere quite so isolated for a research facility. There was no sign of another house in any direction, nothing but the outline of a ruined castle on a headland a good mile away. Astronomy made its home in some odd, distant locations, he thought, but he'd never met one quite as strange as this.

He walked into the big barn and was immediately grateful for the cool, dark interior. There were six people in the big open main room. It was full of PCs and wall charts, nice, classy wooden desks, high-backed executive chairs, and the buzz of people busying about their work. Three of the inhabitants were pushing papers around their desktops. The rest stared straight at him as he came through the door.

"Michael," Bennett said, smiling, and held out a hand.

Simon Bennett was probably in his mid-fifties, stockily built with neatly cut gray hair, a round face, and half-moon glasses of the kind adopted by Oxbridge academics of a certain age. He peered at Lieberman with bright, curious eyes. Bennett was wearing gray slacks, a white shirt, and a red club tie. It seemed incongruous in the surroundings.

The three paper-shufflers looked briefly at them, then left the room without saying anything, closing the door behind them as they went.

"You got many people here, Simon?"

"Thirty-two—not all on this single site, of course. We have another base in the mountains at Puig Roig. That's why we spend so much money on helicopters."

"And . . . um."

Bennett looked puzzled for a moment. Academia didn't always teach you the niceties, Lieberman thought.

"Oh. Good Lord. I do apologize. This is Ellis Bevan, our head of operations. And Irwin Schulz, who runs the computers here, and a lot more than that too. Ellis's work I can begin to understand. I do have to sign off the budget, after all. Irwin, I'm afraid, may as well be talking double Dutch as far as I am concerned but he is, I assure you, a genius."

Schulz blushed. He couldn't have been more than twenty-five or so, Lieberman guessed, a short, slightly overweight figure in a bulging T-shirt and jeans, and sporting round wire-rimmed glasses—all in all classic geek material. He held out a pudgy hand.

"Hey," he said, "I'm just the average propellerhead. Don't believe anything else. You worked at Lone Wolf?"

"For a while."

"Some place. I was there a couple of weeks ago. You people ought to blow your trumpet some more. We got this woman on the case there, Jesus, so bright."

"Sara?"

"You know her?"

"I was married to her for a while."

"Oh."

Lieberman felt like kicking himself. Schulz was blushing all over his fleshy face.

"Hey, that's no problem. We're still friends."

"Nice," Schulz said. "I never understood until recently how tiny the whole solar flare community really is. I guess you guys must know each other real well."

"If only by reputation." Bennett smiled.

Ellis Bevan peered at Lieberman and said, "Good to meet you."

He was about thirty, Lieberman guessed, tall, straight, and muscular, with close-cropped hair and a slightly sour expression on his thin, sharp-featured face. Bevan had the word "administration" written all over him, Lieberman thought, and cursed himself immediately. It was wrong to judge people so quickly, but Bevan had the look of someone you turned to when you wanted to do some firing, when the budget was overrunning, and when the plumbing didn't work.

"Operations?" Lieberman said.

"Yeah," Bevan replied in a flat East Coast accent. "Everything outside the academic part of the project is down to me. Telecommunications. Transportation. Finance."

"And a very good job he does too," Bennett added. "That's the last thing we want on our plates."

"I'm sure," Lieberman said. "So what exactly *is* on our plate?"

The smile disappeared from Bennett's face. "You mean you don't know?"

"Hey. I just got a last-minute call from the Agency saying you people wanted some advice in my field and you were paying real money. That's as far as it got."

Bennett said nothing and Lieberman began to feel he'd lost a point. A real academic, someone who wasn't on the edge of burnout, would, at the very least, have asked.

"I see," Bennett said after a couple of ponderous moments. "These are big issues, Michael, and I don't have the time to go into them all right now. This evening I want to run a full briefing session. Mainly for your benefit."

"I'll look forward to that," Lieberman answered. "You've got a lot of people here."

"Most of them are engineers," Bevan said. "We need a lot of support for the kind of telecommunications rig we're running. You don't need to bring every last academic to the experiment these days. We've got a virtual network running between here, Lone Wolf, and another base we have in Kyoto."

Thirty people to keep the network running? Lieberman still couldn't get a picture of it in his head.

"But—"

"Michael," Bennett said with a thin smile on his face, "we really are very busy. Can you leave your questions to this evening? I promise to talk a lot more then. And believe me, you'll find what I have to say . . . interesting. I just want you to know your role here is an important one."

"Crucial," Schulz said. "We really need it."

"I've followed your recent work," Bennett continued. "It's most encouraging. What we need from you is what you do best. An analysis of when and where the sunspot activity is shifting. We're trying to work out how much of the climatic and electro-magnetic effects we're experiencing just now are due to the changes in the state of the solar disk. If you can give us an idea of where it's headed, we can tune the systems we have to make the most of the position."

Lieberman blinked, surprised to feel a certain wounded pride. "You mean that's it?"

Bennett nodded. "Reports every hour. Irwin will set up a channel on the system later this afternoon. We're all pretty much on a war footing until the zenith has passed."

"Great. So I'm kind of the weatherman here and that's that."

"A very *well-paid* weatherman, Michael," Bennett said quietly. "And it's not exactly clerical work, trying to predict what happens on the face of a star ninety-three million miles away from us. Now, is it?"

"No? You sure Ellis here doesn't want me sweeping up too?" As soon as the words escaped his lips, he wished he had them back. Why must you insist on being a pain in the ass? he chided himself.

Bennett was back to shuffling papers. The interview was over. For today, at least, it looked like his role was to play tourist.

5

Straight-in Approach

Central Siberia, 0448 UTC

You don't just fall out of the air. Ian Seabright knew that, had it drilled into him from the first time he'd left the earth, behind the twisting prop of that long-dead Chipmunk. The aircraft did what it was supposed to do when it lost its source of thrust. It settled into the long, steady glide that was determined by the angle of its control systems and the aerodynamic profile they presented to the air as it flowed over its wings and fuselage.

It was descending at around 2,300 feet per minute, something he soon realized he could confirm by using one of the few instruments on board that didn't require electricity to feed it: the altimeter, with its subsidiary ascent and descent readout, triggered by the simple pressure of the air rushing past the aircraft.

You don't just fall out of the air.

The land below was flat and low—no mountains, no all-covering cloud, and thank God for that. There was time to think this through. There was time to act.

Seabright looked at his first officer seated next to him. Mulligan was a mess, his face mask smeared with dried blood, his white short-sleeved shirt stained too, big sweat patches coming out under the arms. The Irishman stared mutely back at him, not flinching, and Seabright felt grateful. Jimmy Mulligan was not a man to let you down.

Gingerly, Seabright removed the mask from his face, took a deep breath, tried to judge what it felt like. Instinct told him the aircraft was not depressurizing, that it would be okay for him to work without the mask that he found annoying. The atmosphere felt fine. The masks had actually fallen due to some electrical fault, not a pressure failure. What was now pumping oxygen into the cabin was the movement of air through the engines, and that would be enough for now. This would keep them alive as the aircraft continued its descent, and by the time you got down to 18,000 feet or so it didn't matter anyway. There was enough oxygen around at that altitude to keep you awake, keep the blackouts away.

Mulligan waited for the instruction, then took his own mask off.

Seabright spoke rapidly, thinking ahead all the time.

"I want you to go back, find Ali, tell her to get the rest of the crew together, to brief the passengers that we are working on the problem, we expect to have it fixed. But just in case, they should prepare for an emergency landing in around fifteen minutes from now, they should get the drill card out of the back of the seat and memorize every word on it, memorize the brace position, keep aware of what's happening out the window. Tell them they can take their oxygen masks off but they should keep them on their laps, use them if they need to. It might just keep the panic down a little if they don't have those damn things around their faces. Tell them not to expect any announcements. The intercom's down. They know that already, but make sure they don't expect it to come back up. Tell them we're in fine weather, descending onto flat, open terrain, not mountains. And we can see down every inch of the way."

"Sir."

"Then get back here pronto and help me get this bugger back flying again."

"Done," Mulligan answered, then took off his shoulder harness, wriggled out of the seat, and was out the door.

Seabright looked at the blank LCD screens in front of them. Still no sign of life, no indication that there was, anywhere within the aircraft, an amp of usable current. Not even hoping for any joy, he felt the yoke. Dead too. This was fly-by-wire. You needed the power, you needed the servos to shift the ailerons and elevators and rudder, to adjust the flaps and slats that kept the beast on its correct, three-dimensional journey through the air. Without electricity, the machine was locked in whatever attitude it held when the circuits failed, in this case the cruise configuration, which, just then, was the best he could hope for. Had the freeze occurred when they were climbing, the results would have been cataclysmic in a matter of seconds. The aircraft would have set itself a high angle of attack, expecting the thrust to keep it flying, keep it going up all the time at a healthy airspeed. Without the engines, and without the ability to trim for the glide, it would have flown itself straight into a stall in under a minute, shuddered to a halt in the air, ceased to be an object that flew, and turned into one that fell, like a brick, straight out of the sky.

Seabright knew this was a time to improvise. This was a machine—a very complex one, but a machine nonetheless. Its circuits and pulleys and servos, its huge fan-driven engines, the reservoirs of volatile aviation fuel that now sat leaden and useless in its wings, were just overcomplicated cogs in a child's toy. The way you got them working was by finding some means to reestablish the links that made them live. You had to use the tools that came in the box. You couldn't kick-start this beast back into being. You couldn't wind up some rubber band. You had to think alongside the system, not against it.

He was still staring at the dead gray panels, watching the altimeter unwind at the corner of his vision, when Mulligan returned, and that worried Seabright. He was the captain and he was taking too long at this. His mind wasn't working straight. He could have done something. Punched some buttons, tried the radio, punched anything.

Doesn't work like that, Seabright told himself. This wasn't some gigantic fruit machine waiting for the right combination by accident. There were too many sequences available, in the mass of buttons and dials in front of them, for that. You had to think your way through.

"We'll go through the start-up sequence, Jimmy. What's it like back there?"

"Pretty calm." Amazingly calm, he thought, and Jimmy Mulligan wished his head hadn't made that analogy when he saw the people, strapped so tightly in their seats, just waiting. With the same blank, hopeless look you saw on animals making their way to the slaughterhouse.

"Ali's coping," he added. And she was. Of course she was. Just.

Seabright had started to work the gray, lifeless panel.

"Sir . . ."

"I know. It's dead. We don't have time for explanations. Let's just see what happens."

And so they spent a minute racing through the sequence, punching the dead buttons, reading through the list, faster than they'd ever done, so fast the company's chief pilot would carpet them on the spot if he'd ever heard it rushed in this way. Then they activated the final switch, sat back, and waited.

After five seconds, five seconds that seemed like a lifetime to both men, Seabright said, very calmly, no panic in his voice, "Okay, Jimmy. Now we do it the other way 'round. We run through the shutdown sequence. Then we try the start-up once more. See if we can fire something up in this bloody thing."

"Sir . . . ?"

"Jimmy." Seabright glared at him with a fierceness Mulligan had never before seen. "Do you have some other idea?"

Mulligan said nothing.

"Right. Well, let's get to it, then."

It was almost the reverse of the start-up routine. A few extra switches. A few extra procedures. By the time they had finished, the altimeter had wound down to 11,000 feet. It would take another minute or more to run through the start-up routine again. This would bring them down to close to 8,000 feet. There might be time enough to try this thing once more. There might be time to try something else. If he could think of something else, and right now there was nothing in his head except this repetitive set of actions that should, in a universe that worked by the rules, bring the aircraft back to life.

"That's it," Mulligan said quietly.

The two men stared at the dead panel, lost for words. Then Ian Seabright closed his eyes, let his mind look into the blackness there, and wondered: What next? Do we keep on punching in this little chant all the way down to the ground? Or do we just sit back and wait? Let it all happen around us, in this dead plane, with its frozen controls, its burned-out circuitry, and close to 340 helpless people waiting to die?

"Sir."

Mulligan's voice was urgent now. The first officer was tugging at his sleeve.

Seabright looked up, cursed the light coming through the window, the bright, piercing sunlight that made his eyes hurt, then saw something, recognized what it was, and found his mind coming back to him from that black, hopeless place it had found a moment before.

A single light winked on the panel. It was the auxiliary power unit, the tiny jet engine housed in the tail, and it was starting to flicker. Something inside had found the spark and, once it was there, had decided to inhale.

"Come on," Seabright muttered. "Come on."

Then he watched, in hot, sweated silence, as the rest of the panel came slowly, erratically back to life, a life that was as much amber and red as green—but that didn't matter. Seabright could have reached forward and kissed every one of them because what they promised was hope.

Seabright gripped the yoke. Shook it, knowing this was pointless, knowing there was no physical link here, that only the buzzing of electrons down the circuit—if it still existed— could help him fly the plane. It was rock-hard. Still frozen. He kept his hand there, just in case.

"The number-one engine's coming back up," Mulligan said, his eyes flashing over the panels, just a tremor of excitement in his voice.

"It's something. You just watch what happens there. Don't push it too hard yet. Make sure we don't start to lose it again. Once you're happy with that, work on the others. Leave the controls to me."

The altimeter was unwinding more slowly now. Down to around 800 feet per minute, the aircraft's descent cushioned by the single engine pushing out a modicum of thrust.

Time, Seabright thought. Just what he wanted. Then made the Mayday broadcast he'd tried to transmit what seemed like hours ago, made it all the way through, with a reading off the moving map, a reading that looked as if it just might be accurate. Someone came back on it too, a controller with a heavy Middle European accent and an undisguised note of urgency in his voice. Seabright turned down the volume, didn't even think about responding. There were better things to do. They knew there was an emergency. The aircraft was squawking its stricken presence through its transponder to anyone who wanted to listen. He had other tasks to occupy his time.

"We've just got number one, sir," Mulligan said. "I think I can keep that one up okay. The rest are dead."

"Fine," Seabright answered. One engine was better than none.

"If worse comes to worst, Jimmy, we're just going to have to fly this aircraft gently into the ground. I want you to drop the gear at fifteen hundred feet, then give us enough power on the one engine from one thousand to cut the descent rate to something as gentle as we can get. The terrain should be obvious by then. If necessary, we'll use the power to pop us over any obstacles we can see and then get this thing on the ground, and—"

Seabright stopped in midsentence, turned to the horrified Mulligan, and smiled.

"Sorry, Jimmy. I didn't mean to worry you."

"It was you?"

"Oh yes." Seabright grinned. "Oh yes."

The movement was so familiar to them, such a part of the training routine. Out of nowhere, the aircraft had moved out of balance, yawed in the air, slipping sideways, moving them in their seats until Seabright realized what was happening, centered the rudder, brought the ship back into a straight line.

"You try it," Seabright ordered. "Try some right pedal."

The same thing happened, shifting them in the opposite direction, then Mulligan relaxed, let the aircraft take up its natural position.

"I have control," Seabright said, and added, mainly to himself, "and now for the big one."

He pulled back gently on the yoke, expecting to feel it lock against him. This time it moved—only half an inch—and then he let it center again. But it moved. The nose of the aircraft rose gently against the horizon. The altimeter slowed, came down to 7,300 feet . . . and stayed there.

"Airspeed?" Seabright wasn't taking his mind off these controls. He intended to stay on top of these all the way until the moment their wheels gently kissed the ground.

"Three-fifty and settled."

Both men peered out the window, out to pale nothingness, empty, bare rocky terrain. But flat. Flat enough, if it came to it.

"Get working on that map, Jimmy. Either you find me some airfield near here and straight ahead or we're going for a forced landing pretty damn soon."

Mulligan wiped his face with his arm, came away with a mixture of sweat and blood and mucus on his skin, and stared at the display.

"There's a military base ninety miles away; you need to turn twenty degrees to the right."

These were command decisions, Seabright thought. These were why they made you a captain.

"We'll go for it, and take her down on the way if we need to. It's probably the station that came back on the Mayday call."

Then, gently, with a rate of turn that was so slow that no one in the aircraft would even notice it, he moved the plane through twenty degrees to the north and let it settle once more. The airplane moved steadily forward through the sky.

Seabright tried to compose his thoughts. He needed to talk to the people in the cabin. And after that another call—to the airfield ahead, to explain their predicament. To describe, in as much detail as he possibly could, what had happened to them, at what flight level, and where. This was good practice. This was just plain good manners. If something struck your aircraft out of the blue, you told air traffic so they could pass it on to anyone else in the area, make sure they were aware of the danger. There was no other reason than that, Seabright said to himself, and almost believed it.

"We'll make it, Jimmy," Seabright said, then started to work the radio. When the Mayday was done, he called Air Force One again. There was nothing on the frequency but noise.

6
Calvary

Lieberman waited outside the huge wooden entrance doors of La Finca, feeling like a wallflower waiting for a date. The mansion was something. He stood at the head of a long, broad driveway that led inland, out of the estate. At his feet was a vast Renaissance fish pond in golden stone with ancient, crumbling statuary and the odd orange shape bobbing up to disturb the opaque green surface. Beyond the water, which seemed out of place in this arid landscape, a line of cypresses ran like exclamation marks down each side of the road, winding through parched, dead fields of wheat into a narrow valley. The crop moved in the faint wind, a febrile dance without energy. This place had money, he thought. Money and class. But all that didn't buy a respite from this strange hiccup in the climate that seemed to have gripped the world.

When he thought about it, he found it impossible to pinpoint when the weather had gone bad. Meteorology was not his field, and his gut feeling was that it was wrong to judge what was happening with the climate on intuition alone. Stone Age man had probably spent a large part of his life complaining that the weather just wasn't what it was. Maybe there was some neural circuit inside your head that filtered out the prolonged extremes from your childhood and turned it all into an episode of

The Waltons, a little rain, a lot of sun, and then some snow now and again. But as far back as 1995 he had started to feel the climate was changing for real, and he wasn't the only one. Maybe it was global warming, maybe it was some new mischief on the part of El Niño. He had no idea, but this couldn't be just received wisdom. The ice caps weren't melting like crazy, the Gulf Stream hadn't shifted north as the pundits had predicted. It didn't look likely that one day you'd be planting vineyards in Scotland or watching reindeer wander the streets of Paris—depending on your particular point of view—but it was obvious something was happening. And to him it just seemed as if someone had turned the weather dial so that it was always set to full. When it got hot, it got very hot. When it rained, it poured. And when it snowed, the best part of Canada and New England could lock the doors, break out the Molsons, and prime the generator, because no one was going back to work in anything close to a hurry.

This was the hot phase, and it had hung around here for a long time, long before the spot cycle began its early peak. Maybe these things were linked, in the way that cancer might be sparked by a random quark from Saturn zipping through your spleen. But this was no straight-line relationship. No one had yet figured out the way to read those particular runes.

There was the sound of a car scrunching across the gravel and Mo Sinclair drew up in a Suzuki Vitara, Annie in the back. Something different there, Lieberman thought. Mo didn't look as lost and dreamy as she had three hours earlier. She gave him half a smile. Annie jumped out of the open-topped vehicle, grinned, and said, "We've been talking about it and this is the deal."

"The deal?" he asked. He was wearing his Lone Wolf Solar Observatory baseball cap (which he liked to think of as office uniform) and not just out of vanity either. Sunburn was a real danger in this weather. "What deal?"

"We show you Pollensa. You tell us what this stuff is all about. Okay?"

"You mean like . . . everything?"

"Everything."

"Sure." He shrugged. "What little I know."

"That will be nice," Mo said coolly.

So he walked back into the building that served as quarters, back into his bedroom, and picked up the gear he'd need for his little tutorial. Then the first part of the tour began, on foot, the three of them sweating in the incessant heat. La Finca, it turned out, was even bigger than he had expected. Some fancy banking family from Madrid had owned the estate for almost two hundred years before getting caught up in the recession of the late eighties. By 1990, it was on the market, and Sundog— "whoever they are," Mo said pointedly—stepped in with an offer no one could match.

"But why here?" Lieberman asked as they walked over to the clifftop and caught a startling view straight out onto the empty blue waters of the Mediterranean. "What kind of a place is this for astronomers?"

"You're supposed to be telling us that," Annie objected, with the dogged lack of logic Lieberman associated with kids.

"It's private," Mo said. "You'll see on the way out how secure it is. One road in, with a locked guard post, the sea on the other side, and mountains everywhere else. Do astronomers need privacy?"

"Everybody needs privacy," he said.

"Oh yeah," Annie said, laughing. He could hear something tense in her voice and, for the life of him, couldn't understand what put it there.

"And it's not just here," Mo said. "Why do you think they've got two helicopters? There's some kind of place up in the mountains . . . they never talk about it when any of the locals are around. Or to anyone low on the food chain like me."

"Maybe," said Annie, "they're all a bunch of spies!"

"Could be," he said, trying to sound conspiratorial.

They both laughed then. It made Mo look a lot nicer, he thought—attractive, in a strained, skinny kind of way.

She stopped by the low stone wall that marked the boundary of the clifftop. The sea was a good hundred feet below, straight onto rock, no beach here, just the angry, relentless churning of the ocean.

But it was Mo he was looking at.

Just then she was close to beautiful, her long straight hair moving softly in the hot Mediterranean sea breeze. She looked like something precious that had been twisted and marked by some pain he could only guess at, something hard and strong and damaging, but still not cruel enough to take away everything that was attractive about her.

"Nice view," she said, staring out at the ocean.

"Yeah," he said, and looked. It *was* quite a sight. From the cliff edge you could see how perfectly La Finca had been positioned. The main house sat four-square, glowing golden in the bright morning sun, its plain rectangular lines broken now by the points of the cypresses lining the drives, and the smaller trees that marked paths into some adjoining ornamental gardens. A thin winding road led off from beyond the house, inland, rising gently into nothingness.

"That's the way in and the way out," Mo said, watching him stare down the road. "The only one, by car, anyway. There's no footpath except from the cove at San Vicente three miles off to the north, and that takes you through some pretty treacherous ground. Apparently it was mined during the Civil War in the thirties. Go south and you'd need to cling to the mountain for a good twenty miles before you ran into Sóller. And don't even think about coming in by boat. There's no jetty down there, nothing. You see what I mean about privacy?"

"Idyllic, if you like that kind of thing."

"Idyllic is the word, all right. Can you imagine how that banking family must have felt, having to leave all this?"

Lieberman let the question hang there, brooding on other losses.

It was Annie who finally broke the silence. "Let's go into town," she said.

Two minutes later they were sailing along the narrow private road in the Suzuki, the hot wind in their hair. A dour Spanish guardsman came out of his sentry box and opened an electronic green iron gate topped with spikes, a remote TV camera too. Then they were out of La Finca, driving slowly along a winding road, a dried-up rocky riverbed to the right and some low olive fields to the left. Finally, civilization appeared, with more and more country villas—big houses for the tourists and the rich weekend folk from Barcelona and Madrid.

They popped out of the mountains, crossed the narrow main road, and were in the town. Mo drove knowledgeably through a warren of narrow white-walled streets, parked in a space the size of a pocket handkerchief, then they climbed out of the car, Lieberman lugging the rucksack he'd brought with him. Annie took him by the hand, led him through two dark alleyways, before coming out in a large, open square, with a hulking church in the same golden stone as La Finca.

"We have money," Mo announced.

"Their money." Annie grinned.

Lieberman sat down on a battered metal chair, beside an even more battered tin table, and announced, "Beer, ice cream, tapas. Let's party."

"One beer," Mo cautioned. "Then I want some exercise."

"Good," he said, and looked for the waiter. Fifteen minutes later, they were out of the square, walking past the church and a cluster of ecclesiastical-looking buildings. The heat was so oppressive it felt tangible. Lieberman's checked shirt clung to his chest, and he could feel the sweat running in hot salty rivulets down his face.

They turned a corner, and stretching in front of them was a straight paved climb up a small hill to what looked like a chapel at the top.

Lieberman sighed and started to climb. Mo slowed to keep pace with him, always watching Annie, who raced ahead, never quite letting her go. As they reached the summit, he got the point. The sights were astonishing on all four sides. They gazed down into the town with a bird's-eye view. To the northeast was the broad sweeping bay of Pollensa, and, in the opposite direction, the long line of mountains that hid La Finca from the world.

Annie was seated on a stone bench underneath a scraggy cypress, trying to stay out of the sun. They joined her and she looked at Lieberman, smiled, and said, "Your turn now."

"Okay. We keep this short. Then you two can carry me back down that hill, since I doubt I can walk."

"Wimp," Annie said.

"I'm old," he countered.

"Not that much."

"Enough to know you should be wearing something on your head. Take this."

He pushed the Lone Wolf baseball cap onto Annie's head and vowed to stand, as much as he could, in the shade of the cypress tree for the next half hour or as long as it took to bring this brief and—even to him—puzzling situation into the light.

The ground around the chapel was empty. No one else was dumb enough, he guessed, to brave the airless midday cauldron that had enveloped the island. He had his little notebook computer with the presentation notes on and a small portable telescope with an equatorial fork mount. Lieberman took out the scope, attached the fork mount to the body, then fitted the screen of the projector to the frame so that the image came straight out of the eyepiece and fell there, damn near perfect, and visible for everyone to see. They were watching him screw the thing together, and there was genuine interest there, in what he had to tell them, and maybe even in him too. They were *curious*, which he found both refreshing and satisfying.

He flashed a quick smile, stared at the nearly complete telescope in front of him, rolled in the last screw, stood up, and began.

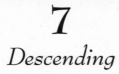

7

Descending

Central Siberia, 0458 UTC

The cockpit door opened and Ali Fitzgerald walked into the cabin. Both men were busy: Seabright, who'd failed to raise Air Force One on the radio, was now peering through the screen; Mulligan was hunched nervously over the panels. Seabright thought he'd detected the shadow of the big 747 with the crest on its side somewhere over to their right. Then it had disappeared.

Finally, he broke away from staring at the bright, featureless horizon and asked Ali, "How is it?"

"The German died," she said softly. "There was nothing I could do."

Seabright looked at his first officer. Mulligan knew what his responsibilities were: Watch the lights flicker and glimmer on the panel, follow every movement of the digital dials on the one working engine. But his preoccupation didn't stop the news from affecting him. In another set of circumstances, he would have stood up and embraced her, tried to share some strength, but this was not the time or place.

"Ali."

It was Seabright who spoke, and as he did he noticed some fire in his colleague's eyes, some blame aimed—where? At himself? Or at Seabright, for taking this initiative, which was surely the right thing, the proper thing here, in this flying tin tube, just struggling through the air at 8,000 feet above the hot, inhospitable land, limping along at close to 150 miles per hour below its normal cruise, with thirty miles still to run to the field and the possibility of safety?

"They need you back there," Seabright said, not looking at her, though there was precious little to occupy his attention outside the window now. The aircraft was flying straight and level, as if it knew the way to go.

"No, they don't," she said abruptly, knowing he was wrong, knowing he just wanted her out of there. People are not stupid. They knew what was happening. They were strapped into their seats, trying not to anticipate this unknown thing called the future, feeling powerless, feeling weak. There was nothing she could do for them, nothing she could do for anyone, even herself.

She pulled down the jump seat from the back of the door, let herself slump into it. There was so much pain in the back of her legs, in her shoulders, it felt as if she'd been carrying around some huge weight on her back for hours. She was twenty-eight years old, and she felt more tired, more weary than she'd ever felt in her life.

The radio barked out of nowhere, so loud and sudden it startled them all.

"Dragon 92. We have you on track for a straight-in approach. Twenty-three miles to run. How are things?"

The man had a Russian accent. He sounded worried, maybe a little scared.

"We have one fatality on board," Seabright said into the mike. "Some sick people too. Cardiac cases, possibly. Can you cover that?"

There was a pause.

"We'll see what we can do," the voice said after a while. "Other traffic in your vicinity. No height, no precise position. Transponder not working. You see it?"

"Shit," Seabright muttered, frantically scanning the sky. "Negative."

The radio went quiet.

"Captain?"

Ali's voice seemed to come from a long way away. Seabright's head hurt; there was pressure getting hard and painful somewhere behind his face. It wouldn't surprise him if he joined the nosebleed club soon, though he'd hardly ever had one in his life outside the rugby field.

"Not now, Ali. We need to deal with this . . . situation."

He wished she'd go away. If it came to it, he'd order her to get out of the cabin, pick her up bodily and put her back behind the bulkhead, out of sight.

She blinked back the tears, and they weren't just because of the way he spoke, which was so unlike him.

"Captain," she said again, slowly and deliberately. "There is something on the aircraft. *On* it."

These were all familiar words but both Seabright and Jimmy Mulligan never thought, in their lives, that they'd hear them in this particular order. Or would have believed how cold they might feel when they were spoken, so quietly, in a voice one of them was slowly coming to regard as something essential, something vital in his life.

"There is something on the roof of the plane," she said.

Seabright looked at Mulligan, tried to read his expression, was ready to force her out of there himself, any way he could. Then both men turned around and whatever words were forming in their throats just died there, dry on their lips. There *was* something on the plane, clinging to its upper skin. And it was getting bigger all the time.

Ali was the first to see it for an obvious reason. She was sitting in the jump seat, behind Seabright and Mulligan, and this gave her an uninterrupted view of the entire cockpit area, right to the top of the big deep windows that ran past the pilots' heads, beyond the normal range of their upper vision.

From here, it appeared as a thin blue electric line, not quite transparent, like a brush stroke of vivid paint an inch or two thick along the top of the screen. It looked, for all the world, as if someone had poured some bright blue screen wash onto the roof of the airliner, then let it spread slowly, gently down the sides, running over the fuselage, then down to the cockpit windows.

The blue light had been almost stationary for a few seconds, though within its body there was movement: some of it rapid, like the coursing of sparking currents through some viscous medium . . . some slower, more liquid, like the gentle undulation of a tidal water flow.

"It looks like lightning," Mulligan said, his head arched back to see the thin line of light.

Then it moved again, visibly, drew forward, fell a good four inches down the window, well within their line of vision now, no need to stretch their necks.

"You can hear it," she said, and didn't even want to think about what this meant.

There was a sound, low but distinct, coming through the skin of the aircraft. It was like the fizzing of some chemical preparation or a power line that had been shorn through, and was now snaking and spitting wildly at anything it saw.

Seabright pressed the mike and said, "Dragon 92, immediate forced landing, we have some form of electrical discharge on the aircraft."

Then listened, not wanting to hear the response, just needing to know. The radio was dead. The antenna was on the roof. It would be one of the first things to go.

He stared out at the left-side window and thought his heart might stop beating. Moving in a parallel path slightly above them, a mere four hundred yards away, was the familiar white shape of a 747, looking equally stricken. Its entire hull was covered in a bright, shifting veil of blue electricity. The crest on the main door and the tail was only just recognizable through the flimsy, unearthly veil of energy.

"Gentle glide, Jimmy," Seabright said. "I don't want to see any more than eight hundred feet per minute all the way down unless I say so."

They would not collide, he told himself, not if they kept their present course.

"Sir . . ."

Mulligan wanted to get this thing out of the sky as quickly

and as efficiently as possible, and Seabright read his thoughts, had been there, gone through that point before his first officer had even reached it.

"I can put her into an emergency descent, sir."

Seabright looked at the man. He was scared, and they didn't have the time for that.

"If we set her up in that attitude, Jimmy, think what happens if the controls lock again or we lose the engine. Or both. So be a good chap, now. Watch the engine. Watch the panel. Let's get out of here."

There was nothing for Mulligan to say right then. He just nodded. And watched the screens. Something was happening there already and it was impossible to judge what it meant. Before, when the panel had gone down, it was as if it had actually died, had felt the lifeblood run out of its circuits, spill out into the atmosphere, and leave nothing behind. This seemed like the opposite. Everything was racing. Every gauge, every dial was coming to life, glowing, winking, brightly, furiously in front of him.

He felt like laughing, in between the anger, in between the red rage that ran around his head. There was something so ironic here. They'd survived being starved of electricity. Now it looked as if they'd be drowned by the stuff, dripping in from outside, down the windows, into the aircraft, into the wings, the control systems, every electronic nerve in its being.

And the fuel tanks too, Mulligan thought. Never forget the fuel tanks.

He watched what was flitting across the panels, not listening to what Seabright was saying, not even letting the words—and they were angry, getting angrier all the time—come close to his head, which hurt, which felt as if it were ready to explode. Because this was something new, this was something you never saw in the books. This was an entire aircraft being swallowed whole by some unknown, shapeless entity that fell from the sky, something blue and hissing, like a venomous electric serpent hooked to the biggest power grid in the world. You didn't read about these things in the books. Nothing prepared you for this, ever.

He felt something on his shoulder, looked, and it was Seabright's hand, shaking him roughly, trying to get him back into line.

Outside, beyond the wing, the 747 was closer now, moving slowly toward them, as if drawn by some gigantic magnet.

Jimmy Mulligan was, above all, a practical man. He took one last look at the gauges, closed his eyes for a second, tried to still his thoughts. His hands weren't shaking when he took off his harness. He felt calm, extraordinarily calm, felt that something inside his head was measuring these seconds as they ticked away so relentlessly.

Ian Seabright, still locked on the yoke, watched the blue fall farther, fall until it was halfway down the screen, far enough for the passengers to see through the cabin windows. Out of nothing more than habit, he wondered what was happening beyond the bulkhead. The aircraft flew on, steady as a rock. He stared out the window. The 747 was still closer. Only two hundred yards. And by the tail a new shape was growing, yellow and fiery.

Ali Fitzgerald had her eyes shut, cradled her head in her hands.

Mulligan knelt down in front of her, took her fingers, and she looked at him. She wasn't crying. In some way she wasn't even afraid.

Then she stood up, her back to the cockpit door. He rose too, felt her arms go around him, felt his face in her hair, against her cheek, soft and warm, damp with sweat, so real, so human it made him want to cry with rage.

She didn't kiss him. They didn't need that, clinging together like this, in some tiny tin cabin, held aloft in the atmosphere by nothing but the whim of the air outside. She just let her mouth brush against his neck, felt the way his did the same against her skin, and both thought, in a single image, of another time, two pale bodies twisting against cotton sheets in an anonymous hotel in an anonymous Japanese suburb, such physical delight passing between them it seemed impossible they could ever grow old or vanish from the face of the earth.

He leaned forward, gripping her more tightly, heard the

sound from behind, unlatched the door, let it fall open, feeling these precious seconds slip away from them, seep out through the fabric of the aircraft, disappear like motes of light dispelled by some greater, all-consuming luminance.

It was like the hot breath of a dragon, so bright and yellow through the pale brown skein of her hair, half-obstructing his vision. The fireball rolled ponderously down the length of the cabin toward them, a perfect golden sphere, roaring as it came, so loud that he could hear no screams above it, with such deadly certainty that he could believe, perhaps, there were none.

Then the dragon breathed in his face, with a heat and searing proximity that took from his head the physical presence of Ali, the faint perfume of her skin, the whispering of her hair, the warmth of her touch, left nothing in its place but the temporary electrochemical stain on the cerebellum that went under the name of memory. And in a second even that was gone.

Twenty miles away, in the control tower of the military base of Bratsk, the two small green marks that Dragon 92 and Air Force One had painted on the ancient radar screen merged. Then, without warning, disappeared altogether.

Five thousand feet aboveground, something glimmered briefly, a vast, fiery, elongated shape, bright and gold against the sky.

Like a halo.

Like a parhelion.

Like a sundog.

8
Toast

Pollensa, 1141 UTC

"You want the good news or you want the bad?"

"The bad," Annie said immediately.

"Okay, you asked for it," Lieberman growled. "You see the sun—no," he interrupted himself so quickly, aghast he could have been that stupid, did his best to interpose his body between them sitting in the shade and the big yellow furnace burning into his back, "no, I don't mean *look* at it. You must never do that. Never. Later, with my little toy here, I'll show you how you *can* look at the sun. Until I do that, don't even think about it. You understand why? It's too hot and it's so bright."

"All right," Annie said, a little disappointed that Lieberman had a serious side to him too.

"Okay, so . . . the *bad* news is," he said, staring at the screen of the computer to remind him how this was supposed to go, "the sun is a star."

He watched the girl's hand go straight up and thought: This could take a long time.

"Stars come out at night," Annie said. "Everybody knows that."

"Annie," Mo Sinclair interrupted, smiling at him with, he recognized, the sort of conspiratorial self-indulgence you got in adults. "Michael here is a professor."

Lieberman wasn't going to let this pass.

"Hey! No problem, Annie. You got a point there. Stars don't come out at night, of course. They're always right there. It's just that the sky's so bright—or they're so dull, whichever way you want to look at it—that we don't see them. The point is the sun is a star too and we get to see that during the day. Now, why do you think that is?"

Two hands went up straightaway (so the grown-up wanted to play this game too; he could handle that). Lieberman picked Mo's.

"It's bigger and brighter than the rest," she said, her smile curling down at the corners of her mouth as if to say: Two can play this game.

"Yeah? That could be one explanation. Not the right one, but it could have been. Maybe when you were nine years old you believed that."

"Me." Annie was scratching at the sky with her hand as if she wanted to hook her hand into the bright blue firmament.

"Okay?"

"It's closer than the rest."

All the way there in under a minute and she didn't look as if it made her sweat. Mo smiled. Not bad. He could think of a couple of schools back home where it might take you half a day to get half that far with a bunch of fifteen-year-olds.

"It's closer than the rest. And one day that will be a bad thing. You see, stars are just like us. They grow. They change over time. Right now the sun is a nice, happy young little star—little and young in star terms, of course, not ours. But one day, when it gets older, it will wake up and decide to do what Main Sequence folk like it have to do, and that's transform. Like a caterpillar changing into a butterfly. One day it will run out of fuel, all the stuff it burns to be a star, and then it will start to change into what stars grow up to be, which is what we call red giants."

"I've heard of those," Annie said.

"Great. So you know what happens then?"

She shook her head. Mo was silent. And he had them, he knew. They'd passed the point of even guessing the answer, were just itching to get on with the tale.

"What happens is the whole thing changes. What we think of as the core, the stuff at its heart, collapses right down into itself, and all the stuff on the outside, what we see in the sky, does the opposite, just races out, goes all kind of red and vaporous, gets really hot, and ends up being this new kind of star, this red giant thing, and that's going to be huge. So big it will be right here, right where we're standing now. On this very spot. Everywhere else on the world too. And you can guess what's going to happen to anything in its way."

There was a pause while they took this in.

"Toast!" Annie said happily.

"Toast," Lieberman replied.

"Cool!"

Mo watched all this, and, right out of the blue, he realized what it was she liked. Someone was giving Annie some attention, someone other than her mother. And why that should be unusual was a question that could have distracted his attention there and then, even with the narrative of this celestial dance starting to run inside his head.

"So what's the *good* news?" Mo asked.

"Hey. The good news is . . . we're all dead anyway! I'm talking a hundred million years away now. Why worry?"

"We could invent the secret of immortality," Annie said slowly, stretching each word out one by one. "Then there'd be a problem."

"Sure. I thought of that. You know, if we get clever—or dumb—enough to invent the secret of everlasting life, don't you think someone might also figure out a way to hightail it out of here? Find a star in another galaxy that's more hospitable?"

"So if the sun is not going to be a worry for a while," asked Mo, "why are we here?"

"*I'm* here because I got paid," Lieberman said quickly, realizing straight away that this was a question he maybe ought to have asked himself more rigorously. "Hey, we all got to eat. And I already told you, if I had any secrets to share they'd be yours. But if you want the long answer, well, sometimes you have to get off your butt and go observe things to learn about them. And when you're a scientist—"

"A professor!" said Annie.

"Yeah . . . yeah!"

He was enjoying the show too.

"When you're a professor, you just have to be ready to up and go when the call comes through. Kind of like Superman, I guess."

A single young face stared at him in silence, eyebrows arching toward the sky, and Lieberman just didn't even dare look at Mo, just knew her shoulders were shaking up and down and couldn't work out whether this was good or bad.

"Don't believe me, huh?"

A man had his pride. These were, as far as he could tell, a nice pair. They didn't believe in kicking a man when he was down, but that didn't put them past nudging him with their toes a little when the occasion arose. It gave you the right to respond.

"Take a look at this."

Then he beckoned them into the light, into the scorching, dry brightness of the day, so hot it burned your skin the moment you stepped into it, and positioned them around the telescope, which was pointing straight up into the blazing yellow eye of the sun.

The projector screen, with its open white panel fixed to the bottom end of the scope, offered an image of the solar disk that wouldn't be harmful to look at. Of all the projections Lieberman had set up for his "students," this one was, as he might have expected, the most spectacular of all.

The freckles on the solar orb were huge now, the biggest he'd ever seen. They were like living amorphous blotches on the burning yellow skin, dark and ugly, and so big they covered maybe a third of the entire surface. What he and Mo and Annie were observing was not the usual single spots, but ones that ran into each other, like they were mating, the dark umbras spawning many lighter penumbras until the picture looked like a blown-up slide under a microscope, the image of some deadly slumbering spore waiting to come alive.

The threesome were quiet; he could feel the sudden chill that ran between Annie and her mother. Without speaking they'd moved closer to each other. He chided himself for doing it this way, wished he'd devised a way to break it to them more gently.

Then, as they watched, one of the spots shifted. The umbra, a region of burning gas a hundred thousand miles or so across, moved. Merged with some other cell-like structure, sat together with it, feeling content, feeling whole, mated, and then multiplied again.

Someone gasped and he thought it just might have been Mo, nice, pained, distant Mo, whose life he'd just invaded, whose world he'd just thrown open with this simple astronomy lesson.

He tried to smile again, said, "Hey! This is just fireworks. Nothing to worry about. Trust me."

But it was futile. Somehow the joy had gone out of the day, and left nothing in its place but the blinding light that beat down on them from the sky, beat down with a relentless, burning ferocity that seared through the skin, seared right into the heart and touched it with the fiery furnace of creation.

9

A Demonstration

Pollensa, 1201 UTC

"Are they alive?"

Annie looked scared.

"No, no, no, no . . ."

Lieberman liked talking to kids now and again, but sometimes the sheer, naive dumbness got to him.

He pointed to the yellow orb on the scope projector screen, trying to make Annie and Mo feel familiar with it, see it for what it was: just an image from outer space, nothing more, nothing less.

"This isn't magic. All you're looking at here is something like a giant light bulb. Lots and lots of burning gases a real long way away. This is a big thing, and it's mysterious too, for sure. But that's only because we don't understand it that well right now. You know what they used to think in ancient times? All sorts of stuff. About how this was a god or something, flying across the sky in his chariot. Hey, people used to think the earth was the center of the universe, and the sun traveled around us, until a few centuries ago. But you don't believe that, do you?"

The girl shook her head.

"Why not?"

"Because teachers tell us it isn't true?"

"Because we all *know* it isn't true," Mo intervened. "It's in books. You're a little young for them now, but later you'll see."

"When I get to school," Annie said a little sourly.

"I'm sure that will happen, Annie," Lieberman said. "Once you and your mom are settled. And you're a bright kid. You won't have any problems picking these things up."

Mo smiled at him, some new warmth there, melting a little.

"What Michael is saying is that what seems mysterious one moment isn't a little later, when we understand it more."

"Which is science," Lieberman added. "Discovering. You know that word?"

Annie nodded her head.

"Course you do. But it's easy to forget what it really means. It's like ticking off something on a list. Once you're sure. And what we're sure of already is that these sunspots are just natural things. Like freckles or something, except in the sun's case they're huge freckles, maybe as big as sixty thousand miles across or more—that is, eight times the diameter of the earth . . ."

And actually, he thought, this particular group was bigger, bigger than any he'd ever seen.

". . . and freckles that change all the time. Which is where I come in. I didn't always do this, you understand. Once, a while back, I messed around with engineering, and other tricks with the sun, though that's a story for another time. Right now I try to figure out which way the freckles are going to go, whether they're getting bigger, whether they might be getting smaller."

"Do they change an awful lot?" Annie asked.

"You bet," he said, and he was on home territory now, heading straight for the finish line. "They come and go, a little like the tide. Not twice a day, like the sea does, but once every eleven years or so."

"Is that important?" Annie asked.

"Depends what you mean by important."

"I mean, does it matter? To us?"

"Well, the sun is a very long way away. Ninety-three million miles, to be exact. Seems crazy to think something that far away could be important."

The girl grinned at him and he wanted to laugh: She really wasn't going to let go.

"You're going to say 'but.' I always know when grown-ups are going to say 'but.' "

"Smart kid," said Lieberman, and she was, it was so clear. "But . . ."

He kicked at the gravel with his toe and wondered how you crammed all this into a few minutes of idle conversation.

"But things sometimes do affect each other in ways you'd never guess. By now we know sunspots affect all sorts of things. Some are obvious, like the big spurts of flame that emanate from the sun, called solar flares. Others are just plain invisible, like magnetism and X-rays, that come shooting through space. Then there's the weather. You cut open a tree that's a couple of hundred years old and you can see that eleven-year sunspot cycle in the rings inside. When the cycle hits a peak, the weather gets warmer, everywhere, and if you get rain too, which we haven't recently, things grow. You can see it inside the trunk. When the cycles were pretty much dead, which was what happened back in the sixteenth and seventeenth centuries for a while—don't ask me why—the world got colder. Europe had some of its coldest winters anyone had ever known."

Mo was the one with the question now.

"Is that why the weather has been so hot these last few years? I thought that was supposed to be global warming."

"Hey"—he threw up his hands—"we're all making this up as we go along. Some of it is global warming, for sure. No one disputes that these days, unless they get bribed by the oil companies. But the climate change seems to be equally linked to sunspots. There's no single reason behind it, just a cocktail of factors."

"And what we're in now is the eleventh year of the cycle?"

That was a tricky one, and Lieberman seriously wondered, for a moment, whether to try to bluff his way through.

"No," he said, opting for honesty. "We're in the ninth. All things being equal, we shouldn't be seeing sunspots like this for a good two years. Something happened, late in 1995, and from that point on we started to see some upsurge in the cycle, real steady, just like you'd expect, only early. And really marked too, recently, as if it was all coming to a head."

"I read about that," Mo said. "And all the awful predictions. Are they true?"

"I do astronomy, not astrology. Yeah, it's true that the peak of a solar storm has an effect on the earth. A cycle hot spot back in the seventies knocked out entire power grids across the whole of Canada. It messes with telecommunications systems too, and we all know how much we rely on those. I guess we can expect some short-term effects but nothing apocalyptic, not unless you think losing TV reception for a couple of hours is a matter of life and death."

"Oh."

He couldn't shake the idea that somehow she was frightened by all this but not willing to admit to it.

"A line of thinking some people are following—and Simon Bennett is your man for this one—is that one factor is tidal. By that I mean that the activity on the surface of the sun depends, to some extent, on the position of the planets to one another. We know that the tides on earth are due mainly to the pull of the moon as it spins around us. Well, the larger planets in our system exert an even bigger force. It makes theoretical sense to think we feel something from them too."

He wasn't really talking for them now, he was talking it out to himself. Mo understood this and encouraged him to continue.

"You're ahead of us?" she asked.

"Yeah?" Lieberman wasn't even thinking of them. He was out in the burning heat and not even noticing it, walking around the courtyard, picking up some pine cones that had fallen from the trees, then placing them carefully on the gravel.

"See, you've got to understand what the solstice is."

He went over to the perimeter wall overlooking the town, grabbed a stray rock, put it on the ground in front of them. Then he held one of the pine cones above his head.

"Imagine the cone is a ball like the earth and the top part of it is the northern hemisphere. Where we are now. We move around the sun, of course, so what I'm showing you is bad science. But it's how we see it from the ground. Each day the sun sweeps across our horizon and when it's there, we've got daylight; when it's on the other side of the earth, we've got night. But the earth isn't really sitting bolt upright like that. It's declined. And that means the height of the sun changes during the year. During the summer solstice it is, at midday, as high in the sky as it ever gets. So we get more sunshine, more daylight, than at any other time of the year, not because we're closer but because we see more of it. Equally, during the winter solstice the same thing happens but for the southern hemisphere. Which is why our winter is their summer. You with me?"

They nodded. They always nodded in these situations, but he was pretty happy with it. He'd explained it more poorly in the past.

"Now, the point is that maybe the heightened effect of spots and flares and all the rest at the solstice isn't just due to the fact that the sun is brighter in the sky and around longer than usual. Maybe there's some tidal effect on us too, messing us about with gravitational pull. And all this accentuates what happens with the weather, and anything else that gets shifted around by spot activity as well."

"Why would that explain how the cycle has shortened from eleven to nine years?" Mo asked. "These are annual events."

"Yeah," he said, and was so engrossed in himself, so buried in the pictures inside his head, that he didn't even realize until later how smart a question it was.

"The point is that if these guys are right, it's not just the tidal influence from the sun we've got to take into account. It's everything. Every other major hunk of rock in the universe."

She was shaking her head. She wasn't smiling anymore.

"I still don't see it. That's always been the case."

"Up to a point."

He reached down for the computer, picked it up, took it over to them, let them look at the bright color screen, and pulled out the sequence, one he was so familiar with, one he'd played over and over again until he didn't need to see it anymore, it lived inside his head.

"Everything moves in the universe, everything is always or-biting everything else, okay? But we know how they move. This is all just mathematics—complex mathematics, for sure, but not beyond us. With this little machine I can show you how the stars looked in Bethlehem on the night Jesus was born. I can fly you past the surface of Mars and look back to see what the earth and our moon are like from there, today, five hundred years from now. It doesn't matter. These things are just some big clockwork mechanism in the sky and they'll stay like that until the big red giant comes along and gobbles them all up."

They didn't say anything. Just looked at him with the word "So?" in their eyes.

"So it's like the old saying about monkeys in a room writing Shakespeare. You keep them running like that forever and once in a while you get something weird. Take a look at this and you'll see what I mean."

On the screen of the computer was a map of the galaxy, with only the major players marked out on it: the sun at the center, the planets around it. They were orbiting slowly, randomly. In the corner of the screen a series of numbers in date format were flicking over, too quickly for anyone to read.

Lieberman watched the display, waited for the moment, then pressed a key. The picture froze where it was and even to them it looked impressive, even to a nine-year-old's eyes there was some awful symmetry here.

The planets formed a line. The earth was on one side, with Pluto, neatly labeled in red, behind. Aligned together perfectly on the opposing side of the sun were four planets, names flash-ing: Mercury, Mars, Jupiter, and Saturn.

"See—we know from studies done by NASA that just an alignment of Jupiter and Saturn can cause a twenty percent in-crease in sunspot activity. When you add in three other planets in what we call the Grand Cross like this, and whatever effects their gravitational pull might have on the earth, maybe you get even more—or less, that's a possibility too. And . . ."

That was enough. He realized it abruptly. They were too quiet and he was just giving it to them too straight, without the caveats.

"And that happens on Wednesday," Mo said, no expression on her face at all.

Lieberman swore inwardly at himself. The date was on the screen. He really shouldn't expect these people to be plain dumb.

"On Wednesday," she continued, and walked around the yard as she spoke, arranging all the pine cones into a row, aligning them with the rock, "we have both this conjunction of planets and the summer solstice. All together."

"Correct."

Lieberman looked at Annie and felt a little happier. He'd lost her. She'd wandered off somewhere else in her head, found this all too big, too distant to bother her, and he was relieved.

"And the reason we're here is to record it," he continued. "For posterity, some kind of solar project—don't ask, they haven't favored me with a full brief yet. We're here to watch, make notes, take pictures. See what we can learn."

Annie had her hand up again, and Lieberman braced for yet another unsettling question.

"I need to go," she said, and he gave an inward sigh.

"Time for home," Mo said. "Say thank-you to Michael."

"Thanks," Annie said flatly, then began the climb back down the steps.

"Wait for us at the bottom," Mo said.

They watched her hop and skip down the hill. Lieberman shrugged his shoulders, felt a little old and stupid after such a rambling display.

"Long time since I gave a school talk," he said, shrugging.

"It was good."

The scared side of her had gone. Maybe it had never been there, really; it was just something the burning day had fired in his imagination. But she was a little warmer. That was no trick of the light.

"You're kind," he said.

"No. I mean it."

"Annie's quite a kid." He hesitated a moment, then ventured, "Is it hard?"

"What?"

"Being on your own."

Mo gave him a frank look. "Annie and I . . . we've been on our own for a couple of years. We have an understanding."

He could think of nothing to say, just nodded. This was not the time to ask, he thought. Definitely not. He started tidying his stuff away.

"Say," he said after a few seconds. "You play tennis? I brought along my long-framed Prince tennis racket, which I prefer to think of as the long-framed tennis racket formerly known as Prince. There's an old court I saw back at the house. It's a touch beaten up but I've got a spare racket. And tennis is quick. We could be over and done in thirty minutes."

She laughed anyway, and looked frankly into his face.

"I'm terrible at tennis," she said, smiling still.

"I'm great but I have no killer instinct, I drown in sympathy for my opponent. I promise to play down to you. I'll promise to lose if you like."

"You're married," she said, and it was a statement.

"Was. Strictly single and unattached these days."

"Oh."

She watched Annie skipping down the steps, following every movement.

"What kills a marriage in your world, Michael?" she said, turning suddenly to stare into his eyes.

"Same thing you find everywhere else, I guess. Time. Boredom. Insecurity. Fear."

"And hitting on women when you're away from home?"

She didn't stop smiling when she said it. This was not, he guessed, a judgment.

"That too. But it's all connected. You'd be amazed how much fear gets to the heart of things, and winds up on the other side with some new label, like lust."

She laughed quietly, and he guessed he deserved as much.

Lieberman's hand reached, automatically, for his head. His thick black head of hair was soaked in sweat. He missed the baseball cap.

"This isn't a move," he said. "I'm just trying to rebuild a few social skills that got lost over the years. Nothing more. Really. If I've offended you in some way, I apologize. I didn't mean to."

"No problem. And thanks for the talk. It was . . . illuminating. And for helping with Annie too."

"My pleasure," he said, meaning it. "And I'll tell you what. They're throwing some briefing tonight. I'll get you invited if you like. We could both find out a little more about why we're here."

"Sure," she said quietly, and looked down the steps, saw Annie waiting there seated on the stone wall.

He shook his head, and softly cursed the way the heat was turning his brain. For a moment there he almost thought she looked scared.

10
Wagner's First Day

Helen Wagner looked at the office and knew it had been swept. It had that antiseptic look that came from polish and machines. People looking for things. People peering into the past. Standard practice when an office in the Agency changed hands under odd circumstances. And something so male about it as well: For all its cleanliness the place seemed untidy, disorganized, just plain wrong.

Until a week before, this had been the home of her predecessor, Belinda Churton, the woman who'd made the post of head of the CIA's Science and Technology directorate—S&T for short—a real job, not just a passing nod at fashion. In eight busy years, she'd screamed at the men who ran the Agency until they couldn't ignore her pleas. And Helen Wagner had followed her all the way, first as a newly recruited graduate out of MIT, then as number three in the formative years of the directorate's rise to glory, when the Internet and biotechnology came out of the lab and fell straight into the hands of crooks and terrorists everywhere.

She gazed at her reflection in the long, deep office window, the image hardened by the dazzling daylight outside. It was an attractive face, sympathetic and intelligent, with sharp blue eyes that never seemed to rest. She wore short, neat black hair tied in a bun, as if to put it in its place and drown a little of her natural beauty. She knew what the whispers were down the corridors, and this was the curse of her looks. This hard, somewhat standoffish elegance belonged, they thought, close to the top of the organization, but not at its helm. She lacked the practical, careworn appearance of the person you expected to find running a department of government.

She wore a gray two-piece suit in light wool, and would take off the jacket, sit at the desk in her cream silk shirt the moment she settled down to the job. Physically, she felt good. She worked out. She looked after herself. She had a strong, curvy body that was guaranteed to turn heads, though she'd long ago stopped noticing. "Keep the body fit, the mind follows," her mother had said over and over again, in the long years of waiting, in the self-imposed exile that followed her father's sudden death. It was the kind of pat, easy sentiment that passed her lips so easily, spoken in that curious accent, a mix of Polish, Yiddish, and American, that never changed. This job, this ascent through the Agency was, Helen knew, some attempt at redemption. She wondered what her father would have thought, and knew such rumination was futile, stupid. He'd died when she was two, when the scandal had broken and refused to leave their door. There was nothing in her memory of that time. Her consciousness began later, in the dead, in-between years, waiting in the shadow of this infamous, vanished man.

Ten years after the Agency had first accused Pieter Wagner, an acclaimed nuclear physicist working at MIT in Cambridge, of spying for the Russians, ten years after they'd leaked the story to the media (lights popping at the front door of their small brownstone house on Beacon Hill, and the constant sight of men waiting outside, yelling questions, never going away), a federal commission had cleared his name, awarded the family close to $10 million compensation, and issued a public apology for the mistake. Which it was. Her father, it turned out, was just the innocent victim of an overzealous employee who thought that a foreign accent and an ancestry in Russian-occupied Poland were, on their own, sufficient grounds for suspicion. The money meant nothing to her, though it would later put her through MIT and pay for a year of research at the Sorbonne. He was gone: wrists slashed with a razor blade in the tiny white-tiled bathroom of the little house by the beach in Maine, the one, she later discovered, they'd rented as some kind of last refuge until the Feds came and broke down the door.

When he was posthumously cleared, she'd sworn she would become a scientist too, had made that oath in her dark, over-heated bedroom on Beacon Hill. It was August 1978 and she was thirteen, already developing a prematurely adult beauty, already aware that she possessed something that made other people uncomfortable. In her own mind this was not a form of revenge. It was all a question of balance. When she joined the Agency, there were no favors, no backward glances, not as far as she could see. She was a scientist, and this was a good science job. If people talked, they talked behind her back, and she didn't even think of listening. The name Wagner had lost some of its topicality, to her great relief. She became herself, a person in her own right, not a portion of his shadow. And then, three years ago, her mother had died, struck down by an out-of-control truck. And the job, which swallowed her, consumed everything she put into it, with Belinda helping every inch of the way, like some surrogate mother and father all rolled into one.

She knew every inch of this office. Today it looked bare, bleak, and soulless. Belinda always had flowers and didn't care what the old guard thought of them. S&T was on the map; it occupied a growing part of the new Langley complex, employing close to three thousand bright young people who'd come out of college and found themselves thrust straight into the melting pot of almost every advanced science known to man. Thanks to Belinda's persuasive powers and her impressive academic record at Stanford, S&T had recruited some of the finest scientific brains she could find, plucked from the corridors of Cornell and Harvard, Oxford and Cambridge, then thrust, without warning, into a world they couldn't hope to understand.

She remembered standing in front of the desk she now occupied, three months into the job, close to tears, telling Belinda she was resigning, that this was no way for any human being to live. The supposed need for there to be a clandestine veil over her life had killed the few tentative relationships she'd started to build. Worst of all was the one, fatal time she'd fallen into bed with a fellow agent and discovered that their professional closeness only made things worse, made her more tongue-tied, more paranoid.

And Belinda had smiled, talked her out of it, as Helen knew she would, had spoken of how these crises came and went in Agency life, were just steps in the natural process of growing into the secret world. Helen had listened to her talk, speechless at the grasp this woman had of her own lowly work. Belinda was so high in the administrative structure of Langley that she could hardly be expected to recognize a junior trainee. Yet, when the moment came, she knew every last detail of the cases Helen had handled, was able to comment on them with such precision this couldn't have been a trick, some quick executive briefing fitted in before the interview just to keep some junior employee on the ball.

When the interview was over, Belinda smiling, extending a hand out over the desk, Helen found it hard to believe she could even have considered leaving Langley. The place was too special. Belinda too. And perhaps, one day, even Helen herself, if she caught enough of her mentor's magic.

It had been around five on a chill January afternoon. When Belinda knew she'd won, she smiled at Helen, nodded across the room, and said, "You look like you need a drink, honey. Watch this. I'm going to let you in on a secret."

And then she walked across the room, over to the sealed glass window, looked out at the bare winter trees, and pulled up a grid in the air-conditioning system.

"You know, three years I've been asking those office guys to fix this vent, and three years they just keep forgetting to do it. There are rules about alcohol on the premises, Wagner, and if I ever catch you breaking them you'll be in big trouble, miss. But right now . . ."

Her hand dived into the vent and came out with a half bottle of Glenfiddich.

". . . I'm prepared to bend a little. After all, what's the point in being the boss if you can't be allowed a little discretion?"

They sipped the whiskey out of plastic cups, and Helen could still remember how it made her eyes water.

Belinda seemed ageless and indestructible, an icon of goodness in the occasionally murky waters that went with the job. Then one day she walked out of the office and was gone for good. All because some Montana crazy felt like making a point. All because you could pick up the tricks of the bomb-making trade on the Web, go out and buy the right fertilizer, rent a truck from Avis, and place your deadly mix of metal and chemical right next to a suburban garage, wait there all night, then detonate the thing with a cheap amateur radio remote control the next morning.

Two weeks later it still made no sense. The FBI was making noises about ecoterrorists, militiamen, and right-wing crazies, but no one had been arrested, and Helen had a feeling that, as the days dragged by, the case was drifting into nothingness.

The director of the CIA, Ben Levine, had called her into his office on the day the news of Belinda's death broke, given her the temporary deputy directorship of S&T, making her the effective head of one of the Agency's four divisions, all at the age of thirty-five. She should have been flattered. The job tasted like ashes in her mouth. She'd never liked Levine, they both knew it, and she could only guess that he picked her because there really was no choice. S&T, like the Agency, was in the middle of some messy executive regeneration. Larry Wolfit, the quiet, introverted scientist who was Belinda's official deputy, should have been first in line, but got passed over. Helen understood, in an unformed way, why too. Wolfit was a loyal, trusted, diligent S&T executive, but lately had seemed detached from the work, bound up with outside interests that took more and more of his time.

It had taken five days for her to go through the added security clearances, get some briefing on how the structure worked inside Langley when it came to dealing with the three other directorates: Operations, Administration, and Intelligence. She'd already met the assistant head of Operations, Dave Barnside, the principal liaison officer for the Agency's active service arm. He was one of the old school, bright, tough, and cynical, pushing his mid-forties and resigned to the idea that he'd probably never climb the ladder any further. Barnside made her glad she was in S&T. The rest of Langley was new to her, and she almost came to resent the insularity that Belinda had built into the directorate, the way it operated outside the orbit of the rest of the Agency, at least as far as most of its occupants were aware.

She took off her jacket, sat down at the large, bare desk, and stared out the window. The weather was dry and scorching again. She wished she'd worn something cooler. The trees looked half-dead; the grass that ran off into the woods beyond the complex was scorched. She was about to scroll through her E-mail and try to put some priority into the day when the phone rang.

"Wagner," she said firmly.

"There's a car coming for you in ten minutes. Barnside and I are going on ahead for the meeting right now. We'll see you there."

Levine's voice sounded as flat and dry as the landscape outside the window.

"Do I need to prepare?"

It almost sounded like a laugh. "No one's prepared for this one. Not even me. We're going to the White House. There's a long day ahead of us."

Then the phone went dead.

Her mind went blank. There was nothing on the agenda, nothing in any of the high-priority E-mails she was now calling up, that could explain this abrupt summons. In her years with the Agency she'd never even been to the White House. It was typical too that Levine had left her in the dark.

"Bastard," she muttered, and got up, hooked her jacket off the peg.

She leaned around the door. Maureen, her executive assistant, had just arrived and was making a pot of coffee.

"It smells great, Maureen, but you're going to have to drink it by yourself. Put all my appointments on hold until you hear back from me. Anything urgent, you can get me on the mobile."

Maureen smiled at her. "My, that didn't take long, now, did it?"

She didn't answer, just walked back into the office and took one last look at the empty desk. Then closed the door and walked over to the window. The vent was still dead, not pumping out an iota of cool air. She picked at it with her long, slender fingers, pried it loose, and lifted up the metal grid. There was a half-bottle of Glenfiddich sitting there, half-full. She picked it up, and thought of the hand that had put it there.

"Jesus, Belinda, I wish to God this was you and not me talking to these people. This feels like one big nightmare."

Briefly, she considered taking a swig from the bottle—for old times' sake—but common sense prevailed and she tucked the bottle back into the vent for another day.

It was a two-minute wait outside the S&T offices in the new wing. Over at the original Agency building that dated back to 1961 she could see a long black limo pulling away, two shapes in the back. Levine and Barnside, she guessed. They could have waited if they'd wanted.

A fawn Chevrolet came up, the driver anonymous behind overlarge Ray-Bans. Helen climbed in, aware that the day was so hot and airless she was sweating and short of breath before she even hit the seat.

When the car was out of the security gates of Langley and mingling with the flow of traffic headed for the city, she closed her eyes and tried to picture the day ahead.

11
A Kind of Love

"Slowly, Joe," Charley Pascal gasped, breathless, feeling his hardness move too quickly inside her. "I don't get so much anymore."

The lithe, strong shape shifted position, his pale, half-Japanese face unsmiling, distant, though she didn't like to think of that. His rigidity became more still. Charley Pascal felt this familiar rushing of the blood, the growing wetness between them, and focused on herself, the way she always did at this point in the act, wondered how different this time was from the last, if you could measure it in terms of the electricity, the moistness between their entwined, coupling bodies.

Joe Katayama was poised over her so carefully, palms down on the bed, back arched, making sure to distribute his weight away from her body just enough to slacken the pain, but not so far as to take away the sparking ecstasy that ran between them. She remembered, when this began, how she'd gently move beneath him, placing the soles of her feet on his thrusting buttocks, extemporizing with the circular motion of his bucking, rearing body.

But that was before.

The best she could do now was touch his chest gently, delicately with her hands, feel for his nipples, hard and tiny, surrounded by circlets of hair, stroke the nape of his neck, hope to taste the rime of sweat there, place her fingers in his mouth, moving in and out across the moistness of his tongue, like a mirror image of this older, larger thing that conjoined their bodies, pushing her hard into the soft white mattress, generating the tinny squeaking of springs from the old wood-framed bed.

This time, she thought, it is different. I won't come. I won't get close.

The illness was moving with such speed now, hand in glove with the events that were shaping beyond the closed wooden door of their room, elsewhere in Yasgur's Farm. The discrete shaft of time that was what remained of her life stood in front of her, dwindling by the minute, and, as it shortened, the physicality of the world diminished, putting in its place some filmy, ethereal appreciation of the subtle, peripheral parts of her existence, unseen before the illness came into her head, began to infect her body.

She closed her eyes (trying, in her mind's eye, to bring the physicality back into their fucking) and felt, somewhere inside her partner's writhing, frantic body, the distant god Gaia work its way into his blood, firing the hardness that burrowed deep inside her. There were no thoughts in her head then, just the sudden, urgent need to hold his sweating flesh, to pull him farther into herself, all the while screaming, screaming.

Joe Katayama released himself and she opened her eyes. The warmth ran between them, so copious she could feel it draining from her, feel the dampness coming through the plain cotton sheet.

She reached up with what strength she had left, took his head, forced her tongue into his mouth, tasting the strength of his life, wondering how much this sudden, unexpected shock of a climax so strange, yet so powerful, might have milked her own diminishing store of energy.

He moved slowly inside her again, hardening. She pushed him away.

"No, Joe," she said. "Too much for me now."

He stared at her with his dark, expressionless, half-open eyes and it perplexed her how little she could sense of what was going on behind this flat, unsmiling face.

"You were different," he said, in a flat Middle American voice, the echo of concern behind the monotone, trying to break through. "Maybe you're getting better."

"No," she answered. "I don't get better, Joe. We both know that. I just change. We're all changing."

As he drew back from her, she felt this hard extension of him leave her body, and wondered at the moistness that it left behind. Not all of it was Joe's.

They lay still on the bed, silent, staring at each other, listening to the breeze outside, feeling the stain on the sheet grow to a dry deadness on their skin. After a few minutes, from somewhere close by, they heard the low, soft sound of people talking, happy, a tiny undulation of applause.

He watched her, waiting. She said nothing.

"You think something's happened," he said finally.

"No. I know," she said, and wished he spoke French; it would, perhaps, help break this communications block that sometimes lay so obviously between them. "I never doubted it, Joe. We're agents. We're channels for something that is so powerful, so real it can't be stopped. It rolls forward, like night after day. Like a tide that's come to cleanse us. Can't you feel it?"

"Sure," he said flatly, and she knew he was lying.

In the end it didn't matter. Understanding wasn't essential. Just acceptance. And she was surrounded by disciples now, ones who didn't question this course they'd chosen. The world was waking up, and in the places she looked, the places that found her too, there was no shortage of followers.

"I need to join them," she said.

He said nothing, picked her up in his arms, carried her into the bathroom, ran the water, tested the heat while she sat in a wicker chair, watching him fondly. When it was full, he lifted her into the bath, joined her, washed her all over, let her do as much for him too as she could.

"So sweet," she said, stroking his damp hair. "None of this could have happened without you, Joe."

"You got inspiration, I got contacts," he said, a brief smile there.

"A leader needs lieutenants," she said. "A vision without a means to its completion is just a dream."

And such dreams, she thought.

He nodded, lifted her from the bath, toweled her dry, dressed her in the clothes she wanted, a plain cotton shirt, comfortable linen slacks. Then took her in his arms and placed her in the wheelchair.

As he bent over her, she kissed him.

"I know this isn't love," she said. "I know it's something else, Joe. Sympathy?"

The dark hooded eyes betrayed no expression. She felt guilty for pushing him this far. He was happier when he didn't have to think. He liked a role, a challenge. He didn't want to have to work out why, just how.

"I don't know what love is, Charley," he said, and seemed genuinely puzzled. "I'd do anything for you. I'd die. Is that love?"

"Yes," she replied, and knew that evened up the lies. Such strength, she thought. There really was nothing he wouldn't do if it was needed.

"I want you to be happy as you go through this, Charley," he said. "It's important for all of us."

"I know," she said, and thought: He still doesn't understand. This is the fire from heaven, this is nature reclaiming its place in the order of things. Her own happiness was irrelevant.

A smile came on her face as he pushed her into the big control room, filled with the whir of the workstations, the quiet low hum of excitement. In her wheelchair, dressed in white, Charley Pascal looked radiant. There were eleven men and women there, all in clean white shirts and pale slacks, applauding as she came in. Tina Blackshire pulled herself away from the screen, grinned at her, acknowledged Charley's smile in return.

"Well?" Charley asked.

"It's down. It was them," she said. "We monitored the first message."

"Good." Charley nodded.

She looked at the clock on the wall, wondered about the zenith, how best to calculate its precise arrival.

"Let's not get overexcited. We've work to do. This is only the beginning."

Tina Blackshire bent back into the computer. The rest of them moved over to charts and other monitors.

Charley pushed the wheelchair over to the window, measuring the strength in her arms (diminishing, she thought). They had everything they needed. Food. Information. The high-speed data links that were, to all intents and purposes, a virtual world, one they could enter and leave at will, with no one seeing their footprints. One they could, when the time was right, remake, forever. This place had no need of fixed geographical boundaries. You could touch a button in Hong Kong and make it flip a switch in Rio. There was a harsh, electronic oneness to it that was its own unmaking, and it removed the need for a physical presence when a virtual one served the purpose better.

Besides, Charley thought as she stared out the window, there were other reasons for staying under this single roof (not hiding, she thought, it couldn't be called that).

Outside the day looked as if it were aflame.

12
The White House

Helen Wagner was rushed through the security entrance of the White House in a matter of seconds, then greeted by a smartly dressed middle-aged woman in a gray suit.

"Your colleagues are waiting for you in the Vice President's office, Miss Wagner," the woman said quietly. "He will be joining you once he gets back from the Attorney General."

The woman wouldn't look directly at her. Helen was sure she'd been crying.

"I'll take you there."

"Thank you."

Her head spinning, she followed into a large lobby where a group of people bustled around, papers in hand, none looking at each other, no one saying much at all, and Helen thought she just might be dreaming all this. The scene had some surreal, inconsequential atmosphere to it.

She was beckoned into a larger office. Levine and Barnside sat there, with two other men, one she recognized as Dan Fogerty, the head of the FBI.

Levine nodded at her.

"Helen Wagner. Acting head of S&T. As of this morning. You're going to have to pick up on this one as we go along, Wagner. Hell, we all are. This is Dan Fogerty. I guess you know that. And Graeme Burnley. Right now the closest we've got to a White House Chief of Staff."

Burnley was thin, with the kind of tidily manicured haircut she always associated with Washington lobbyists. He looked no more than twenty-five. His eyes were pink and watery.

"Hi," Fogerty said, and waved her to a seat. She looked out the window. The White House lawn was still green, the kind of bright, artificial green you got when you watered things in a drought. In the distance a crowd seemed to be assembling: shorts and T-shirts, standard-issue uniform for the searing weather that seemed to be locked in for the duration of the summer.

The door opened and Tim Clarke walked in, shooed them to stay in their seats, and said, "Let's cut to the quick, gentlemen. I know the outline. And I know I'm breaking the rules here. Right after this I go into a meeting of the National Security Council and doubtless you think I should have gone there first, let you brief them, and do things by the book. Well, to hell with the book. If what I think has happened, I'm mad and I'm looking for answers. So who's going to start giving me them?"

Helen couldn't help but stare at him. Clarke had been a sensation in American politics. Lionized for his role in the field in the Gulf War, a successful businessman after leaving the Army, then a fast-rising conservative force among Republicans as his wealth and ambitions grew. It was a classic rise from a working-class American childhood, and the only thing that set Clarke apart was his race. He was black, the son of emigrant Jamaicans, and the West Indies twang still surfaced in his voice from time to time.

All the same, had the Republicans stood a chance in the election, Clarke would never have made it onto the ticket with Bill Rollinson. But everyone—everyone—knew the Republicans were nonstarters from the outset. Until the scandal machine resurfaced one final, fatal time. The Rollinson-Clarke team went from laughingstock to racing certainties in the space of two months, and swept the board when November came. She'd watched Clarke on TV, feeling so proud that a black American had finally reached so far, then checked herself. It was obvious why a black man was there. The white guys had screwed up so badly they were unelectable, so no one cared who the running mate was. And as she watched Clarke move uncomfortably into office—and, according to newspaper reports, get sidelined into speech-making—she guessed the same thought was going through his head too. There was something too pure, almost to the point of naïveté about the man. He didn't push his family to the fore. She couldn't even remember the name of his wife, a pretty, slim black woman, who was always pictured slightly in front of their one child, a boy, as if she didn't want him to step into the limelight and risk getting burned. Clarke somehow didn't fit, and it wasn't just his color. He lacked the sophistication, the guile that everyone took for granted in Washington.

Levine cleared his throat and said, "I think this falls to me, sir. And I wish it didn't. At 0449 our time we lost contact with Air Force One on the way back from Tokyo. She was routed for Geneva. The last confirmed position was one hundred eighty miles east of Irkutsk. We keep constant radar surveillance on Air Force One whenever she's in range as a standard security measure. The indications are that she was in some kind of collision with a British passenger jet around one hundred twenty miles east of the city, but that's only half the story. Somehow both planes were downed by a single phenomenon. We have the same report confirmed from local radar too. They're sending out the Army to look for debris, and they've agreed we can airlift in our own team too. Some pieces of the planes are turning up already, according to the Russians. It's a mess, nothing much bigger than a passenger door, and that burned so bad they don't know whether it's ours or from the British plane. We have a mission on the way, people from the FAA along to take a look. This is Russian sovereign territory but we already have a commitment from the Kremlin that we can take in pretty much who we like so long as we don't take advantage of the situation."

Clarke shook his head. He was a handsome man, thought Helen. He wore close-cropped, military-style hair, gold-rimmed glasses, and a sober, dark suit, and he was big in the flesh, at least six feet tall and muscular. But there was a genuine spark of emotion in his eyes, more than you found in most politicians. She'd seen that on TV. Here, six feet away, it was even more obvious.

"Any hope?"

Levine shook his head. "All the indications are that both airplanes were totally destroyed in some kind of explosion on impact at around six thousand feet. We'll look, but it's impractical to think anyone survived."

"Jesus," Clarke groaned.

Helen watched him. You could forgive someone for losing it a little at a time like this. Who knew what LBJ was really like when they told him Kennedy was dead? And this was somehow much worse. So distant, so huge.

"Run me down the names, Graeme."

Burnley looked at a sheet of paper on his knee, but it was obvious he knew these all by heart.

"The President and First Lady. The Chief of Staff and Mrs. Sawyer. The Secretary of State for Trade and Mrs. Olsen. Congressmen Simons and Bernhard, Congresswoman Lilley. Plus fifteen White House staff members and a crew of seven on the plane."

"And?"

Burnley looked lost. "Sir?"

"The other plane?"

He was lost for words. Levine interjected. "There were three hundred thirty-two passengers and eight crew, sir. We have nationals, most are European."

Clarke shook his head. "Almost four hundred people dead. Someone want to tell me why?"

"Sir," Graeme Burnley interrupted. "There are formalities we have to deal with first."

"They're done, Graeme. I spoke to the Attorney General. I get sworn in right after this meeting. They're working on a TV broadcast right now. Formalities can wait. I want to know what the hell happened, and most of all why we just got robbed of one hell of a President."

"They go beyond that, sir. We need to be thinking about the funeral. The arrangements . . . this will be, effectively, a world summit and you will be leading it. We need to set agendas now."

"No, we don't," Clarke said immediately. "Dammit, Graeme. Bill Rollinson was a man. We have to bury him and his family, for sure. And this nation is going to have to grieve for him too, all of us. But we can leave the politics out of it, for now anyway."

They nodded, in a way, she thought, that said: You have to make these noises, sure, we know. But everyone understood how cool relations between Rollinson and Clarke had been recently, most of it revolving around how Clarke had been sidelined in government. Rollinson would push the black ticket so far, it seemed, and then no further. And as it turned out, in doing so he'd given America probably the last thing he'd ever expected: the first black president in its history.

"And I still want to know what happened."

"Sir," Helen said, and she tried not to blush when they all stared at her, "I did some work on the Mauritius crash last year. When you get down to it there are really only three possibilities in these situations. Either there was some malfunction in the air—mechanical or navigational; or there was a device that destroyed one or both airplanes, or possibly damaged one so much that it crashed into the other; or the planes were destroyed by an outside agency. A missile, ground-to-air fire, enemy action."

"The rest of you I know," Clarke said gruffly, peering at her. "No one introduced you, lady."

Levine leaned forward. "My apologies, sir. Helen Wagner here is acting head of Science and Technology at the Agency. Just started today."

Clarke smiled thinly. "Wagner. I know the name. I guess you get sick of hearing people say that."

"The first time is okay," Helen replied, unsmiling, feeling the eyes in the room upon her.

"First day on the job. Baptism of fire," Levine added.

"Yeah, for all of us," Clarke replied, looking at her. "I can get to that stage myself, Miss Wagner. But where's the evidence?"

"There is no evidence," Levine said, a touch sourly. "First, it's clear that both planes suffered some kind of incident at altitude. Neither should have been at six thousand feet. Both lost contact at around thirty-three thousand feet, so we have to assume some dual incident affected them."

"How far apart were they when they first reported trouble?" Helen asked.

"Ten miles," Dave Barnside said, his eyes on Clarke. "We have an Ops team going through the tapes now."

"Could an explosion cover that kind of area?" Helen asked.

"Nothing you could get on board an airplane," Barnside replied.

"It's inconceivable that both aircraft could have identical system failures at altitude," said Helen. "It must be an attack from the air or ground."

Levine toyed with the papers in front of him. "If it was from the air we would have picked it up on radar."

"A stealth aircraft?" Clarke asked. "We don't have a monopoly on that technology."

Levine shrugged. "No. The Chinese have stealth. And the Russians too. But if this was an attack in the air, the planes would have been destroyed when they were hit. They wouldn't have descended thirty thousand feet intact, as far as we can make out, before disintegrating. It doesn't make sense. And the same goes for some kind of ground-to-air attack."

"Is anyone claiming responsibility?" Clarke asked.

Dan Fogerty pulled himself up in his chair. He looked just like he did on TV: a crumpled academic out of Georgetown, which was exactly what he once was. And the languid attitude and expressionless face hid, she guessed, a formidable intelligence.

"Someone always claims responsibility, Mr. President. I hope you don't mind me calling you that. I don't see why any of us need wait on the formalities. You really have to bear in mind there will always be someone putting their hand up. Thanks to the Internet, they can do it for free just by E-mailing me these days. The news is only just starting to get out on the wires, of course, so the real lunatics are a little way off. Right now, we have three definitive claims. One is from some

Libyan-based organization we've never heard of. One is from a Middle Eastern crew linked to Iraq. And the third is some bunch of ecoterrorists, not that we know much about them."

"Anything there?" Clarke asked, impatience in his face.

"Nothing you can put your finger on, sir. The Libyans and the Iraqis make this kind of claim all the time. Partly to keep us on our toes, partly so that every time something big does happen they can put their hands in the air and say: We did it. The eco-group—I'm getting some data on them. I'm dubious, frankly."

"Any particular reason for ruling them out?" Helen asked.

"The Libyans and the Iraqis have got the wherewithal to do something like this, Miss Wagner. I don't understand how a bunch of tree-huggers can hope to achieve the same. What's their means? You want my opinion? It must have been a bomb at altitude."

Helen watched the way Levine and Barnside were shifting in their chairs, and wondered what was going through their heads.

"Bombs in two planes simultaneously, sir?" she asked.

Fogerty stared at her through owlish, tortoiseshell glasses.

"You have a better explanation, young lady?"

She smiled at him, thought that if someone else gave her the young lady routine she might go crazy, and said, "Not right now, sir. These ecoterrorists: Did they give a name?"

"The Children of Gaia."

"Ah," she said, and nodded. "Gaia. That's kind of a nature figure, I think."

"Gaia, my dear," Fogerty said, adopting his professor pose to the full, "in Greek mythology was the Mother Earth, the daughter of Chaos, from which all creation sprang. There are modern beliefs—cults, if you would have them—which translate Gaia into meaning some kind of spirit of the earth within the universe, as if the planet itself was some kind of living entity in the solar system. Some think this spirit will rise to protect the earth from the damage we seem to be inflicting upon it. I think there are a good many quite respectable, if cranky, tree-huggers who follow this line, and doubtless a few crazies too. The crazies may well be capable of some such thing as Oklahoma. We all know that kind of act takes little in the way of organization and technology. Bringing down Air Force One over central Russia isn't something you can achieve with sacks of fertilizer and a homemade fuse."

Helen listened in silence. For all his intellect, Fogerty clearly wasn't a man to waver from a fixed view of the situation.

Levine shifted uncomfortably in his seat. He needed a cigarette, she thought. It was written all over his sallow features.

"There is one other possibility," Levine said. "Which is why, in fact, I asked you here, Wagner."

"Sir?" she said, thinking she could learn to hate this bastard a lot if he made a habit of leading her blind into heavyweight sessions like this.

"The sun thing, for chrissake. You read the papers, don't you?"

"Right."

Don't bluff, think fast, Helen counseled herself. That's what Belinda taught you.

"So," Levine continued. "You're the scientist. Can there be a link?"

Nice guy, she thought. Asking her to paraphrase an entire branch of astrophysics in a sentence, and one that people were only just beginning to understand in any case.

"It seems unlikely," she said. "It's no secret that we are about to be engulfed by a major solar storm. That happens every eleven years or so, and we usually experience some effects, such as the breakdown of power grids, the loss of telecommunications systems. We know the sunspot cycle is erratic right now. We know that the planetary alignment is disturbing it and altering a broad spectrum of solar radiation and other waveforms on the earth. None of this is new, though this time around their frequency and geographical spread are more diverse than anything we've seen before. That, I suspect, gives you your answer. If there was evidence that the force of the solar intrusions was increasing, and not just the frequency, then I think there is a possibility that the incident had its cause in some related activity. But we have no proof of that, or that airplanes have been affected by this kind of problem before."

"No?" Fogerty asked, eyes wide behind his glasses. "We still don't know what really brought down TWA 800. There's a whole host of unexplained plane crashes in the books."

"But do they match up with the solar cycle, sir? I doubt it. Someone would have made the connection before. There's really no evidence that we are in for much else from this solar storm except some severe telecommunications disruption and an enhancing of the process of climate change, something we have been helping along ourselves in any case. I'm not saying it may not be painful, and it's a fact that disaster response teams around the world are on low alert. But it's not an intelligence issue, surely."

"Really?" Levine grunted. "Then how do you explain the fact that the Russian ground team that's there already reports the wreckage they've found is hot? Radioactive. I got them wiring back to us asking for safety equipment."

Helen gritted her teeth.

"Since I was unaware of that fact until you mentioned it, sir, I can't explain it. When you pass me the file I will happily work on that information."

"Makes more damn sense than Greek gods," Barnside mumbled.

Tim Clarke looked at his watch. "I want an hourly update on this. From all of you. If there is clear evidence of terrorist activity, I want to hear it from you people first, not CNN. And the same goes for any other theories. As far as the press is concerned, this is an inflight tragedy. Graeme, you go see the publicity people. I want the tone of this broadcast right. Let's focus on the loss of a President, not something we still can't put a finger on."

"Sir," Burnley said, and disappeared out the door.

Clarke looked at them all. "You guys work together on this one. I know how you people like the odd border war now and then. This is bigger than all that. You understand me?"

"We both have clear-cut mandates, and we know where they're drawn, Mr. President," Fogerty said, smiling.

"Yeah, you make sure you do. And Miss Wagner?"

He was looking hard at her. She wondered what was going on in his mind.

"Sir?"

"Pursue every angle on this. Every one."

Then the meeting was over. Clarke rose from the table, stared at each of them, and turned to leave.

"Mr. President?" Fogerty said.

"Mr. Fogerty?" Clarke replied at the door.

"I don't have the right words to say this, sir. To become President is an honor, probably the greatest any man can hope for. And to win that prize this way must be one of the oddest feelings on earth."

"You can say that again, mister," Clarke replied quietly.

"What I wanted to say was, you are the President now. There's nothing to qualify that. And I, along with everyone here, wish you well in the job. For all our sakes."

"Thank you for that," Clarke said, peering at him. "I appreciate it."

Then he was gone.

Five minutes later, outside in the corridor, on the way to the car lot, Fogerty smiled at Levine and said, "You were pushing it in there, Ben. This guy's ex-Army. He likes to think you care. He also happens to be the President now. He deserves our respect."

"Clinton appointed me," Levine grunted. "I'm just one more white Democratic appointee who gets his ass kicked out of the way once Clarke gets his feet under the table. You watch, we're in the same boat. Besides, this is just for show under the circumstances. A couple of hours from now he'll feel the weight of all that good old White House paper bearing down on him and sit back into the job. Shame, really. I'd hoped we'd have someone in that job who didn't shake when the wind started to blow a little hard. As for the respect thing, Dan, hell, you know as well as I do, no one deserves it. You earn it, that's all."

Helen marched one pace behind the three men, staring at the wallpaper, wishing she wasn't hearing this.

"He'll make a good President," Fogerty said. "He'll earn your respect. Don't you worry. Not my politics, that's true. A hell of a way to get the job, though. Particularly if you're black."

Fogerty stopped at the front desk and stared at them. "I got someone else to see before I go, Ben. You heard what the man said on this. No range wars."

Levine smiled and pulled out a pack of Winstons from his pocket, started to play with them, waiting for the moment he could light one outside. "Cross my heart. And hope to die."

"Yeah," Fogerty said. "You know, I miss Georgetown. It might be nice to be back."

They watched him head off down a white-walled corridor.

"You did well in there, Wagner," Levine said. "I think he liked you."

"I would have appreciated being told about the subject matter, sir. In particular the radiation."

"Got to learn to duck and weave in this business. That right, Barnside?"

Barnside looked at her and smiled coldly. He was a big, fair-haired man, with the hard, strong physique of a football player, and no niceties at all. Barnside called it how he saw it, and if that meant he came across as charmless and aggressive, he really didn't give a damn. She could understand his rise through the Agency. He was smart, dedicated, and hardworking, with no private life that anyone got around to talking about. Just a bright provincial boy from Arizona who rose through the ranks.

"For what it's worth, Wagner," Barnside said, "I think that solar thing is a crock of shit. Not that I have your impeccable science background to prove it. You want my guess? Someone sneaked some nuclear device onto one of these planes. You wait and see. Occam's razor. Simple explanations. Bombs and bullets. It usually comes down to one or the other."

"In that case," she said, "it's over to you boys in Operations, and S&T can go back to peering into test tubes."

"Now, wouldn't that be peachy?" Barnside grunted.

13
Time Past

La Finca, 1824 UTC

It was early on a beautiful evening in Mallorca and Michael Lieberman was slowly acquiring the idea that it was to be one of the strangest of his life. A few hours before, he'd been staring at the screen trying to make sense of the crazy solar activity figures that were coming down the line. Then the news flash came up on the monitor, intruded into everything without being asked, and suddenly it was as if this remote Spanish mansion were hooked into the feverish nervous system of the Washington machine. Phones rang, people looked devastated, and there was a fever in the air that said this was about more than just the news itself, somehow the happenings in the sky had intruded right into their lives.

He looked through the big glass window at the back of the room and stared at the giant illuminated LCD map of the world set on the main wall of the control center. It was one of those neat ones that painted day and night on the relevant parts, moving with the path of the sun and its elevation in the sky. The universal time was marked in UTC—which he still liked to think of as Greenwich Mean Time—in the corner. You could almost see the summer solstice approaching. The high point of noon was reaching the East Coast of America. A huge curving sweep of daylight, shaped like a breast pointing downward, ran from the North Pole, now in permanent sun, down through the East Coast of North America, through the Caribbean, south past the tip of Tierra del Fuego, to the edge of the Antarctic, where the sun never rose at this time of the year.

This was that ever-moving object midday, where the sun was at its highest, casting its brightness on the greater part of the world. On either side sat, to the right, approaching night, and to the left, rising morning. Darkness was sweeping across Australia, all of Asia, and the southeastern foot of Africa, fast approaching the farthest tip of the Mediterranean. On the West Coast of America it was ten A.M. A fine time to be sitting on the beach in Half Moon Bay, he thought. At least it ought to be, if the sun hadn't been so damn strong of late that you wondered what it was doing to your skin as you sat there watching the slow, strong swell of the Pacific.

He walked out of the room, racking his head for some explanation. People didn't die like this, presidents in particular. The air was still full of heat outside. He walked over to the old stone wall that ran along the cliff edge, parked himself there, watched the motion of the waves, the way the gulls moved on the currents of wind blowing off the ocean. There was a shadow next to him and he wished he could have summoned up the courage to ask her to go somewhere else. Mo Sinclair sat down beside him, unasked, and tossed a pebble over the wall, watched it make a tiny white dot of surf in the clear blue water a couple of hundred feet below.

"You look like a man about to resume smoking after a hitherto acceptable absence," she said.

He gave her a sickly grin. His head was spinning. He didn't feel up to this.

"It's like the Kennedy thing, I guess," he replied eventually. "I was too young for that. Just. But I know what they mean now. And I wish I was thinking about the other people more. It wasn't just Rollinson. There were hundreds of them."

"I know," she said.

"It gets you the same way?"

She nodded. "He's the icon, Michael." She shrugged. "His death makes it all real to us."

"Right."

She watched the smart, troubled face gaze out into the blue emptiness of the sea and wondered why he seemed to take this so personally.

"There's more to all this, Mo. You understand that?"

"How can there be?"

He shook his head violently. "There is more to this. These plane crashes. Why we're here. Some of this craziness I do get. The instability of the weather, we know where a lot of that is coming from. The solar cycle. The crap we're getting from the flares right now. But . . ."

He watched a shining white seabird dive down the face of the cliff and disappear beneath the waves, waited for it to reemerge, and knew he could never predict the point at which it would break surface.

"But we don't know. Give them time."

"Yeah," he said, and flashed a look at her she didn't understand. "We really are overloaded with that here now, aren't we?"

She felt it was time to change the subject. "You weren't always doing this, were you, Michael? I remember you said something to Annie. About designing satellites or something?"

"Oh yes." The bird reappeared on the surface, something silver and wriggling in its beak, and true to form it was nowhere near where he expected. "You ever hear of SPS?"

"No." She looked puzzled. "Should I?"

"Probably not. You're a little young for that particular dream."

He shuffled on the uncomfortable stone wall and wondered why he was digging out this particular sheaf of bad memories right then.

"I'm waiting," she said.

"SPS stood—no, stands—for solar-powered satellite. Back in the seventies, when everyone thought that the oil would run out before long and we desperately needed some alternative to carbon-based fuels, it was quite the theoretical thing."

Mo smiled. "I've heard of solar power. I thought it didn't really work."

"Not on earth. Too costly, too inefficient, although those things may change. What won't change is the weather. You get clouds, you lose the throughput. Plain fact."

She looked at the perfect day.

"It would work just fine here."

"Yeah, but here's not where you need all those millions of watts of electricity. Try Detroit. Or Osaka. Not so good."

"So?"

"So you collect it with a satellite. You put something with huge collection wings into orbit, pick up the juice, beam it back to the earth in the form of microwaves, and close down all the nuclear power plants, stop burning carbon."

"Wouldn't that be dangerous?"

"You mean, do we get the fiendish death ray from the sky? Not at all. All of this was provable in theory by the early seventies. Just theory, mind. It took a bright, inquiring, optimistic mind to turn that into some kind of fact, design the satellite itself, come up with some costings to get it into space."

She placed a hand gently on his shoulder. "This wouldn't, by any chance, happen to be you?"

"No." He looked offended. "Do I come across as that arrogant?"

"A joke, Michael."

"Right. It was a friend of mine. Let's leave it at that. I played my part. Those big wings I told you about? They were mine and mine alone. I was very much into engineering at the time, as much as solar astronomy, the two went hand in hand. Those things that put the juice there in the first place, they had my signature on them. Neat stuff too, even if I say so myself."

She took her hand away and looked into his face. Somewhere underneath the surface there lurked a bright, animated side to Lieberman's character, and she couldn't work out why he kept it hidden sometimes.

"The way you talk about it, I guess it never happened. That must have hurt."

His eyes flashed, and there was a spark of anger there she hadn't seen before.

"Hurt? You don't know the half of it. This friend of mine,

she could sweet-talk the birds out of the trees. She went away, talked to all these gray people in Washington, in NASA. We were at Berkeley then, so they were reluctant to begin with. More money for the hippies, that kind of thing. But then, all of a sudden, we got bankrolled. Right out of the blue, a long-term R&D budget to design and build the thing. All the way through to a launch on the Shuttle, which was still in the planning stage itself back then, of course."

"Whatever came afterwards, that was an achievement, Michael. You should feel proud."

He turned to stare at her, and it wasn't a pleasant look.

"Really?"

She stuttered, "I-if you don't want to talk about it—"

"Hey—" he touched her arm lightly—"I'm sorry. You touched a raw nerve. I apologize."

"So what happened?" she asked, and wondered whether she wanted to hear the answer.

"We began to build it. This friend and me, and a team of some of the brightest people you ever met. And it was like heaven. This was an idea that combined everything you could dream about. Space, exploration, advanced engineering, and guess what? We got to save the world at the other end too. I can't tell you what that felt like. I used to walk through the city, looking at the smog and the fumes coming out of the cars, thinking one day, one day soon, we just pop the satellite in the sky, work out some way of defraying the launch costs, the ground infrastructure, and bang. There we are. Limitless, constantly renewable energy, at negligible cost. Forever and ever. Amen."

"They pulled the budget?"

He just looked at the ocean and said nothing.

"They'll come back to it one day, Michael. If it makes sense like you say."

"Oh, they'll come back to it. You just have to look at the numbers to understand that. It may be fifty years. It may be a hundred. But at some stage we have to realize that this is the only luxury-grade oxygenated planet available to us right now, and we can't keep choking it the way we have this past century.

Nothing else makes the grade, not with the kind of energy demands we take for granted nowadays. Maybe someone will come up with some other way of meeting the bill. Right now this is the only one I know."

"I'm sorry."

He looked at her, puzzled. "About what?"

"That it won't be you. In all probability."

He laughed out loud. "You think that bothers me? Jesus, Mo. Who gives a damn about that? I'm a scientist. I write this stuff so that someone else, a year, a decade, a century down the line, gets to pillage it, make it better, fix the places where I went wrong. Am I pissed we're not doing this now? You bet. But it's not because I don't get to work on the thing. It's because . . ."

"Yes . . ."

"It's because we fritter away our time here, Mo. We're just so blind to what goes on, we veer from gloom and doom on the one hand—the sky is falling, the sky is falling—to thinking what the hell, it's all someone else's job. When really the answer lies somewhere in between."

She looked at her watch. "Aren't we supposed to be getting a briefing or something real soon?"

"Yeah." He didn't look ready to move yet.

"And after they killed the project, that's when you moved into what you do now?"

"I became the sunspot guy. Overnight. A wondrous transformation. No big budgets, no engineering. No teamwork. Never again."

"And your friend?" she asked hesitantly.

He said nothing. His eyes were fixed on the blue horizon.

"Well . . ." Mo glanced at her watch again.

"They *didn't* kill the budget. Just showed us its true direction. I didn't like where it was heading, but my friend stuck with it. It all fell apart a few years ago anyway."

She watched him in silence; this was an interior conversation, not one in which she was involved.

"We were naive," he said. "We were just this bunch of bright kids trying to save the world, trying to tag on this giant pair of wings to a satellite, work on some way of converting all that nice sunshine into a big continuous burst of microwave energy that could take the place of a good number of power stations. We didn't watch the news much. Didn't even take any account of that great speech that Reagan made. March twenty-third, 1983. I stuck that date right into my memory later, when it all became so clear."

She shook her head. "I don't understand."

"We thought we were working on a nice little government project to solve the world's energy crisis. It was all bullshit. We were just little cogs in some huge wheel, and I should have guessed it, should have known from all these guys in black suits who kept hanging around, watching the budgets, making sure everything was kept nice and tight and secure."

The sun was getting low in the sky. There was a hint of coolness in the evening air; it made the skin prickle on her bare forearms.

"I shouldn't be telling you this, Mo. I signed pieces of paper. They made me."

"Then don't."

"To hell with them. It was all a fraud. There was never a plan to put an SPS in the sky. We were just the power plant for Ronnie's bee in the bonnet at the time. Remember the Strategic Defense Initiative? Star Wars, the press called it. A neat little circlet of bite-your-ass satellites spanning the globe. Strictly on a deterrent basis, you understand. Ho, ho. The Soviets throw up a missile, my little SPS unit, now transformed into some kind of orbiting Power Ranger or something, takes it out with microwave, laser, some kind of particle beam, you name it. They had all manner of shit getting tacked on its backside. That's when I found out. I walked in one day and finally got a glimpse of the total design blueprint, not just my part of it. These were war satellites, you'd better believe it. God knows what crap they wanted to build in there, and every bit of it got to live because of what I was making for them. I walked out. Like I said, my friend stayed, and I never did understand that. In the end, SDI itself went down, and all my work with it, I guess. Now no one wants to know about SPS. We just peer ten years ahead and say, 'Looks good to me . . .' It's all such a waste."

And it was, she understood that, just by looking at the pain, the anger in his face.

"I don't know what to say, Michael."

"You don't need to say anything. I'm sorry I dropped that on you."

"No need to be. And after that?"

She knew how to hold on to you when she wanted an answer, he thought.

"After that I got less serious. I got married. Then I got un-married. I floated around the bright world of solar academia doing my sunspot act. It pays the bills. It gets me by."

"But you think it's a waste. . . ."

"Yeah." He thought of Bill Rollinson again, and all those stories about Air Force One. "I think it's all such a waste. And I wish I wasn't so damn stupid, I wish I wasn't here being some kind of weatherman for these guys when there's so much bigger stuff going on around us."

Bill Rollinson and a couple of big silver airplanes falling from the sky, leaving a smear of radiation-hot metal across the earth.

"Oh my God," he said softly.

"Michael?"

But he never heard her. He was staring at the dying sun on the horizon, wondering whether to feel stupid, mad, or both. And who to take it out on first.

14

Argument

"I can't believe these things didn't get run through S&T," Helen Wagner said, surprised by the sudden, unnatural venom inside her voice.

They were in Levine's office. It was approaching midday. Outside the day seemed gripped by a piercing white brilliance. Her head hurt. The air-conditioning sang a high-pitched whine but did nothing to keep out the enervating heat.

Levine and Barnside were staring at her from the opposite side of the table, clearly wishing she were someplace else. There should have been more people in the room for a meeting of this nature, she thought. It was too soon to say that the papers in front of her gave any clue as to the fate of Air Force One, but the possibility had to be there. And Levine was sitting on this. It was all so obvious. He was biding his time, hoping the game would move on before the full story worked its way out.

"First things first," she said. "Why the hell is Operations funding part of a scientific project? Without the knowledge of S&T? Or input?"

Barnside shrugged. He had his jacket over the back of his chair and sat in a white, neatly ironed shirt with a button-down collar and plain blue tie. Sweat stains ran down from beneath his arms halfway to his waist. His hair looked matted with sweat, and a single prominent vein on his forehead seemed more visible than usual, seemed to move physically as he spoke.

"Look, Helen," he said, a note of reasonableness in his voice. "There are territories here. Just because Sundog's involved with scientific data doesn't put it in S&T's court automatically."

"Bullshit," she yelled, and knew her voice was too loud, her tone all wrong. She closed her eyes. The room was stifling. Her headache was getting worse. She looked at Barnside. There was a mocking smile on his face; he won a point there. She was the one who lost her grip.

"We're colleagues, Helen. We need to be able to work with each other on this one."

"Sure, Dave. So turn over the files to me and let me judge for myself."

"Jesus . . ." The vein was throbbing, bright and sweaty on his tanned forehead. "You know I can't do that. At least I hope you know. Do you read the Ops manuals here or what? Work your way into this job, please."

Barnside's face was flushed. He seemed on the edge—they all did, probably, which was understandable in the circumstances.

"I am asking a very reasonable question," she continued. "Why did Operations fund part of Sundog without the knowledge of S&T? Even if there was an operational reason—and I don't accept that for one moment—we should have been informed."

"Like I said. Read the manual," Barnside grunted. "It's under 'need to know.' And 'cell structure.' If we wanted your input, we would have asked for it. But we didn't. If you want corporate niceties, go get yourself a job in the charitable sector."

She glared at Levine, who just shrugged. "Hey, he's right. It wasn't me that rubber-stamped the decision to go into Sundog. Our involvement was low-key and pretty basic. Understand this, people weren't asking us for scientific advice. They were asking us for management and security, some comfort factor."

"And a damn good service they got. . . ."

"Christ," Barnside groaned. "We don't have room for this, Helen. Are you here to help or what?"

Levine wagged a finger. "Enough. Keep a handle on those tempers, both of you. Jesus, it's hot in here. Something go wrong with the goddamn air system?"

Helen couldn't believe how bad she felt. She prayed she wouldn't faint.

"So what happened with security, then, Dave?" she asked.

"Sundog was a low-priority project for us, the entire thing was virtually on ice," Barnside replied. "We're not sitting on it every damn day."

"Great. And now it's out of control."

"No one's saying that," Levine objected. "All they're saying to us is that the space side of things has gone off-line."

She couldn't believe her ears. "Let's put it another way. We no longer have control of the major part of the system."

"Or direct proof that anyone else has either," Barnside said grimly. His eyelids were half-closed.

They all felt terrible in this overheated, airless room—and she sensed it was more than just the heat.

"On the basis of the information you've given me," she continued, "it is my opinion that Sundog, if it were in the hands of a hostile party, could have been responsible for downing Air Force One. It has the military capability. With the solar configuration we have right now, the increase in radiation and general activity, the amount of pure radiation it could generate, God knows . . ."

"That's conjecture," Barnside muttered. "Pure conjecture."

"And in any case," Levine added, "who the hell knows how to use it? Not the Libyans. Not the Iraqis. This just isn't their bag. We'd know if they had that kind of capability. Like I said, Sundog was basically on ice, one experimental satellite in place, three ground stations. The damn thing didn't work reliably when *we* tried messing with it. How the hell could anyone else take control?"

"I don't know," she replied, and her headache moved up several notches. "But the answer's there somewhere. So what about these Gaia people?"

"Cranks," Barnside grumbled. "Are we going through all that again?"

Levine lit a cigarette. She watched the foul-smelling smoke curl into the air, steal what little oxygen there was from it, and wondered whether she might throw up. "We do routine monitoring of a few cults these days, Wagner," he said, the gray fumes seeping out of his mouth. "Makes sense. Some of them are serious bad news. But get this in perspective. There's a big difference between hacking a government Web site and stealing control of a billion-dollar space project. It just isn't a viable notion."

"Depends how smart they are."

"No," Barnside yelled. "It depends on a lot more than that. Equipment. Knowledge. Timing."

"That's your judgment, Barnside. But you're not a scientist, and I am. You should leave that to me. You should have left it to S&T all along."

Barnside glowered at Levine, closed his eyes, felt his forehead, and said, "Will you tell her how things work around here, Ben? Or do I have to do that as well? I really don't have time for this."

Ben Levine stared back at him. The director's bald head was covered in sweat. His eyes looked glazed.

Helen jumped. Somewhere down the corridor a fire alarm was ringing. She could hear people on the move.

"Keep quiet, Dave," Levine said calmly. "Don't make a fool of yourself."

Helen pushed the papers from her lap back onto the table. "We're wasting time here, gentlemen. I've been through the papers you've supplied to me about Sundog. Even a child could see they're incomplete. I don't have details of the security clearances in Spain, the personnel histories of the key players who've worked on the project in the past, managerial reports—"

"Hey, hey." Barnside was waving her down and the sight of his big hand bobbing up and down in the airless space in front of her seemed so infuriating. "One thing at a time, Helen. This is your first day. You're not even equipped with full security clearance yet. We're adapting to Belinda's loss as much as you. Can't you get that?"

She glowered at Levine. "Sir?"

"Say it."

"Did you give me this job precisely because you thought I wouldn't pick these things up? Is that what this is about? Keeping S&T nice and quiet while you try to sweep whatever is out there under the carpet?"

She could have sworn Barnside was starting to laugh.

"I warned you, Ben," the big man muttered eventually. "Just because she looks like a babe doesn't mean she acts like one."

"I resent that—"

"Enough!" Levine hammered a tightly clenched fist on the table. "I will say this once and once only," he announced. "You people have to work with each other. We don't have space for this kind of behavior."

The noise outside the door was getting oppressive. There were more alarms, the sound of people running down the halls.

"It's your call, Dave," Levine said softly.

Barnside shrugged. "Okay, Helen. You're smart. You deserve it. This isn't a question of clearance, by the way. It's simple need to know. You can read about that in the manual. We have an NOC inside Gaia. Nonofficial cover. Someone who doesn't work for us directly but gets paid by someone else and still does the job after all. Been there for over a year and come out with precious little, nothing that links them firmly into this. It's all supposition right now. But we're working on it. And a lot more besides. I'll get the files over to you. And . . ."

Barnside blinked, maniacally, she thought. Down the corridor the commotion seemed to be getting louder.

"I want you to read the manual on cell operation. I shouldn't have told you that. It breaks all the rules, but maybe they're made for breaking sometimes."

"I don't need threats," she said, and heard how shrill she sounded.

"This isn't a threat. . . ."

Barnside's voice was cracking, she thought. This whole conversation was going crazy.

Levine turned on Barnside and his face was bright red. Something happened in the air, like the sudden sharp prick of an invisible needle. All three of them winced, stared across the table. She saw a greasy line of blood appear at Barnside's nostrils. Then the pain returned, and this time it was so real, like a hammer blow in the head, and they were all screaming and yelling, holding their hands to their scalps, wishing away this hidden weight that pressed down on them from the sky, made it feel as if their brains might explode out of their ears.

There was a sound, something electrical, and in the corner of the room the PCs went quiet, then the lights failed, the air-conditioning began to wind down, everything that was modern in the office seemed to lose its lifeblood, the world became acutely still except for this ringing, agonizing and loud, that ran inside and outside her head.

She didn't know how long this lasted. It could have been minutes. When it was over, the weight lifted in an instant, and left behind a sea of different pains and sensations. She wiped her face with the back of her hand. The sleeve of her cream silk shirt was covered with mucus that had poured from her nose. Her eyes, she could feel, were wet with tears. Across the table Barnside's nose was pouring blood; it ran down his face like the makeup of a tragic clown. Ben Levine had his head in his hands, face down on the desk. Somewhere outside a woman was screaming.

Helen looked at Barnside and thought she'd never in her life seen a man so frightened.

Choose your moment, Belinda taught her. Always pick your time.

"They've got it, Dave," she said quietly, getting up from the table, trying to keep her equilibrium. "They took it from you and just delivered the proof. Now you just sit there while I get a doctor. And try not to bleed too much on this nice new carpet."

15
Reunion

They were in the control room, looking flustered, sweating, and when Lieberman saw them he just knew. Mo Sinclair was at his back and he was glad of that. He wanted a witness.

He walked over to Irwin Schulz, whose face was bobbing in and out of the glow of a screen, grabbed him by the neck of his T-shirt, and said, very slowly, very deliberately into his face, "You built it, goddamn you, Irwin. You built that damn thing and that's what's going wrong here, that's killed those people."

Schulz stopped what he was doing and looked at Lieberman with cold, scared eyes.

"They built it, Michael. I just get to come in and try to sweep up the mess. Ask Simon. We're all in the same boat."

"Bennett?"

The Englishman looked sick. His skin was pallid and clung to his cheekbones. Behind him, Bevan was barking down the videophone at a sea of faces on the screen.

"Irwin's right," Bennett said. "We're just the caretakers. They did all that work in the late eighties, Michael. They thought it would be a shame not to see if any of it worked in practice. I'd hoped we wouldn't reach the stage where we'd have to broach this with you. There are security considerations. But obviously that's a little late now."

"So why doesn't it work?"

Bennett bristled. "It does work, actually. As far as we know. It's just that we don't seem to have the keys anymore."

"Not yet," Bevan grunted, his face still stuck in the machine. "We'll be there, with or without you, Lieberman."

"Yeah," Schulz said sourly, and hit the keyboard. "Sure thing. I wish I felt that confident. Take a look for yourself, Michael."

Lieberman pulled up a seat and rolled it around so that he was sitting next to Schulz. What he saw on the terminal chilled him: It was the original SPS design, four big hundred-meter-wide wings trailing in its wake, a cluster of antennae and dishes sprouting out of the front.

"What is it?"

Schulz squirmed. "Imagine the SDI deterrence thing, but with the idea of deterrence sort of put to one side and replaced with some kind of full attack capability. Basically everything you got in the original SDI design—laser, microwave, particle beams—but upped somewhat."

"Somewhat?" Lieberman asked.

"The SDI units were supposed to be able to take out missiles, planes, that kind of thing. This can do all that and a whole lot more too, right down to ground attack, the sort of impact you might get from a tactical nuke. Versatile little weapon. Shame it's a touch temperamental."

"It doesn't work?" Mo Sinclair asked hopefully.

"Not reliably," Schulz replied. "I guess we just upped your security clearance, Mo. You do know what that means now, don't you?"

"Cross my heart," she said, not smiling.

"A little more than that," Bevan added.

"Yeah," Schulz said. "And maybe we all hope to die. Just might happen too. Sundog is true to its name, Michael. A real dog, and a rabid one at that. When they came around to trying out the systems, it was as unstable as hell. Not your part of the thing, that worked beautifully, I might say. Just the rest. Like trying to light a cigarette with a flame gun. Except it could come at you any which way it liked, depending which particular gear you selected."

"This is your business," Lieberman said. "Not mine. If you'd wanted my help, you should have come clean to begin with."

"And you'd have joined us?" Bennett asked.

"Maybe."

"I don't think so," Schulz said, smiling. "We know how you responded when you found this thing wasn't designed to save the world. Besides, we do need that weather report of yours. On an ordinary day, Sundog is just a nasty piece of metal in the sky. With all the crap we have out there right now, and that getting worse by the day, it turns into something else."

"Something that can down Air Force One?" Mo Sinclair asked.

"And maybe a lot worse too." Schulz grimaced.

Lieberman shook his head and wished he were somewhere else, where the room wasn't full of the whirring sound of computers and the heavy weight of despair.

"It's your toy that got broken," he said. "You fix it."

"It's not broken," Schulz said. "That's the point. Three weeks ago we lost the system for an entire day. Completely without warning. One minute we have everything, everything working so smoothly you wouldn't believe it. The next we lose contact and it's as if it's not even there, as if every damn circuit has blown. A day later, it comes back. We scratch our heads, hope this is just some temporary blip."

Bennett sat down and took a sip of water. "Well, it isn't. Six days ago we lost the satellite again. And nothing we can do seems to bring it back."

"Maybe it's a fuse," Lieberman suggested.

Schulz said very firmly, "No, sir! I know that security system inside out, I designed most of it. It's got more failsafes in it than you've got in most nuclear warheads. Nothing could put it out completely. And besides, we've monitored traffic on some of the discrete frequencies we set up for the project. We can't decipher it. Someone must have double-programmed the satellite to accept two different kinds of encoding systems. Sundog is working. It is in place. God knows where this thing's being run from—you need a pretty powerful space antenna to cover that distance—but it's active, of that I can assure you."

Lieberman felt giddy. He didn't want to be here, with these people, who were probably a damn sight more desperate than they were letting on.

"Let me get this clear. You mean you think someone's got control of this thing?"

Schulz looked at Bennett, who stared, in turn, at Bevan.

"We think so," Bevan said.

"Don't you goddamn people take precautions? You're playing with monster toys here, folks. They make nuclear energy look like a box of matches. How the hell can this happen?"

"We don't know, Michael," Schulz said quietly. "But we have some ideas. And we think you can help there too."

Lieberman laughed, and the sound nearly choked him. "Help? You want to sucker me twice? Aren't you people making some assumptions here?"

"No," Bevan said, looking at his watch, then at Schulz.

"At least let Mo and the kid go," Lieberman said. "If this thing can burn a hole in Air Force One, God knows what it could do to us here."

"I can't do that," Schulz replied, shaking his head. "You are one good Unix jockey, Mo, and you're here. This came up out of the blue, and like I said, the project was pretty much on ice when it did. I need you. We can't afford to lose anything on the network we do have working. This thing is coming to a climax one way or another over the next couple of days. I can't ship someone else in. I'm sorry. I really don't think we are in any danger here, but we have to keep what we've got up and running."

"Hey, Mo," Lieberman objected. "Don't rush into this. How do you know you can believe a word these guys are telling you?"

"I don't," she said quietly. "But to be honest, Michael, just now we really don't have anywhere else to go."

Some people bring their own pain with them, carry it around in a little pack on their back, he thought. He wondered what

had happened to this woman to make her think that life was
just like that: You walked around waiting for the next bombshell to drop on your head, shrugging your shoulders when it
came, smiling wanly and muttering, "Okay."

"Well, that's your choice, but as far as I'm concerned you
guys can take a hike. I'm out of here in the morning. If you'd
had the decency to tell me some of this before I arrived, maybe
I would have given it a second thought. But since you spared
me that, I am out of this."

In the corner, Bevan smiled and simply said, "No."

"We need you," Schulz pleaded. "We need you more than
you can even begin to guess."

"Tough," Lieberman said. He heaved himself upright, feeling old and stiff and cross. He felt a touch faint, and the room
was shifting a little.

In the corner Bevan was still smiling. And checking his
watch.

"One other reason, Lieberman. It's about time. Someone
made an appointment and we ought to keep it."

"What appointment?"

"Two more minutes," Schulz said, his face pleading. "That's
all, Michael."

The computers blinked and whirred constantly.

"No more."

Schulz beckoned him to the biggest workstation. A video
camera sat on the top. It was just like the rig in the bedroom,
except larger, large enough to take in all of them if they wanted
to have a video-conferencing party.

Lieberman sat down, nursed a glass of water, then turned to
Bevan and said, "Gimme a clue."

"Someone you know," Bevan said. "We think there's someone in this you know pretty damn well."

"We have packets," Schulz said, staring at the screen. "We
have packet activity and I think that means something's coming through and . . . oh boy."

They looked at the screen. Something had gone wrong. The
picture was too big, too much of it was occupied by this leer-

ing, dominating face, and there was nothing Schulz could do about it, however hard he slapped the keyboard.

"Oh boy," Lieberman echoed, and thought to himself: Sometimes your past does catch up with you in the most unexpected of ways.

Charley Pascal had cut her long dark hair savagely, so that it hung off her head in a ragged urchin crop, and it was hard to decide whether it was the kind of thing that cost you a fortune from some fashionable new salon off the Champs-Elysées or the sort of mess you ran up at home with a cutthroat razor, a cheap mirror, and a bad mood. Her eyes were the same, big and open and perfect, looking right into you, laughing all the time. There were creases at the edge of her mouth. She looked like some fashion model running a little past her time, and straight to seed with it.

"Why, gentlemen," Charley said. "Mr. Bennett, Irwin, a couple of you I don't recognize. And Michael Lieberman. Dear Michael. They have you too? I suppose I shouldn't be surprised."

"No one more surprised than me," Lieberman said, trying to think this one through.

"Fooled again, huh? They just keep doing that to you, don't they? Never mind. It's all going to change. Everything is going to change, in ways you can't even dream of."

"Oh," he said. And thought how odd it was to feel your life jumping between two discrete, distinctive periods in time, each with its own particular reality.

"This some kind of a payback thing? Aren't we a little old for that stuff? You stole the toy you gave them, Charley. Haven't you proved your point?"

"Oh Michael. You know so little," she said, laughing, and the French accent was still there. "Have you people been following what's happening in the world? Do you think I'm talking about payback?"

Simon Bennett said, "So what are we talking about, Miss Pascal? If what you say is true, you have caused us some concern these last few weeks and no small amount of expense. I'd very much like to know why."

She was grinning so close to the camera it couldn't quite focus. Maybe that was deliberate, Lieberman thought. Maybe she was trying to block out the background, hide any clue as to where she might be broadcasting from in that wonderfully indistinct place they called cyberspace.

"Are you happy, Mr. Bennett?"

"My happiness is irrelevant, Miss Pascal. Could we kindly come to the point?"

"Happiness is the point, Mr. Bennett. You don't understand that now but you will. Very soon too."

"Hey, Charley," Lieberman said, "what's the problem here? Because this sounds crazy to me. We got all this shit stuff coming from the sky, we got bright people here. We can think this thing through. We can learn things, for chrissake."

Charley Pascal's face loomed down at him from the wall, a good five feet high, and Lieberman really thought he'd cracked it then. She didn't look crazy at that moment. Her face relaxed, almost as if she were relieved about something, and he could remember what she was like when she first walked through the doors of the research lab in Berkeley almost twenty years before.

"Poor Michael," she said in the end. "Still as lost as ever."

Lieberman looked at her and felt this moment hanging in the balance.

"Please, Charley. I don't give a damn what's gone under the bridge here. We can work this out. You give me a chance. You trust me. What do you want us to do?"

She laughed. It wasn't a sound he liked. Then she picked up a cigarette, lit it in front of the camera, blew smoke into the lens.

"The same thing I want everyone to do, Michael. Prepare. Everything comes around in its own good time. Life. Death. The cycle of nature. Sometimes you have to burn the corn to the ground to make sure the crop that follows prospers. Think of it that way."

Charley Pascal did that laugh again, the one that made Michael Lieberman feel cold, then said, "Oh, really, Irwin. You never give up. You have any luck?"

Schulz went red.

"Charley?"

"With all that low-grade snooping you're doing. Oh hell. . . ."

She reached forward, her face disappeared, and they heard the sound of a keyboard getting hit. Then she came back on screen and said, "Irwin, you ever hear of the ping of death?"

He nodded. "Surely. They had that when I was at college. That stuff is old. You could ping someone, anyone, out on the Net, provided you had their IP address."

"That's right, Irwin. And what happened when you got pinged?"

"Well"—he couldn't understand where this was leading—"someone took your system down. But all that's impossible now, 'cause we don't let any executables past the firewall, and even if we did—"

"Irwin?"

"Yeah?"

Lieberman watched Schulz's face. He was puzzled. Something was coming through on the monitor he didn't understand.

"Welcome to the new world," Charley Pascal said, and then the screen went blank, her face dwindling into a fast-vanishing dot, there was a popping sound, and, one by one, every terminal in the room died, slowly, mechanically, on the hot, fetid air.

"Fuck," Schulz muttered, in a way that made Lieberman think this was a word that didn't pass through his lips that often. "Holy fucking fuck."

And then, from a far corner, a sound. One of the terminals came back to life, lines of zeros and ones scrawling across its screen, and from the speaker the tinny sound of a guitar and a female voice. It was Sheryl Crow, and the mysterious way Charley had sent this thing, unbidden to them, from God knows where out on the Net, meant that only the first line came through, just looped around itself continuously.

Singing, "Every day is a winding road . . ."

Bevan came over to him, stood so close that Lieberman could smell the sweat on his body.

"We need your expertise. We need your insight. You knew the Pascal woman. Pretty well, huh? And now she wants to

screw the world. Who knows? Maybe these two things are connected."

"Bullshit," Lieberman said, and went back to the briefing
room, picked up a bottle of red wine.

"Bullshit," he said again, then headed for the door, left them
there, staring at his back for all he cared, thinking about how
he'd get out in the morning. Walk if need be.

Outside it was a glorious Mediterranean night, the air hot
and aromatic with the scent of wild herbs. The sun was dying
out to the west, a gorgeous sphere of gold and red embedded
in the velvet sky. The stars were out, so clear in the sky, alive,
sparkling. The evening hummed with the skittering of insects
on the hot, dry breeze. It would be another airless, sweat-filled
night.

He half-walked, half-stumbled over to the clifftop, sat on the
wall, drank from the neck of the bottle.

"Don't want company," he said out to the sea when he heard
her footsteps.

Mo Sinclair sat down next to him on the wall, looked at him
with that accusing feminine expression he felt had probably ac-
companied his birth.

"We can't go, Michael. You heard what they said."

"Watch me."

"You don't have to like them. They need us."

"Really?" he grumbled, wheeling around to face her. "Now
they do. But not when they were setting up this stupid piece of
shit. Who do these people think they are, putting their fingers
into a pile of stuff like this? Perry goddamn Como singing
'Catch a falling star and put it in your pocket'? Jesus, they set
out to do this kind of thing and they show no respect. And
when it all goes wrong, they turn around to the likes of you and
me and say, hey, this is your responsibility, you're the one to
blame."

"I heard what Bevan said. That was a stupid and thoughtless
thing. I told you he was an unpleasant man."

"Hell, I didn't mean that."

"Then what did you mean?"

"Doesn't matter. Will you leave me alone? Can't a man even get drunk around here if he wants?"

She glared at him.

"Hey," Lieberman said, "I don't get it. We only met today. And there you are giving me that contempt thing just like we've known each other for years."

"I thought you were different," Mo Sinclair said, and turned on her heels, headed back to the mansion.

"To hell with 'different'!" Lieberman yelled at her disappearing back. "You know what they do to different people in this world?"

She didn't answer. Pretty soon she was gone, inside the mansion.

"Turn them into Charley Pascal," he said quietly to no one, watching some distant lights bob up and down on the sea, now glittering under the brilliance of a nearly full moon. "That's what."

Then slowly poured the remains of the bottle of wine over the rocky wall.

16
Colorpoint Shorthair

Sunnyvale, Northern California, 1842 UTC

"What the fuck do you call that?"

Pete Jimenez stared at the picture in the cheap plastic frame with chili peppers and sombreros on it, the sort of mass-produced item you picked up in the tourist stores at the airport. There was a growing sneer of distaste wrinkling his pockmarks. It was too hot in the room. The freeway leading out through Silicon Valley to San Jose was packed with slow-moving cars full of angry people. The world felt ugly just then, felt at the end of its tether, writhing underneath the relentless burning brightness of the sun.

"Looks like ET with fur on," Vernon Sixsmith said, and wiped his brow. The air was stuffy and thin, as if there weren't enough oxygen in the atmosphere.

"Yeah. And not much fur, at that. Not much of anything here I can see. I guess we should stand down the SWAT team. These guys bill heavy by the hour and I don't think we got much for them to do here."

"Yeah," Sixsmith said. "In a minute. No hurry."

They hadn't expected much of the apartment. Barnside had had men crawl over Charley Pascal's place before. The address wasn't hard to find. The Pascal woman had quit the Sundog research team in Sunnyvale a year ago, after a long bout of absenteeism and a string of arguments with the management. By that stage, they guessed, she'd picked up all the information she needed.

At some stage too, she'd quit the apartment, continuing to pay the rent but, as far as they could work out, living somewhere else, probably with the rest of the Gaia crew, probably in the Bay Area, but no one could be sure. The woman was just plain elusive.

The apartment was in a block of buildings put up to cater to the growing single population of the Valley, the army of bright young computer things who were flocking in from all over the world to feed the digital industries that ran from close by San Francisco airport all the way out to San Jose. Charlotte Pascal was long gone, every item of clothing with her, that much was obvious on their first visit. Jimenez and Sixsmith fine-combed the apartment, opened the drawers one by one, looked under the cushions, talked to the solitary neighbor who was still around—a dopey-looking German girl with close-cropped blond hair dyed partly pink—and found out nothing they didn't know the moment they came through the door. Charlotte Pascal had walked out of this apartment three weeks or more earlier, with the rent paid up until the end of the year, and she hadn't told a soul where she was going.

All this was a week before. Then Barnside sent them back again. Jimenez watched Sixsmith taking the call from Langley, and the look on his face said it all: My, what a persistent man.

Barnside asked for a closer look, so that was what he got. Jimenez flicked through the letters that had stood in the box in the apartment block mail area. Credit card bills, junk circulars, flyers from the local Chinese restaurant. Charlotte Pascal had nothing that could even count as personal in her correspondence, and the oldest item dated back to May 24. Jimenez shook his head and said, "Vernon, we're wasting time here. We can get the lab people in, see what they say, if Langley's so keen."

"Yeah." Sixsmith nodded. "In a month's time when they get around to typing the stuff out. You heard what Barnside said. He wants this stuff now."

"Well, maybe he can tell us how we're supposed to get it, because for the life of me I don't know. This woman looks like she was some kind of hermit or something. No letters from boyfriends. The German kid says she never saw anyone coming or going ever. She thinks maybe Pascal wasn't even here most of the time she was supposed to be in residence. And just take a look at this apartment. What do you get out of it? It's like . . ."

"It's like she cleared it all out knowing we were coming," Vernon Sixsmith said, trying to think this through, trying to put himself in the woman's shoes.

He walked over to the angular metal framed bookcase that still had some things in it: a couple of Stephen King paperbacks, some books on solar physics with titles he didn't understand, and a copy of something called the *Linux Bible*. And on the top shelf—this had nagged him ever since Jimenez pointed it out—the picture of a cat alongside a cheap tourist ashtray from Acapulco, a three-inch model of the Eiffel Tower that looked as if it had been cast in lead, and a pair of Mexican salt and pepper pots made to resemble desert cacti.

"Ugly fucking thing," Jimenez said. "The frame and the animal. Who the hell would want to bring that home from vacation?"

"A cat lover, I guess," Sixsmith said, and took the photograph down from the shelf, turned it over, unpicked the back, took out the print.

"Hey," Jimenez grunted, "that's not some piece of tourist junk after all. That's her cat."

"You don't say?"

There was nothing on the back, not the photographer's logo he'd hoped for. But this was a posed picture, Sixsmith was sure of that. The animal was seated against a pale blue background, the sort you got in studios, and it was craning its long, almost hairless neck as if someone, just out of reach, were holding out a piece of smoked salmon, teasing it into a nice pose.

"Get that German kid in here again, Pete," Sixsmith said, still staring at the picture.

A few moments later Jimenez was back, standing behind the German girl, making movements with his head that said, This kid is *not* cooperating, this person has not yet joined the Friends of the CIA.

"You know what that is?" Sixsmith said, holding out the picture.

"Cat," the German girl said flatly, her voice sounding mannish, not even looking at the photo.

"Yeah. I know that. But any cat in particular? Was it her cat? Miss Pascal's?"

She shrugged her shoulders, stayed quiet, and Jimenez walked out from behind her, smiled, and said, "You know, for someone with no green card who's been working illegally and has a couple of ounces of dope stashed behind the CD player, you are being mighty unhelpful, young woman."

"Fucking cops," the girl grunted. "I got a green card. I earn more money than you two put together. And I don't use dope. Go see for yourself if you really want to rifle through my panty drawer."

Sixsmith closed his eyes for a moment and wondered how much more of Jimenez he could stand. Then he said, "Fine, thank you very much. Now, before we declare war here, can I repeat myself? All I want to know is this: Is that Charlotte Pascal's cat? And if so, what the hell is it?"

She thought about it just long enough to irritate them. "Sure. It's her cat. Loved the goddamn thing. Something rare too. Weird name. Let me think."

Sixsmith prayed that Jimenez wouldn't blow this one.

"Colorpoint Shorthair," she said after another infuriating pause. "Name of Michael. I guess I should have known she was gone for good when it stopped waking me up at night scratching on her door and meowing. She never let the damn thing out of the apartment. Scared it would get run over, I guess."

"This kind's rare?" Sixsmith asked.

"So she said. Cats aren't my thing. I took her word on it there."

"Thank you."

"Can I go now?"

"Surely." Sixsmith smiled, wondering what this was worth. "And thanks for your cooperation."

The German girl went back to her apartment, leaving the two men fuming silently at each other in Charlotte Pascal's onetime living room.

"Well," Jimenez said in the end, "we know what kind of cat she likes."

"Yeah," Sixsmith muttered, but he was already dialing, straight through to the Agency information desk, where some clerical assistant in the city office sat permanently glued to the computer.

"Sixsmith here. I want you to look up a breed of cat for me."

The line went dead for a moment, then a young female voice said, "A cat?"

"Hey, you can hear me! Do we get to do some typing now too? A Colorpoint Shorthair. I want you to see if you can pull out some names of breeders, owners' associations, any kind of links you got."

"Colorpoint Shorthair," the woman said, then paused for a second or two. "My, that is a pretty pussy. Looks like ET."

"I been there already, friend. You got some numbers we can call?"

He heard typing down the line.

"You ought to be grateful for this stuff," the voice said down the line. "Most of the networks are down right now. Only a handful of us can access anything. That sun thing, I guess."

"I'm waiting."

"Yeah. Got a whole list of registered breeders here on the Cat Fanciers' Association site. Where do you want me to cut this off?"

"How many breeders have you got in the Bay Area?"

"Ten, fifteen or so."

"E-mail them straight to my pager. We need to start calling right now."

"Okay. One more thing as well."

"Yeah?"

"Got some number in the city for the secretary of the Northern California Colorpoint Shorthair Owners' Club. Mrs. Leonie

Hicks, fine-sounding address out in Pacific Heights." She gave him the phone number.

"Got it," Sixsmith said, and cut the line, then dialed straight out again. An elderly female voice that sounded like the rustling of old tissue paper said, very cautiously, "Yes?"

And Sixsmith was so glad he hadn't handed this one over to his partner.

"Mrs. Hicks? Mrs. Leonie Hicks," he said, his voice a little higher than usual.

"Yes?"

"My name is Harold Levinson. I do so hope you can help me."

"If I can."

"You see, it's about poor Charlotte's cat. It's a beautiful Colorpoint Shorthair called Michael."

"Finest cat in the world, Mr. Levinson. A feline *sans pareil* is the Colorpoint Shorthair, but then you seem to know that already."

"Quite. And so loyal too. Which is the point. You see, Charlotte moved out of her apartment next door to me in Redwood a month or so ago and took Michael with her. And now—I just don't know how to explain this—the poor creature has come running back to his old home, looking very sorry for himself. And I just don't know how to return him, you see, since Charlotte, in her hurry, never left me a forwarding address."

"My oh my," said Mrs. Leonie Hicks. "These cats never cease to surprise one."

"So I was wondering if you could help."

"Mr. Levinson, my home is always open to any Colorpoint Shorthair in need of a bed for the night. It is pedigree, I gather?"

"Well, I am sure that is most generous of you, Mrs. Hicks. But I was rather hoping you might have Charlotte's address. Her being so fond of this kind of cat, you see. I was wondering if she just might be on your books."

The line went quiet and then the tissue paper rustled again.

"I don't think so, young man."

"Can you check?"

"No need. I know all our members. We meet quite regularly. And I am sure I would remember a name like that."

"French woman, kind of pretty, worked in the Valley."

"I'm sorry."

Sixsmith pressed the mute button, looked at Jimenez, and said, "Shit."

"Well, thank you, ma'am."

"My pleasure. And remember, if you need a home for that poor creature . . ."

"I will," said Sixsmith, thinking fast. Then added, "Oh, one more thing. Charlotte had this beautiful picture of Michael taken in some studio somewhere. It's a real work of art. Clearly someone who understands cats. You don't know where I might go to get something like that myself, do you?"

"Now, there I can help you. If you want a portrait of a cat, there is only one man hereabouts who can do the job. Henry Lomax. You wait there one minute."

Sixsmith pulled the phone away from his ear and sent up a little prayer. One minute later, Mrs. Leonie Hicks was back with a number. Two minutes after that he was speaking to Henry Lomax, who remembered this job so well, since it happened only two weeks before. Sixsmith scribbled something down on his pad and cut the call.

He looked at Jimenez. "Two addresses. Sunnyvale. And 2314 Ravel, that's on Potrero, he says, he delivered the pictures himself."

Jimenez grinned. "Hey, man, we're rolling!"

"Yeah," said Sixsmith, and put the picture of the cat back on the shelf. It was crazy, he knew, but he didn't like the way the thing kept staring at him.

17
Charley Pascal

Tim Clarke sat at the end of the table in the Pentagon bunker, dressed in an open-necked shirt and jeans, and stared at the group that had assembled around him. This was a subset of the National Security Council, with the additions he'd demanded and the live video link to La Finca. He wasn't feeling good about the team. It was an ad hoc amalgam of different agencies, different skills, no one quite meshing, no one quite understanding the prolix nature of the problem.

He'd decided against inviting the military in the form of the chiefs of staffs and the Defense Intelligence Agency. This wasn't a military threat, nor, at this point, would a military solution seem appropriate. He had the FBI to handle the internal situation, but there was no evidence that Gaia was necessarily resident in the U.S. anymore, and if they were, the Bureau had few clues about where to start looking for them. The Agency, from what he'd seen, knew more than anyone else, but that was still vague. Then there was Sundog itself. They'd patched through to the control room in La Finca, and the live video of Simon Bennett and Irwin Schulz sat on the bunker wall, alongside a digital world map showing the movement of daylight across the globe. They looked lost, academic caretakers of a half-forgotten project who had suddenly found the doors to their lab flung open to the world, and a bunch of strangers walking in, taking over the desks.

The conventional notion of security wasn't made for this world. There was something so global, so intangible, about the way the threat had emerged that it had outwitted them, and all they could do was stare at each other accusingly and wonder where next to punch the air.

His training told him you left these situations to the professionals. In his gut, Clarke knew that this would be a dreadful mistake. The zenith was now less than thirty-six hours away, and the growing presumption was that, whatever Gaia wanted to do, it was the peak of the cycle they would choose for the act. There was no time now for the infighting that would resume the moment he stepped out of the room. So instead he had to lead, directly, with no room for argument.

"Let's start this off with something we can all understand," Clarke said slowly. "What the hell happened in Langley this afternoon?"

Helen Wagner scanned the papers in front of her. "Data is still coming in, Mr. President, but it's already clear that the area of the CIA headquarters was subject to some intense kind of solar radiation around midday. The burst lasted, as best we can estimate, six minutes. We had massive electrical failures in the buildings, we're still missing some telecom circuits, and it may be several hours before we can hope to get back to normal. And it's not just Langley. There's telecom disruption through the DC area."

"I'm not interested in the power supply. What about the physical effects?"

She shook her head. "We don't know accurately what was in this burst, sir, so we're still in the dark. There was a huge increase in ultraviolet rays during the period, equivalent to standing out in the sun for the best part of a day. It's the unknown elements, the X-rays and the electromagnetic emissions, that are hard to call. The best guess of our physicians is that they are responsible for the illnesses. Mostly these are associated with a sudden rise in blood pressure—physical discomfort, headaches, nosebleeds, the triggering of cardiac incidents, and the like. If the radiation level had been on a Chernobyl level, we'd have monitored that, of course, but more importantly we would have seen other symptoms by now—vomiting, physical side effects. This thing gives you a nasty shock, and repeated doses would doubtless trigger carcinogenic occurrences, just as much as standing out under the sun all day. But it's not deadly in itself, unless you have a preexisting condition. The real lasting damage may well be to the systems we take for granted. We have entire network backbones down and they don't seem much willing to come back up."

"It's Sundog, Mr. President," Schulz said from the screen. "It's all Sundog. The mix of rays is exactly what we got in the trials, and one reason why we half-mothballed the thing in the first place. It's dirty stuff and damn hard to control. But you got to remember this thing is a bunch of weapons, not just one. She's got hold of the transmission feed too and she can use that to mix data into the beam, foul up the telecom networks with all sorts of crap on top of the magnetic disruption you get anyway. Like the biggest computer virus you could think of."

"We had to do some pretty fancy rerouting just to keep any of the network upright," Helen added. "But we shouldn't take that for granted. We have to assume we could lose a lot of our telecom infrastructure at any time when the satellite is in range. And we're still some way off from the zenith. What they're throwing at us on all fronts now is nothing compared to what we could get tomorrow."

"Understood," Clarke said. "And on the ground?"

One of the NSC staff people Clarke didn't recognize cut in. "The local authorities have the situation in hand outside, sir. There may be a curfew in selected DC areas tonight if this sparks unrest. Right now the TV stations are swallowing the line we're feeding them, that this is some kind of power outage. I don't know how long we can hold that, but we'll keep it as calm as we can."

"Casualties?"

Helen said quietly, "We have two staff reported dead of heart attacks. There are some automobile crashes on the freeway. Reports are still coming in."

Clarke shook his head. "This is so accurate. How'd they do that?"

Schulz's voice came out of the system. "It's not a big deal, sir. The energy goes in a dead-straight line. Provided you can work out any refraction through the atmosphere, it's a simple calculation. The fact that they brought down two planes when clearly they were going for Air Force One maybe means they're refining it now."

Clarke looked at the mute, immobile faces in the room. He knew the makings of despair when he saw it. "So who are these people? What do they want? And what can they do to us if we don't give it to them or find them in time to take this little toy back out of their hands?"

There was an awkward silence around the table. Clarke gazed stonily at them. "My, this is an unpopular assignment. Since we don't know the answers to those questions, can someone kindly tell me who the hell these people are?"

"I can give you some background, Mr. President," Barnside said, and hit the presentation panel. Two photos came on the video screen: one of a smiling, attractive woman in her thirties, with long black hair and a pale, intelligent face. The other was of Charley Pascal, as they now recognized her from the recording of her conversation with La Finca. It was possible—just— to believe these were the same woman, but they had to use their imaginations. Something had happened to this woman over the intervening years, something more devastating than mere age.

"Charlotte Pascal," Barnside said, looking at the screen. "Age thirty-nine. Born Bordeaux, France, been working in the U.S. on a green card since 1983. Came to California to study at the Lone Wolf Observatory, then got a job directly with the Sundog Project. She left Sundog twelve months ago. She had full security clearance inside the project, so as far as we can tell there's nothing she doesn't know about how it works. She had an apartment in the Bay Area. We got some people checking out various leads. Seems she hung on to the apartment, even though she hasn't been using it. Presumably she's had some contacts with Gaia going back a long time. These people must have some kind of base. Maybe she just visited part-time, then moved in when she felt she had enough to quit Sundog."

"Why does she look so different in the two photos?" Burnley asked.

"She's sick, physically sick, it's obvious," Helen said immediately.

Barnside glowered at her. "The first is her original passport picture. The second is from her brief appearance on the Net this evening. We made some inquiries. It appears that a year or so before Pascal left Sundog she was diagnosed with some form of incurable brain cancer, anaplastic astrocytoma."

He'd no sooner said the words than Helen Wagner was keying at her palmtop computer.

"I guess that didn't help with the instability," Barnside continued.

"You can't make assumptions like that," Helen said quietly. "There are some nasty symptoms—nausea, fainting, the gradual loss of the use of your limbs—but you can't assume that someone with brain cancer is, per se, irrational. Or incurable."

"Well, thank you," Barnside muttered. "The incurable part comes from her ex-physician, by the way."

"Where the hell is she?" Clarke asked.

Barnside grimaced. "Immigration shows she left the U.S. back in January and returned at the end of March. No record of her departure since then, so we think she's still here."

"So when did she start talking to these Gaia people?" Clarke asked.

"The Children of Gaia. That's the name they use. We don't know," Barnside answered. "We only really started monitoring minor cults a couple of years ago, so we had some catching up to do there."

"Scalable terrorism." Clarke stared at the CIA and FBI teams assembled side by side at the table. "Guess you guys took a while coming 'round to understanding that option."

"In the beginning, sir," Barnside replied, "this wasn't terrorism. The Children of Gaia seemed to have a few people in at the start who were loosely connected with Heaven's Gate in San Diego, the cult that committed suicide over the Hale-Bopp comet. I guess you'd call them fellow travelers. Heaven's Gate swallowed the assumption that Hale-Bopp hid a spacecraft, and the cult members could rendezvous with that by killing themselves, moving from one plane of consciousness to another. The Gaia people didn't go for this space thing. They were loosely associated with a covert ecoterrorist alliance known as Siegfried. This linked various groups—people raiding animal research establishments, targeting the meat trade, the chemical companies, anything to do with hunting."

"Like Dan said. Tree-huggers." Levine nodded. "Militant anti-abortionists and the like."

"That's not quite correct, sir," Helen intervened. "From what I understand, I think you'll find these people get nowhere near the abortion debate. To them, man—at least modern man—is the enemy species. We despoil the planet. We interfere with nature. The idea of abortion is probably neither here nor there to them. They take what they think of as a broader view of the issue."

"Maybe," Barnside said. "But let's stick to what we do know. You're talking serious computer geek territory here. They use the Net to communicate and recruit new members. To them, what they read on the Net is real, and the *New York Times* is pure fiction. They are separated from most everything we regard as normal life. And as far as we can work out, Pascal is now their leader, maybe has been for some time."

"This woman designed part of Sundog?" Fogerty asked.

"A *big* part," Schulz said from the screen. "Charley knows this project inside out. She was one of the brightest people we had and she was there right from the beginning, when it was still, on the surface, a solar energy project. She worked on everything, from programming right down to the design of the hardware. We didn't change anything significantly. She knows how we work. If she has the keys, she can do what she likes right up until the moment we take them back."

"And the people with her?" Clarke wondered.

Barnside shrugged. "Our guess is thirty, forty at the most, and we're real short on detail. Probably living together now in some kind of commune. We lose track of them after a property in San Diego they vacated around the time Pascal left Sun-dog."

Clarke stared across the table and they watched, waited for him to speak. There, at least, Helen thought, he had won a kind of victory. He had the authority, had stamped it on the gathering through his own physical presence, not the badge of office.

"Will someone tell me what kind of people they are? Can we deal with them?"

Helen was there first. "Smart people. With no lives. No family. From what we know, we think there's ex-programmers from Microsoft, Apple, Cisco, IBM, Netscape. . . . We're not slouches in this area, Mr. President. We can match them. Given time."

"Time. Let's leave that to one side for now, Miss Wagner. What do they want?" Clarke's voice echoed in the silent room.

Fogerty rifled through the papers in front of him. "In a word, sir," he said, " 'prepare.' "

"What the hell does that mean?" Clarke asked heatedly.

Fogerty shook his head. "That's all it says on the E-mail we got after Air Force One was lost, Mr. President. That's all she said when she made that call to La Finca. We've heard nothing since."

Levine rapped his hand lightly on the table. "We need intelligence for this. More than anything."

"Wagner?" Clarke asked, and he could feel the ripple of resentment in the room.

"We need intelligence, sir," she agreed. "But we need understanding too. Maybe if we can find out what drives them, that might help."

"So what do you think?"

"I'm not a psychologist, Mr. President. But if you want a guess . . . consider Pascal's condition. She's dying. She's surrounded by people who are probably willing to die for her too. And none of them mind. Their own lives—and by extension those of everyone else—are unimportant. That doesn't mean they're out to be mass murderers—"

"She shot down Air Force One, for chrissake," Barnside grumbled.

"But not without reason, surely. We need to understand their view of the world and what they think it's becoming. My guess is they see themselves as agents, of Gaia, if you like. Of the earth. Of some moving force in nature. If you feel you're unimportant yourself, maybe the entire human race becomes unimportant. And what matters is something bigger. The planet. The universe, maybe. Perhaps they're looking to return us all to some kind of state of grace. It's as fundamental as that."

Fogerty smiled at her from across the table. It felt distinctly odd. "If you're right," he said, "then surely it's obvious what they want. Not the end of the world. The beginning of it. Eden. A return to the garden before it was spoiled, before we bit into the apple."

"There were just two people in Eden, Dan," Levine said quietly.

"Well, maybe you'd need more than that," Fogerty added. "A few more."

"It's not possible," Helen said. "She could cause a lot of damage. She could kill a lot of people, take down networks, destroy financial markets, maybe . . . hell, create chaos for a while in any case. If you add in the extra energy we're going to see at the zenith, then maybe there is the power inside Sundog to destroy entire cities, I guess. But we'd still be back after a while. We wouldn't forget how to make the internal combustion engine, how to organize the fabric of society."

The room went quiet, and that made her feel cold.

"Are we all so sure?" Fogerty asked. "Imagine walking out of this building into a world with no jobs or electricity, no money, no transportation, no workable form of government. Would it all go back to normal just because someone, three months down the road, found the on switch at the power company? Not necessarily. From her point of view, perhaps civilization—what we think of as civilization, at any rate—is a thin veneer on the mob, and the more we take that veneer for granted, the easier it is to bring the walls tumbling down when it disappears. Just look at Rwanda. Look at Albania, any number of former Eastern Bloc states. As I reminded you all once before, Gaia is the daughter of Chaos. And it's from Chaos that everything springs anew. That's the real threat, Mr. President. What comes after. She's betting that it pays to burn your house down now and again, because what gets built in its place has to be better than anything that went before."

"Won't get that far," Barnside said quickly. "We can stop these people."

"How?" Tim Clarke asked, and the question almost sounded rhetorical.

Barnside glanced at the monitor. "You secure at that end, Bevan?"

The thin pale face nodded.

"I would appreciate it if this is kept out of any briefing beyond this room, sir. We have someone inside," Barnside said, staring at Helen Wagner, daring her to intervene. "We've had someone there for a while."

"Then why the hell don't we know where they are?" Clarke asked.

"No contact, sir. Maybe it's too dangerous, or impossible. I don't know. But once this thing starts to move further, we'll have news. Mark my word."

"You'd better be right," Clarke said, shaking his head. "You people keep me posted on the hour and when anything significant develops. And let's tailor this for the press as much as possible. As far as the public's concerned this is just one big worldwide computer crash. Let them write to Bill Gates, for all I care. That's all. And Wagner? Find out what makes these people tick. Find someone who can explain that to me."

Inside La Finca, Irwin Schulz watched Ellis Bevan mop his brow, watched Mo Sinclair following the video link at her workstation, unseen by the camera on top of the main monitor. He wondered how soon he could wake the deeply slumbering Michael Lieberman. Then he put that thought to one side, caught Helen Wagner's attention on the monitor, and said, "This isn't enough. We need to talk to NASA and activate that Shuttle idea. We need to talk to them right now."

18

Potrero

San Francisco, 2034 UTC

Ravel meandered over the crest of the Potrero hill like a thin strand of hair struggling across the top of a bald head. At the summit, it almost didn't make it. The road came up from the direction of the city, turned into a dead end for cars, then narrowed into a jagged footpath through low trees and scrub, set on a good sixty-degree drop, until the terrain became a little less vertical farther down and the street returned. In the confined, pedestrian part the houses were timbered and individual, some tiny, some low, sprawling mansions. Vernon Sixsmith couldn't, for the life of him, work out what kind of neighborhood this was. Whether these ramshackle timber boxes, some big enough to accommodate an entire commune in the wild old days, would fetch upward of a half a million dollars on account of their cuteness, or this was just a piece of Potrero that got passed by in the gentrification process and was left to go ragged at the edges all on its own.

The SWAT squad arrived first and hung around at the dead end of the street, out of sight, just watching the house, waiting for orders. The penetrating afternoon heat made their armored vests feel like dead weights, caused the sweat to work up beneath the black uniforms, sit, greasy and constant, on the skin. An advance surveillance team of two, posing as Pacific Bell linesmen, had started working on the telegraph pole one house down from where Charley Pascal and maybe the rest of the Children too were now living. They were wired and live, and any moment now Vernon Sixsmith hoped to hear from them. Even from here he could see the gear they were using: a directional audio amplifier that would pick up any sound in the house, even the creaking of bedsprings (and they'd heard that one often enough). Plus a wireless tap on the line that could detect a single ring and, with a touch of luck, the number on the other end.

Sixsmith screwed his eyes shut, tried to squeeze away the constant headache, and picked up a pair of binoculars from the back seat of the car. He took a few steps, stopped to look at the sky: pale, cloudless blue, nothing in it but the yellow fire of the sun and the faint, distant trails of airliners painted high in the atmosphere. One thing he liked about San Francisco was the temperate weather. That was why, he thought, they got a touch fewer crazies than LA. Normally it was just a little too chilly to get really worked up about things. But something seemed to have changed these past few months. The year had begun with some of the worst floods Northern California had ever experienced. A week or two later the heat wave began. Constant dryness, constant sun. The sort of weather that might never end.

He shook his head, then concealed himself in the shade of a dusty oleander bush and looked at the house. It was single-story, painted a pale pastel shade of green, with ragged roof tiles in need of some attention. The window frames were white flecked with brown where the wood was showing through. The front garden was a mess of overlong grass and discarded household goods: an old freezer, the remains of a washing machine, a cheap, off-white sideboard that had cracked at the seams and now moldered in the deep grass like a corpse getting flyblown. All in all, this was a nice road, Sixsmith thought. The neighbors must have loved having Charley Pascal move in.

Correction: Charley Pascal and her cat. The Colorpoint Shorthair was still bugging him. He felt sure that if he closed his eyes he'd see its face—ET with a touch of fur—staring straight up at him, straight into his head, and saying, all feline aggression and spark: *Yeah?*

The earpiece crackled and he watched the phony linesman's mouth moving, down the road. "We got activity," the surveillance man said. "Someone's playing music."

"You hear how many of them are in there? Which room?"

The distant head moved. "The music's too loud to make out anything much else. It's in the right-hand front room. That's all."

Sixsmith swore quietly to himself and was aware of the way Jimenez was smiling thinly at him, saying: This is your call, partner, your decision. The handbook asked for proof there was someone in the house before the SWAT people could wade in. Otherwise the suspect just might be around the corner shopping for groceries when they pulled out the mallets and handguns. He might watch from the end of the street, laugh dryly, and be gone with the wind.

But the handbook didn't really say what to do when there was nothing but music in a house that looked as dead as a corpse.

"Wait," Sixsmith said. "Tell me the moment it sounds like someone is changing the music or you see movement."

Jimenez looked blankly down toward his feet and let out a long sigh. Sixsmith stared down the street, at the house. It was really grubby. Which was strange. Houses normally took on the characteristics of the people who owned them, in one way or another. The Sunnyvale apartment was neat, clean, and impersonal. This place looked like it was the home of someone who was making a statement: *I am dropping out of this place, I don't care what it looks like, I don't give a shit what you think.*

The earpiece crackled again. "Phone call. Front room left."

Jimenez smiled, didn't look at him, and took out his handgun.

"Patch the call through to me," Sixsmith said, and ignored the low curse that Jimenez threw at the pavement. It was a French voice, nice, female, sounding pleasant. This could be someone talking to her mother or her best friend. It was all so calm, so anodyne, so everyday. This was the elusive Charlotte

Pascal talking about shopping, about going out, someone at the other end of the line hardly getting in a word, just coming in with the occasional, "Really? You don't say?"

Sixsmith listened for close to twenty seconds, cut the line, nodded to Jimenez, and said, "Let's go, front room left." Then watched the team work their way down the hill, Jimenez by his side. These guys were specialists. You left the initial stuff to them. And inside a minute it was done. The front door of the house was through, the front windows too. Hooded men were inside—no shooting, Sixsmith thought, that was good anyway. By the time the pair of them had walked down the hill and were standing at the front gate, the SWAT team leader was back outside, hood off, right glove off too, blood pouring from his wrist.

"Cut myself on the fucking window," the man said, glowering at the wound. "This isn't me. Too fucking hot to think out here. Stitches, I guess."

"So?" Jimenez asked, cutting the sentence off as quickly as he could manage.

The man shrugged. "The phone call was a tape. Left on repeat, cycling 'round and 'round. Like the CD player. Some clever stuff hooked into the PC. Just to make the place look occupied."

"Shit," Sixsmith said, and thought: This woman is so on the ball.

They walked inside. It wasn't as grubby as Sixsmith expected. In a way, it looked as if it had hardly been occupied. There was a mattress on the floor of the main room, a low coffee table with the CD player on it. Sheryl Crow was coming out of it a little less loudly now that one of the SWAT team (who was a fan) had turned it down, not completely off. In the corner was a desk with a PC and a phone connected to it. The computer was on: A geometric screensaver bounced slowly from corner to corner like a Ping-Pong ball moving through sludge.

A thin young SWAT guy with ginger hair came in, smiling, trying to be helpful, and said, "Nothing in the mailbox except junk circulars. Not a piece of mail in the house as far as I can see. No clothes in the drawers. No pictures. Nothing personal at all."

Jimenez sniffed the air. He could always tell which SWAT people wanted to cross into plainclothes work. They were so friendly. "Can't even smell the fucking cat, Vernon," he grumbled. "And I got a sensitive nose. That cat never even lived here, if you ask me."

Vernon Sixsmith wished Jimenez would shut up about the cat. He stared at the floor: bare boards, looking a little pale, unpolished for years. Something on a single, slightly raised nail. He bent down, picked at it. A piece of red fabric. Sixsmith stared at it closely, then pulled a plastic bag from his pocket and tucked it away for later.

"Someone had the carpet up," Sixsmith said. "Took it away."

"Maybe the pussy peed on it. Maybe the fucking cat peed all over the place and that was that, they just had to move out and get things fumigated. That would explain why I can't smell nothing."

Over in the corner the PC started whirring, coming to life.

"Shut up, Pete, for chrissake." The screensaver disappeared, to be replaced by a small yellow circle.

"Jesus Christ," Jimenez said. "What the hell is that?"

The SWAT man, still trying to be friendly, shrugged at him. "The screensaver shit they get on these things right now, who's guessing? I bought my kid some PC for Christmas down at the Good Guys. Two weeks later he's knee-deep in beaver shots. The Good Guys? I ask you. And him ten years old."

"Some of us started at nine. Early developers."

"Yeah." The SWAT man laughed, and Jimenez thought it could be real good fun to jerk this one around a little.

Sixsmith glanced at the computer. The image had changed. It was bigger now.

"Say," Jimenez said, "you heard the one about—"

"Shut up, Pete."

"Okay, you're thinking. I recognize the signs."

The cat bothered Sixsmith. "What did that photographer tell me about the pictures he took of that cat, Pete? Remind me."

"He told you he took 'em and delivered 'em here. Two weeks ago."

"Yeah. And Pascal made out like she moved out of Sunnyvale three weeks before that?"

Jimenez paused, puzzled. "Yeah . . ." Then looked at the computer. It had changed again. The image had grown. It was now clearly a medieval sun, with a face in the center. Not a pleasant face.

"So," Sixsmith said, "she had the picture taken, went back to Sunnyvale, and put it on the shelf, even though she wasn't living there."

"Guess that's the sum of it."

He thought about the bare floorboards and wondered aloud, "Now, why would she possibly want to do something like that?"

And the SWAT guy looked at the computer and said, "Ugly or what?" The image filled the entire screen. It was the color of gold. The face was huge and full of apocalyptic fury at its center. Vernon Sixsmith suddenly felt hot and cold at the same time, stared down beneath his shoes, and said, "I think we'd better get the fu—"

Then watched the earth erupt at his feet.

19

Tina Blackshire

"Smile for the camera, Charley." Tina Blackshire ran around Charley Pascal with the little Sony video camera, crouching down to the level of the big wooden couch where she sat, almost regally. Charley Pascal hadn't wanted to be filmed in the wheelchair. This wasn't a matter of conceit, she said. They had to be careful not to give anything away.

"When do we do the real thing?" Tina asked. She had a plain, blank face, almost unintelligent, Charley thought, although this was deceptive. She had been with them almost a year. She knew Unix. She knew the Web. Tina could handle low-level hacking tasks as easily as someone else might set out a spreadsheet. And she had no family, no friends. She was like everyone else inside the Children: alone, unattached. Capable, Charley thought, of putting that distance between your puny, temporary body and the greater, everlasting glory that lay beyond.

"Joe said after," Charley replied a little sharply, not wanting questions just then. "You have to be patient, Tina. He just wanted me to try the video out. Get some shots they could splice in if they needed them."

Tina nodded, a broken, fragile expression, the invisible bruise of the gentle rebuke hidden somewhere in the pale, flat contours of her face.

Charley wore a plain white cotton smock. She smiled. Tina always made her smile, even when she had this infuriating childishness about her. She was twenty-five or so, had worked in database programming for Oracle in the big black buildings in Redwood City, just down from the San Francisco airport, until she threw in her job and came to join the Children full-time. She had a high-pitched, girlish Valley accent that broke into falsetto too easily when she became overexcited. She was slim, almost without breasts, and nearly six feet tall.

Once, Charley had taken her to bed, just out of interest, boredom maybe, knowing that Tina would never dream of saying no. They had tried this strange, half-serious mix of sex and affection, all tentative fingers and gentle probing, no passion, no excitement, just touching, feeling, sensing. Afterward, when Charley questioned her about it, Tina said she was a virgin. These things hadn't happened in her life. There was always some work to be done. What social contact she got was through chat forums on the Net, not in the real places of the world that Charley, before she got sick, had frequented. There were so many like that in the Children, it only seemed fair to Charley that she should spread her own experience among them.

In time, she had thought, she would take Tina back to bed, pushing it all the way, as far as she wanted, seeing how long the fragile smile stayed on the plain face when the question of penetration, of real fucking, arose. Somehow it never happened. Over the past year, Charley had screwed almost every member of the Children. Most had enjoyed it too, though some were uncomfortable, merely submitted themselves. This was part of the sharing, part of establishing the relationship (of love, of control too). She was their mother figure, and their leader. She knew their bodies, the taut, anxious ones, the slack, frightened ones, she had tasted their sweat, their semen, their salt hair, consumed them with her love, her passion. But never Tina again. It made her wonder.

"You look so lovely," Tina said, then touched her hair, sexlessly, reached for the mirror-backed brush, stroked gently, fine bristle moving through shining black. The bright reflections of the hot day skittered around the room as she moved. Charley closed her eyes and enjoyed the sensation. This was the world slowing down, she thought. Every day is a winding road. . . .

Joe Katayama walked through the door. She looked fondly at him. The rest of the family were still outside, crowding hopefully behind.

"They want to watch," he said.

Quiet Joe. Loyal Joe.

"It's not possible. You know that. Too many risks. If someone were recognized . . ."

He nodded. "Okay. I'll tell them." Then he went out and closed the door behind him, returning shortly afterward. She didn't need to ask their reaction. People followed Joe, as they followed her, and, when she thought about it, this could annoy her. In their passivity, which was part of their innocence, lay some streak of laziness, something that might one day pass for a lack of resolution, cowardice even.

"Tina," Charley said, stopping the brushing with her hand. "Joe and I need a moment alone."

"Sure." She looked so happy. There was a radiance in them all, she thought, now that everything was going so well.

Joe watched her leave. "How do you feel?"

She thought about it. "Strange. A little elated. Some trepidation. But not frightened, no. I don't believe I could be frightened with you around."

He just looked at her, said nothing.

"Joe?" It was hard to extend any depth to these conversations with him. Intimacy didn't frighten Joe, she thought, it was simply something that he didn't want to embrace.

"Yeah?"

"Do you remember a point where this all turned? Where you knew what was happening? And you couldn't go back?"

"No," he said immediately.

"When I quit Sundog, left the job, moved in full-time with the family. That happened for me. There was a day when I woke up and felt this thing moving through me. We were talking loose stuff at the time. Thinking about little things, small acts that no one would ever have noticed. And I knew we could do more. That it was down to me, to lead us through it."

Her head was fuzzy from the illness and the dope. "You were there then?"

"Yeah," he replied. "I remember that time. We were waiting for something to draw all the threads together, Charley. You did that. Don't ask me how. I'm not that bright."

She held out her arms, he bent down his head, let her embrace him. "You're bright, Joe. Bright and loyal and true. The best lieutenant I could ever ask for. Even when it gets hard."

He kissed her softly on the forehead, pulled back from her body. "I can do it, Charley. I thought about these things a lot. And no, I'm not bright. But I know you got things worked out."

"That's *her* strength, Joe. Gaia did that."

"Right."

"And you remember turning that corner?"

He thought about it. "No. I remember feeling lost, wondering whether there was any purpose in anything. And then coming 'round to realizing you did see it, and it all made so much sense. You got the revelation, Charley. For the rest of us, it all came a little more slowly. We didn't have the gift."

"No," she said, and thought: Someone has to lead, always.

"You're sure about this?" she asked. "We ought to be sure."

He nodded. "I'm sure."

She stared at the closed door. "I think I knew already. Intuitively. But there was something that prevented me seeing it. This is a human condition, Joe. One of our failings. The animals know better how to trust their instincts. Perhaps we can relearn these things when the world gets to start anew."

"You're right," he said, and she watched him thinking wordlessly, realized there was something of the animal, feline and strong, inside Joe Katayama all the time.

"Everything else is there?"

"Sure. The Web page just needs the movie in it and we'll upload it. We're planning to shift the address constantly. They'll see it, but they won't see us. No problem. We'll be like a TV station with a broadcast to the world, but no one will have a clue where we're coming from."

"Good." And this was the moment, she thought, much more

than the time they pressed the button on Air Force One. This was when the awakening, the rebirth began.

"Let's have this done," she said.

Joe Katayama went out and came back after a minute with Tina Blackshire. The girl looked radiant. Her eyes shone, were a little misty. Beyond the door, before it shut, Charley could just make out a small crowd of figures, waiting.

"You'll let me watch?" Tina asked breathlessly.

"Yes." Charley nodded. "We need you, Tina. We all need you."

The pale, vapid face looked puzzled, but flattered too. "I never dreamed I would be part of this. . . ." She came over, touched the white gown.

"You brushed my hair so beautifully, Tina."

"It's like being there," she said, her voice trembling into falsetto. "Like watching the sermon on the mount, or seeing Buddha or something."

"I'm not a god, Tina. None of us are gods."

"No," the girl said, kneeling at her feet. "I know. You said. We're all part of the greater god. Gaia. And the spirit of the earth."

"We come from the earth, we return to the earth. You know that, don't you?"

"Yes," she said quietly.

Charley reached forward and touched her, felt her breast. The nipple was hard. Tina looked at her, wide-eyed, not knowing.

"It's the feminine within us that is the source, Tina. It's important to remember that. The masculine is important, but only as a facilitator. It's the feminine where the godhead lives, for all of us. We ignore that and we cease to be alive."

"Yes."

"The world springs from the female, which tames, humanizes the male. Creation is joy, the start of the cycle. You know about creation?"

"Sure." Her eyes looked as if they might pop out of her head.

"And you know about our unmaking? How the cycle ends?"

"Yeah," she replied softly. Then jumped. Joe Katayama had turned on the video camera, which was now attached to a tripod. It had burst into life with a loud mechanical crack.

"You know what you're going to say in the broadcast?" she asked, wanting to change the subject.

"I know."

"You have no notes?"

"I don't need them."

"Wow. You want me just to sit here? I'll be in the picture?"

Charley smiled. The girl took her hand. "Be brave, Tina. We all have to be brave."

"Sure." Joe moved the tripod a little closer, played with the viewfinder.

"It's on," he said. "Don't worry if you make any mistakes. We can edit it on the machine."

"Yes," Charley said, and closed her eyes. She wanted to feel the planets whirling in her head. She wanted to see the trails they made through the stars. But they weren't there.

Charley Pascal opened her eyes and said to the camera, "The earth doesn't belong to us. No one gave it to mankind, no god, no creature from outer space. There are no explicit mysteries, there is no deus ex machina. We are what we have become, we are what we have made ourselves. And the earth is what we have made it too. That's the implicit mystery. The earth is its own spirit. It loaned itself to what we call life, not just man, but the animals, the plants, the birds, the creatures of the seas. And only man betrayed this earth spirit, which we call Gaia. Only man."

She licked her lips. They were dry. Tina Blackshire's hand squeezed hers nervously. "This cannot continue. You know this yourself. If you look in your heart of hearts, you understand this world, the world man has made, is unsustainable. We destroy a little more each and every day, and the cycle of that destruction increases each year. We extend our own lives upon the planet unnaturally, and destroy it as we do so. The world is soiled by our presence. We have squandered the gift that Gaia gave us, and for what reason? Greed. Insanity. The thrusting, covetous male principle that has come to live unchecked inside us. We are out of balance, and we have spread that imbalance to the earth."

Charley Pascal looked into the dead eye of the camera and tried to imagine the world listening to this message, relayed by the TV stations posted across the Internet, stopping the traffic, halting the conversation in bars everywhere.

"We live temporal lives with no view to the future, no appreciation of the past. And if you think about it, you know that we must be reborn in the fire. This isn't a new beginning for our race, we're not butterflies emerging from the chrysalis. Our place is here. On the earth. But as part of a different order of things. We must destroy to create. We must go back to go forward. We must dismantle this false fabric of civilization and return to another time, when humanity was young. I need to open your eyes and I know this will be painful. Some will die. You shouldn't think of yourself, but of your children's children. Of the world they will inherit. Without greed and fear. Without oppression and pollution. The world Gaia granted us, and we, in our foolishness, destroyed."

She waited, and Katayama closed in with the zoom until nothing but her face filled the lens. Her expression was hard and cold and threatening. "We have the power of the sun in our hands. Ask your governments. They will deny it, but they know this is true. We have killed the President of the United States, we will give you more signs so that you can prepare. And prepare you must. This is a new era. This can be a new beginning. We will, for a short while, have the chance to throw off the shackles that bind us. On the zenith, when the sun is at its peak, the sky will burn. We will destroy this artificial fabric of your lives. We will raze cities. We will sear the artifice of man from this planet. And in its place we will put truth. Nature. Reality. Don't look to the TV stations and the newspapers to tell you what to do. They won't be there, not for a while. Look to yourselves, your own hearts. And afterwards, when the governments and the dictatorships have no chains around your legs, when the sky is clear and blue, and the air is fit to breathe, you will thank us. You will rebuild humanity, and the world we inhabit, and you will do it well."

In our memory, she thought. She smiled, then beckoned to Katayama to pan out, move slowly back in the room. "This is yet to come. There are evil men who will try to seek us out and kill us to prevent this happening. This is pointless. There is no time. And we have right upon our side. They infiltrate their agents in our midst. Thinking we are some kind of god, they try to plant a Judas among us."

She bent down, awkwardly, toward Tina, felt her hair. The girl looked at Charley, looked nervously at the camera, lost for words.

"This isn't going to happen," Charley said, and motioned for Joe to cut the video. There was an awkward silence in the room. Tina broke it with a pained smile. "That was great."

"No," Charley said, gazing into her face. "Are you one of us now?"

"Oh yes!" Tina seemed lost.

"Can you feel Gaia? The mother?"

"I guess so," she said quietly.

On the other side of the room, Katayama had parked the camera, leaning on the tripod, taking in the whole scene at the sofa, the two women, one still, one crouched awkwardly on the floor. Charley Pascal looked across at him; he nodded. She touched Tina Blackshire's face. The skin was hot and pale and damp.

"This isn't for any reason of betrayal," she said. "Not for that at all."

Tina Blackshire blinked. "Betrayal?"

"You don't need to say anything, Tina. It doesn't matter. None of us matter as individuals, only as a whole, as a family. And you are a part of that, whatever has happened between us."

There were tears in the girl's eyes. She didn't know where to look. Joe Katayama was moving across the room, taking care to keep out of the way of the camera.

"I don't know what you mean, Charley. Betrayal? I . . ." She wiped at her face with her bare arm. Her eyes were glassy. "I didn't like making it with you, Charley. It was nothing personal. That's all. I didn't really want to do it."

"Nothing matters anymore, Tina. Nothing except the gentle sleep, in the arms of the Mother."

"Charley," she sobbed, "maybe there are things we could talk about. Things I could tell you."

Joe Katayama stood over her, reached down, and placed his hands on her shoulders. She went quiet on the instant. His thumbs felt like hard sheaths of muscle against the tendons of her neck.

"We all go in peace, Tina," Charley said. "How many can expect that?"

"Charley?"

Tina Blackshire's voice was slurred. Joe Katayama's thumbs found the two carotid arteries in her neck, pushed there, insistently, not hurting, just relentlessly, not letting go. Tina Blackshire found that, with the pressure, came something that ran beneath the threshold of pain, a gentle, rhythmic compulsion to close her eyes, relax into the thrumming sound of her own heart beating, trying to keep her alive.

"In sleep there is peace," Charley said. "And this peace comes to us all in the end. There is nothing to fear. Making and unmaking are part of the same process. From our bodies springs a new world."

Tina's eyes were dry now. Her mouth had turned cold and tasted metallic. The room was fading, and the shadows were the color of blood. "Mother," she said, her voice the thin rasp of shriveled autumn leaves on arid ground.

Joe Katayama bent down, wound his arms around her neck, stiffened his upper body, then, in one single, sweeping movement, twisted hard, snapped the spine. There was a harsh, inhuman breaking noise. The girl died with a grunt, a sudden, animal expulsion of air from her lungs. Katayama relaxed his grip. Her head hung off her shoulders at an awkward, sickening angle. A sudden gush of blood came out of the corner of her mouth, ran thickly down her chin. He let the body slip gently to the floor. A brown stain was spreading down Tina Blackshire's pale shins, underneath the simple floral shift. There was a distinct smell in the room. Katayama walked over and turned off the video.

"Give it to them to edit, Joe," she said. "Then tell them about Tina. You did well."

Katayama nodded, his flat face expressionless, although she was sure something was moving there inside him. He took the cassette out of the video camera and headed for the door.

Charley Pascal looked at the body at her feet, fallen in an odd, unnatural shape, like a rag doll that had been dropped on the carpet. There should have been something to cry for just then, but she couldn't figure out what it was.

Day Two
June 20
The Children

20
Michael's Call

La Finca, 0251 UTC

Michael Lieberman came to, wondering where he was and what was making the noise. He jerked upright, felt his head wallow around as if it were about to fall off his shoulders, and reached for the light. Over on the other side of the bedroom the computer monitor was flashing, and a sound like an old Bell telephone was coming out of the speaker.

He dragged on a pair of jeans, walked over, and punched the keyboard. "I think you got the wrong number. It's the middle of the night here."

"No," Helen Wagner answered, in an unemotional East Coast voice. "You're Michael Lieberman. There's no mistake. I'm sorry to disturb you at this hour. Irwin gave me your address. We have to talk."

"We?"

"My name is Helen Wagner. I'm acting head of S&T—that's Science and Technology—for the CIA in Langley. I don't expect that to mean much to you."

Lieberman glanced away from the screen, shook his head as if that might help to clear it. The woman was familiar from somewhere.

"Professor Lieberman. I have bad news for you. I'm sorry. There has been an incident at Lone Wolf."

He wanted to throw up. He wanted to pick up this piece of plastic and glass and hurl it onto the floor. "An incident?"

"We had no idea they were capable of inflicting this kind of damage. It looks as if they hacked their way into the internal network somehow and wound up the internal power generator way beyond its limits. We got a minor explosion and a major fire. Sara will be okay. I'll give you the number for the hospital. She was the only one there when they hit it. Maybe they thought it would be unmanned. It was just bad luck."

"This isn't true," he said. "You people lie all the time."

Helen Wagner blinked back at him. The CIA didn't really look like this, he thought. The CIA looked like Ellis Bevan, all coldness and deceit. "I wish I was lying. A few hours before this they blew up a SWAT team that we hoped was tracking them, and there we are talking real explosives. People are dead. They seem to be able to pick and choose between the technology they use. So far they've killed the President and a couple of hundred people with Sundog, wiped out some agents on the ground with Semtex, and managed to screw up one of only three working control units for Sundog with some kind of computer attack. It makes you wonder what's next."

"Washington?" Lieberman asked blankly.

"We had a major telecom blackout and something like an intense magnetic storm just after noon. It was some kind of directed beam from Sundog. More disruption than real damage. My guess is that they are working to understand what they've got hold of, and conserving it too. It wasn't meant to handle the kind of energy they must have had to throw at it to bring down Air Force One. If they want to save it for the zenith unscathed, and that seems to be their aim, they need to be sparing when they use it."

Lieberman shook his head. This was all too much. "What the hell are you talking about? Sara's hurt?"

She looked at him and said softly, "I'm sorry. Too much at one time. I'm not good at this. You were still pretty close. I didn't know that."

"Yeah. Close." He looked at her as if to say: *What do you expect?*

"Sara was trapped for a while in the debris after the power plant went up. You should call the hospital and find out more. I'll give you the number."

Lieberman nodded. People getting sick. People getting hurt. These were things he never handled well. "Why are you telling me this? Why not Bevan? He's one of your goons, isn't he?"

She smiled, and it looked genuine. "Professor Lieberman—"

"Drop the professor part. It makes me feel uncomfortable."

"Michael," she said tentatively, "this is a very fluid situation. None of us was prepared for this. And we're not in control, not one little bit. We don't run the timing. They do. It's a little . . . unusual for us. At least for Operations here. I'm a scientist. Like you. I don't really get mixed up in those things."

"What do you really want?" he asked.

"I wanted to break bad news to you."

"Yeah. And nothing more? Please. My head hurts."

"And ask for your help," she said. "Bevan said you planned to ship out in the morning. I want to talk you out of that. It's important you stay on board. We need to cover every option there is for taking Sundog out of their hands. You could help a lot there."

Lieberman wished he could shake from his head this image of Sara lying in a hospital bed. "I have to go back home. I should be near Sara."

"Michael," the woman said, "her husband is with her."

"Oh. Right."

"And she'll be fine. Don't take my word for it. Call her. It's important you stay part of the team."

"Important for who?"

"All of us. This is an international issue now, Michael. It's gone beyond the murder of the President and his staff."

"Not my fight, Miss Wagner."

"Helen. Please."

"You've got all these people. In Washington. All over the world. They can fix it."

"I wish you were right," she said quietly. "We're doing our best but we still need you. You designed what makes this thing work, Michael."

"Thanks. I really appreciate being reminded of that."

"It's a fact. I know you would never have done it had you realized what they really wanted it for. But isn't that a little academic now? And we do need your input on the sunspot cycle. They're bound to wait until the absolute zenith until they start to have their fun. And I need to know when that will be because the force they have in their hands is incalculable. When will it peak? When can we expect them to throw the big switch? Will it be midday UTC or what?"

Lieberman was aware that these thoughts had been running subconsciously through his own head too. The entire game might come to hang upon them. "These things walk hand in hand, the solstice and the planetary alignment. It's like bringing a camera into focus using a couple of different lenses. Bennett's right about that, I'm sure. Last time I looked, you got the sunspot zenith coming around forty-five minutes after noon UTC."

Helen Wagner sighed. "Which is about as bad as you could get. The power of the storm will be at its peak."

"You're making a lot of assumptions. That Charley really means this thing. That she has the wherewithal to do it. And that we'd all be sitting here with nothing happening even without Sundog, and of that I'm not sure at all."

"Not really," Helen Wagner said, no expression on her face. "We don't need to make that many assumptions anymore. Like I said, things have changed while you were sleeping. She's made that side of things a little clearer."

"Don't tell me about it. I don't want to know."

She looked at him. Lieberman felt himself being scrutinized. "Why are you like this? A bright guy. So detached."

"Because I'm tired. And sick of being told lies all the time."

She shook her head. "It's not that."

"I don't do shrink stuff at two in the morning. Sorry. Is this conversation over? I have to pack."

"We need you."

"No, you don't. You need people like Bevan. They're trained for this sort of stuff."

"We need your expertise. More than that, maybe, we need your insight into Charley Pascal. I have plenty of people here who'll walk around waving guns in the air. Operations has a few of them lying dead in the street in San Francisco right now. But something tells me that's not going to help us here. We need to understand this woman. What she wants. Why she got involved with the Children. And you know her, Michael."

"*Knew.* A very long time ago. And this is crazy. It isn't like her. Not the Charley I knew."

Helen Wagner shrugged. "People change, Michael."

"Not that much. Not deep down." She looked sad, he thought, resigned.

"I have to show you this," Helen Wagner said. "It isn't a pretty sight. But you need to look. You need to help me understand."

"I'm out of here."

"This is bad, Michael. This could be everyone's worst nightmare. We thought we could keep this under wraps as much as possible, keep a lid on people's fears. But you're right, Charley's smart. After hitting Lone Wolf she put up a site on the Web. It's got her stated aims—sufficiently hazy so that we can't second-guess the detail—and some other stuff too. I believe you when you say she wasn't like this when you knew her. But something shifted inside her. She's sick, physically, and I think in some way she relates what is happening in her head to what is happening in the universe. People no longer matter to her. And she wants to hurt us, all of us, in a way we'll never forget. She thinks that she can somehow send a wake-up call to the human race."

Lieberman shook his head. "That's not the Charley I knew."

"Take a look at this. We downloaded our own copy. The real thing is getting so many hits on the Web you'd never get through. There's something else too. We had someone inside. Charley found out. She E-mailed us a little extra, a picture of the body. If you're feeling up to it, click on the image. If you need more proof, that is. I won't nag. But you have to ask yourself this: Can you really stay apart from what's happening? If you do that, will you ever forgive yourself?"

"I told you," he said, "I'm out of here."

A Web page came on the monitor. Brightly colored text and

background, the words *Children of Gaia* in red, and beneath a simple message: *Prepare.*

Lieberman shook his head and said, "You people . . ." He clicked on the enclosed image she had sent straightaway and thought: She knew that was what would happen all along, she planned it just like that.

Half an hour later, a vodka in his shaking hand, Lieberman called the hospital in California on the videophone. Sara Wong had a bandage around her forehead, a big livid bruise showing up on her right cheek, and what looked like the makings of a serious black eye above it.

"Hey. I leave you alone for a little while and see what happens? Hell, Sara. What do I say?"

"You ask how I am."

"I can see that from looking. Does it hurt? Can I do something?"

"No." It was the look again, as if this were somehow his fault.

"I wish I was there."

"Why? It's not so bad. Talk a little, Michael. I'm tired. I was about to go to sleep."

"Right. So I'm out of this place. This whole job was just some kind of cover for a spook thing and I'm through. I can maybe get a plane to Madrid, be back home in a day or so."

"Oh, Michael . . ." Yeah, he thought, he got the message.

"They spoke to you, huh? The Wagner woman." Sara winced (and this was the pain he was giving her, not the physical side of things, he knew that).

"Of course they spoke to me. Someone attacked the goddamn facility, it looks like it's been firebombed. What do you expect?"

"Don't believe what they tell you. Don't believe a thing."

"Really." Her face looked tired, a little sour now too.

"No. You recognize that woman's name? She was in *Time* the other week. The spook appointments page or something. She's Pieter Wagner's kid, the guy the men in black hounded to death way back when. I just double-checked on the Net. Can you believe that?"

"I remember that story. Maybe she thought it was a good job. Maybe she thought that, if they got better people in there, mistakes like the one that screwed up her father wouldn't happen."

"Yeah." Always thinking the best of people. Sara all over.

"Is that so hard to believe, Michael?"

"For me it is."

"Then that's your cross. Christ, it's nearly fifteen years since you walked out of that project like someone had stolen your very life. Don't you ever get over things?"

"She told you to say that."

"So what? There's something bad happening in the world right now. You have to trust someone and it might as well be them because just now I can't think of anyone else. Either that or you just hide in a deep, black hole somewhere and wait for it to go away. Is that what you want?"

Lieberman drained the vodka glass, poured himself another.

"That's going to help, Michael. Why don't you just take the whole damn bottle, let it give you some comfort down there in your hole, with all those demons. Just let someone else take the responsibility for getting on with the job."

"You don't mean that, Sara. I want to be home. I want to see you."

"Christ." Her voice got louder. It made him sweat in the lonely, airless bedroom, the sound of the Mediterranean washing in from the window.

"Michael. I don't want you here. Not because they told me to say that. Not because they asked me to persuade you to help them. It's simpler than that. I have a new life now. I have a husband. And I don't want you here."

"Right." The same old ritual, a few thousand miles apart.

"Believe me," she said, eyes closing. Dog-tired, he thought, she wasn't faking that, or anything else either if he were to be honest with himself. "Believe that, Michael, if you believe nothing else at all."

21

Precautions

Langley, Virginia, 0311 UTC

Helen Wagner left the S&T block and headed for the old building and Levine's office. Larry Wolfit, Belinda's deputy, now hers, was by her side, a tall, slender man, dressed in a checked shirt and jeans, brought straight back from a few days' vacation by the crisis. He was a few years older than she, quiet, thoughtful, not given to hasty decisions. When the news of Belinda's death broke, Helen's first thought was that they would make Wolfit acting head until a permanent appointee was found. If he was disappointed by their eventual choice, it didn't show. When she considered it more carefully, she guessed it was predictable he didn't get the job. Wolfit was too introspective for the likes of Levine, maybe, and—she didn't enjoy the thought—too smart as well.

"We haven't had the conversation, Larry."

He gave her a wry smile and strode out across the road. Wolfit had been somewhere in Yellowstone when they tracked him down, working on a wildlife renewal project that seemed to occupy most of his spare time. He was still wearing his mountain boots. It gave him an odd, rural air in Langley's neatly manicured environment. The office had nicknamed him Wolfit the Wolf Man, and it seemed so inappropriate. He looked like a college professor on a hike, tall and thin, with wispy fair hair that was falling fast. He could have swept aside what was left to hide the baldness, she guessed, but that was the kind of personal touch that probably never occurred to him.

"No need," he said gently. "I wasn't looking for the job."

"All the same—"

"Really," and he gave her a fixed stare. "And besides, to be honest I've been thinking about quitting anyway. Not that now's the time. This work I've been doing, it's getting a sight more interesting than I ever expected."

She knew, in a loose fashion, what the work was; everyone in S&T did. Larry Wolfit was involved in some scheme to reintroduce wolves into parts of the Rockies where they'd been chased out by man. It was an unusual hobby for an S&T employee, she thought, and she couldn't help but envy his energy and his commitment.

"We can talk about this later," she said. "Interesting hobbies don't necessarily make interesting careers, Larry."

He smiled and, for a moment, she thought Wolfit was humoring her. "I wouldn't describe it as a hobby. We're starting to learn things there that are pretty amazing. I wouldn't be surprised if it leads to some large-scale wolf reintroduction schemes pretty much everywhere before long."

"I guess we need to manage things better."

"No," he answered swiftly. "We have to unmanage them. That's the big lesson. We just go back to something like the status quo, then get the hell out of there."

She watched the big shape of the main block loom up out of the darkness. "Speaking of wolves . . ."

Wolfit grinned. "Please. If they could speak, they'd be offended. Wolves are highly social, team-oriented animals, with a strong sense of what we would call duty and loyalty. They wouldn't flourish here at all. Which is one more reason why I'm thinking of going."

And that would be a loss, she thought, one she would try to avoid. They needed people with Wolfit's qualities: intelligence and the ability to think outside the box. She'd copied everything they had on Sundog to him for his arrival and he was already up to speed on the situation. His insight was, she knew, going to be vital.

The night was hot and airless. It made her catch her breath as they walked purposefully across the quadrant. They sky was clear, bright with stars, pregnant with some power Helen Wagner could only guess at. She had been racing to catch up on the subject of solar energy these past few hours and felt she had a reasonable brief under the circumstances. But there were so many holes in the subject, so many unfilled doubts, even for someone like Lieberman, who seemed to know it by heart. With the best will in the world, they had to guess their way through this one.

Lights burned throughout the Langley complex but they were alone on the walk. These spaces between the component parts of the Agency could be huge, she thought. They turned into the old block, walked to Levine's first-floor office, entered, saw the acting director waiting there, Barnside next to him, and she wondered how Belinda would have handled this. Only one way: directly. This was, in some sense she did not understand, some kind of struggle, between her and this static, slow-moving traditionalism that Levine and Barnside personified. The difference was generational. Both men failed to realize that the ecosystem around them was changing, the threats were different, and the old, simple, forthright solutions didn't apply anymore.

She led Larry Wolfit into Levine's office, breathed in the smoke from his cigarettes, saw them seated at the table, watching her, uncomfortable, almost sullen. Then she sat down, looked at their faces, and said, "How the hell did they get to know about that poor kid? Where did that come from?"

Barnside sighed, a long low moan, reached for a can of Coke on the table, took a swig. His shirtsleeves were rolled up, his face looked lined, older. "Jesus, Helen. Do you have to be so predictable? No one said Ops was a safe ticket. We're not pushing keyboards. This was a field operation. Everyone knows the risks."

"Great. Now that that little speech is out of the way, can I have an answer? How the hell did they find out?"

"She'd been out of touch with us for months," Barnside said, shrugging his big shoulders. "Something went wrong. The most likely explanation is that they tumbled to her some time ago and waited for the right moment. Maybe she was a bad choice. I wouldn't deny that. The point about these people is that they are from outside. We never put them through much formal training. That's what gives them their value—they don't wear the uniform."

Helen Wagner took a deep breath and knew that what Barnside said made sense. That didn't stop it from bugging her.

"We got an inquest running on the girl," Levine said. "Nothing more to know about that at the moment. Let's talk about some broader issues. These Gaia crazies have got all this equipment in the sky. Like some kind of death ray from outer space, the way these Sundog people talk about it. Why did they do all this hacking to get into the Lone Wolf unit?"

She nodded. "It's an interesting question. They want to disable the dome—that's the unit that was developed to house the Sundog antennae and control equipment. We know Sundog can disrupt telecommunications and produce some pretty nasty physical side effects. It's got lots of gears. They could have thrown at Lone Wolf what they threw at us." Helen was thinking on her feet. It didn't come naturally.

"So why didn't they do that?" Barnside asked.

Wolfit looked up from the papers. "I spent a couple of hours going through the records of what happened during the Sundog trials. The reason the thing got abandoned was that it was so damn hard to control. It had all manner of attack media in there—laser, microwave, particle beam. You could create anything from a sea of white noise to a radio or network blackout. Even real damage on the ground—fire, high magnetic and radiation fields. What they threw at us was something designed to flex a muscle or two, I guess, and it happened to coincide with a peak in the sunspot cycle. Maybe that was lucky. I wouldn't want to rely on it for taking something out entirely, and clearly they wanted to do that with Lone Wolf."

Helen nodded. "I agree. We didn't know how to control Sundog with any degree of accuracy and my guess is Charley doesn't either. And this just gets all the more unreliable as we swing up to the zenith. Even without the satellite we could expect some pretty visible effects on the earth in any case. If they can tap into that, then they probably could hope to bring a dome down, but not quite yet, not with any certainty anyway."

"Makes sense," Levine said. "So. Why did they do it?"

"It may have been just a demonstration of their strength," Helen responded. "They threatened some signs that would persuade people to prepare when they put up the Web site. Maybe that was a sign. There's no way of knowing. They haven't even claimed responsibility yet."

"Or?" Levine asked.

Helen grimaced. "Or it's the start of an all-out war to remove our capability to talk to Sundog in any form. The Children clearly have their own facility somewhere. It would take money to build a replica of a dome, but the equipment is available on the open market and Charley sure knows how. I've got the FBI tracking through contractors to see who's been buying the right sort of installation. They want to take us through the zenith using their own dome, but they have to live with the possibility that we might regain control of the network. If they take out our three control centers, that's impossible. In fact . . ."

She turned to the monitor and keyed in the La Finca address. After a few moments, Bevan's face came on screen. "Is Irwin there?"

"A moment." She waited.

"Hi," Irwin Schulz said, looking exhausted.

"We need to understand more. Let's say the Children somehow manage to take out the two remaining domes. Then they program the satellite to do its worst through whatever installation they have and destroy that. Is there any way we can get back on it?"

Schulz licked his lips and said, "Not from the ground."

"What if we start building a dome right now?" Levine asked. "As a precaution?"

"No time, sir," Schulz answered. "It takes a month or more to bed these systems in."

Levine stared at Barnside. "Put some heavy-duty security

teams on site in Kyoto and La Finca. And scour everything there, make sure there are no little surprises waiting for us already."

"Irwin," Helen asked, "you think it takes a month to get one of these things working? That's after you get all the equipment."

"Oh yeah. It's a real pain."

Levine looked at her. "Well?"

"Charley Pascal basically had a blueprint for an entire dome in her head, is that right, Irwin?"

"Sure. She designed most of it."

"So if she wants to do this quickly, surely it makes sense to copy everything right down to the last nut and bolt?"

"The telecom equipment's heavy-duty but standard."

"Maybe they built a dome too," she said. "Is that a possibility? Maybe they got the same kind of design just to make it easier. Could they do that, Irwin?"

"I guess so. If you found the contractors."

Levine stared at her, cast a sideways glance at Barnside. "Good work. We pass that over to the Bureau. There can't be that many people who can build one of those things."

"Irwin," she added. "Mail me the plans for the dome, and the names of the contractors you used."

"Sure."

"So what are we getting from your guys, Dave?" Levine asked.

Barnside shrugged. "You got the list. The President tied our hands a lot, you know. Insisting that this really was a Bureau job."

"Yeah. I heard. But no one knows for sure they're inside the U.S."

"I think," said Helen, "we have to assume that's a probability. We have no evidence that there is a foreign government in play here, and they surely would need that level of assistance to try to produce a dome abroad."

"And here you just go buy it from the catalogue. Wonderful," Levine grumbled. "It doesn't mean we sit on our hands and watch this game go by. The priority's clear. We have to take every step to ensure nothing happens to the two remaining domes. Talk to the military, the politicals. See if we can get air exclusion zones, whatever, put around these things. And sweep every last inch of them."

Barnside shook his head at Levine. "We're not going to get an easy ride over any air exclusion requests. The President is taking this through the UN Security Council right now, they're in permanent session. He's not having an easy ride."

"So we're the bad guys," Levine grunted. "Again. What's new? Pile everything you've got into those places. I do not want a repeat of Lone Wolf. Understood?"

They nodded. Levine gave her a baleful glance. "I got a gut feeling Operations isn't going to get us out of this one, Wagner. The best they can do is keep the fire damped down. What about S&T?"

"We have things to work on. The possibility of the dome. Also the appearance of the Web site. That has to use some conventional network and IP addressing system. There are ways of cloaking your location, but we have people looking at it."

Wolfit shook his head. "I don't want to hold out unrealistic hopes, sir. These people know what they're doing. The idea they might leave a loophole that lets us find them through the Net has got to be a touch fanciful."

"Yeah," Levine said. "But no one's perfect. You give us somewhere to search. It's a start. I got to see the National Security Council now. I got more briefings on the go than minutes in the day. Dave, you take the FBI liaison meeting in the morning. Communicate anything of moment in it to Wagner straightaway. You hear?"

"Sir." Barnside nodded.

Levine watched her, and she couldn't work out what he was thinking. "You think this Shuttle idea has got some mileage?" he asked in the end. "It's a hell of a risk."

She didn't try to hide her doubts. "We can probably get the thing up there in one piece. The problem is what we do then. Unless Lieberman can come up with something, it's pointless. We won't get anywhere near it."

"Twist his arm," Barnside said.

She thought about the deep, intelligent face she'd seen on the monitor. "I don't think it works like that. He has to find his way there on his own."

"Scientists," Levine complained. "Worse than working with goddamn movie stars. Barnside's right. Twist his arm. Do whatever you can. Then try to get some sleep tonight, the pair of you. It may be the last we get for some time."

22
Nature, Rising

Yasgur's Farm, 0432 UTC

She watched the needle go into her arm, closed her eyes, let her head go back, and sighed. Joe Katayama looked into her face, checked the dilation of her pupils, then felt her pulse. The morphine dose kept getting stronger all the time. It had to be watched carefully. And there were times too when he had to say no. They needed her in full control. She understood the system better than anyone. Outside, in the control room, they had enough pure programming skill to run a small corporation. But Charley had the vision, and the breadth of knowledge too. She could turn her hand to hexadecimal one moment, and offer an expert interpretation of the data coming through the feed on the sunspot cycle the next. They couldn't function properly without her.

She opened her eyes and understood the way he was looking at her. There'd been a time when the slow, warm comfort of sex had helped, but that was behind her now.

"Joe," she said, and reached forward, stroked the tanned, muscular strength of his forearm. "No more."

She wore a white shift and lay on the large white bed, soaked in sweat from the heat that seemed to issue in waves from the white painted walls of the farmhouse. She had slept quickly, a deep, narcoleptic sleep, after Tina's death. When she awoke, she found Joe had curled up beside her and lay like a tight, fetal ball, looking so much younger, no cares, no fear in this place his sleeping being had found. She had watched his body, the way his chest moved slowly with each long, patient breath, and wondered at the space between them. Joe Katayama was ever-present in her life, she relied upon him for so many things, personal and physical, but practical too. Yet in some way she still felt he was a stranger.

Awake now, he was his old self, watchful, waiting, always ready to obey. He didn't seem disappointed by her refusal. "Whatever you say. You feel worse? Is there less feeling?"

"It's partly that. But things move on, Joe. From now on I think we begin to leave the body behind. We start to get closer to the Mother. When we make love . . . it's like being back in the Garden, like Adam and Eve. But they were children, Joe. We're growing, changing. We need to focus on that."

"You're right," he said flatly, and slipped off the bed, pulled on his jeans, began to dress. Charley shrugged on the loose clothes that were still lying at the edge of the bed, let him carry her to the wheelchair, comb her hair, then push the chair to the bathroom.

Afterward, she asked, "How are they feeling?"

Joe Katayama thought about the others. They were, effectively, in his care now. Charley's ability to control them through anything but the force of her will was slipping. This didn't worry him. They were loyal, faithful. Or, to put it differently, they didn't think much beyond the confines of the farmhouse. All they saw of the outside world was what appeared on the monitors in the room, and these images were so distant, so intangible. Reality began and ended at the door of Yasgur's Farm. This was their great strength. He shrugged. "They'll be fine. It shocked some people. Billy Jo. Anthony. The weaker ones."

She smiled. "You have to get rid of that way of thinking, Joe. Those days are over. It's not their fault they're shocked. We're all shocked. We all weep for Tina. And ourselves. But more than anything we weep for the earth. We're nothing next to her."

"I know," he said. "I kind of told them that. Besides . . ." He hesitated.

"Besides what?"

"Where could anyone go? We're here. We're safe. If anyone tried to leave until it's time, I'd know."

"You always think in terms of force," she said, and wondered whether he resented the comment. "It's not necessary anymore, Joe. They won't do anything we don't tell them."

"Maybe not."

"It won't happen. They couldn't do it. And okay, if you like, you won't let it happen."

She pushed on the rails of the wheelchair. Joe opened the door into the control room. It had a low, active buzz about it, people hovering over computer monitors, watching newscasts, printing out papers, posting them on the whitewashed walls. There were fans scattered throughout the room, setting up a perpetual hum of motion, a flow of thin air that scattered papers, made your sweat feel cold on your brow. Maybe it was like this in a war, he thought.

The constant movement stopped as she entered. The family gathered around her. She smiled at each of them, taking care to look into their eyes, seeing there a mix of emotions, fear and uncertainty, without doubt, but loyalty and commitment too. On her signal, they stopped work, came and gathered around her wheelchair, silent, waiting.

"Tina would have betrayed us," she said. "She was placed here by those who wish to kill us. We had no choice. And it was finished quickly. Now we have to focus on why we were put here, why we were given this chance."

No one spoke.

"Günther?" Charley said. "I thought someone might wake me. I gather Lone Wolf went according to plan."

"Sure." Günther had shoulder-length hair and a soft, formless face. He spoke with a marked German accent. "We didn't want to disturb you unnecessarily. The dome's out, Charley. Here, we got running copy from the news wires." He passed her some paper off the printer. She scanned through the words, smiling, then stopped when they mentioned the casualty.

"Charley?" one of the women asked. "You okay?"

"Sure. Someone was hurt?"

"Yeah," Günther said. "I read that. Some woman who worked there."

"I knew her. You see? This thing can take from us all. We all have our price to pay. It's what we must sacrifice for all these centuries of waste. Do any of you doubt that now? Can't you feel this motion inside you?"

She closed her eyes and rocked slowly, backward and forward in her chair, to some unheard rhythm, her stricken body moving with such conviction a couple of them in the room started to copy the motion.

"What do you feel, Charley?" Joe asked, watching them, not her.

"I feel the sun and the moon and the stars. I feel the earth stirring. I feel nature on the rise. Humanity in its proper sphere." She stopped suddenly, opened her eyes, stared at them, incredulous. "Don't you feel it too?"

"Sure," said Joe.

"I feel it," Günther said. "Whenever you're around, I feel it, Charley. So strong. Moving."

"Me too," someone else echoed.

"It's only natural," Charley said, "you should have doubts. We're fighting a war now. We're fighting for the Mother. It scares us. And soon we'll begin to leave this place, wait for what comes next. This is only the beginning. The fire and the chaos wipe this slate clean. Afterwards we need voices that can be heard, when the TV and the newspapers aren't there to spread their lies. When people discover they can look into their hearts again and find what's there."

"We've got to go anyway," Joe said, looking at them. "They'll find us, one way or another. We have to separate. For good."

"But . . ." Billy Jo stood by one of the screens, mouth half-open, looking lost, Charley thought. "What do we do, Charley? What happens afterwards?"

"We get a second chance. The earth, Gaia, gives us that. Don't expect miracles, Billy Jo. They'll get their TV sets back, probably sooner than you might think. They'll bring in their newspapers and their police. But all that doesn't matter. We're going to open a hole in the sky, one so big that people will be able to see what we see. After that nothing will be the same again."

She held out her arms. They came to her, touched her flesh, her clothes, covered her in kisses. When they were done, when they stood back to look at her, she was soaked in tears. Joe Katayama nodded across the room at Günther.

"Make the call," he said.

23
The Golden Dome

Kyoto, 0447 UTC

George Soames looked at the dome in the midday light and felt, as always, a sense of pride. Like the two other Sundog domes, this was a perfect geodesic, a "Buckyball," named after Buckminster Fuller, who had conceived the idea of the perfect geometrical dome. It sat on the northeast edge of Kyoto, on a low hill of bamboo and scrub, ringed by a ten-foot-high security fence, accessible through a single narrow guarded road.

As local director of Sundog, Soames had supervised its construction down to the last detail. The telecom equipment the project required was expensive and delicate, though not particularly rare—most parts could be bought "academic retail" for those who had the money and the sources. And Buckminster Fuller's geodesic was ideal to contain the dishes safely and securely, out of sight from prying eyes. Thanks to the advanced lightweight material of the dome, it gave sufficient radiation cover to keep the prefecture happy when it came to safety regulations too.

The unique structure seemed custom-made for the project. Nothing could match its strength and efficiency. The dome was cheaper to cool and heat than a conventional building. And the greatest part of all for Soames, who loved Kyoto dearly, regarded himself as half-Japanese after twenty years in the city, was the color. The fabric had to be treated to contain the radiation created by the operating equipment inside. This wash of protection left it a mature burnished gold, not quite the same tone as the Golden Pavilion a few miles away, but close enough to let him rename his baby the Golden Dome.

Soames admired the scene in the morning's radiant light. It was hard to remind himself that there was a job to be done here. With a sigh he flipped open the screen on the satellite videophone and looked at Irwin Schulz's tired face.

"Hell, Irwin. There's nothing wrong here. We checked it a dozen times. I've had the embassy spooks go over it, every last inch. We've cut the Net connection, just like you asked. The dome works, and everything inside it."

"You got the hardware people in too? To check you really are logged off?"

"Yes. How many times do I need to look at this plug to see whether it's wired or not?"

"I'm not doing this for fun, George. How many people have you got there?"

"Me and about ten from the embassy, the five permanent security staff, and a bunch of people from the local police station. And frankly this is starting to make me feel a little embarrassed. Can I go home now? I can see why we need all this activity but it makes me feel uneasy. You know as well as I do we're just a mirror. We don't have all that big stuff you guys have to deal with at La Finca and Lone Wolf."

Schulz's face disappeared, to be replaced by someone Soames only knew as "the new guy."

"In case you forgot, Soames, these people just took out the Lone Wolf dome in a way that just shouldn't have been possible, damn lucky someone didn't get killed too," Bevan spat down the line. "You'd be doing us all a favor if you took this a little more seriously."

"Fuck you, and the horse you rode in on," Soames answered. "I'm taking this deadly seriously. It's just that there's nothing more we can do here. And that's not my opinion, it comes from your guys who've done the rounds. There are no devices here.

No signs anything's been tampered with. And the perimeter's secure."

He watched the shirtsleeved security men walking the length of the wire, checking every inch again. "What the hell else are we supposed to do? This is Kyoto, not California. We have a lower jerk count, in case you didn't know. And you just keep making this assumption that, because these crazies hit Lone Wolf, they're bound to hit us next."

Schulz's face reappeared. "It's not an assumption, George. It's a precaution."

"You think these people are capable of taking out all three domes? One by one? What they got out there? An army or something?"

It was Bevan again, and he looked mad. "We don't know."

"Well, son, I don't think I'm going to be finding out any answers for you here. We got this baby wrapped up tight. No one comes in, no one goes out without one of your nice embassy people looks them up and down."

"George?"

Soames couldn't help staring at the dome. It looked so beautiful in the bright sunlight. He was around the back of the thing, by the smaller, secondary door. "I hear you, Irwin. Is that creep done with me now? Those people always give me the heebie-jeebies. Yeah, I know. They're a necessary evil."

"People are getting hurt," Schulz said. "Treat this seriously. Take care."

"Sure," he said, his mind wandering. "I keep telling you, Irwin, this is Japan. We never imported that stuff here." He stared at the outer skin and frowned.

"George?"

"Wait a goddamn minute, Irwin. You guys getting air miles for these calls or something?"

Damn contractors, George Soames swore to himself. Every week they were supposed to come and clean the dome. Top to bottom, make sure the exterior was spotless, make sure every last rip in the fabric got mended. And here he was, one day after the visit, looking at the biggest blemish he'd ever seen in the dome skin since it was completed.

"I'll kill those guys," Soames muttered, then walked the six feet that stood between him and the dome fabric and looked again.

"Irwin?" Soames asked.

"What is it?"

"This fancy videophone of yours good enough to let you see a decent picture of something?"

"What?"

"If I knew that I wouldn't be asking the question. Something stuck to the fabric."

"Jesus," the voice from the videophone shrieked, "get the hell out of there. Leave this to security. They get paid for it."

"Don't piss your pants. This thing's no bigger than a matchbox. Maybe it's just part of the gear from something inside that got tacked onto the fabric."

"Call the goddamn security guys!"

Soames looked around. "Typical. Can't see a damn one of them right now. Tell you what. This thing's up at about six feet or so. Too high for me to try to take it off, but if I hold up your fancy phone here maybe you can get a good look at it."

Soames stretched his five-foot-three frame to the maximum and tried to point the lens of the phone at the object on the skin. Then, to make sure it didn't penetrate the skin in some way, he opened the small secondary door with his smartcard, pushed it open, and walked inside the bright, gleaming interior of the dome, looked at the skin from there. It was unmarked. Soames was beginning to feel pretty mad. With a grunt, he walked back out into the sun, leaving the door open, and called Schulz.

"You see it? As far as I can make out it just looks like a plastic box, it doesn't go through or anything. Something shiny on the side. Like I said. No bigger than a matchbox. Beats me. Where the hell are those security guys?"

Back at La Finca, Ellis Bevan stared at the dark object on the screen and shook his head. "Means nothing to me. Why doesn't that moron do what we keep telling him to and get someone to look at it?"

"You don't know George," Schulz muttered. "He sort of loves that thing."

"Well?" Soames bellowed. "I'm waiting."

"Hell, George, we don't know," Schulz replied. "Will you just walk around and find those guys, please? We could be wasting precious ti—" The videophone went quiet.

"Irwin?" George Soames beamed. "I knew you'd come up with something. You're thinking. I can hear it from here."

"How well can you see the front?"

Soames stretched on tiptoe. "Pretty well."

"Looks to me like there's some kind of shiny plastic panel there? Just like the kind you get on the front of a TV remote?"

Soames grinned. "You got it. Someone stuck a TV remote on the side of my dome. I'll disembowel the bastard when I catch hold of him."

"Let's think about this," Schulz said slowly, feeling hot, trying to sort through the possibilities. "Did you put any alarm systems in recently? Some surveillance points?"

"What? We got permanent security supplied by the embassy. Cameras every fifteen feet or so along the perimeter wire. What the hell would we need a burglar alarm for?"

Schulz closed his eyes, squeezed hard, then glared at Ellis Bevan. "You have any clue what this is? Why anyone would use a simple infrared device on the exterior of a building?"

Bevan shook his head. "Not a one."

"George," Schulz said slowly. "Just walk away from that damn thing, find the security people, and leave it to them. Okay?"

"Bull," George Soames answered, and stuffed the videophone into the pocket of his neatly pressed blue shirt. "No bastard goes around sticking bugs on my dome."

He jumped up once, then twice, and finally got his hands on the thing. The little black box came away easily from the skin of the dome and sat in his hand. He turned it over. There was a little clasp for a battery compartment, held fast with a single Phillips screw. He swore mildly, then walked back inside the dome and picked up a screwdriver from a bench just inside the door. He worked on the cover, flipped it, opened the back, and looked at two shiny new AAs sitting in a row.

"Would you believe it?" he said into the big empty space, then took the videophone out of his pocket again. "Hey, Irwin. Take a look at this thing. It is a goddamn TV remote. Now, who the hell has been messing with my dome? That's what I want to know."

Irwin Schulz stared at the picture on the screen, thought about the two batteries and the infrared eye on the front, then said, "Okay. What you do is you take out the batteries. Then you pick that thing up and throw it as far as you can and start running in the other direction. You understand me, you get—"

"What?" George Soames's face came back at them, wrinkled with a puzzled frown. "You hear that noise outside? Sounded like a mosquito farting or something. Damn if that makes sense. No civilian traffic around here for miles."

He felt cold in the constant midday sun. The whine kept getting louder. He looked through the open doorway. It was coming from the sky. There was a tiny black dot there.

"Where the hell did those security guys get to? Never there when you need 'em, when I get back to the emba—"

"George?" Schulz's voice asked, a tinny sound coming from the phone.

Soames didn't reply. He just stared up through the open door at the bright blue sky. Coming straight down at him was something that was moving so quickly it was hard to focus on the shape. "Damn me if it isn't some toy plane," he said to no one in particular, clutching the little plastic box all the more tightly in his hand.

"Get out of there!" Schulz yelled.

Then the picture made a lurch and all Schulz could see on the monitor was tumbling scenery: grass, the bright fabric of the dome, what looked like the red and white wings of a model airplane. There was the sound of something breaking, George yelling in pain, what might have been an explosion, then a hissing noise that went on and on.

Schulz watched the monitor, his heart in his mouth, trying to stab at the keys on the workstation, calling for help. He'd just got through to Langley when George Soames's face rolled in front of the camera. It was distorted now, the skin a livid red, eyes bright, bloodshot, and terrified. His tongue protruded between his swelling lips like a fat red lump of tortured flesh. In one swift, convulsive movement, Soames vomited on the ground repeatedly. And then was still.

24
Return Call

Somewhere over the other side of the world, he guessed, an incoming message icon was flashing on a screen. This was a crazy way to communicate. He'd no idea where he was calling, what was at the other end. Then Helen Wagner answered. Michael Lieberman looked at her calm, tired face and felt some kind of decision being made for him.

"Hey, I thought I might be waking you up. Returning the favor."

She smiled. "Not exactly. I had half an hour on the sofa in the office. We have more than a hundred people working on this outside the door, and that's just S&T. How's Sara?"

Lieberman blinked. "She's fine. Resolute, you might say."

"And the bad news. You heard about Kyoto?"

"Yeah, I got it from Irwin. He's really cut up, knew the guy there. So that's two down, one to go. What the hell happened?"

She winced. The small movement made him realize how effortlessly attractive Helen Wagner was, and he couldn't help but wonder how this must have hindered her career in the Agency. "They planted some kind of homing bug on the dome. We don't know how. Then they used a toy airplane loaded with VX nerve agent."

"That's the stuff Saddam was fond of, right?"

Wagner gave him a look that was only a touch short of condescension. "We all have VX, Michael. It's not rocket science. They wanted to penetrate the dome and make it unusable so they had some minor explosive charge in the plane. As it turned out they didn't need it. The local director had the door open anyway and the damn thing went straight inside. He took a direct hit, which has to be one of the worst ways to die. They knew what they were doing. This is a persistent, highly localized nerve agent. It's going to take up to sixteen weeks to clear away the residue from the vicinity, and we won't be able to work efficiently in the dome for a good four to five days."

"What about breathing apparatus?"

Wagner did give him a condescending look then. "You think we could run this operation wearing space suits? Do you want to try that right now in your control room?"

"Sorry. I'm dumb in these matters."

Wagner favored him with half a smile. "Think yourself lucky. It's the best way to be."

"Hell of a weapon for a bunch of ecoterrorists to use."

"Perhaps . . ." The thought had occurred to her. "I don't know. Maybe they were trying to make a point. The cult that attacked the Tokyo subway had much the same view, you may recall. Except they used Sarin, which is around one-twentieth the strength of VX and nowhere near as persistent. They were trying to get their hands on anthrax and the Ebola virus too."

Lieberman shook his head. "This is one scary world you inhabit."

"Same world as yours."

"Really. If you don't mind my saying, you people didn't do much of a job protecting Kyoto. Are you going to do any better here?"

She looked nervous. "We're still trying to get our heads around this one. The President said something that really struck me. This is all outside the loop, outside anything we've prepared for. As much outside as having aliens land, except we have at least some contingency plans for that."

"Really?" he asked, half-agog.

"Of course. It would be irresponsible not to. But the President's point was that these people are as foreign, as incomprehensible to us as aliens. And they're of our own race, of our own making. You want to know the really scary thing? I know how they feel. In some ways I sympathize. We are making a mess of the planet. We are out of control. And . . ." She went silent.

"And what?" he asked.

"We're all distanced from one another. It doesn't matter to them that they can cause real harm, real hurt. Somehow it's all just a game. No, not a game, they're deadly serious. It's all *apart*. We've replaced real communities with virtual ones, and some piece of humanity disappeared in the process. I'm thirty-five and single and you know what I do when I happen to have some chunk of free time you might call leisure? Read a Web page about mountain climbing. Instead of damn well going out there and doing it."

"So this is the insight part of the conversation, huh?"

She laughed. "Oh dear. Did that sound deliberate? It wasn't. Really."

She found herself enjoying this conversation, tired as she felt. There was something insidiously likable about this man.

"Okay," he continued. "So let's think about Charley. You know who these people are?"

She shook her head. "I wish."

"Let me tell you. Just ordinary people. People like us. They're bright. They're educated. They probably come from nice middle-class parents who gave them everything they ever wanted. A good education, a nice car, the works. They've got no real gripes with society. No one took over their country. No one oppressed them. They have no political philosophy they think can change the world for the better. So why do they do it?"

Helen Wagner closed her eyes and knew exactly what he was going to say.

"Because they have no lives, none to speak of," he continued. "And we've all been like that, from the sixties on, searching for something we thought had been promised us. Then usually getting older, getting responsibilities thrown at us so often we forget we ever dreamed things could be different. Except these kids had this new world, of PCs, of the Internet, come up and open its arms, welcome them in, and say: *Hey, this can be home.* This can provide anything you want. People who agree with you. People who hate you. People who say they love you. Even virtual sex—whatever that might be—if you want it. And suddenly they were a part of this unreal thing. Learning Linux when they should have been sitting watching a baseball game. Hacking Web sites instead of dating. Thinking theirs was the reality and ours was the illusion. And it's such a waste. Because they're wrong. No clever stuff here. They just took a blind turning and it's eating up their lives."

She watched him fall into silence on the screen and wondered, "Was that Charley?"

"Oh yeah. And more. You want the gory details?"

"Only if you think they're relevant. And then only if you want to."

He watched the light growing outside the window. One more day to the zenith. And somewhere, maybe inside him, was some key they could use to reach Charley.

"When the scales fell off my eyes over that damn satellite I went a little crazy," he said, not looking at the screen. "Charley and I were just colleagues until then. Really. Then that big bombshell struck and I just felt stupid and used and mad. I wanted out. She wanted in. And the crazy thing was that when we both fought like that, we wound up, one way or another, having an affair too. Professionally we went in two different directions. I chased anything that was the opposite of solar satellite design I could find. She picked up her security badge and went in to finish off the job. The new job. This lasted six months."

He picked up the glass of water on the desk and drank. It was warm and tasted dusty.

"Did that bother you?"

He gazed at her picture on the screen. This woman didn't mind asking the big ones. "No. Nothing bothered me. I just didn't care after I left the project. Charley did, for sure, and that puzzled me. I couldn't see why she was hanging on. Me, I just let the dice fall wherever they rolled."

She watched his pale, still outline on the screen. "And now you'd like to run away again?"

"We'll come to that. The important thing you need to know is that Charley is the one person I met in all my life you attach the word 'genius' to. When we met, she knew more about just about everything—solar physics, astronomy, even electrical engineering—than anyone I ever encountered. And she had such insight into things. She could visualize a problem, not just see it as some algorithm waiting to be fixed. I became the person who tried to put a few boundaries around the places she was going to. Not easy. That woman would take on anything, work all the hours she had to see it through."

She waited; he was struggling for the words.

"You have to remember," he went on, "Charley had all this intellectual capacity and it was packed inside this person who looked like an airhead, who looked like she ought to be posing for the front of some fashion magazine. That made it really tough for her to get taken seriously. The funny thing was it made it tough for her to date too. Poor kid got the worst of both possible worlds. People looked down on her work because they thought she was a bimbo. And out in the real world, where real people live, they just looked at this model-type woman and thought: Hey, let's leave this to the rich kids 'cause I can't afford that kind of dinner date."

"She has some sense of separation. They all have. Do you think she was in love with you? For a while maybe?"

"No. Not at all. But maybe, looking back, I represented some kind of chance of normality for her. Bizarre as that seems. Being close to genius you're close to madness too. Maybe after that it all just went downhill, she retreated into herself, the work. And one day got hooked up with the cult, and the computer thing really took over. Maybe, and this does bother me, she just thought of this all along, and that was why she kept on working for them even when they came out into the light and said: *Surprise!* I keep trying to think what drives her now. And I just don't know."

He stared back from the screen, serious, dark eyes peering at her. "Does that help?"

She shrugged. "I'll run it past our specialists here. I'm really grateful."

"Say what you mean."

"My God, I am a lousy liar, aren't I?" She smiled and stared at her notes. "We can't reach her. She's beyond that. She's smart and she's absolutely determined in what she's trying to do. There's no room here for negotiation, talking her into some other path, because we don't have anything she wants. Either we take back Sundog or they're going to do what they say. It's as if we're some kind of beta version of what they believe the planet should be. They think they can throw away a lot of the code in the hope that whatever comes back in its place has to be better than anything that preceded it. Which seems a pretty shaky premise to me, by the way."

He nodded. "That was my feeling too. Charley came from all that European tradition, you know. She went to the Sorbonne. She knows what the prerequisites of revolution are."

"Chaos. A word I'm getting to hear a lot."

"It's a nice, pat, easy way out of things."

"And there's no damn point in wasting any time contemplating it either," she said. "So you've looked at the new solar data?"

"Yeah."

"How bad is it?"

" 'Bad' is a subjective word."

"Not right now," she said quickly. "We don't have time for semantics. Maybe I didn't make myself clear, but we've got the makings of a world in crisis out there. This is filtering through to everything, the financial markets, the information infrastructure, everything. This has the potential for real natural disaster, if it deserves the word 'natural.' And one on a global scale we've never witnessed before."

Lieberman peered quizzically at her. "You're sure about that last point? No. Don't answer. Okay. The forecast is terrible. The way things look I expect that anyone with a piece of colored glass will be able to see a lot of activity with the naked eye by midday today. After that, it gets hazy. It's easy to predict the trend, hard to say whether we get there slowly or in one big rush. The trend is that there will be some spot-merging, and that will produce one giant beauty. The biggest we've ever recorded, covering maybe half of the surface of the disk. Maybe more, when we get to zenith."

"What does that mean for the strength of the emissions?"

"Not my field. You need to ask Bennett."

"Come on."

He shrugged. "Take what you got in Langley and multiply it by ten, twenty, a hundred times. I don't know. And think what it is then, because I'm guessing it may be something different. There's all sorts of crap mixed up in this stuff. It could manifest itself as heat, radiation, high-level electromagnetic fields, pure plasma . . . hell, I don't know. It could be a heat wave that puts out the TV, it could be a firestorm that wipes out Manhattan. You tell me."

"Jesus," she sighed.

"And the truth is, I think we could be in trouble even without Charley and your little toy. This thing is so powerful, and the way we've been treating the atmosphere we're so vulnerable. Just out of interest, I looked up some of the times we've had some combination of spot cycle and syzygy to match it. That requires a lot of guesswork. But I'll tell you one thing. We did have something like this between 2600 and 2700 B.C. Ring a bell?"

"I'm not a historian."

"Me neither. I just remember it from some of my self-taught classes in atheism. That's thought to be the time of the biblical flood. Noah. The animals went in two by two. That kind of thing."

"That's myth, surely, folklore."

"Yeah. That's what I told myself too. The trouble is these old guys had learned to write by then. You don't just get the flood story in the Old Testament. It's in the Gilgamesh book as well. That's Sumerian. And there's hard evidence there was flooding in the region around that time. We also had some kind of conjunction around 1650 B.C. That was the year the volcano erupted in Santorini, one of the largest eruptions in human times. It changed the face of the Mediterranean. The power structure. Everything."

"I remember," she said.

"And just one more. If you take things back too far, the dating gets a little ridiculous, of course. But we do have firm fossil evidence that whatever it was that brought the Cretaceous era to an end occurred at a time of intense sunspot activity. It's there in the rings of the cretaceous vegetation."

"That was, what . . . sixty-five million years ago?" she said quietly.

"Yeah. Which is why I wouldn't rely on my computer alone. And, as I'm sure I don't need to remind you, the end of the Cretaceous marked the extinction of the dinosaurs too, in ways we still argue about. Suddenly. Instantly. Conventional wisdom is starting to say that it was a meteor impact that caused it, and the Yucatán Crater in Mexico is the proof. A ten-kilometer meteor, to be precise. And maybe that's right. Or maybe it was something pretty much like a meteor that the sun spat out, some big ball of plasma. I don't know. There aren't any dinosaurs left to ask."

Helen Wagner caught her breath. "You think Charley's made that calculation too?"

"You bet. Hell, I'm amazed it's not all over the Web right now. And you can see how that knowledge would work on Charley too. It makes her feel part of something bigger. But it's disappointing in a way too. If we've really only had three major catastrophes through solar cycle and planetary syzygies over the last sixty-five million years, maybe we ought to come out of this one with little more than an extra suntan. If I can still hope to read Charley right these days, this data is saying to her that she probably needs to give the thing a little push if she wants to be sure the world really can start all over again. Maybe give the ants a chance this time. And don't kid yourself. She wants to do more than cause some stock market crash. She really does want to change things for good. This is cataclysm, nothing less."

She was quiet. The office suddenly felt lonely and cold.

"There's a storm on the way," he said, "and it's coming whether we take back your little toy or not. Maybe it just scorches us a little. Maybe it passes us by altogether. And maybe we get the Yucatán all over again. I don't know. No one knows."

"It's not my toy."

"I know," he said, shaking his head. "I apologize. It belongs to all of us. We just got greedy. Thought we could tame that big golden ball of fire and make it run our TV sets for free."

She looked at his face, half in shadow on the screen, and wondered at the amount of trust that seemed to exist between them. "So do we have your pleasure for this event, Michael?"

"I guess, Helen," he said, unsmiling.

"I'm glad about that."

"Don't be. I mean, where the hell are you supposed to hide when the sun god comes to call?"

She nodded. Thought twice about this, and said, "This is really useful. But I need more from you."

"I haven't got any more."

"But you have. We're working on every way we can to get Sundog back under our control from the ground. We've got any number of teams out there trying to track down Charley. I've got to cover every angle. We're putting up a Shuttle in a few hours. I need you to find us some way to take the power source away from that thing directly, in the sky if we have to."

Lieberman couldn't believe what he was hearing. "Wait a minute. That was the first thing I asked Irwin and he said there's no way we can go near this at all. He made it sound like you've got the Battlestar Galactica up there. If you try to shoot it down, it can intercept the missile. And take out whatever shot it in the first place."

She nodded. "That's true. It's one smart weapon. It could take out the Shuttle if Charley detected it on launch. Then there's an automatic defense system that will attack anything substantial that comes within a half a kilometer of it in space. That still leaves us room. If we can get into orbit and power down the Shuttle before the automatic system comes into play, we could get a couple of astronauts close to the thing. The trouble is, as far as I understand it, they can't touch it, and any weapons they might carry would be detected. And we have to find it. The damn thing is built out of polymer, like you see in stealth devices. We're not even exactly sure where it is right now, though with those huge wings you designed for it I think the Shuttle ought to be able to track it down."

"Jesus, Helen. You're just sending these guys to their deaths."

She sighed and Lieberman saw the sadness in her face. "That's a possibility. They know it."

"So why?"

"We need options. We calculate there's a ninety-second window after launch when the Shuttle could come under direct attack from the main weapon systems. If it escapes that and gets into orbit, it can edge in behind Sundog and give us a chance."

"To do what?"

"That's what I need you to figure out. Imagine we do take the ship within half a kilometer of the satellite with all the systems down. And after that, we could place a couple of astronauts in extravehicular activity up to ten meters from the satellite without triggering any automatic self-defense systems."

"Then what?"

She shook her head. "Any weapon would be detected and, in all likelihood, immobilized immediately. No, we have to shut it down without touching it. That's the only possible solution and you have to know how, you designed that entire power system. I need you to clip those wings, Michael."

He was genuinely affronted. "Nothing else while I'm there? A cure for AIDS, maybe?"

"You don't mean it when you say that kind of thing."

"How the hell do you know?"

Helen Wagner's eyes held him on the screen. "You called, Michael. You care. And you can find the answer. You just tell me what you need to get there."

25
In the Air

Above New York, 0734 UTC

Tim Clarke watched the lights of the city recede beneath the fast-rising helicopter and was glad to be gone. The mute, baffled reception he'd received from the Security Council was depressing. Perhaps they recognized the note of desperation in his voice.

He looked at the close circle of advisers around him. These were people he'd inherited from Rollinson, and when times got back to normal some would change. They knew that. But they were good, solid, dependable men—all men, he thought, something would have to be done about that—fine in a conventional crisis, lost a little in this one. Governments ran on rail lines, Clarke thought, mapping out the future on the basis that it was all predictable within limits. When something came along that wasn't in the contingency plan, suddenly it all fell to pieces.

"Those guys want some news from the Bureau, Dan," Clarke said, looking at Fogerty seated opposite him. "We can try to sweet-talk them into keeping calm right now, but you got the mood in there. They think this is our baby. They think we're the ones who got them into this, and we ought to be the ones who get them out. In their position I guess I'd feel much the same."

"Sir." Fogerty nodded. "We're pushing every resource we've got into this. But I'm not going to lie to you. These people have no criminal records, no terrorist background. They're not the kind of folks we're likely to follow as a matter of course. If the Agency had kept that damn plant they had inside there, or leveled with us in the first place—"

"No time for range wars. Don't you people get it? This is a crisis with the clock running. Maybe this is just a storm that will blow over. But we've all seen some of the reports coming in from Wagner. The power these people have in their hands is, as far as I understand it, massive. The odds are that if we don't do something in the next twenty-nine hours or so Bill Rollinson's funeral will be the last thing on our minds. We've got to focus on stopping this thing happening, nothing else. Okay?"

He watched them nod at him and thought: They still don't get it. "Dan, do you think Wagner's right when she says there's no negotiating with this woman?"

"Absolutely, sir. Our psychological profiling people back up everything she says. This woman is resolute. She's not looking to bargain. She sees herself, and the Children, as being part of some inevitable, natural process of rebirth. She's looking forward to this. Nothing's going to stand in her way."

"And that stuff about what might happen even if we do get Sundog back?"

Bryan Jenkins, the White House scientific adviser, coughed and said, "A lot of this is speculative, Mr. President. There's no real way of knowing."

Graeme Burnley winced. He didn't like stepping on other people's toes. "Sir, we have clear indications that other governments are perceiving this as a major threat too, and have no better idea of how to tackle it. Why do you think we got such a relatively easy ride in there over the detail? They're just as much in the dark as we are."

"That was easy?" Jenkins asked, incredulous.

"Maybe easier than we deserve," Clarke said, staring at his hands.

The helicopter flew down the security corridor, out into the night, back toward Washington. The rhythmic pumping of the blades and the noise inside the cabin reminded Clarke of the Gulf, a decade before, though it seemed much less than that. There was a lot of time spent inside the bellies of these machines then, and it was easier: You had someone to fight, you had an objective. Now it was like punching shadows and wondering whether you might break your fist on your own face instead.

"What about the Shuttle?"

"We can launch, sir," Jenkins said. "If we knew what we could do if and when we find the damn thing. Sundog's probably at greater altitude than the Shuttle would normally operate. But we can overcome that. NASA had a high flight modification in the works and it's ready to roll."

"You got volunteers to man it?"

"I could fill it five times over. NASA put it straight on the line how risky this thing was. It didn't stop anyone. We've picked the two best pilots we know and the guy with the most EVA experience."

"Come again?"

"Extravehicular activity. Spacewalk, in plain language, Mr. President. But we still need this Lieberman guy to figure out what these people could do up there. This thing is purpose-built to withstand all forms of attack."

"You mean we can't get anywhere near it?" Burnley asked.

"It can detect other vehicular activity within a kilometer," Jenkins explained. "But if we kill all the main systems barring light telecom on the Shuttle, then drift it into the vicinity, we ought to get under the detection system. It's based on engine heat and electrical activity, nothing visual, thank God. The same goes for getting near the satellite through an EVA. We can probably put a guy real close to the thing, provided he isn't using anything it can pick up. Even a blowtorch would trigger a response, and by response I mean something major. The standard would be high-intensity laser, which would kill instantly and could take out the Shuttle too."

"So what can we do?" the President asked.

"Turn off the power generation system. If this Lieberman guy can figure a way. He designed the thing and it's real clever stuff. If that's down, Sundog grinds to a halt in minutes. This thing just eats power. But we've no word on how you can do that without being able to dismantle part of the installation physically."

Clarke thought about the queue of astronauts inside NASA waiting for the opportunity to dance around this deadly, poisoned ball of plastic and metal in the sky. "It has to go. Even if we haven't figured out what to do with it. We have to cover every option."

In two hours he would be going on live TV to announce the emergency measures: the suspension of all civil aviation flights and public ground transportation, the closure of all nonessential government buildings, and orders barring the opening of all but vital private sector offices in the major cities. All of these measures would run from noon indefinitely, although the idea in the broadcast was to emphasize that, if everything "went according to plan," the restrictions would be lifted by late the following day. And most other heads of state were following the same line. Trying to balance caution with the need, the overriding need, to avoid an outbreak of panic.

"Dammit," he said, "I wish we could shut down the markets. And the Net too. We can keep a handle on the newspeople here. Make them act responsibly. But it's useless if someone can just turn on a PC, go to that damn Web site, and read it all for themselves. Plus all the other rubbish out there."

Dave Barnside, hidden away in a corner at the back of the cabin, said, "We've looked at it, Mr. President, and it's just not possible. There's no practical way of pulling the wire on that thing. It's designed to be impregnable."

"So are the markets," Fogerty added softly. "Who knows? Maybe she'll take them both down for us."

"I don't think so, not the Net anyway, that's where these people live," Clarke said, watching the lights on the ground move slowly beneath them. At night, the land was so anonymous. The Children could be anywhere. Even far beneath the helicopter, listening to the distant swirling of its rotor blades, running the show through some control installation hidden in the woods, all down some humble little piece of copper and maybe a dial-up connection with AT&T. "From now on we run this from the Pentagon bunker. I want the White House cut down to essential staff. Move my family out, Graeme, take them somewhere secure. Until this thing is through, we stay in the Pentagon. I want no unnecessary air travel, no one out of the bunker unless they need to go."

"Sir."

"Don?" Millington, a brigadier general from the Army seconded to the National Security Council, nodded. "Make damn sure they don't touch that last dome. Make that your top priority."

"Absolutely, Mr. President," Millington replied, the braid on his uniform glittering in the darkness. "We got clearance from the Spanish to join the air cover and they've agreed to a temporary exclusion zone now. No one gets in or out of there without our knowledge."

Clarke looked at Barnside. "Can they do what they did in Kyoto?"

The Agency man shook his head. "We believe that's impossible, Mr. President. We have the Spanish site wrapped up. In Kyoto they put some kind of infrared locator on the dome to get there. That sort of weapon's no use in mountains of the kind we're talking about here, even if they could get close enough, and they can't. Also, there's definitely no locator on the Spanish dome. We've fine-combed every last inch of it, and the surroundings."

"Where the hell," the President asked angrily, "did they get that VX shit from anyway?"

Jenkins sighed. "If you know chemistry, can get a line inside a fair-sized chemicals company, and have enough money to set up a small lab, it's not that difficult, sir. We've had people making Sarin in one room and LSD in the other. You can pick up the recipes like that off the Net."

"Jesus . . ."

"I advise," said Millington, "that we put our air bases on alert for when we do track down these people. If we get a location at home, we can take them out very rapidly, shut this whole thing down."

"Yeah?"

The cabin went quiet. They were descending. And there was something new inside Clarke's voice that gave them all pause for thought, something close to bitterness.

"You guys," the President went on, "you kill me sometimes. That really is all you want. A neat little name and address. And then off you go, sending in your people and your airplanes, bombs a-bombing, guns blazing—I got the details of that stuff in San Francisco, by the way, Barnside. Real clever. Are you thinking out of your dicks or something? You know something? I'm the dumb-assed moron you people used to send on these jobs. And I never asked why. Not once. I was as plain stupid as those suckers you got out in the field right now."

Clarke could feel the heat in his face and he didn't mind who saw it. If they thought this outburst was unworthy of the President, he didn't care. This wasn't a time for niceties.

"It's a question of maximum response, Mr. President," Barnside replied. "How else do you deal with these people?"

"Bullshit. You guys haven't got your head around what's going on here yet. None of you. Forget 'dealing with these people' for a moment and get back to the matter at hand. And that, unless I'm mistaken, is getting us all through the next few days as much in one piece as possible."

"Sir," Millington said, "if we cauterize the source—"

"Aw, Jesus. *Cauterize?* Don't give me that crap. I know what you guys want. A carte blanche so you can walk out of here and do what the hell you like. Well, you aren't getting it. Understand? Sure, maybe the world is that simple. All you do is find these people, bomb the hell out of them, take out their dome, and we all go back to the way we were. But let me ask you this: What happens if we do that, then find out they have got some way of taking out the Spanish dome? What happens if we do that and discover they've locked that goddamn thing in the sky in some way that all your computer geniuses combined can't pry it open? What if they just turn out to be a lot smarter than we thought? Consider that. They know we can blow them to pieces if we track them down. Do you think they care? Of course not. If they did, they wouldn't be in this position in the first place."

The cabin was silent. Dan Fogerty looked out the window and saw the illuminated shape of the White House far off in the distance.

"They've already thought this through," Clarke said softly. "Taking them out won't make any difference to what's going to happen. May be just what they want, for all we know."

"So, Mr. President," Fogerty asked, smiling as he broke the silence, "what do you want us to do?"

"Think a little. Find these people. Take them alive. Hand the keys to their installation back to Sundog, just in case they need them. And save your testosterone for your girlfriends. That too much to ask?"

Fogerty could see the dry grass of the White House lawn swirling under the downdraft of the helicopter blades, the line of cars waiting to greet them, rush them back to their various, scattered offices throughout the area.

"Sir," he said, and listened to the low murmur of confused approbation that followed.

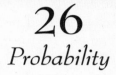

26
Probability

Geri Southern stood behind the counter of the blackjack table in the Bird of Paradise Casino on the Las Vegas Strip. She watched the distant Mirage volcano spit fire for what seemed the ninety-ninth time that night and wondered whether the short-cut croupier's uniform and the nasty fishnet tights just might leave permanent crease marks on her body. The tall, thin tourist on the other side of the table gave her a halfhearted grin. She stared back, with as artificial a smile as she could muster, and said, "You want to play? Or you just here to look?"

This graveyard shift was not one she liked. All the drunks. All the losers, eking out their last remaining dollars. And then there was this emergency thing that got big-time on the news. It was all so complicated. The President dead and some black guy there in his place. Phone systems, television networks closing down. Like it was the end of the world. No one could decide whether this would be good for Vegas or bad. The airport was closing in a couple of hours, but most people seemed happy to book in a few more nights in the hotel, party some more, see how it all panned out. This was Vegas. Why worry?

"Thinking about it," the man said, big mouth opening wide to show his teeth. He looked about thirty-five but something told her this was deceptive. Probably a good ten years younger, she thought, but he wasted it with a geek crewcut, a cheap khaki shirt, a thin, ugly face, and bad dentistry.

"You hot in here?" she asked.

He was sweating heavily. "Yeah. Lousy air-conditioning."

"Normally it's pretty good. It's just we got a real spell of desert weather right now, I guess."

He was sucking on a free gin and tonic and there was a decent bulge in his money belt. Must have been playing somewhere, she thought. This wasn't a night to lose anybody. She smiled again, a little more genuine this time. "If you play we can talk some."

"Yeah. I know."

He looked disturbed, nervous. "I could teach you things," he said.

"Really?" Had that been a yawn? She wasn't sure. She didn't care.

"Useful things in your kind of work. For example, what do you think the odds are of you dealing out the fifty-two cards in that deck as a perfect hand to four different people here—ace to king in all the suits?"

"This is blackjack, sir. You get two cards only. We try to keep things simple."

"I know that," he said, a mite testily. "But just guess."

"Oh." She tossed her blond hair back so he looked at it a little harder. "I don't know . . . maybe, say, two times ten to the power of twenty-seven to one. Something like that."

He grinned, twitched a little, puzzled. "Pretty good. They teach you that stuff?"

She stared at the next table. A red-faced couple in matching satin shirts were starting to play heavily, sucking on long drinks, swaying on the plush seating. It must be something in her face, she thought. It just attracted the failures. "Vegas is kind of an educational sort of place. You'd be amazed what you pick up. So you want to play?"

"Five cards from a fresh shuffled deck. What are the odds on getting sweet nothing there, you think? As a percentage this time."

"I'm not getting paid for this, sir."

He put a twenty on the table. "Make like you won it off me. It doesn't matter."

She thought about it. Took her hand off the little security button under the table. Then pulled the twenty over to her pile. "A little over fifty percent, so one in two hands is a bummer."

"Hey! You got a feel for these things." There was another bill in his hand. She smiled. Maybe this would be a good evening. "Okay. That was easy. Now it gets tougher. A single pair."

"From what? Five cards? Somewhere over forty percent."

"Good." He nodded. "Forty-two-point-two-six or so, if you want to be strict, but that's close enough." The bill sailed over the table. "Now for something harder."

"Sure," she said, wearying of this a mite. "But if it's tough, does the money stay the same? It doesn't seem quite fair."

A couple of people had stopped by the table now, sensing something odd was happening. As long as she logged this as winnings no one would mind. They had this on the camera anyway. Linda, the hatchet-faced security woman with the physique of a squat wrestler, had joined the crowd. Linda nodded tentatively, as if to say: A little further, see what happens.

The man took out a bunch of bills. She couldn't see how many. "A straight. Five cards in a run, suit doesn't matter. Again, fresh pack. Same rules."

"About a third."

"Excuse me? I didn't quite make that out."

"About a third of one percent, three times in a thousand," she said, more loudly this time.

"Good." He threw the bunch of money across the table. "You all hear that? We've gone from almost every other deal to three times in a thousand in a couple of quick steps, and you people are still not getting it."

Linda the security woman stared directly at her, and Geri Southern knew what this meant: So he's some anti-gambling weirdo here to make a point. What the hell? He's throwing money at us.

"Okay," he said, and opened up the money belt, poured a pile of bills on the table, let them lie there for a moment so the crowd could take it in. Geri Southern tried not to gasp. Just a glance told her the denominations. There was probably a good twenty thousand dollars looking at her right then.

"Now we go for the big one. And when I ask, I want you to think about this. Not just the answer, but what it means. A royal flush. How about that? Just a plain royal flush."

"A hundredth of a percentage point," she said.

"Aw Jesus!" he yelled, and she wasn't sure if he might not burst into tears. "Is that the best you can do? You didn't even try to think."

"I got it wrong?"

"Yeah."

"Do I get another try?"

"Nope," he said, scooping up the money. "What kind of a dumb fucking question is that?" His voice went high and squeaky. " 'Do I get another try?' Jesus, you people are unbelievable. How many tries do you think we get on this planet? You think we should've given Hitler another try?"

Linda the security woman was on the radio now. Pretty soon the weirdo would be back out on the Strip. And, Geri thought bitterly, what was left of his money would be with him. He scooped up the bills and walked quickly around to her side. "Let me tell you . . ." He peered at her name tag. "Ge-RI!"

"Sir . . ."

"Let me tell you the odds on a royal flush. One five thousandth of a percent! One turn-up every half a million deals. And you know what's really rich? You people know, in your guts, that's the truth. It's all so distant you don't even care. But sometimes these things do come up, oh yes. There's one coming up right now and you morons do nothing except sit back and play the goddamn slots."

Geri looked beyond the crowd. A couple of security men were on the way. Not rushing. The guy didn't look dangerous, and it was good policy not to scare off the ordinary Joes. Besides, in a way it was amusing.

Then the man scooped up some of the money, thrust it down the front of her costume, looked at the big-denomination bills sticking out of her pretty cleavage, and said, "You listen to me,

Geri! You take that money and you get yourself in a car and you go drive out of here as fast and as far as you can. Because the biggest royal flush you're ever going to see in your life's on its way here and it's going to scorch and burn you all. All! You hear me?"

They were laughing, she saw. All of them. Even the security guys ambling over, thinking this was one good tale for the bar after work. The man stared at them, not believing it. "You all run from here. You just go. All that stuff you saw on TV, that isn't even the half of it. I can't tell you more than once. I can't."

He stared at the pile of dollars on the table, then threw it into the crowd.

"Holy shit," Geri Southern said, as the area around her erupted. In a matter of seconds it was bedlam, people kicking and screaming, yelling obscenities, fighting for the bills. A fist flew out from somewhere, caught a big blowsy tourist on the jaw. Linda the security woman had someone in a neck hold. People were rolling, scrabbling on the carpet for the money.

The man just looked at her, then shoved some more bills into her hand. "You think I'm crazy. But I'm not. Believe me. You got to go. There's a hard rain gonna fall around here, fall everywhere. Someone just rolled the dice up there in the sky, Geri, and what they got at the end of it is real bad news."

"Mister . . ." she started to say, then fell silent. He didn't look crazy at all. He was crying, the tears rolling down in two continuous streams that stood like melting icicles on his pale, pockmarked cheeks. He put a finger to her lips. "Just go," he said, half-sobbing.

Two black-sleeved arms came from nowhere, jerked him backward, locked him in a hold. She could hear the sound of handcuffs getting slapped on. From somewhere there was the noise of the internal alarm. Cops, she guessed. Quite what you could charge the guy with was beyond her.

Linda the security woman came over, breathing hard. Geri Southern stared at her. She had a bad nosebleed and what looked like a formative black eye. "Fucking weirdos. We're going to have to tag all this money, check it with the cops, honey. God knows where the jerk might have got it from."

"He said to treat it like it was won at the table," she said, half-hoping.

"I heard that. I know. Once the cops say it's okay, then it's clean. You get your cut."

Geri felt her throat go a little dry, pulled the bills out from between her breasts, and said, "He gave this to me. This wasn't won."

Linda the security woman stared hard at her, the line of blood running down from her nose, over her beefy lips, into her open mouth. "I'm going to pretend I didn't really hear that. You know where the money that goes across this table belongs. You don't really want to try and argue that one with the management, now, do you?"

Her head was swimming. He wasn't crazy. Not normal crazy, anyway.

"Take a break, Geri. Straighten up."

"Yeah," she said, and walked off to the staff quarters. It had the makings of a long night.

AN HOUR LATER the man sat in the interview room in the Las Vegas Metropolitan Police Department's Southeast Area Command and stared at his hands. Mike Carney, the duty lieutenant, glowered at Sergeant Phyllis Simpson and said, "You pulled me out of a budget meeting for this?"

Simpson swallowed hard and answered, "Sir, we had those standing orders come through that said to look out for people making noises about this kind of thing."

"Bad moon rising," the man said. "The world's coming to an end. You got a cigarette?"

"Sure. What's your name?" Carney asked, throwing a Marlboro across the table. "Where did you get all this money?"

"My business."

"Fine. You're free to go. Please don't cause any more disturbances in casinos. Some of these guys get upset by that kind of behavior and deal with it directly themselves. Which can be a touch less caring than the service you get from us."

The man puffed hard on the cigarette, not a normal smoker, Carney thought, he looked so uncomfortable with it. "What?"

"You can go. Okay? We've no reason to hold you, and you've no reason to occupy our time."

"Bullshit!"

Simpson tidied the money back into a big plastic evidence bag and pushed it over the table to him. "This money is clean as far as we can tell. My advice would be to get it into a hotel safe-deposit box as soon as possible. Vegas is a nice, safe city in the main, but it's not a great idea to tempt people."

He shook his head. "Stupid, stupid bastards. Don't you understand me? Something's on the way here. Something awful."

"Like what?" Carney asked.

"Take a look at the sky. Ask your people in Washington."

"Right. It's this sun thing, huh? We had some more of you people earlier in the week. They said it was God and the end of the world. That right? Do we get Elvis too?"

"Not God," the man said quietly. "Not your kind of God anyway."

"So," Phyllis asked, "how is the world going to end? I've always been a little curious about that one."

"Fire," the man said plaintively. "Don't you know anything?"

Carney wished for one brief, sweet moment he'd lived in the days when you got to kick people from time to time. "Okay. You're out of here—now."

"No!" He was almost in tears again. "You got to believe me!"

"Why?" the cop yelled. "Why the fuck do I have to believe you any more than I have to believe all the other loons who wander in here because they've got nothing better to do?"

"Because it's true."

"Hey," Phyllis interrupted. "Look at it from our point of view. You come in here. You won't give us your name. You won't do anything except sit there telling us the world's going to end. And you won't go. We can get you some help. We can call someone if you like."

"Help?" He shook his head. "You can help me? If you knew how dumb that idea was . . ."

Carney rapped softly on the table with his knuckles. "Time's up, pal. We got better ways of occupying ourselves."

"What's left of it."

"Yeah. Anyway, the short of it is you're out of here. Now, do you want to walk? Or do you want to be carried? Your choice."

"All I want is for you to listen."

"Sorry," Phyllis Simpson said, and touched his arm. He really was going to burst into tears, she thought. It might be best to get in the Samaritans.

"You go tell your people I know about Sundog," the man said, head bowed. "You tell them that and see if they want to speak to me."

Phyllis took her hand off the man's arm and looked at Carney. Then she pushed over the closed folder in front of her and watched as he opened it and read the single sheet of paper there, with the Bureau seal on the top.

"This been in the papers? On the Net?" he asked her.

"No, sir."

"Right." He bent down, tried to get into the guy's line of vision, which seemed to be pitched directly at the tabletop. "Hey. Cheer up. You just won something. You got my attention."

"I have? You do surprise me. Tick-tock."

"What?"

"Time just ticking away."

"Right. So this Sundog thing. What do you mean by that?"

"Ask your bosses. They know."

"It's a start, I guess," Carney said, then pushed the piece of paper over the table. "You can read that if you want. It's an alert from the FBI. Asks us to pick up people going around making unusual predictions of the end of the world—great request to us, I'm sure. We'd fill every cell we've got. And it gives us some clues as to what turns just your average Joe crazy into someone they'd like to speak with. That word 'Sundog' is one of them. Congratulations. You won. We got local Bureau guys here. I'll call, but if you want my opinion, they'll bring people in for this.

It seems pretty important to them. So you probably just got yourself a couple of days in custody."

The man stared at the piece of paper, blinking, and said, "You got another cigarette?"

"No. Or rather, yes. But you're not having it. No point now, is there?"

"As a favor?"

Carney looked at the man. The room stank from his sweat. "Jesus, I don't believe this," he said, and threw another Marlboro over the desk, then watched the man's hands while he lit it. "Make that call, Sergeant."

He was almost choking on the cigarette. "Why are you doing that?" Carney wanted to know. "Hell, I don't think you even smoke."

"Lot of things to fit in."

"This being the end of the world and all that?"

"Sort of."

"Sir," Phyllis asked, "who exactly do you want me to speak to?"

"Never mind. I'll do it. I need a break from this."

"So," the man said, half-choking on the cigarette, then stubbing it unfinished into a grubby tin ashtray, "you really are going to call the FBI?"

"You heard, chum," Carney replied.

"Good. Then that's me done. Some go early, she said. The best are always the first to go."

Tears started to roll down his cheeks. Underneath the table, out of view, his hand was shaking as it came out of his jeans with a ball of silver foil.

"Who said that?" Phyllis asked.

"Nemesis," he mumbled. "Look it up in a book. She's the one who gets you for hubris, but I guess you dumb people think that's something you pick up in a Greek deli."

Carney looked at Phyllis Simpson and shrugged his shoulders. "I'm forgetting you said that, friend, I'm just saying to myself: This guy knew the magic word."

The man put his hand back on the table, unrolled the silver foil, took a handful of pills out of it, popped them into his mouth, closed his eyes, and started to chew and swallow, chew and swallow. All so quickly that there was nothing they could do to stop him.

Phyllis Simpson watched him and started to curse herself. "What's that?"

"Digoxin," the man mumbled, his mouth full of white, mangled pills. "You believe those Heaven's Gate guys used barbiturates? Now, they really *were* crazy."

She darted a worried glance at Carney.

"Shit," the cop said, got up, walked around the table, took the man by the neck, and yelled, "Cough those fucking things up now."

He started choking. Carney shoved his fingers down his gaping throat, waited to hear him gag, then screamed, pulled his hand out. "Fucking bit me! Simpson. Get the paramedics in here. What did he call that stuff?"

"Digoxin," she said, reaching for the phone.

He swung the guy around in the swivel chair, stared him in the eye, and said, "Listen. Either you cough those things up now or I hold you upside down until you spit them out. Now, what's it going to be?"

The man wasn't crying anymore. "Fucking cops," he said, his face going red, voice slurred, breathing labored. "Can't you even let a man die with dignity?"

"No," Carney yelled, then picked him up under the arms, let him stand for a moment, and punched him hard in the stomach. The man creased over onto the table, gasping, coughing, retching. "Spit those fuckers up. Where the hell are those paramedics, Simpson? They on coffee break or something?"

"Don't try to make him throw up. It's not the right thing to do. I did poisons in training. Digoxin is digitalis. We can't deal with this, Mike. He needs medical help."

The man slumped back onto the table, groaning. Phyllis Simpson walked over, felt his forehead, looked into his eyes. "Can you see okay?"

The man shook his head. A thin dribble of opaque yellow vomit trickled out of the corner of his mouth. He yelped, then farted. The room filled with an obnoxious smell.

"How much did you take? Come on, now. It's not too late." Simpson tried to ignore the stink. He was shaking, and Phyllis had an idea it was halfway between an involuntary spasm and laughter.

"Enough," the man said, then rolled out of the chair onto the floor, mouth open, starting to choke on the stream of puke that kept coming out from inside him. His eyes were popping out of his head. His body was going into convulsions.

"What they tell you about this?" Carney asked. "In training?"

The man puked a real bellyful onto the floor. Shit stains ran down the seat of his pale chinos.

"You can pick these things up anywhere. They use them to strengthen the contractions of the heart. Too much and the system just goes haywire." The convulsions were getting worse, she thought. She let go and he twitched a whole revolution across the floor, spraying bile everywhere.

"Is it bad?"

She looked at him. "What do you think? From what I recall, they said that anyone who survived the first twenty-four hours would probably pull through."

A noise was coming out of his mouth, not quite human. It sounded like an old door with rusty hinges, a low, slow exhalation of sound, dying away into nothing. Then he twitched, a sudden spasm that went the length of the body, pulled his hands up into a rigid, rabbitlike pose underneath his chin, opened his mouth wide, face white and waxy, eyes popping, and went still.

Phyllis Simpson turned away and stared at the wall.

"Well," said Carney's voice behind her, "I think he just missed that one by—oh—twenty-three hours and fifty-eight minutes."

The door opened with a bang and two paramedics walked in, beaming. "Phyllis!" the first one said. "And my favorite lieutenant. Now, you people been beating up on the good people of Vegas again or wha—"

They stared at the body on the floor and fell silent.

27
Tactics

Michael Lieberman sat on the steps at the front of the mansion, watching a handful of soldiers mill around the helipad. From this distance, it was hard to see what kind of troops these were—American or Spanish. When you put people inside khaki and gave them a gun, they all looked much the same. On the flat parched grass of the clifftop two helicopters sat side by side, the rotors on the nearest turning slowly in a leisurely windup sequence. He winced. Airplanes he could handle. Helicopters, with their noise and constant vibration, always seemed somehow unnatural. These were his least favorite form of transportation.

Ellis Bevan came and stood by him. He was wearing a gray shirt and slacks of an identical color. The best uniform he could muster, Lieberman thought. "Where are they going?"

"The mountain," Bevan said, his flat, expressionless face already soaked in sweat. The day had developed with some fierce, burning vengeance in its belly. This was the hottest yet. It was impossible to escape the ferocity of the sun anywhere, even in the close, damp, humid dark of the mansion. "If anywhere is going to come under attack, it's there."

He looked Bevan in the eye. "You're sure?"

"Oh yes. That's where the dome is. And close by we have another control center too. It duplicates what we have here to some extent, and handles all the telecom traffic with the satellite. They could reduce this place to rubble and we'd still be operational. If they are going to hit somewhere, it's on the peak."

"Hope you're right this time."

Bevan tut-tutted quietly to himself. It was a small, infuriating gesture and succeeded in making Lieberman feel immature. "You're still mad at the way we lured you here?"

"I don't like being lied to."

"If we'd told you the truth, would you have come?"

"No."

"So you get my point? Also . . ." Bevan fell into silence, watched one of the helicopters maneuvering into the sky.

"Also what?"

"You knew this woman. Maybe you had some involvement too. We couldn't rule that out."

"Jesus," he grunted. "It's nice to have your trust, Ellis."

"You're bad at seeing other people's points of view, Lieberman. It makes it hard for you to work alongside others."

"Thanks for the analysis. I wish it was original. So, speaking of teamwork. These guys with the guns, they're answerable to you now? My, your empire grows and grows."

"It's a security issue. Do you think I should leave this to Schulz?"

Lieberman laughed. It was a good answer. "No, of course not. But this is a waste of time. Charley's too smart to start lobbing missiles or something at us."

"You're probably right," Bevan said, watching the helicopter disappear along the coastline, out over the iridescent blue sea. "That doesn't mean we just sit here doing nothing. Speaking of which . . ."

"Yeah, yeah . . . I know. I was just taking a break from looking at those damn screens. When I designed that thing we used models and paper and stuff. Not so much in the way of computers. It all looks so different from what I remember."

Bevan eyed him and nodded. It might even have been a gesture of sympathy. "This idea of crippling Sundog through the Shuttle isn't going to happen, is it?"

He didn't like the note of pessimism in the man's voice. "I'm working on it. You people have asked me to disarm some little scorpion you've invented, one that can bite me the moment it knows I'm there, and, guess what, I don't even get allowed to touch it. If it was easy, I wouldn't be here, now, would I?"

Bevan let his dead blue eyes wander over the desiccated corn fields. "I wouldn't argue with that. We need all the hands we can get right now. And if it means anything, I'm glad you're one of them."

"Thanks," he said, and meant it.

"And one more thing. If people liked me here, I probably wouldn't be doing my job. Bear that in mind. You think we should get back to work now?"

Lieberman shrugged, got up, and followed Bevan into the big barn. The control room was only half-manned. Maybe the rest were up on the mountain. To his astonishment Annie Sinclair was seated at a terminal next to Irwin Schulz, who was almost beaming at her through his thick glasses.

"Annie?" Lieberman asked. "Are they running the new Barbie CD-ROM on these things now or something?"

Her eyes flashed at him, wide open, astonished. Offended. "I hate Barbie. How can you even say that?"

He threw up his hands. "I believe you, I believe you. But what is this? Where's your mom? And why are you making out like a geek? Do you want to turn into Irwin or something?"

"Annie's no slouch at Unix," Schulz said, his eyes not leaving the screen. "Don't knock it. You never know when it might come in useful. More than a Barbie CD-ROM anyway."

"So," the girl asked, "if I want to make it to super-user I need to have another password, one way or another?"

"Yeah. But that's enough for now."

"Okay." In a flash of keystrokes, she logged off the system, turned to them, and said very seriously, "Mom's in the briefing room, Michael, waiting for you. I'm going to have some breakfast now, if you don't mind."

He watched the little figure go out the door into the sunlight and shook his head. "So what's wrong with the Barbie CD-ROM? Will someone tell me?"

"Context," Schulz muttered. "That's all. Annie has picked up a lot. She knows enough to log on, find files, even get onto the network. And you want her to talk Barbie?"

"Great, another geek in the making."

"Bull. It's not that hard. Most kids can use a PC these days. What's the big deal?"

"I don't know. All I know is there is one."

"Luddite," Schulz said, half-laughing. Lieberman followed him into the briefing room, noting the presence of Bennett, Mo, and a couple of silent-looking types he guessed were pals of Bevan's.

"Michael," Bennett said, smiling, "we're so glad you changed your mind."

"Yeah."

Mo just looked at him. He didn't like the expression on her face. She seemed scared. He sat down and watched Bevan go to the whiteboard and scrawl the single word *Security* on it.

"We all know what's happened in Lone Wolf and Kyoto over the last twelve hours," Bevan said. "And you don't need a crystal ball to guess that the dome here is next on the list for these people. I want you to know that we will stop them. And I want you to understand what these security measures mean for you and the people on your teams. The Sundog people know each other. You haven't met Captain Suarez, who is our liaison officer from the Spanish military. . . ."

One of the seated soldiers nodded at them. He was young, about thirty, Lieberman guessed, thin, with a slender dark mustache on a nice-looking tanned face.

"And John Capstick here is U.S. military liaison for the duration."

The other one smiled. Blond crewcut, bright sparkling eyes, a physique out of a football team. "Lady," Capstick said, smiling at Mo, "gentlemen."

"Between them," Bevan continued, "our two friends have upward of sixty armed men, mainly on the peak, which is where we perceive the principal threat to be. We have emergency orders which will allow all officers to arrest anyone they find in the restricted area, and shoot if they don't cooperate. And we have an air exclusion zone covering the entire western mountain line of the island. These crazies will not get through."

"You bet," Capstick said, grinning.

Lieberman felt faint at the man's optimism: He really did think this was one cushy number. "So now we know how Charley won't try to wipe us out. Is someone going to tell me a few ways she will?"

"Michael," Schulz said softly, "we have to take these precautions. I know it's unlikely, but you have to see why we can't ignore them."

"Sure. But you know she won't come at us like this. Why the hell would she need to when she's got your neat little magnifying glass in her hand?"

"True," Bennett said. "But we're taking precautions against that too."

"She didn't use Sundog to take out Kyoto," Bevan said. "There's a lesson for us there."

"Yeah. The lesson being that was then and this is now. Maybe she thought there wasn't enough solar activity to let her damage Kyoto when she wanted to hit it. But take a look at the latest projections. Pretty soon everyone will understand this is a global event. There's a whacking great beauty spot about to appear on the face of the sun. When she has that in her grasp, who knows what she can do?"

"Whatever it is," Bennett said, "it's predictable. We may not know what the precise mix of radiation will be, but we can protect against it. When this meeting is over we'll start to put a lead covering over the roof of the control block. That should make it safe for us."

"Should?"

"Michael," Schulz said, "we don't say this is perfect, we're saying it's as good as we're going to get."

"Right. So all we need is for me to figure some way to disarm Sundog, without even touching the damn thing. Or get the system back on-line and keep our computers running through this storm that Charley's helping along the way. That's all. These soldiers here—you're just putting those guys out there to fry."

"We know the risks," Capstick said.

"You do? Wow, well, that's more than I do. And what about you, Bennett? You're just about the world authority on this stuff. Do you know what these poor suckers are risking by standing out there under the sun like that? A lot more than some missile up the ass is my guess."

"Michael . . ." It was Mo this time.

"Hear me out. I don't know if I can work some magic with the Shuttle. I do know we have to cover the basics. Mo, a systems analyst of all people should know what we need to do in this situation. We need to secure what we have. We need to know that something that gets knocked out can be replaced or revived one minute later. How the hell do you communicate with the control center up there and the dome anyway?"

"Microwave," Bevan said. "And don't worry, we're putting in a landline."

"It's a start. Now tell me. If she hit your network right now, how long would it take you to get the thing back up?"

Mo shrugged. "Ninety minutes. Two hours."

"Can you cut that? I mean, I'm no geek, but can't you just unhook one of those workstations, make it into some emergency system, and then leave it by the network with the cable unplugged so that it stays free of anything she sends our way?"

"Yes." She nodded. "It's not the normal way—"

"Let's do it," Schulz said, grinning. "That's a great suggestion. And I want that on the peak too. Ellis will sort out the transportation."

Lieberman blinked. "Excuse me? We have something in the air out there that brought down Air Force One and you people are thinking of flying civilians around in one of those damn jumped-up dragonflies? Are you insane?"

"We can't do it all from here," Schulz said. "We have people up there already but no one with high-level system administration knowledge. It's okay. If it's a problem I'll go."

"No way," Bevan said firmly. "You're needed here. This won't be a problem. It's just fifteen minutes up there, fifteen back. You'll be okay."

"So why aren't you doing it, then?" Lieberman asked.

"Dumb question. Because I don't know how. And because I'm needed here too."

Mo Sinclair stared at the notepad in front of her. She was really scared, he thought, and this was about more than just personal risk. She was scared for them all. And all because he had to open his big mouth. "It's all right," she said. "I'll do it."

"Lieberman," Bevan said. "You weren't happy with the visuals on the workstations here. You didn't think they were that good."

"Sign of age. I never bought this virtual reality thing."

"Up on the mountain we've got a twentieth-scale model of Sundog. Perfect in every detail. You think that might help?"

"It might." He got the point and it was nice of Bevan to make it. "Maybe I ought to take a look at this elusive dome anyway."

Schulz scribbled some notes on his pad and passed them over the table. "Some ideas of my own, Michael. I wondered whether we couldn't hang a power cable down onto the solar cell system. Short it or something."

He stared at the doodles on the page. He'd run through the same idea himself and rejected it as unworkable. "I really need to get into those control circuits, Irwin."

"Not possible."

"How long do I have on this?"

"The latest we can schedule the Shuttle launch is for 1500 UTC. I need you to come up with something over the next three hours. We're arranging a video briefing with the crew anyway. If you have any ideas, we need them. Either way, the launch happens, but if there's any special equipment you want along, we need to know then."

"The crew? Volunteers, huh?"

Schulz nodded. "Apparently they're queuing up at Canaveral for the privilege."

Lieberman stared at his hands.

"You'll have something to give them, Michael," Schulz added. "I just know that."

28
The Red Mountain

The pilot wasn't part of the military operation. He was, now that Lieberman thought about it, the same English guy who picked him up at the airport on the way in. Until you got close up and saw the wrinkles, he looked about twenty-five. No, correction, Lieberman thought, nineteen. He wore a T-shirt, faded jeans, and filthy trainers.

"You're all coming?" The pilot grinned. He had one of those odd estuarial accents that seemed, to Lieberman, to have become the Queen's English these last few years.

"You really know how to fly this thing?"

"No," the pilot said. "But I'm learning fast."

Annie was crouched down by the machine, playing with something. It was a magnifying glass and she had it aimed right at something on the ground. A thin wisp of smoke was curling up toward her face.

"Hell, Annie," Lieberman muttered. "Burning bugs is wrong. Don't you know that?" He stuck the folder of papers he was carrying between the glass and the sun, watched the smoke disperse, and got an angry stare from down below.

"Wasn't a bug. Just some grass."

"All the same, this place is like a tinderbox. The last thing we need is a fire."

She glowered at him and mouthed the word B-O-R-I-N-G.

"Sorry. In spite of appearances, I am a grown-up."

Annie looked at the pilot's right arm. It was thin but muscular, and a big blue tattoo sat on the skin. "What's the tattoo?"

"Army helicopter corps. I used to ferry men in masks around Northern Ireland in the middle of the night, looking for other men in masks. Before I became a civilian, that is. You should hear my war stories sometime. They're good."

"You look too young. What's your name?"

"Why, thank you. Bob Davis. What's yours?"

"Annie."

Davis looked at Lieberman and Mo. "Why don't you just stay here while we pop up the mountain, Annie? I mean, this isn't really a pleasure trip."

"I've never been in a helicopter before."

"Plenty of time for that later."

"I've plenty of time for that now," she said firmly.

"Right."

"We stay together," Mo said quietly.

Davis shrugged. "Well, don't say I didn't try. Ladies in the back. Strap yourself in tightly. You, sir, are next to me. We'll have you up there in fifteen minutes flat, no problem. And today there is no sightseeing. I have my orders. We stay in the air for as short a time as possible. Okay?"

Lieberman hooked the videophone over his shoulder and wished Schulz hadn't been so insistent they carry it. The thing was like a small video camera on a leather sling and it was heavy. Then he climbed in, his heart sinking, and listened to the blades beginning to spin. Some rusty mechanism in his head was trying to shift gears.

"No need to be afraid of flying." Davis grinned, looking at him. Lieberman tried to smile back. "Now, crashing . . . that's a different matter," the pilot continued. "Crashing scares me shitless, to be frank."

"Thank you, Bob," Lieberman said, then turned around, blew a big kiss to Annie.

"What was that for?" she asked.

"Inspiration," he said, and hit the mike. "Irwin?" His stomach began to churn as the craft lifted off, seeming to struggle in the meager, steaming air.

"You've got an idea," said the voice in the headset. "I can just tell."

"Maybe. Now tell me. What if I don't cut off all the power. Only, say, eighty percent or so. Would that be any good?"

"Fine by me. Once the thing is getting less than fifty percent from the panels it goes to sleep for fifteen minutes. Then, if the power doesn't come back, it goes into suspend. When it's sleeping, it's still lethal—there's enough power there to bite you. When you reach suspend, the thing truly is harmless. We can climb all over, do whatever we like."

"Sounds good."

"So . . . ?"

"So let me call you when I've looked at this model and given it some more thought."

Lieberman turned to the pair in the back and shone a big grin on them. They looked mystified. The big broad sweep of the Mediterranean appeared to their right. The golden stone of La Finca and the dry, brown fields around it disappeared beneath them. The machine clawed its way into the meager, hot air and even he had to be impressed by the majestic isolation that surrounded them. The mountains ran sheer to the sea on both sides of them, the tumbling rock too steep and arid for anything to live there except some gaunt scrub vegetation, the occasional wild goat, and, wheeling around close to the cliff edge, eyeing this distant mechanical bird, the odd soaring eagle. It was the same as they got higher. He kept expecting to see some corner revealed, some sign of human habitation brought into view by their fast-increasing altitude. None came. This line of primal rock was uninhabitable. Nothing but the wilder creatures of the earth could flourish on these bare sierra escarpments, and just to satisfy himself of the fact he wriggled until the phone was in front of him, pushed the on button, and looked at a blank screen.

The pilot laughed. "Won't work here, mate. Blocked by the mountains. Unless you've got some line-of-sight chain—like they set up for the microwave back at the mansion—you're lucky to get a squeak out of anyone. Even air-traffic control until you get out of the top."

"But I thought they said there were other aircraft around here," Lieberman yelled. "How the hell do you keep out of their way?"

" 'F-16s active above and below you,' " Davis chanted in a bad American accent. "Jesus, some of these people they've shipped in are dorks. Listen to me. They have short, stubby wings. And we've got rotors. We are different. Watch." Without warning, the helicopter lurched upward and to the left, climbing at a dizzying pace toward the sheer rock face, now gleaming orange in the midday sun.

"No tricks," yelled Lieberman. "We got a kid on board."

"Oh yeah," Davis said, shot a glance at Annie, and saw how she was loving this. "They said to come the fast way. And this is it."

The craft skirted the flat, beetling face of the mountain, cut in close to the rock no more than ten feet away, then veered directly into the sierra, Lieberman thinking this really was the end, until the face opened out into a narrow, craggy col leading inland.

"Keep cool," Davis said. "I know this run like the back of my hand. If you look down, on the scar there, you can see some ruined shepherd's huts, maybe even a ruined house. Got to be a hundred years old at least. Some life they had then, eh?"

Lieberman stared down, saw the little piles of rock rushing beneath them, felt giddy trying to work out these different sensations of height. The rock escarpment could have been no more than fifty feet from the glass of the windshield. The long, dramatic descent behind, down to the deep blue waters of the sea, seemed to stretch forever, so far it would take years to fall into those crystal, limpid depths if this fragile mechanical apparatus dissolved around them.

"Hold tight," Davis said, the words jerking them back from the window. Ahead was a flat rock face. It seemed impassable, and the helicopter was headed directly for it.

"Bob . . ." Lieberman said quietly.

"Shush," the pilot answered, and ran the engine up several

notches. They were moving forward quickly now, rising on a steady incline. And Lieberman knew, with everything that had stood for certainty in his life, they weren't going to make it. "Bob!" he yelled, and wondered what you did when you found yourself in the air with a madman. You couldn't grab for the wheel in this flimsy hunk of metal. He hadn't the faintest idea how it came to stay in the air, let alone guide itself.

The craft was now less than thirty feet from the bare rock slope, and the distance was closing fast. Lieberman looked in the back and saw Mo and Annie silent there, eyes wide open, waiting, and tried to smile. Thinking to himself all the time: These Gaia people probably don't mind dying, not at all, and maybe don't mind taking someone with them.

Ten feet.

He looked at the pilot. No expression there. The ridge was coming up, and as they approached, above and to its right, he saw something new, something man-made, golden, and circular, emerging like an artificial planet cutting through the horizon.

Five.

You get too scared in these situations, Lieberman repeated inwardly. The dust was blowing up from the ground, billowing around them like a sandy cloud that stained the lower windows of the helicopter until, to his horror, it was impossible to see the rock below at all.

"Bob," he said quietly, no other words alive in his head. Then, with all of them, he thought, rising in their seats to help the thing along the way, they were over. The helicopter cleared the ridge—how much to spare? He didn't even want to think— and he breathed deeply. Then, for the first time, he truly thought he was going to throw up.

The helicopter had almost come to a halt. They dangled over a sudden, blood-chilling drop of a good thousand feet down into a jumble of misshapen rock. To the right, towering above them, was the dome, like a giant honeyed golf ball attached to the landward side of the sierra peak.

"Almost there, folks," Davis said quietly, and dropped the craft forward, tucked into the rock face, following the curving line of the bare cliff down toward a bluff that sat six hundred feet or so beneath the dome, large enough to accommodate what looked like a prefabricated white single-story building and a small helipad. A scattering of tiny dark figures watched their approach, rifles in their hands.

"Welcome to Puig Roig," the pilot said calmly. "That's Mallorquin for the 'red mountain.' Now, we have some queer currents at this point, so just hold on, and don't be surprised if this isn't exactly the smoothest ride you've ever had in your life."

With that, he twisted the helicopter around sideways and edged in a descending arc toward the helipad, curving it around at the last moment to land square in the center of a big painted H. The dust was swirling around them as high as the doors. "One minute. For the rotors," he said. And stared at Lieberman, then at the pair in the back.

"Apologies," he said. "It's normally a touch more enjoyable than that. But they said to keep this as short as possible. So I came the way I normally use on my own."

John Capstick was walking toward them, beaming. The pilot turned away, started to examine the landscape. Lieberman found it hard to look at anything but the dome, perched on the peak several hundred feet above them. By comparison the low, white command center seemed puny.

"Beautiful day, beautiful day," Capstick said, watching them get out of the helicopter. "You'll be giving us a return time on that detail, of course."

"We need two hours and forty-five minutes," Lieberman replied.

"That's very precise."

"Call me superstitious," Lieberman replied, "but I know when that big yellow thing in the sky is starting to get angry today, and I'd rather be on the ground down there when it does."

"Good idea," Capstick said. "Noted. So what are you people here to do? And who the hell's looking after the kid?"

Annie glowered at him.

"She's with me," Mo Sinclair said, not smiling. "Check with Irwin if you like."

"I will, I will." Capstick smiled. "Now, the pilot guy I know is staying with us until you folks want out again. So that leaves you."

Lieberman couldn't take his eyes off the complex. "Just the standard tour, a good look at the satellite mock-up and whatever it takes to get up to the dome. Plus I think we're supposed to have some video conference with a couple of spacemen. An economy lunchbox and a bottle of San Miguel will do."

"No alcohol on site. I'll find someone from the admin team. This is all Greek to me."

The pilot was smiling at Capstick with a knowing, impertinent expression.

"Can I help?" Capstick asked.

"You're happy with this, then?" the pilot said.

"You mean the security status?"

"Yeah."

"I'm content. Yes."

The pilot just looked at him. "What's that on the hill over there? Those ruins?"

Capstick followed his line of sight. "Old shepherd dwellings or something. Don't worry. We've checked them. We've checked every pile of stones you can see. They're all dead. No money in agriculture, huh?"

"I thought that. Until I took a closer look."

"Really."

"We're above the grass line here. What are the sheep supposed to eat? Rock?"

Capstick paused, thinking. "They're old. Maybe they predate the climate change."

Lieberman took an appreciative look at the pilot and said, "Climate change doesn't happen that fast. How high are we?"

"Four and a half thousand feet."

"You should think again," Lieberman said.

"So. You two are the smart guys." Capstick looked thoroughly pissed.

Lieberman shrugged.

"Maybe shepherds used to use machinery too," the pilot said.

"What?"

"Take a look. There's rusted iron. And workings. At least I think that's what they are."

"Workings?" Capstick nodded. "I knew that."

"Mines. The rock formation underneath the dome. If you want my opinion, someone's mined tin or something around here long time ago. Probably mined this whole area. This ridge included."

Capstick looked impassively at them. "Interesting thought," he said flatly.

29
Canaveral

"You mind me saying something?"

Bill Ruffin, the commander of the Space Shuttle *Arcadia*, had a broad, friendly, intelligent face, short, spiky red hair, and a wry, seen-it-all grin that seemed to fill the entire screen.

"Nope," Lieberman mumbled.

"Can we cut the awe stuff out, please? I expect it when we do the school visits and that. But not now."

"Right." Lieberman detected something close to a ripple of laughter from Mo next to him in the big control room on the mountain. "It's just that—"

"Yeah, yeah," Ruffin said amicably, waving a giant hand that bobbed up and down on the wall monitor. "You always wanted to be an astronaut. Join the queue. Next you'll be asking me how we get to do a dump up there."

"Commander . . ."

"Professor . . ."

"Look. I get airsick in elevators. Nothing would get me where you're going. But do you really know what you're in for?"

Ruffin reached down, pushed a button, and the two other members of the Shuttle crew came up in windows beside him. "In case you forgot, my name is Bill Ruffin. Four missions, two as a commander."

He pointed to a stoic-looking, thickset black guy with a shining bald head. "This is David Sampson. Three missions too. Best Shuttle pilot we got on the planet right now, present company included. And this . . ."

The third was a woman, dressed like the rest of them in standard NASA ground uniform. She wore close-cropped blond hair and had a thin, intense, impatient face that kept looking at you as if to say: *And then?* "Mary Gallagher. Four missions. Just as many EVAs. Do we know what we're in for? I guess not. But . . . hell, Mary, you tell the guy."

The woman leaned into the camera and said, "Professor, we put this damn thing there. If anyone gets the right to turn the off switch, it's us. Okay?"

"Not to mention the fact," Ruffin added, "that we also happen to be the best-qualified people around for the job."

"Agreed, agreed," Lieberman said. "Look, I know when I'm beaten. I just want you to understand this isn't exact science. I'm making this up as I go along, so if you people see some holes in it, then holler."

The three heads nodded above their white uniforms and he knew that, at least, was going to happen.

"The problem," Lieberman continued, "is simple. We need to turn Sundog off without touching her, and that, I have to tell you, isn't easy. I assume, Irwin, you still hold to the view there is no way we can get back into the control system directly and do something from earth?"

"Not that I can see right now," Schulz said on the link from La Finca. "Charley has that tight in her hot little hand and isn't letting go."

"In that case, we really have only one option. We need to turn off the sun. We need to starve Sundog of what makes her work, wait for her to run down first into sleep, then into shutdown. Then, if I understand the system right, you guys can get your tool belts out and go to work on her."

Bill Ruffin smiled and said, "Neat idea, Professor. How do you propose to do that? My information was that thing's burning brighter than ever right now."

"Shades. You just get out your sewing kit and start making some shades."

He'd stared at the model in the command center for almost an hour trying to work it out beforehand, and still he couldn't spot a flaw in the idea. The part of Sundog he knew best, when he saw a physical representation of it, was almost exactly as he remembered. The satellite hung in space powered by four giant black solar panels on the sun-facing side, with most of the active gear pointed down toward earth. It looked like a huge metallic windmill slowly cartwheeling through the sky, and all you need do—*all?*—was work out the measure of the dance and move into two-step with it.

"Sundog runs off four solar wings, each a hundred meters long and twenty wide. Now, you people don't need to worry about how much energy that generates or what kind of technology sits in those wings. All you need to know is this: It's big and fast and it's optimized to suck out every last jumping joule out of whatever sunlight falls upon it. And the other side of that equation is that it has no latency. If, for some reason, the light fails—and Sundog was predicated on the idea that this couldn't happen, of course—this little beast assumes it's got big internal problems and starts to turn itself off. So what we do, is this. . . ."

He pressed a button and the badly drawn graphic came up on the screen. "Shades, four of them, a little oversized compared to the wings themselves, with a central hub so that they maintain the same ratio to each other as the wings. Your engineers can figure out the best way to pack all this into something you can get into the Shuttle. You need some kind of light-absorbing or -reflecting fabric and a means to erect all this in situ. I thought maybe some kind of gas system, like they use to inflate tents. Or poles, whatever."

Ruffin looked at the image on the screen and said, "I get the idea. This is just like erecting some big kind of cover for the wings, except that we put them back from the panels and cast them in darkness."

"Precisely. So we get that in place, we maneuver it over the wings, we synchronize it with whatever movement there is— you can do that by hand. And we wait."

"Won't kill all the light," Mary Gallagher said. "There's bound to be some ambient illumination getting around."

Schulz chipped in, and Lieberman simply adored the enthusiasm in his voice. "Doesn't matter. Like Michael said, this is a high-performance system. If it's getting anything less than fifty percent of what it expects, it can't function properly, it goes straight into the sleep sequence. You can hold that frame a couple of meters off the wings themselves and it's still going to kill the thing. And quickly too. Maybe fifteen minutes to sleep. Another fifteen to shutdown."

Ruffin looked at Lieberman. "Surely the wings on the satellite can angle themselves. They're supposed to tune to the best source of light they can find. As soon as we move the shades in place, they'll just start shifting Sundog around trying to dodge it, and that could make things real awkward for us."

"That's why you need the hub," he said. "If you tried to do this one shade at a time, that's precisely what would happen. You'd be chasing the thing all over the place, and the three other panels would continue to power it while it tries to improve the angle. Doing it my way, we assemble all four shades together out of synch with the wings, forty-five degrees around from their position. Then turn them into the blackout position all in one go when we're ready. Just like lining up a couple of kid's windmills. Sundog goes from perfect sun to near-total darkness in a second or so and there's nothing in her code that tells her this can be anything but some kind of system failure."

"Smart." Ruffin nodded. "Shame you can't be there to watch it."

"Yeah, thanks. Actually, I do want to watch it. Can you put cameras in or something?"

"We can relay from *Arcadia*," David Sampson said. "And I can put out a floatcam to sit alongside you and feed back live video. If that doesn't trigger something, of course."

"No problem with radio or video," Schulz confirmed. "I just don't want you using any powered tools in the vicinity, and you're going to have to cut everything but the bare essentials on the Shuttle while you're close."

"Interesting . . ." Sampson said.

Lieberman watched the three astronauts. Something was going on between them that they weren't about to share at large.

"How much time will that give you? Drifting in like that?" he asked.

"I need to work that out," Sampson said. "I can't match the exact trajectory of Sundog without using some power, of course, but if I come in slow I can get damn close. Provided we make sure we've got long lines out there to these two guys, we can reel them in nice and clean after maybe forty-five minutes or so, with some room to spare."

"That's enough for us," Ruffin said, and Mary Gallagher nodded in agreement by his side. "Let's take this part as read and let the engineers get on with the details. Once we have the system shut down, where do we go from there?"

Schulz took over the graphics feed on the conference and zoomed in on the side of the satellite. "There's an access panel here. We'll upload all of this so you have it with you, of course. You need an anti-torque driver to get in there, then a smartcard and an access code. Once you're there, it's a simple shutdown sequence to take Sundog off-line altogether. And then we're done."

Lieberman waited for someone to say it. "Not quite," he added, when the line stayed silent for longer than he could bear. "There's one massive solar storm going on up there right now, Irwin. Ordinarily you wouldn't dream of launching a Shuttle into all that crap."

"Our problem, Professor," Ruffin said flatly. "If worse comes to worst, we just burn some gas and move on over to the dark side. Nothing can touch us there."

"Maybe that would be a good idea anyway, after you're done," Schulz said.

"Yeah," Ruffin agreed, and glanced at his watch. "As soon as those guys have finished with their sewing, I want to be on our way. We've got a rough sector estimate for where that thing is up there, but it could take us a little while to find it, and when we do we have to come at it from the top, just so it doesn't get too grouchy. We need all the time we can get."

"Good luck," Lieberman said, and suddenly felt foolish.

"Hell, Professor." Ruffin grinned. "What's luck got to do with it?"

30

In the Pentagon

Washington, 1044 UTC

The war room was up and running, and to Helen Wagner it felt deeply strange. This was a military location. They had senior representatives of the forces on tap, waiting silent and a little resentful in the wings. Tim Clarke was calling meetings when he felt like it, forcing the pace all along, taking a decisive control of the response. But the way the situation was shaping, it was the intelligence services and the team assembling around the Shuttle that seemed to be making the running.

Clarke, she guessed, knew this would happen, and picked the Pentagon bunker because it was neutral ground. There could be no range wars here. Your troops were too distant, sitting down the end of a video-conferencing line, to give you any comfort. There were safe areas, in Langley and at the Bureau, he could have chosen. But the Pentagon evened things out, and one of the side effects was that no one felt at home. Dave Barnside and Ben Levine sat side by side, looking gloomy. Dan Fogerty was opposite with a couple of Bureau people she didn't know. Lieberman was live from the peak, Schulz was on-line from La Finca. She sat next to Barnside, trying to feel part of that particular team.

Clarke looked at the faces around the table, nodded at her, and said, "Situation report, Miss Wagner. Where are we with the Shuttle?"

"It looks optimistic, sir. We have a way to neutralize the satellite. *Arcadia* is in prelaunch sequence right now."

Lieberman raised a finger on the screen and began speaking. "Basically—"

"Spare me the details," Clarke interrupted. "I really don't have the time. How hot is it getting out there?"

"We're doing okay, Mr. President," Lieberman said. The latest hourly projection sat on the giant screen on the wall opposite the conference table. "I think the levels are pretty steady right now and they'll stay like that for three hours or so."

"Good. What's happening on the ground?" Clarke asked.

"Minor telecommunications disruption," Graeme Burnley said. "Nothing we can't handle. We're getting some criticism for overreacting, to be honest, Mr. President."

"Let them moan," the President said. "I'd rather overreact than underreact."

"And this hiatus is temporary, right, Michael?" Helen asked the image on the wall.

He nodded. "You bet. After this quiet period, my guess is that the spots will start to grow and join again and the effects of the storm will be correspondingly greater."

"Bigger than anything we've had before?" Burnley asked.

"I'm an astronomer, not a fortune-teller. There's no way of knowing that. It's obvious that the radiation level is linked to the state of the sunspot activity, but it's not a straight-line relationship."

"Guess, mister," Clarke said. "This isn't an academic exercise."

Lieberman hesitated and took his eyes off the screen. Tim Clarke had a habit of staring at you until he got what he wanted. At least a video link gave you a break from the heat in his eyes. "My guess, for what it's worth, is that it will be big, and continue to grow right up to the peak, which is a little over twenty-four hours away. By the zenith, this will be larger, more serious than anything ever recorded. Even without the toy Charley stole, we could be in trouble. This isn't just some passing heat wave. It has all manner of poisonous crap inside it. Add Charley into the equation and I just don't know. It could be radiation. It could be direct heat. We're dealing with a cocktail of solar particles that could turn up in any form they damn well feel like. The death ray from hell or just a very bad day on the beach. None of us knows, not even Charley. That's why we abandoned Sundog in the first place, remember. It was so damn unpredictable."

"A straight answer," Clarke said. "I appreciate that."

"So what do I tell these business guys who keep phoning me?" Graeme Burnley asked. They all stared at him.

"Tell them to stay at home and watch TV," Lieberman answered from the wall. "For as long as it lasts. We're in the phony war stage now. It won't go on for long."

Clarke nodded. "Let's hope the Shuttle idea works out, but it doesn't mean we let up on any other options. What about tracking down the Children?"

Dan Fogerty cleared his throat and read from a piece of paper. "It's slow, to be honest, Mr. President. We've drawn a blank trying to trace any equipment-purchasing pattern that would match up with someone trying to set up their own transmission facility. Maybe they sourced this abroad. It's a possibility. But we do think they bought the wherewithal for a dome. We found a company outside San Diego specializing in geodesic structures. They say a bunch of people came to them two months ago with plans and specifications for the component parts for a unit that pretty nearly matches up with the Sundog model. Placed the order, paid cash, and collected a week later. The billing address is a phony, of course, and we're getting nowhere with an ID on the people at all. But the specs are too close to the Sundog model to be a coincidence. This is Gaia, all right."

"You're pouring men on that, I trust, Dan," Clarke said. "You're going to find where they went with that thing."

"Sure," Fogerty said. "It's happening. But there are a couple of points to remember. This is a kit. These people turned up with their own pair of trucks and took it away with them. They could transport it pretty much anywhere in the country and erect it on site."

"Not the sort of thing you'd miss," Barnside said quietly, looking across the table. "A forty-eight-foot dome."

"Not if it was in a built-up area, Dave," Fogerty agreed. "But think about it. They could site that almost anywhere the entire length of the Rockies, and who would know the difference? Remember that A10 that went missing a couple of years back? That took us two weeks to recover when it went down in the mountains, and it was one big pile of metal."

"So how do we track them down?" Clarke asked. "They've got to be using this thing. What about the transmissions?"

"We're flying AWACs over the less densely populated areas, sir," Helen replied. "But that's one big job, and I imagine they're being very careful about when they use the dome to transmit right now. Does that make sense, Irwin?"

"Sure. If they've replicated the dome and the gear inside it, they don't need to stay on the line long. You could reprogram the entire instruction set in under thirty seconds, and then switch off. I hate to tell you this, but unless we get real lucky, those AWACs are burning fuel for no good reason."

"Keep them there," Clarke said. "What about the dome we still own? You're sure that's secure?"

"As sure as we can be, Mr. President," Barnside said firmly. "We know what we're up against now. If she can break through this, she really can work miracles. We've put the men and resources in there, picked the place clean. And from what I understand, she doesn't have anything to throw at us from the sky."

"Not yet," Lieberman interjected. "I don't think you people quite get it yet. We don't know what this is going to be like when the spot activity gets hyper. We don't have the books to tell us. She could just turn that beam on us here and there'd be hell to pay one way or another."

"Maybe," Clarke said, "but there's no point worrying about things we don't understand or can't affect. Just make damn sure that place is as tight as you can get it. We lose that and we are in trouble."

"Sir," Barnside said, scribbling on a pad.

"This Vegas thing, Dan," Clarke asked, "is there anything in it?"

Fogerty looked uncomfortable. "Hard to tell, sir. A guy starts talking about the end of the world. Mentions the word 'Sundog.' Then kills himself. I mean: Why?"

"Maybe he was trying to run away?" Helen said, knowing it didn't make sense.

"Then why did he kill himself? Second thoughts?"

She caught Lieberman's eye through the video link. "Michael. Can you remember if Charley had some links with Vegas? Anything at all."

"She hated it," he said. "We went there once. For a Dylan concert at Caesar's, believe it or not. The concert was okay but the town—she loathed it. The tackiness. The venality. It's the last place on earth she'd choose to be."

"We need to ID this man," Fogerty said, "and we're working on that one. Newspapers. TV. Everything, not that we're handing out the real story. If we can prove some link, we may have a start."

"Assume there is a link, Dan," Clarke said. "What next?"

"Big area, sir." Fogerty grimaced. "We can focus the AWACs, do some aerial reconnaissance."

"We can start doing that now, surely," Helen said. "I checked with our own imaging people. We have digital photography of every last square foot of this country. We can set them working on that straightaway."

"Sure," Fogerty said. "But think of the scale of the task. Nevada, Utah, Arizona—it could be any of the three, and you're talking massive areas of bare rock there. Even if we knew what we're looking for, how long would it take to find it? Photo reconnaissance is a long-term exercise, not something you can pull up in an hour or two."

"We do know what we're looking for," Schulz said from the screen. "A dome. You've got these photos in digital form, right? I assume you have some kind of reconnaissance software that can search images on the basis of recognizable shapes."

"Sure," Helen said. "We developed it ourselves. Runways. Camouflaged buildings."

"Then set it up to look for a geodesic. Even if it's camou-flaged you're going to get an outline." Helen scribbled some notes on her pad. This was straight up Larry Wolfit's street. The room was quiet. They were all waiting for Clarke.

"We're getting somewhere," the President said. "Maybe we can kill the satellite. Maybe we can take them. If we're in luck, we do both."

"Sir," Helen replied, and looked at the faces around the room. There was some hope there, she thought. They were moving in on Gaia at last.

31
Capital

Yasgur's Farm, 1131 UTC

"Martin never came back? We never heard from him again?"

Joe Katayama shook his head. Charley Pascal smiled at him, the slow, strained smile he recognized as an expression of some real physical pain inside her. In the main room of the farm-house, where the Children worked around the clock talking to the satellite, monitoring the wires, there was a slow buzz of excitement that was fast approaching anxiety.

"Everything moves in its sphere," Charley said as they sat alone at the edge of the room, watching the work go on. "Everything has its purpose. We need to start moving people out, Joe. It's killing everyone to be glued to these screens. We need to start dispersing."

Katayama pulled out a sheet of paper. "I'd been thinking much the same way. I got some preprogrammed routes they can follow, vehicles lined up, air tickets, train tickets for when the transportation gets back to normal. They know what to do. Spread the word."

Charley almost laughed. "They don't need to spread the word, Joe. We're not evangelists. You don't understand."

Some small fire lit behind his eyes, and Charley thought: He has a temper; it just stays beneath the surface most of the time.

"No," he replied, face hard and expressionless, "I guess I don't. I thought that, when it was over, when we'd dispersed, that was what we did next. Pointed the way."

She did laugh then, just to see if she could get a response, but the flat Oriental face stayed unmoved. "Meet the new boss. Just like the old boss. I don't think so. We've done our teaching. We can help. People can advise, point the way if it's needed. That's not why we're here."

"Why is that?"

"To cleanse," she said softly. "To purify. The way a farmer burns the stubble at the end of the harvest. The way an artist scrubs a canvas when a painting goes wrong. There's a god in all this, Joe, don't forget that. Not a god that lives in the sky with some long white beard and a list of commandments. The god inside us. All of us, every living creature. And when we purify, that god comes out. She doesn't need our help. It happens. Even though they'll get their TV stations back on the air before long. Even though their armies don't go away. The real revolution starts in the heart, when we start to see the world around us for what it is: chaotic and fragile, ruined by our own endeavors."

"You put a lot of trust in people," Katayama said.

"No," Charley said swiftly. "I put a lot of trust in my god. Let's get moving, Joe. Start to thin the ranks." She pushed her chair around across the room and touched the arm of someone punching away at a keyboard. He stopped, beamed at her. "How goes it, Sam?"

"Like a dream," he said in a monotone English accent. Heads turned, faces smiling. No need for concern, she thought. The Children were a family, would always remain a family, even when they'd dispersed. There was peace in the room, in spite of the heat that seeped in from the windows, rose from the humming terminals, enveloped them all. Peace and a resolve to see this through. "Good," she said.

Against her instincts, she had spent time learning the workings of the financial markets. It was necessary to understand what you sought to destroy. Sam Lambert had been pivotal in this. A former English stockbroker who had quit his job to work for a ven-

ture capital company in Palo Alto, he knew so much about the
way this digital flow of capital worked, moving around the world
in some obscene impersonation of the sun itself, twenty-four
hours a day, never resting, never failing—until now.

The markets were like flowers, blooming for the sun.
When the earth revolved and placed them in daylight, they
opened their petals, let the life flood into them, raced and ran
through the bright, waking hours. Then, eight hectic hours
later, they felt the day start to grow darker and chill, wound
down to sleep. And as one bloom closed, another one opened,
following the daily circling of the sun's light upon the earth.
It was a permanent, unchanging process, one that had been established decades before. What made it different now was the
technology that threw an invisible electronic thread between
each of those points on the globe, made it possible to trade in
Tokyo from a desk in London.

This changed the nature of the exercise entirely, linked
every part to the whole. To make a trade in London, however
small, however local, was to throw a pebble into the gigantic
pool of international capital that swilled around the world, taking little heed of governments and currency restrictions, circumventing them by some quicksilver body swerve that got
you where you wanted by some other route. It might add a few
milliseconds to the transaction, taking you through some ca-
bling in Panama or Cayman instead of Berne or Bonn. But you
got there. Everything got there, pretty much.

This digital nervous system was the financial world. And
without it, Charley had come to realize, the complex fabric of
modern money was merely a blank and empty page, a tabula
rasa demanding something be written upon it, with precious
little there to use as ink.

"See how it's moving," Lambert said, as much to the rest of
the room as to the figure in the wheelchair. Tokyo had closed
well down, not disastrously so, but enough to give the Western
markets, which had to follow the game, sufficient jitters for a
few nervous stomachs. Sydney and Hong Kong had drifted to
a close along much the same lines. There were minor markets
in Western Europe that opened before London. But no one

was in any doubt about where the big players lay. The way the world was structured, London had the job of defending this game, until New York chipped in halfway through, opening the day as the sun rose over Manhattan.

Charley Pascal sipped a chamomile tea and watched the way thing were being sold, not heavily, just at a measured rate, just out of caution. Then, with no emotion in her voice, asked, "Sam. Take a look at Zurich, will you? Tell me what you think." And before he could answer, added, "No. Before you reply, take a look at Amsterdam too."

Lambert started hammering the keyboard, staring fixedly into the screen. "Unbelievable," he said.

The numbers on the screen were, literally, incredible. They represented the largest and fastest fall on the smaller exchanges he had ever seen. Not just Amsterdam and Zurich. In Paris and Frankfurt and Brussels the local index was tumbling through the floor. Across the world in Singapore, which thought it was heading for a quiet close with only a little backdraft from what had happened in Tokyo, the Straits index was now plummeting too. It was as if they had all walked to the edge of the cliff, then jumped. And any minute now they would take the Footsie with them.

"Look at the money markets," Charley said. Lambert switched the table onto the screen. It was the same old story. People rushing to the dollar, the mark, and the yen, even gold, hunting for security and letting everything they perceived to be weak collapse behind them. The pound was in freefall, already pushing par with the dollar. The Euro followed suit, plummeting to new lows.

This was the biggest market in the history of the world. It spanned the globe and ran through fiber-optic cables and geostationary satellites, it pulsed twenty-four hours of the day. And it behaved with the same mute, unchanging instinct of a herd of beasts. There was a name for this, and it was one that Charley, as she had watched the markets these last few months, had come to understand. It was a depressive supercycle, of the kind that was around in all the great crashes, in '87 and 1929 too if someone had known how to recognize it. And all it needed to push the supercycle over the edge into complete economic collapse was a little help.

"What's the state of the storm, Louise?" Charley asked a blond girl at the next terminal.

"Coming up good. As good as we've seen."

"This is just nervousness, Sam," Charley said. "That's right, isn't it? Nothing we've done?"

"The nervousness is caused by our presence," Lambert replied. "But you're right, the systems are running pretty well in themselves. There's some disruption from the solar activity, but it's not a cause in its own right, we haven't fed any disruptive data into the Net."

Charley Pascal leaned back in her wheelchair, closed her eyes, felt ecstatic. "Open the gates, Louise," she said quietly. "Not all the way. Just enough to throw a wrench in the works. No fire. Not yet."

"Done." The girl was smiling. They were all smiling. Twenty or more people in the room, waiting, the keyboards silent for once.

Charley Pascal closed her eyes and tried to imagine what was happening in space at that moment, tried to feel the way this tiny slice of that gigantic sea of energy flowing through the universe was being channeled toward the earth.

"Well?" She lifted up her head and looked at Lambert. A small crowd was gathering around his terminal; she could hear the fast, hot chatter of their excitement. Sam Lambert's face was a picture: half-glee, half-horror. There was still the thrill of the trader there, even after all these years. It was like jumping from a plane without checking if there was a parachute on your back, she guessed. Or Russian roulette.

The lights shifted and flickered on the monitor. It was Singapore that went first, taking down the overnight trading lines that still ran after the market close. One moment the figures were on the screen, with some frantic agency copy underneath them. The next they were gone. No "network down" announcement. Nothing.

Moscow was the next to fall. In exactly the same way, twenty seconds later. Zurich followed and shortly afterward Frankfurt.

Then, so quickly it seemed to happen simultaneously, Amsterdam, Paris, and Brussels. The panels on the monitor that should have carried a miniature stock chart were empty, just black voids, while the live part that remained, the London market, and the prospects for Wall Street, whose turn it was next in the game, just raced and ran and screamed at them.

The stock screens went blank. The Children watched, waiting breathlessly, to see if something would return. Finally, Charley spoke. "What do they do now, Sam? What are their options?"

"I don't know. They must have contingency plans for this. They can keep the markets closed on a temporary basis."

"Good. But what does that mean? For these people? For this old order of things?"

He tried to imagine. "They can rebuild. They can suspend trading until they are happy they can control things."

"But this is capitalism," she said. "This is global capitalism, without frontiers. It feeds upon the ability to move money instantly, digitally, anywhere, at any time. And we are removing that nourishment, we are destroying the cogs and wheels of this particular machine that entraps, enslaves us all."

"I know," he said.

"So what happens?"

"Collapse," Sam Lambert said. "Absolute, bloody chaos."

"The mother of us all." Charley Pascal grinned and threw her arms around him.

32
Martin Chalk

Washington, 1232 UTC

It didn't take long at all for an ID to come through. Forty minutes after the Bureau put the picture of the dead man on the internal net, the phone rang in the Pentagon bunker and Dan Fogerty started to smile, furiously taking notes all the time. A hurried conference was put together in a quarter of an hour. Tim Clarke was back at the head of the table, and this time, Helen Wagner thought to herself, the military men were starting to look energized. *Targets.*

"We have a lead," Fogerty said. "The office in San Jose picked the guy up from missing persons. His name is Martin Chalk, age twenty-six. Used to be a postgrad student at Berkeley, something to do with quantum mechanics and fusion. Then a year ago he dropped out, joined the Children. His family complained to the local police station and then to us that he'd been kidnapped, brainwashed, the usual thing. He was living with the Children in some commune they had in San Francisco."

"Did you check it out?" Clarke asked.

Fogerty looked uncomfortable. "The local cops did that, sir. The guy was twenty-six. And very bright. He knew what he was doing. He was able to come and go as he wanted. There was no way they could intervene. This is a free country."

Clarke sighed and shook his head. "You're sure about the ID?"

"Oh yes, sir. Last year Chalk took part in some kind of eco-protest on the Golden Gate Bridge. Climbing up the pillars and sitting there, holding up the traffic until the cops came and talked them down. He got fingerprinted after that. The records are still at the station. He was never charged, which is why we would have been a little slow to pick up on them through the main print database. But we double-checked. And we know that he moved on to San Diego, presumably to be near the Children, because there was still some correspondence after the arrest, when they were thinking about whether to prose-cute. This is the man."

Clarke surveyed them all and Helen was astonished. There was a smile on his face, and this was such a rare thing it made all of them, even the Agency people, feel rewarded. "That's great work, Dan. We can work with this. We can do something. General Barksdale?"

"It has to be somewhere near Vegas," Barksdale replied. "We need to start putting people in place right now."

Clarke nodded. "Right, we need—"

"Sir?" Even the President was staring at her as if this were an unwarranted interruption.

"Miss Wagner?" Clarke looked coldly at her.

"Are we asking ourselves enough questions about this? We don't know why this man was in Vegas in the first place. We don't know what drove him to talk to that woman in the casino or kill himself."

"This isn't your field, Wagner." Levine scowled. "If you'd got as many years in Operations under your belt as some of us around this table, you'd know that the simplest explanation is always the best. People are a lot less smart than we think."

"So," she continued, "what we are being asked to accept is that this man somehow left the Children, made his way to Vegas—how we don't know—issued this warning, and then, for some reason, killed himself."

"It doesn't sound so implausible, really." Fogerty smiled.

"No? And he just happens to be someone that we can identify so easily? Someone who has prints? A police record? It seems to me that if they wanted to give us a sign, if they wanted to lead us in the wrong direction, this is one great way of doing it."

"That's bull," Levine said.

"Not necessarily." To Helen's astonishment it was Fogerty who came to the rescue. "There's a possibility this is some kind of game. Or it could be something genuine. We just don't know. But what we do know is that it's the best—in fact the only—lead we have. Even if this is some elaborate kind of trick, we may still be able to pick something up from it. We now, at least, have a chance of narrowing down our focus. You can't expect us to dismiss that."

"No," she answered, thinking. "I agree."

"The important thing is to be ready," Fogerty continued. "We need to have a high-level team in place when we need them—and I'm not leaving this to anyone local. We're going to have to ship them in, and that's going to take . . . how long, Jim?"

A thickset man in a USAF uniform looked at his watch and said, "We can have a team on the ground within five hours of departure. There's no civilian air traffic today because of the emergency. We can take you straight into the domestic airfield in Vegas. I'll position helicopters there that will enable us to go on to pretty much anywhere in the vicinity in the space of an hour or so once you give us the target."

"Right, Miss Wagner? Are you any closer to locating this target through reconnaissance?" Clarke asked.

"We're looking, sir," she answered. "We need to do some reprogramming. It won't begin in earnest for another three hours or so. That's as tight as I can push it."

"Push it tighter," Clarke said. "And hell, the bottom line is simple, surely. This guy is the one proven link with the Children we've got. Do you people have any more about to pop out of the woodwork?"

No one spoke. "Well, then, there you are. If something better comes in—and I don't see much hope of that written on your faces—we have the resources to cope with it. In the meantime, prepare to get a team down to Vegas that can go in, take hold of these people when we find them, and secure whatever installation they have there intact. Intact! Do I make myself plain?"

They all nodded.

"I have to go along," Helen said. "I need three or four people from my team with me."

"No," Barnside grunted, "if anyone goes along from the Agency it's someone from the operational side."

She blinked. "We are going to have to take control of whatever equipment they have down there, and do it quickly. I don't want to risk trying that down the line. I've got MIS people who are going to be essential. But I need to be there."

Clarke looked at her. "I take your point. But what about the imaging? I don't want you sitting on the asphalt in Vegas if it means any slippage there."

"We have an excellent team chasing that, sir. I can breathe down their necks as easily from Vegas as I can sitting in a bunker here."

"You make a good case," Clarke said. "Organize your people. Take whoever you want."

"Sir," Barnside said testily, "we can't have Agency staff out in the field without an Operations presence. If you're agreeable I'll accompany Assistant Director Wagner."

"This is an FBI operation, Dave," Dan Fogerty pointed out slowly. "Remember our orders. No range wars here."

"Guaranteed."

"You're happy with that?" Clarke asked.

Fogerty nodded. "Sure. Provided we all know where the chain of command lies."

"It lies with me, Dan," Clarke said. "Ultimately. And let's not forget the purpose of this. At the risk of repeating myself, gentlemen, we need this installation in good working shape and, if possible, these people alive. The Shuttle can't be our only option. Understood?"

The door to the bunker opened and Graeme Burnley walked in, face taut with trepidation, a couple sheets of paper in his hand.

"Good." Clarke got up from his chair, not waiting for them to answer. He looked tired, Helen thought. He looked impatient, and that was dangerous in any leader. "By my watch you'll probably be getting into Vegas towards midday local. Let's see if we can get this thing wrapped up by the end of the afternoon. And then get back to some nice easy problems, like running the country. And burying Bill Rollinson. Until we do that, nothing starts to get back to normal."

They watched him go. When the door closed, Ben Levine grunted, "The little guy looked like he'd eaten a frog. I wonder what the hell was wrong with him."

Fogerty watched them from across the table, and Helen was struck, not for the first time, by the contrast between the two: both relics of the previous administration, one an old pro, risen through the ranks, the other someone who crossed over from academia and, to an extent, never ceased to treat this as an intellectual exercise.

"You should get yourself one of these new smart pagers," Fogerty said, pulling something out from his jacket pocket. "This damn thing was twitching like crazy all through that little conversation we just had."

Levine's eyes hooded over. "What's it say?"

Fogerty looked at the screen and smiled. "It says the markets have just gone. Right down into the gutter. Best avoid those falling bodies on your way down to Vegas, gentlemen. Hard cash is the currency of the day from now on."

33
Departure

"Quite a setup." The pilot nodded at the control center, so white under the scorching afternoon sun that it made Lieberman's eyes hurt.

"Oh yes." Lieberman was fresh from the video conference and finding it hard to focus on all the things running through his head. And wishing he could push one abiding image out of his mind. That of *Challenger,* rising into the sky on a hot day in 1986, punching into the blue heavens on a column of smoke and flame, then exploding like some giant firework that burned a big black hole in the stomach of all the millions who saw it.

Bob Davis tossed his dying cigarette over the edge of the precipice, then immediately reached into his shirt pocket to pull out another one. "And not a bit of it works. We are in a mess, aren't we?"

Lieberman bristled. This quick, easy cynicism was something he knew all too well himself, but it just wasn't appropriate. He'd been all over the site, spent the best part of an hour poring over the scale model of the satellite. Leaving the motives to one side, what Sundog had achieved on the mountain was astonishing. They had created an entire operational nerve center and placed it in a remote, secure location, out of prying eyes, yet linked through enough state-of-the-art communica-

tions gear back to La Finca, straight out into the big wide
world.

And Bevan was right. La Finca was, to some extent, peripheral. The low, modern command base was the key. It was set a
few hundred feet beneath the dome itself, on a long, protruding rock finger that was broad enough and flat enough to take
both the building and the vital helipad. The dome sat remotely
above everything, glowing in the sun like some huge golden
golf ball perched on a giant rock tee stabbing upward at the
sky.

Lieberman had taken the tiny funicular that linked the control center to the dome, sat in the flimsy metal cage as it
climbed the hill, feeling the sweat cling coldly to his shirt, looking out across the mountains, across the island, inland toward
the bay of Palma beyond. When it came to a halt, he stumbled
out onto the summit, keeping his eyes away from the un-
guarded edge. There wasn't a single thing inside the dome that
he understood, but it was impossible to be anything but impressed.

"Don't knock it," he said. "This is a work of art. It's not their
fault someone stole it from them."

The man coughed and spat over the edge. "I'll take your
word on that. It's just the bloody awful security that bugs me."

Lieberman watched him draw heavily on the cigarette. "I
guess they thought the whole thing was pretty much in moth-
balls. You think it's that bad?"

The pilot looked at his watch. "Oh yes. We'd best be going.
If your earlier feelings about the time to leave still hold."

Lieberman felt like kicking himself. The sheer sophistication of Puig Roig had entrapped him. The video conference
meant he'd missed the last cycle update. It was a miracle
Bevan wasn't screaming at him already. Worse, he really had no
idea whether the cycle had worsened. There had been so much
to see. "Damn. Five minutes. I need to check something."

And drag Annie and Mo away from this too, he added quietly
to himself. There was such a buzz, such frantic energy being
poured into the complex, that you could get swept up in it all
and let the hours drift away into nothing.

"I'll see you at the machine," Davis said, then launched a cigarette over the cliff edge and walked off toward the helipad.

Lieberman strode into the control room, took a snatched look at the incoming data on a free monitor, then found them still head deep in the system. "You've got to cut that. It's time to go."

"Not now," Mo said, not even taking her eyes off the screen. The big American was over in the corner, talking to a couple of the staff people who'd shown Lieberman around. He was glancing at them.

"Exactly right now. GI Joe is about to come over here and call off our departure slot if we don't move this minute."

She pulled herself away. "Does that matter, Michael? We're here. Nothing's happened. And it's past the peak. Surely it's obvious. We're safe here."

"You're right. It's just that I hate flying so much I want to get it out of the way as fast as I can. And whatever that thing is you're doing . . . I'm damn sure you could both accomplish it all down below."

She thought about that. "That's true. Now, anyway. I'm glad Irwin did send me up here. This network was on the point of collapse."

"Good. Now can we go, please?"

"Done," she said, and started to log off.

Capstick walked over and said, "Are you folks on your way? If you're not out of here in five minutes I'm closing that window. And God knows when it's going to be open again."

Lieberman felt something inside his stomach jump and asked, "What happened?"

"Nothing like Kyoto, thank goodness. But we've got all hell let loose out there. Something's infected the stock markets. They're through the floor everywhere. The President has suspended all trading until further notice, most everyone else is following. Some big worries about currency effects too. Everything trying to rush into gold, not that it's easy to buy anything."

"Have they claimed responsibility?"

"You bet. Right there on the Web site. As pleased as punch about it. The news wires say this could push the entire world into a recession, and those loons are sitting up and applauding themselves."

"I guess they have a different agenda."

"They don't care," Mo said. "They just don't give a damn."

"Right," Capstick yelled, heading for the door, motioning for them to follow. "But the bottom line is I need you out of here right now. Along with the crash, we've got a major telecom failure throughout the northern latitudes right now. The closest it's got to us is Toulouse, but I'm not taking any risks. If this comes any farther south we lock the doors and shut ourselves in for the night. I'm happy we can keep the link with La Finca now we've backed up the microwave dishes with a landline. But I'm sure as hell not having people flying in and out with some electromagnetic storm going on. Get one of those helicopters down on us and it could put this entire center out."

"Thoughtful of you." Lieberman nodded, shielding his eyes as they came out into the ferocious heat and light. "No problem. We're gone." Mo and Annie followed in his wake, moving as quickly as they could. Capstick nodded as soon as he saw they were on their way, then was gone.

"You think anyone got hurt?" he asked no one in particular. "All that guy could think about was money and hunks of equipment. Jesus. Maybe Charley's right, in some way. We do deserve all this."

The engine was winding up. "You don't mean that, Michael," Mo yelled over the noise, and touched his arm.

"No?" So hot. So complex. So much in this place he didn't understand. "Let's go before GI Joe changes his mind." They climbed into the helicopter, Annie smiling at the pilot, who winked back at her.

"If you want to go the quick way, Bob, it's no problem with me," Lieberman said over the noise of the engine. "So long as you don't mind me throwing up along the way. Seems there's some major telecom breakdown out there. Capstick wants us out before it reaches here."

"I heard," the pilot yelled. "He's an idiot. This thing is spreading west, not south. It's taken out the main lines in New York, for God's sake."

"All the same."

"All the same, you relax. We have one little thing to do, and then we're home." The helicopter lifted off the ground, sending up a skirt of dust that briefly obscured everything, then cleared. They were hovering, stationary, ten feet off the surface.

"What little thing?" Lieberman yelled.

The pilot threw a headset at him, motioned him to put it on, did the same himself with a pair tucked into the pocket by the seat, then shouted backward over his shoulder, "Sorry, my loves, only one extra pair in this beast. You just talk among yourselves."

Lieberman put the cans on and was amazed by the difference. The sound dulled to a mute swell, and Davis's voice came through as clear as a bell. "What little thing?"

The helicopter moved slowly sideways, thirty feet or so until it was hovering stationary again, this time over the stomach-wrenching drop down to the foot of the valley. "Bob. What the hell are you doing?"

Davis shifted the stick gently, the engine note changed, and he replied, "Satisfying my curiosity." The pilot looked over his shoulder. "Don't worry," he said loudly to Mo and Annie. "We just have to make one pass and then we're gone."

Lieberman felt his guts start to wind around and around themselves as the machine slipped slowly beneath the level of the ridge and down the rock face some fifteen feet in front of them, another thousand feet of nothingness below.

"Meaning?" he asked.

"Meaning I spent the last three hours watching those bone-heads play security men around this place, and I have to tell you the only suspicious device they'd ever manage to find is one that consists of a big black ball with a fuse coming out the top and the letters B-O-M-B painted on the side. It's pathetic."

The helicopter was completely beneath the line of the ridge now. Lieberman could see that the center was built on a huge overhang of rock that had somehow been left behind in the natural erosion of the original mountain. "Bob, they checked those places you mentioned. I saw them doing it. They put a team down with ropes and stuff, and looked inside."

The thin face glared at him. "The obvious ones. Don't you think these people expect that? It's in the bomber's psychology. You pick the places you know people will look. And put the real nasty somewhere else altogether. Somewhere you'd never think of looking."

Lieberman watched the cliff face move past them at a snail's pace, felt the vast gap between him and the ground below turn into something physical, something he could touch. "Make this quick, for God's sake."

"One pass, that's all. Around the ridge. And I'm probably wrong, let me say that straightaway. This is doubtless me just being downright awkward."

"You said it," Lieberman replied, and tried to stifle a burp.

The machine moved another few feet along the cliff face. They were now beneath the massive spur of rock, in the shadow of the overhang that supported the command center. And there was nothing to see. Nothing at all. He felt Mo's hand on his shoulder.

"What's going on, Michael?" He shook his head. The pilot was trying to work the radio, cursing all the time.

"Problems?"

The pilot grimaced. "It's blocked by the mountain. I can't even talk to them if we do see something. I'll just have to break off."

"Bob . . ." Lieberman wanted to yell at this man, wanted to seize the stick on this thing and guide them gently, swiftly down to solid earth. Hanging like this in the thin and burning afternoon air was insane. "There is nothing here. It's straight underneath the outcrop. You couldn't get at it even if you tried. That's why they didn't look."

"No?"

The helicopter swung around a corner of the rock face, and the pilot said, "Then what the hell is that?"

Lieberman looked at it in silence. As they shifted around the mountain, it was coming into full view, with the machine now edging toward ten feet from the mouth. And there was no mistaking this. Below, through the glass panels beneath their feet, you could see the winding, narrow track, invisible from a distance, that led to the place. This was some kind of disused, ancient mine entrance, an opening that spanned a good thirty feet in diameter, with nothing but blackness beyond.

"Bloody idiots," Davis said. "I knew they should have looked here. There could be any number of these things hidden in the lee of the peak."

"What are you going to do?" Lieberman asked.

"What can I do? We'll fall back to the other side of the valley, I'll be able to radio them from there, and then we're going home. I'm damned if I'm hanging around here doing their dirty work for them."

"Sounds good to me. You think that—"

And he stopped, pulled the headset off, knew that this was more important than anything else right then. Mo was screaming, over and over, frantic, hysterical, and for a moment he couldn't see why. "Look!" she yelled.

In the mouth of the opening, emerging from the blackness, was a solitary figure: a woman dressed in khaki overalls, moving slowly forward into the light. Lieberman blinked. She had bright red hair, so bright it seemed unnatural.

"Oh Jesus," the pilot said quietly to himself, then hit the throttle. The helicopter pitched up and started to move backward, turning slowly on its axis. Lieberman stared at the woman, trying to work out what this strange, shapeless thought was that kept running around the shadows in his head.

"She's not armed," he said. Then he put the headset back on, repeated, "Bob, she's not armed." The helicopter was moving so wildly now, thrusting them from side to side, he thought he might lose all contact with what was up, what was down.

"She doesn't need to be," the pilot said quietly, and then the sun was on them, pouring through the glass canopy of the machine. "Base One."

He yelled into the mike. No one returned the call. *"Base One!"*

Climbing, turning. Lieberman didn't want to try to work out which way they were even facing now, so he focused back on

the fast-disappearing mouth of the mine in the rock face instead. The figure was no longer there. The machine popped up
above the flat level line of the helipad, fifty feet away, still as-
cending, still shifting back toward the sea.

"Base One!"

"Base One, we read you," said a bored voice. "You're supposed to be long gone from here, friend." The engine
screamed higher; it felt as if they were being pulled into the
sun.

"You have intruders in a tunnel underneath the facility," the
pilot yelled. The radio was quiet for a couple of long seconds.

"Location?" It was Capstick's voice.

"A disused mine about three hundred feet below your level,
just around the corner of the overhang, going back into the
mountain. If you have people at ground level, they can get in
through a path that leads up from the valley. You may need
ropes."

"Can you get there?" Capstick asked.

"We've been there, mate, and we're not going back. We can't
land and we can't do a damn thing except sit there waiting for
them to start firing."

The line went dead. Lieberman looked at the pilot. The engine had lost some of its frenzy. The machine was edging back
over the valley, rising steadily, on its way home.

"Hold position," Capstick said.

"Negative, we have civilians on board."

"Well, put them down somewhere, man. We need you to
point these bastards out."

Lieberman looked at Mo in the back. She was terrified, plain
terrified, with Annie clinging to her. And Davis was wavering.
Military men, he thought. It was hard to shake it from your
blood.

"I can't just leave them," the pilot said. "If I find somewhere
close by I can . . ."

You can what? Lieberman almost asked the question. It
seemed a reasonable one under the circumstances. But there
was something in the way, and it was half-noise, half-light too.
It sat, ominous and golden between all of them, like a fiery

beast taking in breath. And then it roared, exhaling, screaming, loud and blinding, blotting out everything else there with its vast, shimmering presence.

The machine bucked and wheeled. The pilot was wrestling the stick, forcing the throttle ever higher, trying to climb away from this thing. And beneath them, everywhere, was dust, a huge, swirling ocean of brown, alive and billowing, racing out from the ledge beneath the command center, out toward them, with powdery fingers and fiery breath.

Lieberman looked at the base and thought: This is a sight that lives with you forever, stays imprinted on the cells of your neural fibers until they cease to function.

A bright, searing line of fire ran from the foot of the outcrop, close to where they found the mouth of the shaft, diagonally upward and inward, toward the massive heel where the projecting spur met the mountain, eating the rock like a fissure in a volcano, rising, destroying, weakening as it ran. There was a second explosion, a ball of fire roaring out of the rock. The pilot looked nervously at them. "Brace yourselves, the shock comes after."

Lieberman watched, clinging to the door handle in the helicopter to try to minimize the discomfort of the buffeting. The spur of rock on which the center stood was failing, its integrity destroyed by the blasts. Tiny, distant figures, like racing ants, ran around the crumbling buildings, tried to cling to the structure, unable to second-guess which way it would twist and turn as it crumbled into dust. He watched and thought: Charley? Maybe the CIA woman is right. People do change that much. And then the view was obscured by a vast, billowing cloud of dust that raced toward them, the engine was screaming, the helicopter fighting to gain some height.

When it hit, it felt as if they were lifted by some giant, omnipotent hand that picked them up, gently at first, then with an awesome strength, and shot them up toward the sky. Just as suddenly, they were free, the machine was released from this violent, swirling force. The cloud was falling away beneath them. To their right, he could see the distant line of the sea, still and blue and placid. In this rush upward, the flimsy, forced engine of the helicopter and the sudden blast of air that came out of the valley had taken them over the peak, and they were now limping erratically out toward safety.

Lieberman watched the pilot fighting the machine, with his hands, with his feet. There were strange noises coming from above them. The helicopter seemed incapable of tacking a straight line down toward the scrub in front, down toward land. He pushed his arm behind his seat, felt their hands grip him.

"We'll be okay," Lieberman said. "Don't worry. We'll be okay."

The pilot looked at him and Lieberman felt cold. He was scared too. "This thing's buggered, mate," Davis said. "If I don't put her down straightaway, it's going to come apart on us in the air."

The engine coughed. Something metallic flew down in front of the glass. "Shit," Davis said, and pushed the stick forward, falling, hunting, turning the craft around, looking for somewhere flat enough to land. Lieberman watched the earth rise up to meet them. They were descending at something close to forty-five degrees now, he reckoned, and still there was nothing but sheer rock on either side. Annie started crying in the back. Or it may have been Mo. He didn't want to find out.

They veered to one side, and Davis was pointing. "See the ridge?"

He couldn't even make it out at first. Off in the distance was a tiny spur of flat rock ending abruptly in nothing. It seemed incredible that they could even dream of landing there. Lieberman clung to the door handle, looked across the cabin. "Okay," he said. The man's eyes said it all. And in a long, halting swoop, the helicopter half-flew, half-fell out of the sky, skimming the steeply inclined rock face, catching strands of scrub as the life died in its airframe.

The pilot took his right hand off the stick and grabbed Lieberman's arm. "We come in running. As soon as you can open the door, get these people out of the back. Take your belt off now."

Lieberman shook his head. "You want the belt off?"

"Please." His eyes were begging. "We have one chance with this. If it goes over, a belt's going to do you no good. If we manage to stay on the straight and level, I want you out ASAP, and clear of this bloody machine. Understand?"

Lieberman nodded and looked at Mo and Annie. "You heard?" It was Mo who was crying. She seemed more scared than Annie in some way he couldn't quite understand. Something snagged the machine, bounced them briefly out of their seats. Lieberman looked at the pilot, fighting the controls, all arms and legs, and thought: This is one way to go, so wrapped up in the mechanics around you that the idea of moving from life to nonexistence never really enters your head. Then the world turned upside down, there was screaming again, and something louder, the constant, ear-piercing screech of metal meeting rock, blood on the glass in front of him, pain shrieking in his head. And, in a moment, stillness.

He opened his eyes and looked across the cabin. Davis was breathless, holding the stick; above them the rotor was slowly winding down. They were on an incline. Not a gentle one.

Davis still looked scared. "You're bleeding," he said.

Lieberman felt his head. The scalp was damp and sticky.

"It's okay."

"Good. Now get out of your side, mine's too close to the edge. Go carefully. Keep your heads down, that blade is still alive. Get well clear of the machine once you're out. I'll follow you. *Now move!*"

He didn't need to be told twice. Lieberman kicked open the door, saw the thin line of flat rock of the tiny plateau between them and the edge: no more than eight feet. He grabbed Mo by the arm, took the strain as she eased down onto the ground, then did the same with Annie. He looked again at the pilot. It was hard to tell. Even if he was hurt he wouldn't want to show it. "Let me give you a hand."

"For God's sake, man, get out!" The metal skeleton of the machine grumbled. Lieberman kicked and pushed and was out the door, let go of the frame, and heard it groan.

"*Michael!*" Mo yelled.

He registered the noise and knew, in an instant, what it was. The helicopter was shifting, off the plateau, off the edge. Their weight had changed the balance. It was slipping away from

them, the pilot locked inside. He wheeled around and saw just
how bad it was. The ridge was less than twenty feet wide, and
the machine had moved so far to the left that half the frame
now hung over the precipice. Davis was struggling to get out of
his belt, and every time he moved, the machine tilted gently
farther toward the edge.

"Stay still," Lieberman shouted, and grabbed hold of the
land-side leg, now rocking gently toward the sky. The pilot
looked at him, afraid.

"Easy for you—"

"Shut up and stay still. I'm thinking."

The helicopter rocked once more on the cliff ledge, Davis
instinctively leaned inward, and Lieberman knew he couldn't
hold this thing, all of them couldn't stop it from tipping over
when it decided to go. One hand on the strut, the other working feverishly, he undid the cord on the videophone. "Mo, help
me. Please."

She took the strap, unthreaded it from its fastenings, and
pulled it clear. Extended, it ran to almost three feet, all solid
nylon, strong too, he guessed. He threw it inside the cabin.
"Are you free of the harness yet?"

Davis nodded. "I think so."

"Good. When you're ready, take the strap by both hands and
come toward me. This thing is going to fall away from under
you pretty quickly. Know that now. But I can pull you free if
you do your part. Understand?" Davis nodded.

"Your knee is trapped behind the stick thing," Annie
screamed.

"Yeah."

Davis struggled. So much stuff inside this thing, Lieberman
thought. It was hard to believe he could avoid every wheel and
pulley and projectile as it fell past him.

"On my three," the pilot said.

"You're still behind the stick."

He nodded at Annie. "I know. . . . One."

Lieberman took up the slack. The helicopter groaned.

"Two . . ."

Mo and Annie weren't watching this. He knew that, without having to see it.

"Three!"

And Lieberman thought his arms would be pulled from their sockets. Davis leaped up in the cabin, banging his head on the roof panel, yelling wordlessly, fighting with his legs. The machine began to topple over, creaking, sighing.

"Kick your leg free," Lieberman shouted. "Your leg, man."

It was like a fight, a brawl. Davis was battling every piece of metal in the cockpit, and each stood in his way. Suddenly the aircraft pitched violently upward, the strut catching Lieberman in the face, the sky went dark for a moment, the strap fell free from his hand. He clutched at his eyes, wanting to scream, listening to the groaning metal, the rush of air, the sound of this huge contraption tipping itself into space.

"Michael," Mo said, something in her voice bringing him back down to earth. He looked down. Mo was flat on the rock, the strap in her hands, Annie holding her ankles, being dragged gently toward the edge of the precipice. He leaped down to the ground, added his hands to the strap, held firm, dug in his toes, felt the movement slowly come to a close.

"You're heavier than you look, Bob," Lieberman yelled. "I don't know how long we can hold this." Something grunted from beyond the ledge. It was too hot. The sweat was running from every pore, making the harsh plastic weave of the strap cut into their hands. A dead weight tugged on the line, like a giant fish, then Davis's angular face appeared, inch by inch, at the cliff edge, then one arm, pushing upward, then a second.

The pilot rolled over onto the rock plateau, came to a halt on his back, closed his eyes, and let out a long sigh. Lieberman felt Mo's body come close to him, put an arm around her, felt Annie too, held them both, not knowing who was sobbing, who was laughing right then (and still something nagging away inside). When something like sanity returned, he opened his eyes and saw Davis watching them.

"You're bleeding," the pilot said. "Cut on the forehead. Stitches, if you ask me. Any other problems?"

"No."

"And you two?" Mo and Annie looked just fine.

"Good. Well, Professor, it seems you came off worse. Now shall we see if we can get that little toy of yours working before we burn to a crisp?"

"You bet." Lieberman retrieved the videophone from where he'd left it. He turned the thing on and they stared at colored snow.

"I guess it's time to walk," Bob Davis said, and started out for the goat track that led down the dry, rocky escarpment.

34

Something Visible

"They could still win this war," Tim Clarke said quietly on the portable videophone parked on the dressing table in Helen Wagner's bedroom. "You both ought to understand that."

He was on his own again, talking to Helen and Schulz, circumventing normal channels as usual. Clarke hadn't melded with his advisers yet. There was something between them, she thought, something that might even amount to mistrust. In his own head, she thought, he had calculated the time scale of events and decided there was no room here for niceties. Either he led directly, from the front, or the response descended into committees and meetings. It was a high-risk strategy, but she could understand why Clarke was following it. He was still a stranger in the Oval Office.

"There's someone inside, sir," she answered, pushing some spare clothes into a bag. "They're second-guessing what we're doing. They seem to know so much. And don't forget about Belinda Churton, my predecessor. Someone killed her, and she'd be doing a much better job here than me."

"Maybe, but I'm not sure we want to be diverted by that right now. And by the way, you're doing just fine. I'd tell you if I thought otherwise. You got your team right for this little trip of yours?"

"I think so. Barnside handles the practical side. I got Larry Wolfit, my number two, with some of his computer team too. If we get their installation intact, we can get it back on our side, don't doubt it."

"I wouldn't dream of it. You and Barnside going to manage to get along out there?"

Clarke was quick to spot these things, she thought. "The protective older figure act gets a little wearing sometimes, to be frank."

"Yeah. I guess he can be a real pain in the ass sometimes. But then, so can you."

"We'll cope." She threw some things into the bag as they talked, trying to picture Barnside in the field. Maybe he got a new kind of fluency, of naturalness out there, found his true environment, like a seal rolling clumsily off the land into the ocean and finding how easy it was to swim.

"You do that," Clarke said. "We've got the world on a knife edge. There's no room for personal stuff. Yesterday all we got was phone calls asking when we were going to bury Bill Rollinson. Now the phone doesn't ring so much anymore. People are retreating behind their own borders, back into their shells, wondering what the hell is going to fall from the sky next. Nothing works. Not the markets, not half the telecommunications north of the equator. I got the UN on my back like it's my fault, and half of that is because the phone lines between New York and Washington still work and we're the only people they can call. And if these Gaia people are right, things are going to get a whole lot worse tomorrow, in ways no one seems sure of. Isn't there anything else we can do on the ground now that the Spanish base is down?"

Schulz said, "The Shuttle's our best hope, sir. Failing that, we're going to have to find them and take over their unit. That's the only other option."

"There's nothing you can do to resuscitate La Finca or Kyoto, Irwin?" Helen asked.

Schulz shook his head. "Not in time. Kyoto's still full of that VX crap and it's going to be a couple of days before we can put people in there safely, a week or more before we can rely on what we have here."

"What's the timing on the storm?" Clarke asked.

"Not good," Helen said. "As far as we can tell. Lieberman is still missing. We don't know whether he got out or not."

"There's people been seen in the mountains," Schulz said. "But we haven't made contact yet. It's a big, wild area out there."

Clarke grimaced. Behind his dark, thoughtful face they could see the bright midday light in Washington, the corner of what looked like the seal of office. All these icons, Helen thought, and their power on the wane.

"Where are we now?" the President asked.

"You just have to take a look out the window, sir," Schulz said. "This thing is clearly visible with the naked eye if you use a filter. And our guess is the peak is going to be big. Huge. Whatever effects we've seen so far, whether Charley caused them or not, they're nothing compared to what we might get from now on, with or without Sundog. We face massive disruption of telecom, power grids, maybe some geological activity too. Add in what Charley has under her belt and I think you could see localized peaks of radiation, maybe up to the strength of serious physical human damage. At this kind of level, it's hard to predict exactly what Sundog will spit out. We never envisaged its use in these circumstances, but she's got a lot of different levers she can throw—microwave, electromagnetic emissions, particle beam."

"When does it peak, Irwin?" Helen asked.

"Too erratic to be exact, even if I was confident we had the right people to guess that one. Sometime between 1200 and 1250 UTC tomorrow, that's my best guess."

Clarke swore softly, then said, "So what you're saying is that we've got a little over nineteen hours to get this thing back? Or she can do what the hell she likes?"

"No, sir," Schulz said, genuinely puzzled this point hadn't got home to them yet. "What I'm saying is what Lieberman said, and no one seems to be listening. You have an emergency on your hands whatever happens. It just gets a whole lot worse if we leave Charley holding that magnifying glass in her hands."

And with that, Schulz made an excuse and was gone. The line to La Finca went dead.

Clarke sighed. "He's a smart guy, Helen. If he's right and we have a big problem either way, maybe you should be staying here."

"No, Mr. President," she said, glancing at her watch. It was a twenty-minute drive from her house in Rosslyn to the national airport where the Agency Gulfstream would be waiting. There was another twenty minutes to spare. Time was ticking beneath their feet, and she didn't like the look on Clarke's face. It had a touch of the confessional about it. "We have plenty of people capable of handling a natural disaster. What we need to make sure of is that we don't have an unnatural one that's much worse on our hands."

"I guess so."

She stole him a glance that said shoo. You weren't supposed to treat the President like that; but then, the President wasn't supposed to call you in your bedroom while you were packing. "Excuse me a moment." She yelled out into the hall, "Martha? Will you feed the cat while I'm gone?"

"Sure thing, Helen," said a middle-aged voice from the hall. "It'll be a pleasure."

Helen smiled at the videophone. "The world champion cleaner. I'm a lucky sort of person."

"Good. You're going to need it. Even after all I said, there's one hell of a goddamn range war brewing over this thing. If this goes wrong, a lot of people go down with it. Me included."

She moved out of the range of the video camera for a moment so that he couldn't see the concern on her face. "I didn't hear that, sir."

"You deaf or something?"

"Sir, this is a crisis we have to deal with, one way or another. I don't even want to think about failure, about some kind of retribution."

"That's agreed. But if this does fall apart someone is going to have to draw a line in the sand. We're going to need new beginnings. And, in case you hadn't noticed, I am driving on this one. Not the military. Not the intelligence community. I chose to take control here because, in my judgment, that was the right thing to do. If that judgment proves wrong, I go. No one needs to push me."

"Sir," she said firmly, "do you think it was the wrong judgment? Do you have doubts?"

"No. Not for a minute since this began. But that doesn't mean I'm right."

"These are extraordinary circumstances, Mr. President. They merit extraordinary solutions."

"Yeah," he replied, and shrugged. "You're right. Forget what I said. Sometimes I just need to talk out loud, and right now I don't have a family here to inflict that on. Back to business. And the range war."

"Over what?"

"Who goes in there and takes control. The Agency is shipping down an HRT. They leave just before you in some fancy damn 767 they keep for the purpose. Meantime the Army is calling up a Delta Force crew from Fort Bragg. And I know those guys very well. They'd eat you and me for breakfast and chew on the bones."

"You don't need both of them. They'd just get in each other's way."

"Exactly. And I would have told them so if I'd found out earlier. So what do you think?"

She threw the last few clothes and a washbag into her traveling case and zipped it closed. "Who, exactly, *is* HRT, sir?"

"HRT is the Hostage Rescue Team," Clarke replied. "They took a lot of stick after the mess at Waco. And that was their call. Fogerty says they're more than just hostage rescue. You think that's on the ball?"

"I guess so. As my colleagues are forever pointing out, though, Operations is not my field."

Clarke nodded. "You got a good enough grasp. We need these people, Helen. But if we get a line on this dome, my guess is you and Irwin—and Lieberman too, if he's still alive— stand more damn chance of turning it around than any number of hard-assed soldiers. You can talk."

"I guess it depends on what you see as the threat."

"Meaning?"

"Are these people going to be armed and dangerous? And I think the answer is: Not in a conventional terrorist sense. Look at the profile of the guy in Vegas. Look at Charley. They're smart enough to plant bombs, screw up systems, but they're not soldiers."

"I agree." Clarke nodded. "If we thought we'd have to fight every inch of the way in there, then Delta would be the only option. But we won't. We need to enter the place with as little damage as possible, then contain and control it."

"Pretty much like a hostage situation."

Clarke nodded. "My feelings exactly."

"The military won't like hearing it," she said, glancing again at her watch.

"The military can do as they're damn well told."

"Either way, the problem is time. They know we don't have a working dome or the chance of owning one now. In theory, they might be best placed to set the satellite up to do maximum damage, destroy the dome they have, and get the hell out there. They could disappear in Nevada, Utah, Arizona . . . we'd never find them."

"Is that likely?" Clarke grimaced.

"Maybe not. I talked to Lieberman about this. Charley's no fool. She can read the signs as well as we can and she knows this cycle is so erratic she can't be sure how to hit the peak. My guess is she'll hold it to the last possible moment."

"The longer she holds on, the more likely we are to pick up a big bunch of people like that," Clarke said.

"Maybe. But Charley's dying anyway, so I guess she thinks she's special. The volume work they needed—setting up the systems, stealing their way into Sundog—that's done. A couple of people could run that thing through the peak. Whatever the truth, the clock's fixed. We will probably wind up going in during darkness, sir."

"Well, that has made up my mind," Clarke said. "HRT it is. You put soldiers in the dark and pretty soon everybody starts winding up dead. That's what we teach them to do."

"Sir?"

Helen Wagner, to Clarke's amazement, was actually tapping her watch. He couldn't help smiling. "It's okay. This isn't TWA. They don't go without you, I promise."

"All the same . . ."

"One more question, Helen. We're assuming we do find their base. How much confidence do you have in this imaging idea?"

She took a deep breath and replied, "I'm confident we can track down potential objects. And that, given time, we could track down the dome. It's all a question of time. We don't know how many ordinary, similar objects will show up. We have to eliminate them first. Larry Wolfit knows this field better than anyone. It's not our only avenue either. We have people on the ground too. That part of the world is big and empty but it's still hard to start a commune and build something like that without someone noticing."

"I hope you're right."

"I hope so too," she said, thinking how Clarke had grown in stature over the last day and a half. She recalled the way Levine and Fogerty had talked when they left the White House at that first meeting. There were plenty of people who expected Clarke to fail, and they had underestimated this man, enormously. In a way, she guessed, he was doing a better job than Rollinson could. As a former military man, he knew when the bull was being ladled out, and when to cut to the quick. And though the strain was there, he rarely let it show.

"You go catch that plane."

"Sir," she said, and took the hint, reached over, switched off the phone. If you thought about things too hard, Belinda Churton sometimes said, you muddied the waters, made it all murkier than it really was. The thought that came into her head when she looked at Tim Clarke's tired, conscientious face was a grim one: I can't do this. I don't have the experience, the will, or the courage.

And she knew what Belinda would have said right then too: *If that was the case, honey, why the hell do you think I chose you?*

"Right," she said, and picked up the bag, walked out into

the hall, headed for the door. Martha was dusting some furniture. She stopped, smiled, and said, "You going for long?"

"I don't know. Business."

"Oh, wow, business, forget I ever asked, don't want those
men in long black cars around my house, no, sir. . . ."

The words drifted out onto the dust in the living room,
unanswered. In this soulless, antiseptic room, Helen felt too
aware of her solitary existence. It seemed as if the only footprints on the pale, perfect carpet were her own and Martha's.

"I'm sorry, honey. It's serious, isn't it?"

"I have to go."

"This is about this sun thing, isn't it? Some situation. You
know, if I hadn't been able to walk here and get back home in
daylight I couldn't have come today. It scares me. Scares everyone, not that they'd let on. I got Frank sitting at home, putting
up his feet, saying this is just some free vacation time, courtesy
of the government. But it's not that now, is it? You know that. I
know that. Even that dumb-ass knows that. People are frightened by all this. It's like the ground suddenly starts moving
under your feet after all these years of staying solid. You go sort
that nonsense out, huh?"

"I'll do my best," she said softly, walked over and kissed
Martha on the cheek. "Take care of the house while I'm gone.
And Frederick too."

"Damn cat don't need taking care of. Thinks he owns most
of Washington, that creature does."

"I'm going, Martha."

"Am I stopping you?"

Helen Wagner opened the door. Immediately the phone
started ringing in the hall. "Damn."

"Hell. You answer that phone. I'll take that stuff of yours out
to your car, wait there to see you off."

Helen handed the bag over, watched Martha walk purposefully out the door, then picked up the phone.

"Wagner?" Levine sounded angry.

"Sir, I'm sorry—"

"You're sorry. We're supposed to be cleared out of here in
three minutes' time."

Her mind wandered; she looked outside. Martha was walking down the path, carrying the small green bag, her lips pursed, whistling. The sound came faintly to Helen through a half-open window. The day shimmered in a miasma. So much heat, so much lassitude in the hot, meager air. A battered Toyota pickup was parked next to her Ford. The Toyota looked out of place, as if it had just come off a farm truck somewhere.

"I had a call from La Finca," she said. "Lieberman is still missing. We're going to have to re-create the solar activity projections without him and pray we don't need any modifications to the Shuttle gear."

Levine was mad. "Fifty damn people dead there, and the President kicking my ass all over the Pentagon. Wonderful."

There was no one in the van. She looked at the nearby houses. No one mowing the lawns, tidying the flower beds. Something stirred in her memory.

"Those imaging people got us anything to go on yet?" Levine bellowed. "I mean, we should be having this conversation on the plane, but I got people to brief right now."

"Nothing so far, sir."

Martha came to a halt next to her Ford, looked at the sky, pulled a sour face.

"Well, then, you get the hell down here now and let's get moving. We can talk some more in the air and . . ."

There were sacks in the back of the pickup: sacks and sacks and sacks, all full and neatly tied at the neck.

"Shit!" she yelled, dropping the phone, then ran for the door, stumbled over the coffee table, screaming, words that made no sense, just trying to get Martha's attention. It seemed to take an age to get outside. Her limbs were made of lead. The sun bore down on her like an invisible dead weight. Down the path, yard by yard, Martha with her hand on the door of the car.

"Martha!"

Not looking back at the house, the black woman pulled the door handle, opened the rear door, threw the bag in, turned, and smiled at her, puzzled.

"Run," Helen screamed. "Run!"

Footsteps, someone walking. She felt for her purse. There

was a service pistol somewhere inside. She had no idea if she could remember how to use it.

Martha walked up and said, "What on earth is the matter with you?"

And a man in denim overalls strode up to the back of the pickup, pulled at one of the sacks, heaved it off the vehicle, onto the ground, grunting. Something like sand spilled out of the mouth.

"Who the hell is he?" she panted.

Martha shrugged. "Some guy doing some building work on the house next door. If you spent a little more time at home you'd get to notice things like that, young woman."

"Right." And this picture in her head—of Belinda Churton, blown to pieces—just refused to go away.

"Gimme the keys," Martha said. "One minute to lock up, make sure that cat of yours is happy, and I'll drive you over to the airport. You look like you could use some thinking time on the way."

"Thanks," Helen said, climbing into the passenger seat. And prayed she could stop shaking by the time she reached the plane.

35
Phaeton

In front of them a line of poplars stirred gently in the tenuous evening breeze, making a sound like distant running water. The day was dying slowly in a wash of ocher, and the small town seemed deserted. With Bob Davis leading the way, they walked over the tiny Roman bridge and sat down in the battered plastic chairs parked outside the bar.

"Beer," Lieberman said, pulling out the videophone, trying to clear his head. They'd walked for miles through heat that defied imagination, a fierce, burning wall of air that was too thin, too hot to breathe. He punched away at the plastic, missing the buttons he was aiming for, and announced, "If this damn thing still doesn't work, I'm going to stamp on it here and now."

The bartender came out of the deserted, dark interior. Mo chattered Spanish at him. He looked miserable.

"I hope your gadget works," she said when he went back inside. "He says the phone's down."

"They heard the explosion?" the pilot asked.

She wasn't looking at Davis when she spoke. "They heard. He says people are scared, Michael. There's talk on the radio about some kind of international crisis, and he doesn't understand it."

"Join the club." Lieberman's head hurt. He could feel the dried blood pulling at his scalp. "Correction. I have had the last piece of scaredness scared right out of me. I am numb. And if that bartender knows his job, I'm about to get even number still."

Three San Miguels and a Coke arrived at the table. He looked at Annie. She seemed a million miles away. Exhausted, he guessed. It had been a long, slow climb down from the mountain, trying to catch the attention of the occasional passing helicopter, trying to make the videophone come to life. He downed the beer almost in one swallow, ordered another, then turned on the phone. "Come on, Irwin. Just this once."

Gray static on the screen, audio scurf out of the speaker.

"Come on. . . ." The LCD found some color, a picture came together out of dots. Schulz stared back at him from the screen, goggle-eyed.

"Jesus Christ, Michael. We thought you were dead."

"Not quite. Four of us here: me, Mo, Annie, and Top Gun Mark Two. Please send someone to get us. In a nice, earthbound vehicle, nothing with rotor blades."

"Sure. Where are you? Things are happening. You okay?"

He looked at Mo.

"By the Roman bridge in town. Outside the bar," she said.

"You hear that?"

"Yeah. That's a long walk from the mountain."

"You're telling me. And my head hurts. I guess you must have been too busy to look for us that hard."

Schulz seemed offended. "Not so. We had guys out there. Charley let off one big bang. We're only just managing to assess what's left."

"And?"

Schulz looked grim. "Let's put it this way. I'm awfully glad NASA has run with that sunshade idea of yours. They're on countdown to launch right now. I'll run a link through to you. We're pretty much out of it as far as talking to Sundog's concerned. Whatever they had up there took out the command center."

Lieberman sighed and tried to replay the picture in his mind: the tongue of flame leaping out from underneath the promontory, the long, low concrete building starting to lose its form. And people running everywhere.

"Many hurt?"

"Yeah." Schulz nodded. "But it could have been a lot worse. And you guys got away. You don't know how good that makes me feel. Personally and professionally. Those sunshades could save us, Michael. And they have other leads back home too. They think they may have an idea where Charley is running this little show from."

"Thank God for that. Deserves a drink or two."

"Don't even think of it. We've got work for you here. *Arcadia*'s about to get on her way. I'll patch through the live feed. Helen will be delighted to hear you're going to be around to hold their hands. She's en route to Vegas right now."

Vegas? Lieberman couldn't work out why that made him feel uncomfortable. "Okay. Just send us the limo." He switched the phone off, wondered where the beer had gone, and looked around to order another.

"Please don't," Mo said, putting her hand over the glass. A nice little feminine gesture, he thought. One he'd seen more than once in this world. This was a long day, Lieberman thought. So much traffic through his brain.

The pilot was swirling around the dregs in his glass. "You think he could be right? If they get back that other dome, we could do something with it? Even if the Shuttle idea doesn't work?"

"Maybe. If, if, if . . ." He looked at the videophone. The screen was blank. Schulz still hadn't switched through the live image from the Cape, and he'd no idea how long it was to the launch. Somehow he didn't want to know. That image from almost fifteen years ago still lived in his head: *Challenger* dying in a giant shower of flame. He stared back over the road, toward the valley that led to La Finca. It was a pretty spot, low orchards, a few smart villas that bespoke money. But on this side of the track it was all local: cheap tapas, terraced houses, old, beaten-up cars. There should have been kids playing soccer in the street. There should have been people.

"What a mess we've made of this," he said. Swifts darted

overhead, their chattering coming back in soft echoes from the stone walls.

"Is that of anything in particular?" the pilot asked.

"Everything in particular."

Inside, in the dark interior, there was bottle upon bottle lined up against the bar. Brandy and vodka, gin and all manner of local stuff. A man could have a good time here, he thought. A man could bring the curtain down in style, talking to the sun god all the while.

And in the end, he thought, there really was just the one thing to decide: which sun god you happened to be addressing, which one was looking down on you from the burning sky and wondering who put these bugs on the face of the earth.

There were so many to fit the bill. Apollo and Hyperion, Helios and Ra, Mithras and Hiruko. Every race that ever lived seemed, at some stage of its mayfly existence, to have come up with its own particular solar deity. The sky must have been full of them, arguing over who got there first.

And, Lieberman thought, his gut going cold because this stirred some long-dead memory he didn't want to face, on a mere mortal scale there was Phaeton too. He couldn't remember why it took so long for that corpse to rise up from the dry and dusty dregs of his memory. There had been a time (when Charley was bright and healthy and optimistic and the world seemed young) this name ran through his head almost every day.

Poor, stupid, mortal Phaeton, son of Apollo and some passing nymph. Star-crossed Phaeton, who cornered his dumb, adoring dad and wheedled out a promise that, just this once, he could drive the chariot of the sun across the sky and keep the universe in balance. There was something so human in this nagging request. *Hey, Dad, can I borrow the Jaguar? Aw, come on.*

And something human in Apollo too, in letting the kid go, even though he knew this was fated. The horses and his impetuosity would betray him, the course would be wrong, the earth would catch fire, and, with a thunderbolt from Jupiter, Phaeton would, to use Annie's apt expression, be toast. Phaeton, who was warned not to fly too high or too low, to steer the middle path, to do as he was told, to ignore the basic rule of being human: *I screw up, therefore I am. Hey, we've got to make progress somehow.*

There were those who thought the myth stemmed from some real event, like a meteor, some cataclysm from the sky. The legend said that the Libyan desert was created when Phaeton crashed to earth, that the scorching heat of this encounter forced up the blood of the Ethiopians and made their skin pitch-black. The Euphrates and the Ganges boiled. The poles were on fire. It was only when the earth herself, Gaia, daughter of Chaos, a family Lieberman felt he was starting to know well, spoke to Jupiter and called in a few favors that someone sent out the celestial Uzi and delivered a touch of holy retribution.

This was crazy. You didn't need to rationalize a line. Phaeton was all of us. This foolish, ambitious fragment of the universe— child of the sun, child of the earth—was each of us, the very essence of humanity, all the stupidity, all the vanity, and that bright, sparking thing called ambition, that curiosity, that urge for the truth.

We were Phaeton all along, but the toys got bigger, and with them the stakes. Every culture had its sun god, and every one its cautionary tale too. Of the mortal who flew too close to the fire and paid with everything he had. And the funeral oratory that followed, the one that said: *Dumb kid, hapless kid, stupid kid. But you got to hand it to him. The moron was a tryer.*

It lived inside every one of us. It was what made Rocky keep getting in the ring, remake after remake. It was what made you think you could shoot some souped-up chunk of metal into space and steal a little piece of that holy flame, make it all your own.

Catch a falling star and put it in your pocket.

Oh yeah? Bigger toys, bigger stakes, with the same dumb mammal flailing through the ancient ceremony. This was being human, having some insidious, endemic thing that lived inside your soul and never let you rest. The world was just some giant room filled with buttons marked "Don't Press," all manner of hell and damnation sitting on the other side, and we couldn't even hear the dybbuks jabbering beyond the door. Bring on the celestial idiots. Send in the clowns. And leave the earth to clean up the mess.

"What are you thinking?" Annie asked. He was so lost in this reverie, the question seemed to come out of the sky.

"I was thinking of an old story I used to read when I was a kid. About this dumb little brat called Phaeton, who thought he was bigger and stronger than he really was. And found out the hard way what happens when you mess with things you don't understand."

Mo nodded at the ground. "I remember that story."

"Shame a few more people didn't."

"You don't mean that, Michael."

"No?"

"No. You're as much a part of this as any of them."

"Bullshit." He hardly had enough energy to be angry. The sun seemed to have stolen it from his body during the long, exhausting day.

She was adamant. "You don't think we should just sit in dark corners, never finding out about the world. You're saying that what that myth means is that we're small, we're powerless, we're insignificant, and we should know our place in the order of things? I don't think so and you don't think so. That's what Charley thinks and she's wrong."

He was silent. She was right.

"And one more thing. You forgot the real point of that story."

"Being?"

"The love that Zeus felt for Phaeton all along, even when he went bad. A human love. One that surprised, maybe even alarmed him. To be weak and mortal and still believe. . . ."

"Well, that's gods for you. Stroke them with a little humanity and see where they wind up. Extinct."

She cast him a sour look, reached over, and stole the remains of his beer. "You really do sound like those people sometimes. And that isn't you."

He peered into her lean, tanned face, no emotion on the surface there, some kind of brittle hardness, like an eggshell, between her and the world.

"They're coming," the pilot said. Across the main road a jeep was kicking up dust.

Lieberman closed his eyes and shivered, trying to let these churning, feverish thoughts subside into something he could handle. Something scratched at his attention. It was the videophone coming suddenly to life, the small flat screen filling with a picture that seemed so familiar: the distant white gantry of the launch pad, the Shuttle there, hooked to the back of the booster rocket like a limpet trying to hitch a ride to the sun. But this Shuttle looked different. Bigger, like the old one on steroids. He recalled what he'd heard about the altitude requirements. Someone had strapped the mother of all engines on the side of this beast and now it was ready to blow. Smoke was billowing out from the base of this giant machine. Lieberman was trying to remember what Schulz had said about the envelope, how long it would take this vast hunk of metal, and the three small human beings inside it, to escape the gravity of the earth, to move beyond the point where Sundog and Charley could peer down from space, run out a thin, poisonous finger of power, and turn them into fiery atoms.

Mo got up from the table, walked around his back, put a soft hand on his shoulder, so close he could feel the warmth of her breath. Davis shuffled his chair around, watched the drama begin. It sounded like a video game through the tinny speaker of the little phone. There was no hint of the vast mountain of energy that sat beneath these three, distant human beings. Then the Shuttle began to move, the camera following it, rising into the blue Florida sky, incandescent white beneath the power of the sun.

"Fly, damn you, fly," Lieberman whispered.

And it did. For some period of time none of them could assess, the white shape rose in the sky, discarding the booster, rolling on course, pushing in a quickening vertical drive, getting smaller, heading for orbit. Heading for the game.

The screen went black for a moment, then Schulz was back, grinning with a wide-eyed ferocity. "You got that?"

Lieberman nodded, and felt the way Mo was hugging him.

"We're moving, Michael," Schulz said. "We can win this."

"Yeah," Lieberman said, and wondered how stupid his own grin looked.

36
Flying West

Airborne, northwest of Las Vegas, 1724 UTC

Clear desert, in every direction. Helen Wagner watched the empty plains roll beneath her and wondered why she couldn't close her eyes and get some rest. Barnside was sleeping thirty minutes after they left Washington, Levine not long behind him, right after he pulled together the briefing, made one last, uneasy conference call to the President. She watched them recline in the comfortable seats of the Agency jet, mouths half-open, and envied this effortless switch they had on their lives. There were just the three of them on the plane. Levine said both the HRT squad and the Delta Force team would be on the ground at Mc-Carran a good hour before the three of them got there. Sitting on the asphalt, staring mutely at each other, waiting for someone to win the day, she guessed. There would be no changing Clarke's mind on the idea that HRT would be the ones to try to cast a nice, gentle net over the Children, of that she had no doubt. But that didn't stop someone in the military from making one last bid for glory.

Tired of watching the ground slip past, she went to the back of the plane, sat in the communications center, keyed in her password, browsed through the pile of messages there. She clicked on the one from Schulz marked urgent, and got the news about Lieberman.

"Thank God for that," she muttered, then shifted the rest of the E-mails into the pending tray and called back to Langley. Stuart Price took the call. He looked flustered.

"So what's the problem?"

Price blushed. "Too much data or too little. It's the same old story with imaging. If you make the capture criteria too narrow, you get no hits. If you widen it just a little, in this case we're picking up everything from people's circular swimming pools to drainage tanks."

"Can't you refine it in some way?"

"How? A circular object near a building? Plenty of those. A circular object away from a building? That's more promising. We're trying that. We've got some two hundred or so potential leads but before I even let you close to them I want to see them checked against what we know of them from public records. Most are turning out to be existing licensed structures."

"Understood."

"And in the meantime I've drafted in a team of trained photo analysis people from the Pentagon. Just to look at the pictures with a human eye. Still beats any damn computer I know of, and the more minds we have working on this thing, the merrier."

Price went quiet, glanced off screen.

"Stuart?"

"I really ought to get back to this."

"Say what you want to say. Please."

"The point is . . . I have to be honest, Helen. We read the newspapers. We watch TV. I know how bad this situation is, and it worries me to think you're relying on us to pull something out of the coals. If you have something else that can narrow this down, then we might be able to get somewhere. Without it, we're just looking for that proverbial needle in a haystack. Give me a couple of weeks and that would be fine."

"We don't have a couple of weeks."

"I know. Let me put it another way. I'm real glad the Shuttle thing's going well. I think we should focus our hopes on that."

A good man, she thought. Working his heart out. "We are.

They still have to track Sundog down, and the damn thing was purpose-designed to make that hard to do. It's got some small position-adjustment power systems of its own, so it's not even that easy to come up with a particularly accurate ballpark estimate based on last known position. So you see, we can't rely on that alone."

"I hear you. I just want you to be realistic about what we can achieve here."

"I am. One last question and then we're done. How's the network holding up? How confident are we it can withstand this storm?"

"Search me. The MIS guys are going around the place clucking like hens, but that's nothing new. There's lots of bad shit going on out there right now in the public networks. But that doesn't affect us so much. Remember your history. They built ArpaNet to withstand a nuclear attack. I guess they have ways of keeping us running through this, even if we get some glitches along the way."

"I hope so. I'll leave you to it now," she said, smiled, and cut the line.

She looked at her watch. Another ninety minutes or more to go. They were late. But in any event, it hardly mattered. It looked as if they would be waiting on the ground, watching the sun set over Nevada, with nothing to occupy their time unless the Bureau had come up with some lead on their own.

She opened up the private information channel Langley had set up for the operation. Lieberman's last report was almost six hours old. She keyed the button for La Finca and Schulz came on the line. "Hi," she said. "I heard the good news about Michael."

"Yeah," Schulz replied, half-grinning. "Nice to have some breaks anyway."

"So when do we get to see a new report from him?"

Schulz shrugged. "Ask him yourself."

The picture changed. Lieberman came on the screen. He looked whacked. The wound on his scalp bristled with stitches. "Whoa. It's the slave driver from Langley. Do you ever give up?"

"No," she said, looking somewhat amazed by the question. "I'll remember that."

"How's Sara?"

"I called when I got back here. She's okay. Iron constitution, she needed it when she married me. She's worried, of course. About everything but herself. So what's new?"

"Good. And you look . . . alive. Does it hurt?"

"You're too kind. Not that much."

"The Shuttle's going to work, Michael, I just know that. But we still need to cover all the options. So when do we get that cycle report?"

He made a face. "Ten minutes. Half an hour."

"Great forecasting there. Mind giving me a little peek?"

He sighed. There was a pleasant relentlessness inside this woman you couldn't resist. "You mean as far as the natural stuff is concerned? Dry and bad and nasty. Everything I thought was going to happen and some more. Heavy radiation, electromagnetic disruption. Massive UV values. You're going to be handing out some warning on general things like skin cancer and such?"

She nodded. "They're going out already."

"Sorry. I haven't had a lot of time to keep up with the news. Well, you tell people to stay indoors and catch the show when it comes out on video a few years hence. This thing is lighting up for the big one tomorrow."

"What time? When will it peak?"

"Read my figures when I've done them. What I said initially still holds. I guess around 1210. Which is about as close to the solstice as you can get. It's still fluid, fluid enough to make Charley want to wait before pressing the final button, I imagine. But I think it's pretty certain that people on the Prime Meridian running from a little north of the equator up to maybe the tip of Scotland will get the brunt of it. Then it will start to die, only slowly, so you can expect a big wash of radiation and whatever else is inside that thing sweeping right across the northern hemisphere. We won't be anywhere close to normal until around 2400 or so. Which means it will affect everything from the Prime Meridian west right into the Pacific in some way or another. That's the real battleground Charley's got for tomorrow: London to Tokyo, and every place in between. And please, don't ask me what happens when she turns the magnifying glass on. What they got on Air Force One. What you got in Langley. All that at industrial strength, plus a little more I wouldn't care to guess at."

She went silent, knowing there was something he wanted to say.

"You're really sure about this Vegas thing?" he asked finally.

She shook her head. "Why do you ask? No, as it happens. But we know the guy who killed himself here was one of the Children. It's a lead. It's the best we can do at the moment without some hard intelligence. Like I said, we need to cover every option."

"I understand that."

"But?" she asked, puzzled.

He tried to smile. It seemed to be his lot in life to bring people down sometimes. "I don't know. The idea of Charley in Vegas sounds odd to me. You be careful. I like these conversations. I'd prefer them to continue."

She looked flustered, in a way that Lieberman couldn't help but find amusing.

"Is that a CIA blush, my dear?"

Helen Wagner's face did go noticeably pink right then. "Dammit, Michael. Time and place."

"Okay. That's a deal," he said, feeling a touch guilty for embarrassing her this way. "Hey, you want to see something that proves how careful we all ought to be? How different this world is starting to behave right now?"

Lieberman's face disappeared. She heard him speaking off camera to Schulz.

"Yes?" she said to nobody.

The tanned, intelligent features came up on the screen again. "I got to move this little camera thing from the monitor to the window so it's looking outside, not at my ugly face. Won't take a moment."

She waited, watched the moving image on the screen, then closed her eyes. "Do I really want to see this?"

"Sure! This isn't *The X-Files*. This is real."

In the Gulfstream jet moving effortlessly toward Vegas, she took a good look out this distant window in a remote Mediterranean farmhouse. The sun was setting in a sky the likes of which she had never seen. It was gold, burnished gold, mixed with a bright, sparking, rolling overlay of green, like an electric curtain, a dancing light show in the heavens.

"Tell me I'm not going crazy, Michael."

"Of course you're not. If you lived in Iceland you wouldn't think twice about seeing this. The Aurora Borealis. The Northern Lights. And as fine a show as I've ever seen. You'd almost think this was the opening night of something new."

"Don't say that," she whispered.

"Hey, there you go, off on an *X-Files* trip again. This is pure physics. The Aurora are nothing but the solar wind burning up in our atmosphere."

"In the Mediterranean? It's rare even in southern Canada."

"I told you we had an industrial-strength dose of this stuff right now. Wait your turn. I'd wager the puny contents of my solitary bank account you'll be seeing this across a lot of the northern hemisphere tonight, probably tomorrow night too. Though Vegas may be pushing it a little far south. Sorry to disappoint. And you know something?"

"What?"

"It's beautiful. In a kind of cold, cosmic way."

"Beautiful?"

"Yeah. Like a sign. The times they are a-changing. Remember that one?"

"Not my generation, Michael."

"Or mine really. 'Your sons and your daughters are beyond your command.' Maybe the generation doesn't matter that much after all."

"I have to go," she said, seeing, somewhat to her relief, Levine and Barnside awake and in conversation at the front of the plane.

"Right," he said. "Just don't get scared by what you see in

the sky. That's natural, whatever we think. It's what's inside us that's scary. Sure frightens the life out of me."

She looked at this strange image on the monitor—the Mediterranean sky alive with gold and a dancing green curtain of arcs and bands and coronas of strangely colored light—and said, "I'll take your word on that."

37
Beneath the Green Sky

La Finca, 1842 UTC

Bennett looked a broken man. He sat in a corner of the control room, nursing a tumbler full of Scotch, silent, hardly watching what was going on. Lieberman nodded at Schulz. "Is the old guy still with us?"

"Up to a point. Bevan really chewed him out about security after we lost the dome. Can you believe that? Like it's his fault? Now that it's up to the Shuttle and whatever they can run up in Vegas, I guess he feels out of it."

"Speaking of the devil, where the hell is he?"

"Out with what remains of the military guys," Schulz replied. "Looking for anyone who's still up there. After that we go quiet here until some word comes back from the Shuttle. The military go back to Palma in case they're needed for crowd-control duties. Nothing left to guard here, I guess. All they're thinking about is tomorrow, what happens if we get it wrong and the storm does hit. Understandable, I guess."

"They come across anyone else up there on the mountain?"

Schulz sighed. "A few. You look tired, Michael. To be frank, you look terrible. Why don't you get some sleep? When the Shuttle comes up with something, we'll wake you. Until then, we're pretty much out of this show."

The latest activity report was done. It was available on the network for Helen or anyone else who had access to it, and the signs were as bad as Lieberman had feared.

"What happened to Mo?" he asked.

"I think she went upstairs too. Her kid was absolutely out of it, from what I saw. You could all do with some sleep. If—correction, when—*Arcadia* finds that thing, you're in the driver's seat."

"I know." Lieberman's head hurt. And only part of it was the wound.

"Take a break, man. Think of that as an order, and be assured I'll be shaking you awake before long."

"Sir," he said, making a fake salute.

"And Michael?"

"Yeah?"

"I hate to ask. You and Mo? Is there something going on there?"

He blinked. "Are you serious? Under these circumstances?"

"No, I didn't mean it like that. I just thought there was something a little weird between you when you got back."

"We got blown out of the sky and had to walk a million miles to find you people. Plus I confuse her, I guess. I'm a confusing sort of person."

"Say that again. Is that why you two can't look each other in the eye?"

Some things you forget, Lieberman thought. Some things just hang around in the back of your memory, waiting for you to give them a little nudge. "Is that right? Search me."

He shuffled off out of the barn, back to the mansion, past the quiet bunches of soldiers who were waiting under this strange green light, then slowly climbing into the trucks taking them back to the city fifty miles away. His head was hurting. He was feeling tired, but alert too, something harrying away at the back of his consciousness.

The bar was empty. He surveyed the lineup of bottles, then picked up some mineral water, threw a few chunks of ice and lemon into the glass, poured himself a big one, and went upstairs. He walked into his room feeling dog-tired, the drink slopping over the edge and splashing onto the tile floor. And

jerked upright, stopped by the bed. The big double doors to
the balcony were open. Outside, lit by the strange sky, Mo Sinclair sat on a simple white chair, back to him, a glass of something in her hand. From this angle she looked so thin,
unformed, like a teenager.

He coughed and said, "Did I come into the wrong room or
something?"

"No," she said, turning around, half-smiling at him. "The
door was open, so I used it."

"So I see."

"I've been drinking your vodka."

"Permission granted. Don't be offended if I don't join the
party."

He went over to the balcony. She'd changed. She was wearing a thin red shirt, old and weathered, and cheap jeans cut off
at the knee. Her hair was wet from the shower. She could have
been sixteen, he thought, if you didn't look too close. Her face
was naked, shorn of expression.

"I couldn't sleep," she said. "Not right away. And there's
nothing for either of us to do until the Shuttle finds something."

"And Annie?"

"Like a log. Do any children suffer from insomnia?"

"You're asking me?"

"Yes."

"I don't think so. They tend to accept things for what they
are. You need to grow up a little in order to fool yourself you
make a difference."

She looked at him, and she wasn't a kid just then, he
thought. She had all that knowledge and intuition inside her
that women seemed to possess just when you hoped they were
looking the other way. "All that easy cynicism, Michael. Is that
really you?"

He gulped at the water, and wondered about the vodka before pushing away the thought. "Sometimes."

"You should have had kids, Michael. You're good with them.
You can talk to them like a grown-up and on their own level

too. That's a gift. I can feel Annie coming out of her shell a little more every time we meet."

"Why's she in that shell, Mo?"

"Jesus." She gulped at the drink. "We don't take the long
way 'round to questions these days, any of us."

"Blame it on the weather. It shines right through everything."

"Not quite. Annie's like that because of me. Is that what you
want to hear?"

"No. Because I don't really believe it. We all get sidetracked
in our lives sometimes. Me more than most. There are times
when you should blame yourself. And times when you have to
accept that some days it just rains. None of us controls as much
as we like to think."

"No," she said. "Maybe not. But I'm grateful for the way you
talk to Annie. Like she's real. Not some ornament around here.
Can't we leave it at that?"

He pulled up a chair, planted it next to hers on the balcony,
looked at the sky, and felt like a jerk. She was scared and he
should have known that, would have known too if all the right
parts inside him had been working as they should.

What scared her were the Northern Lights that stood above
them, rolling and dancing, ageless, formless. There were reasons for this exhibition. They stood at the back of his imagination, hard and cold and factual, reasons that talked of all those
extra protons and electrons that the sun had emitted colliding
with the upper atmosphere of the earth, racing toward the
magnetic poles and giving off their mutual energy in this psy-
chedelic panorama that took your breath away, made you feel
small and powerless beneath its vastness. But reasons belonged
in the plain, all-seeing light of day. Sometimes they never followed you into the dark, unfamiliar rooms where you needed
them.

This was the biggest Aurora he had ever seen, at any lati-
tude. It flowed like a continuous greenish blue curtain to the
north of them, its lower hem a fringe of violent ruby red. Inside, the fabric seemed to be alive, seemed to move and pulse
and breathe.

They stared at the lights, so bright they made the stars in the south invisible in the radiant night sky. She was shivering, he could see that, and it wasn't that she was cold.

"Take it easy, Mo. It's no big deal."

The usual night noises were oddly absent, with few bird calls, only a gentle rustle of hot air across the dry grass. And beneath it all, like some distant, mystical orchestra, the sound of the lights. A gentle fizzing and crackling that was like static, the rustling of electricity.

She reached up, covered her ears, trying to stifle this sound from the sky. "I don't want to listen, Michael. I can't stand the thought of being underneath all this. Not being able to hide."

"You don't need to hide. This isn't Charley. This is natural. Being afraid of this is like lying awake at night worrying someone is going to turn off the gravity and send us all cartwheeling off into space. Even if that were a possibility, fretting over it would be pointless."

She watched the green electric curtain pulsing, alive, above them, and said, "You know these things. They make sense to you. All I see is . . . insanity."

"No. You see change. The world changes. We get used to thinking that we control those changes but that's an illusion. It's always been changing. It's not what we have to be frightened of. It's what's inside ourselves when we realize how tiny we are against all this."

Did this reassure her? He thought there was no way to tell. She kept something tight and close and private inside her, something that rarely saw the light of day.

"You're scared for Annie," he said. "You needn't be. It's people in the cities that need to be scared. When things break down, people damage each other. Charley knows that. She's not going to bother with us anymore. We're too small."

"I'm scared for all of us. The world scares me. Michael . . ."

Gently, gingerly, she put her arms around his neck, cradled her face against his skin. She was warm. There was moisture there. A dim memory, he thought: It was a long time since a woman had cried against him. A dim memory.

"What happened today—".

"Shhhh . . ." He put a finger against her lips, felt the warm, dry skin. "What happened today is in the past. We got out of there. We survived. We will survive."

She moved her face closer against him; he felt the hard, damp sharpness of her teeth on his neck, her fingers running through the back of his hair. Mo Sinclair kissed his cheek, pulled back, and he found himself staring into her strained, expressionless face.

"Michael," she said, "I can't be alone just now. I can't be."

Something like electricity ran between them, mirroring the fire in the sky.

"This isn't a good idea," he said, and she was rising already, back into the room, taking off her shirt, walking over to the bed. She was wearing nothing beneath the old red fabric. Her breasts stood small and taut against her thin, straight chest.

"We don't have time for ideas. Don't think, Michael. Feel."

He took one more gulp of the water, tried to force some sense into his head, looked at the sky, and decided this was futile. "You sound like me," he said, out over the balcony to no one but the dancing, raging sky. "You sound just like the old part of me, not my favorite part."

Something clicked inside his head. Something that gave no way back. He rose from the chair and started to remove his shirt, his jeans. She was in the bed now, beneath the single sheet, her body just visible through its flimsiness, her face stained by the green light coming in through the open windows. She held out her hand. Pleading, Lieberman thought, and something now slumbering inside him asked: *Why?*

He sat on the side of the bed and pulled back the sheet, down to her breasts, staring at the dark, small nipples, soft as he touched them, not stiffening. He pulled the fabric down farther, revealing the long slender body, the color of fading copper, too tanned, a triangle of dark hair.

"Don't think," she said, and reached for him, felt the developing stiffness at his groin. "Please."

He let his head break free of this baggage of adulthood, shrugged off the last of his clothes, and climbed on the bed, touched the gentle rise of her stomach, bent down, licked her navel, felt the taut, tight lines of her stomach, her thatch, the damp, inviting sweetness it concealed, kissed her hard, hand raising now, into her long, dry hair, eyes closed (not in the green light, not in the green light), felt her legs submit, moved, was above her, inside her, gently shifting, rocking, probing, feeling.

And there was so much to feel: This part of being alive was hot and fevered, slow and ecstatic. In the faint green light that filtered into the room there lived a frenzied line of electric delight that brought them, moaning, screaming, fighting to some swift, elemental climax.

Her eyes were closed. She smiled, delicately, a tiny corner of her mouth turned upward, like a piece of punctuation on a physical page, and it came to him how new this was: to see her in some senseless delight, to know that within her taut, strained being there lived some small, insensate oasis of carnality, unfettered, wild, free.

Like this, she was truly beautiful: satiated, content, made whole by their joint coupling. He stayed in this place, relishing the fleshy warmth between them, becoming ever more conscious of it again. A voice inside his head said: *Don't think, feel.* And the pictures, the images of the day rolled behind it, in counterpoint, like a slow-moving video.

Michael Lieberman felt himself hardening, and the fire of procreation began the urging again, starting to order his hips, his groin into motion. Breathless, he pushed himself away, felt himself come free, with a small ache, pulled back over her body, rolled over onto the bed.

She opened her eyes and this was the old Mo again, closed, mysterious. "Michael," she said, looking into his face, some hurt there inside her voice, "I thought . . ."

In the green light now she looked different. Her eyes rolled, like those of a frightened animal. She stared at the ceiling. Lieberman reached over, touched her face with his fingers, gripped her chin, forced her head around. "Mo," he said. Tears now, forming like transparent pearls at the corner of her eyes.

"Don't," she said, trying to snatch herself away.

"I know."

It was there so clearly now, like a photograph inside his head, and he wondered why it took so long to make sense of the image.

"You know what?" she answered, and there was as much fear in her voice, he thought, as there was aggression.

"You recognized that woman," Lieberman said, still working to understand these words himself. "On the mountain. In the mouth of the mine. You knew her."

She closed her eyes, tight, so tight, and shook her head from side to side, so fast, so hard her hair went flying around like some whirling, wispy halo.

"You saw," he said quietly. "And you thought you could fuck that memory out of my head too."

38
Slipping

Airborne, northwest of Las Vegas, 1749 UTC

"McCarran Tower, this is November Five Seven Eight Whiskey Sierra." The pilot let go of the PTT button and listened to the static, called again, then tried another frequency.

"Something local?" the copilot asked from behind impenetrable Ray-Bans.

"Probably. Give it a minute, Mike." The distant city rolled out on the desert plain in front of them, dead flat in the valley between two arid mountain ranges, unmistakable across the clear, cloudless desert sky.

Mike pressed the button and made another call. "Still static."

"Shit," the captain said. "I feel a command decision coming upon me."

"The woman did say to call her if anything like this occurred."

"Yeah, I know. But it doesn't matter if we have to go into McCarran blind, for God's sake. They grounded all the commercial airline traffic for today. Hell, you go talk to her."

"Sure." Mike unstrapped his harness and went aft. Helen Wagner was on the videophone and she looked angry. "We got some static, some interference," the copilot said.

"Tell me about it," she grumbled. On the screen in front of her Lieberman's face appeared intermittently. Most of the time the image was filled with junk: white noise and distortion.

When it was clear, she didn't like what she was seeing. Lieberman looked ashen and as miserable as sin.

"When you're ready," the copilot said, and went back to the cockpit, feeling relieved.

"Michael," she said, "drop the video. Just put this over to voice. Maybe we'll get more over." The screen died altogether, and, for a moment, the sound with it.

Then Lieberman said, "Is that any better?"

"A little. But it's not great."

"No," he replied, in what was close to a distant, unintelligible mumble, "same for you. What's the problem? Everything else seems clear this end."

"I don't know. Some local interference here possibly."

"This is electromagnetic, remember that."

"I will," she replied, and became aware of Barnside and Levine at her shoulder.

"You'll do that," he yelled through the noise. "I've been thinking about this. Charley said she'd give us a sign. And she hasn't. She's got something up her sleeve, something that comes straight out of the sky, not a box marked Semtex. It will be electromagnetic. It has to be. And this place you're going— a nice big network of wires and high-intensity, open-air electronic devices in the middle of the desert—is one hell of a location to try it out."

"I know this," she answered, trying not to sound too touchy. "Is that why you called? Because if it is, we're going over old ground and I've got better things to do."

The line went dead. Then Lieberman said, "Keep your hair on. Are you sitting down?"

"Go on," she said testily.

"We've found someone here who was one of the Children. And then made it here. They put her into La Finca as some kind of spy. She knows them. But we need to handle this thing carefully. I don't want some gooks just treading all over this woman because that won't do any of us any good."

Levine looked at Barnside and said, "Get that guy of yours hooked into this conversation. This is his damn job. Not some goddamn academic's."

"Michael," she said. "Calm down. Take this slowly."

"I am calm, Helen." He didn't sound it at all, she thought. "I have found someone who was one of them. And was told to come here, get inside this place."

"She did that?"

"She's here. But she says that's as far as it went. She didn't do anything. She's scared. Of you. Of them. And scared for herself, her kid. You need to treat her right. Otherwise she'll just stay quiet, clam up."

"I understand. . . . Michael?" The line went dead in a big burst of static.

"You still there?" he said eventually.

"Yes."

"Look," Lieberman continued, "I don't know how much she has to give, and this isn't going to be easy. But if we try, if we're patient, we can work something out."

"Patient?" Levine snorted. "You hear the guy? This woman could put us on the line with Gaia. Who the hell does he think he is?"

"Who was that?" Lieberman's voice asked out of the speaker.

"One of my colleagues."

"Right. I guess I'm being dumb here, huh? You people are just going to break out the leg irons and beat it out of her."

"No!"

Levine said, "We'll do what it takes. What the hell does he expect?"

"I heard that," Lieberman said, only half-intelligible through the noise. "And you listen to me, whoever you are. You guys may enjoy running around with hard dicks and guns hanging out of your pants. But it hasn't done you much good so far, now, has it?"

Levine swore. Then glowered at Barnside working the radio on the other side of the plane, a headset clamped to his ears. "That guy of yours asleep or something?" Barnside said nothing, just carried on talking quietly into the mike.

"Listen to me," Lieberman said. "If we take this slowly, easily, I think we can bring her around."

"I hear you, Michael," Helen said. "Just trust us on this one."

"Trust you?" The rest of the sentence disappeared in a sea of white noise. She saw Barnside dragging the headset off, wincing with pain.

"Give it a moment..." she suggested. But the aircraft bucked beneath them and she almost retched as her stomach rose up inside her body. It felt as if the plane had dropped a thousand feet or more in a single second, hit something hard below, and was running along some solid, rough ledge cut into the air. The impact scattered every loose object in the cabin: notebook computers, writing pads, pens, papers, mobile phones. She clung to her seat, desperately trying to fasten the strap, and watched Levine and Barnside struggling to do the same. A hand gripped her shoulder. It was the copilot.

"Belts," he said. "I want you all strapped in right now."

"We're talking," she objected.

"No one's talking, lady. The comm systems just went stone dead and we don't even want to think about what might have gone with it. This is no big deal. We got plenty of altitude and we could just glide into Vegas from this height if we wanted. But there's something turbulent out there and that means we want you tied. Now!"

She wished she could see beneath the opaque Ray-Bans. This man looked scared, she thought, and that was rare in a pilot. "I asked you to tell me if we had problems."

"Please..."

She unhooked the strap, got up, holding tightly to the seat, tried to smile at him, and said, "You have a jump seat. I'm taking it. And that is an order."

"Go for it," Barnside yelled, buckling himself into his seat, and gave her what she hoped was a look of encouragement. "You heard the woman."

"Shit," the copilot muttered, then turned his back on them, worked his way to the front of the cabin, holding on tight to every seat as he passed it, and pushed open the cockpit door. A sea of light the color of gold flooded through it, then he was dragging her with him, pushing her hard into the tiny jump seat, strapping himself in, and pulling down the military-style harness that sat above it.

"Make it tight," he said. "You can wear these too." He pulled out a spare pair of sunglasses from a pocket in the cabin and thrust them at her. She put them on, took a deep breath, and looked ahead.

Still trying to believe her eyes, she gasped, "What the hell is that?"

The captain turned around and smiled. "We were rather hoping you'd be telling us that, ma'am."

On the horizon, suspended over the southwestern portion of the city, level with their own altitude, stood a vast, elliptical golden shape, like a miniature sun stretched and distorted by gravity. It ran almost the breadth of the valley, joining the mountain ranges on either side of the flat, strung-out urban area, and shimmered, motionless, in front of them.

"What do they say on the ground?" she asked, already knowing what the answer would be.

"All communications are down," the copilot answered, tapping away at the buttons in front of him. "We haven't a clue."

"Can't you even listen?"

The copilot turned his sunglasses on her. He reached for the panel and upped the volume. The sound of static, screeching, meaningless, filled the speakers. "I've been dialing through everything, from the McCarran tower through to local radio on the NDB frequency and they're all the same. Beats me. I never had interference that could run clear through from UHF to AM."

The captain eased back some more on the throttle. The aircraft had slowed, she now realized. They didn't know enough to turn it around, but they wanted more information before heading straight toward the object. It sat several miles away from the commercial airfield, which she could see clearly now, directly in their flight path.

"Ordinarily," the captain said, "I would have suggested that was some kind of optical illusion. You get this thing called a parhelion, a sundog. Caused by crystal diffraction in the atmosphere. Harmless."

"I know what a parhelion is," she replied. "And this isn't one."

"No. I guess the interference ought to tell us that. You wouldn't expect that from an optical illusion."

"So what is it?"

"Search me. But one thing I know is we're going nowhere near it. I'm keeping this altitude just so we're nice and safe and as close to the airfield as need be."

She stared at the object in the sky. The color was changing occasionally. At the perimeter of the ellipsis it turned blue and green in flickering waves of flame.

"If I didn't know better," the copilot said, "I'd reckon that was ball lightning."

"Not that anyone knows what ball lightning is," the captain muttered. "Or has ever photographed it. Or proved it does exist. And, if my memory serves me right"—he stared at the golden shape ahead of them—"it's generally supposed to be about the size of a soccer ball."

"Yes," she said, and found it impossible to take her eyes off the object. "But it is some kind of lightning." The aircraft rocked again. Not so bad this time. There was a sound close by, like escaping air.

"Shit," the copilot said, and started to press gingerly at the bank of switches and buttons in front of him. Vegas lay in front of them like a giant lightning conductor, the metallic spine of the Strip running through its core. Silence invaded the cabin. On the panel the lights went dead. The two pilots stared at each other.

"It's moving," Helen said. They looked ahead and saw that the rim of this miniature, elongated sun was now almost completely blue. What looked like flames or wild electrical discharges ran flickering along the skin.

The captain watched it for a second or two and came to a swift decision. "To hell with McCarran. I'm taking this thing into Nellis whether they like it or not. And fast."

She watched them run through the checks on the panel, push and pull the levers in front of them. Nothing much seemed to be working on the plane. The nose had slipped beneath the horizon, and the pilot was working the machine physically, with his hands, with his feet. The smell of ozone, of burning wiring was starting to became noticeable in the cabin.

"We lost the flaps," the copilot said quietly. "No power, no flaps."

The captain shrugged. "Oh my. Well, I always did want to do this with someone else's ship." And he turned the wheel full to the left, then kicked in hard with the right rudder, putting the plane into a sharp side slip. The aircraft jerked itself uncomfortably around in the air, the nose twitching to the right, no horizon visible, and it felt as if they would fall out of the sky any second. She watched the altimeter. It was unwinding at three thousand feet a minute. This crazy attitude made it difficult to see what was going on in the city. The wing obscured the view. All there was out to the left of the plane was a sheet of gold and flickering blue. She closed her eyes. The plane, the world seemed out of joint. She tried to think of Michael Lieberman, and what he had said. He was probably right. They attacked this problem as if it were something that could be cured with conventional force, conventional procedures. Charley Pascal was smarter than that. Even more, she was only part of the problem, almost a symptom of it.

Her head hurt. Maybe a nosebleed was imminent. She screwed up her eyes, tried to will away the pain. Then felt the plane move again, swing forward, back into balance, return to something like normality. Against her instincts, Helen Wagner lifted her head and saw a long, empty runway approaching quickly in front of them, military planes parked either side of the extended finger of asphalt.

The copilot operated a lever on the floor and something shifted with a bang beneath them. "Gear down," he said.

"*All right,*" the captain muttered, and toyed gently with the wheel. The aircraft kissed the ground with scarcely a noise, and began to decelerate along the asphalt runway of Nellis. She didn't want to look but there was no avoiding it. To her left, the fiery ellipse was descending, streaking blue and green and red as it came to earth.

"Lightning," the copilot said. "Has to be."

"I think," she said, "we should get out of the plane. As quickly as possible. Get away from anything that is flammable or liable to attract an electrical discharge."

The copilot's opaque sunglasses were fixed on her. A line of blood stood hard and red in one of his nostrils. "You mean we just stand out in the open, ma'am? And wait for this thing to come our way?"

39
Shared Love

"It's a bad place," Günther said. "It deserves what's coming to it."

Sundog was primed now, sat in the sky with fire in its belly. The solar cycle was on the rise. Charley felt nervous. All the tests, all the minor experiments they had conducted—everything before had been a prelude to this event. They had learned so much, how inflexible and difficult to control the satellite could be. They had learned too how important it was to monitor the flux of the cycle, to time the moment they captured it precisely so that they stole as much of its energy as possible.

But there was still too much guesswork, and the cycle itself was so unpredictable. Time was running out for them as much as for anyone else. They had to be realistic, they had to accept that there were limits to what they could achieve. This was a gigantic instrument of destruction, but it concerned her that the precise way in which it would manifest itself was still, to some extent, in doubt. In this mix of fire and radiation, this whirring digital demon that slipped into the networks of the world and devoured them from inside, there remained uncertainties. Some experiment, some proof was needed, not just as a sign for the world, but also for her own peace of mind.

"No," she said, bringing her mind back onto the small circle of figures around her. "This isn't a time to think of good and bad, Günther. We're not avenging angels. We're not punishing anyone. This is about a change in direction. A return to a natural order. Equilibrium. Balance."

She closed her eyes and smiled: It was a bad place all the same. She could remember the gaudy, heartless streets, the phony smiles they met everywhere, the tawdry glamour. Vegas, it seemed to her, epitomized what was false and dishonest and wicked about humankind. That it should present such an opportunity to make the sign gave her no regret whatsoever.

Billy Jo asked, "What will happen to them? Will they all die?"

"We don't know," Joe Katayama, sitting cross-legged on the floor, said. "How can we? Not all of them. Maybe not even many. That's not the point."

You could think and you could dream and you could calculate, Charley thought, but in the end there was always the mystery. People misunderstood the signs: It was believing that the mystery could be removed that led you into seeking your own petty godhood in the first place.

"We walked in darkness," she said. "And then Gaia gave us hope, gave us light. For everything. For the world. Can't you feel it?"

Joe Katayama said, a thin smile starting to crack his face, "I can feel it." And someone else too. In a moment, there was laughter in the room, and it was genuine, she knew that. It would be strange if they didn't feel some foreboding, but still there was a close, compelling certainty that drove them forward. They remained a family even in the face of this forced dispersal.

"And you think," Günther said, "that we really will change things? So soon?"

She nodded urgently. "Of course. Why would we be here otherwise? This is a world ripe for change, Günther. Like a caterpillar emerging from the chrysalis. Think how much we have achieved already. Closing the markets. Shaking the apparatus of the state."

"But," Billy Jo said, "people aren't exactly changing right now. I've been following what's going on through the Web, on TV. People are scared. But I get the impression that for some of them this is just a way of getting a free day or two off work while they wait for the government to fix it. Like a power outage or an earthquake."

"What do you expect them to say?" Charley replied instantly. "That their world really is about to end? Change happens in your heart. Unless it begins there, it means nothing at all. And we will touch their hearts, we will make them look at themselves with fresh eyes."

Joe Katayama said, "It's a point, Charley. Maybe we ought to have told them a little more."

"No," she said. "People are blind. People are stupid. They want proof. So we'll give them proof. And when it happens, it will be so big, so unavoidable, they'll know."

They didn't argue. They never argued these days. "The proof starts now. In Vegas. And here too. We have to move on. We have to disperse."

They watched her, hanging on every word. "We all know, through this shared love we possess, where this leads. We can't inflict this damage, this pain on these people—and that will be real—without showing them that we share it ourselves. This is our shared grief, our common legacy. We all move forward, hand in hand, to this fate."

There was silence in the hot, airless room. Some were holding hands. Most looked happy. In this state, such closeness between them, it became easy to think with a single mind, she thought. It was when people were separated, moved outside the family, that they ran the risk of becoming lost.

"We will redeem ourselves, like them, in pace with the world. Joe?" He looked up at her from the floor, a thin smile on his face, content, she thought, like all of them. And he would be the last to leave the nest. He was needed to see this final stage to its conclusion.

"Yes?"

"How many of us are there now?"

"Twenty-four."

"Twice the number as there were disciples," Charley said, happy, relishing the love in their faces. "Slowly, over the next eighteen hours, we disperse. You must leave the farm, go back into the outside world. The die are cast here. We've got the programs to prime Sundog. Someone has to stay, see it through. From now on you must start on a new journey. What we've achieved is good and important. But people will kill you for it if they know. Until the awakening, until they see this is a new beginning, we remain silent. We remain apart. We wait."

Billy Jo put up her hand. There were tears in her eyes. Charley watched them roll down her cheeks. Tears of joy, she guessed. There was, in this fast-diminishing space in front of them, a hard, gripping form of ecstasy that wouldn't let them go.

"You're dying, Charley," Billy Jo said. "We won't see you again."

"We're all dying. I'm no different than any of you, except that I have this knowledge that lets me say goodbye to you now."

"All the same. I thought I'd be here. I thought I'd hold your hand."

Charley touched the soft white cotton of her shirt with pale, shaking fingers. "I wish it could be like that. But we can't jeopardize the very reason we're here. We're smaller than Gaia."

Günther nodded. "Charley's right, Billy Jo. This is the way it has to be."

"Okay."

"Only love lies between us," Charley said, "and that love survives wherever we are." She leaned down from the wheelchair, took Billy Jo's hand, and Günther's too. "If you like, if Joe is agreeable, you can be the first to leave. Together."

They looked at each other and smiled.

40
Trompe l'Oeil

Room 2341 of the Mirage Hotel looked directly south along the Strip, out past Caesar's Palace in the adjoining block, with its marble figures and fake porticos and colonnades glistening white in the midday heat, past Bellagio, New York New York, and the big gleaming hulk of MGM, with the towers of Excalibur and the peak of the Luxor pyramid in the distance. Somewhere beyond that, Sam Jenkinson dimly recognized, was the airport where they had arrived, jet-lagged and exhausted, from England two days before. But no circling planes marked its location. The emergency had arrived in Vegas.

They were in the new Dali wing of the Mirage. Here everything was surrealistic. The elevators looked as if they had been modeled out of naked flesh. The clocks melted on the wall (and still worked). Even the waitresses, wandering around the floor area trying to sell you cigarettes and Keno tickets, looked like something out of a nightmare: huge feathered tresses, gold swimsuits, bizarre makeup, but not on their chests; their chests gleamed out into the big casino room everywhere, twin peaks of flesh, bobbing between the tables.

He stared at the big golden sky down from Luxor, took a swig of rum and Coke, then looked at his wife. Marion Jenkinson was fifty-seven, one year younger than her husband. She lay on the bed dressed in a pale red and lime-green polyester jumpsuit, one she bought the day before from Emporio while he was in the bar. Her clothes matched the room. The standard lamp was in green verdigris copper, twisting around on itself like a serpent. The bathroom door had some painting on it that looked vaguely familiar: a woman, half-naked, turning to sand. And on the ceiling, watching you all the time, huge, staring eyes, Dali eyes, with big eyebrows and, as a recurring motif, that twirled-up waxed mustache. He gazed out the window, looking puzzled.

"What's wrong, Sam?"

"Nothing. . . ."

Marion Jenkinson climbed off the bed and came and sat next to him at the window. "It's very bright out there." In the distance, beyond Luxor, somewhere close to where the airport ought to be, he guessed, the sky was simply golden, as if the sun were so bright it had turned into a local corona.

"It's moving," they said, almost in unison.

He shut his eyes for a moment. The day was so bright it began to make the back of his pupils hurt with a pain that was like a long, slow bruise. When he opened them, the huge golden shape was directly behind the Luxor pyramid, and it was vast, like the filament from some vast light bulb. As it got closer, it appeared more complex too. An incandescent blue, like electric flame, ran along its skin.

"What is it, Sam?"

"I don't know." He surveyed the street. No crowds, no lines of people. Hardly anybody at all. It was a hot day, he thought. Maybe everybody would stay indoors to watch this kind of show, whatever it was.

"It is fireworks," she said, and he was aware of her arm on his shoulder.

"I suppose so." And thought: No.

The storm—it was some kind of storm, he thought, it had to be—was now engulfing the peak of the Luxor pyramid, and from its underbelly fell what looked like giant gleaming hailstones, hundreds, even thousands of them, pouring out from the churning guts of the thing, down into the dark glass, down to the ground. Then it moved on. The great golden cloud was swamping the fairy-tale towers of Excalibur. It was impossible to see what was left in its wake. The shimmering golden ellipsis covered everything behind.

He looked across the street. As he watched, the lights started to go out. First on the Flamingo, then on the Imperial, finally on Harrah's, opposite them. There was a distinct electronic ping in the room. The TV died. The air-conditioning died. The sudden, unexpected silence seemed to occupy the entire room. Outside, the golden cloud had reached Caesar's. Spheres the size of soccer balls were tumbling down from its livid underbelly, some spinning on their axis, the movement visible by a whirling filament of streaks in their sides, some pure gold, all the way down, a few turning pale, dying in the sparkling air.

"Sam . . ." she said.

"I'm thinking, woman. Give me time."

The cloud moved on and on. He went to the door of the room, threw it open, stared across at the elevator. A bunch of people stood around it, banging the buttons, swearing, looking frightened, some pushing at the door to the fire stairs. Marion was at his shoulder.

"I can't go down them stairs," she said. "Not twenty-three floors, and who's saying it's safe in there anyway?"

"Nobody." He pushed her back into the room, wishing she'd be quiet. Behind them the window was now pure gold. The cloud was enveloping the Mirage, and with it came the shower. They sat on the bed and watched the light show outside the glass. The painted eyes on the ceiling, so many, bright and huge and vivid, seemed to be laughing at them.

The picture outside the window was changing. The light was no longer quite so solid. Elements were moving in it. Maybe this was how they formed, he thought. Maybe this was the beginning of the ball shower. She clutched his hand. Her skin was wet with sweat. The temperature seemed to have climbed ten degrees. There was a thin, acrid smell, like ozone, and, above them, a chirruping, fizzing noise that seemed to fall down on the room, with a physical movement, like rain.

"It can't get in," she said. "It can't break the window, for God's sake."

"Right. We just wait. It'll soon be over and then . . ."

Making a sound like a nest of snakes, a gleaming, fiery ball appeared at the window and hung there, as if it were looking at them. It was a good three feet across, blue light flickering across its skin, and revolving slowly, like a globe turning on its axis. Briefly, it rose a few feet in the air, as if it were examining the sea of eyes painted on the ceiling.

"Shit," he said quietly.

"Sam, it *can't* come in."

"No."

The ball came down to their level, came right up to the window, so close he expected to see the skin pushed back, like a nose pressed up to the glass. Then it moved forward again and he thought she was going to snap off his hand. It was protruding through the glass, two-thirds of it outside the room, one-third in. And growing. Moving. Behind it, two more spheres had appeared, were hovering in the same way, like mute animals, catching the scent of prey.

There was noise like the firing of a small gun, and then the first sphere plopped through the window, hung in the air, eighteen inches off the ground. The room was filled with the sound of hissing; it seemed to come at them from every direction. The smell of ozone was unbearable, and there was a sense of heightened atmospheric pressure, the sort you got when a plane was landing. He looked at his wife. Her nose was bleeding profusely. She had her hand to it, her mouth open, the blood dripping in.

"Sam," she said thickly. And then it was gone. The ball raced past them, heat brushing their legs, into the open door of the bathroom opposite, skittered around the four walls, hovered over the toilet, and disappeared over the edge of the bowl.

"Bloody hell," he said. A blue light hovered over the pink ceramic unit and steam was rising from the hidden water. Then the basin exploded with a roar, ripping off the half-open door, sending shards of porcelain blasting through the room. They ducked beneath the bedclothes and waited for the noise to die down.

"One down," he said, gingerly coming out from beneath the sheets. Outside, the brightness seemed to be diminishing. "It's moving past us. It'll soon be gone."

The two spheres still danced outside the window. One made a little bob, then popped through the glass, no noise this time, it was as easy as stepping through a shower. The second followed and they stood at either end of the long window.

"Get under the covers, love," he barked. "Get some protection if one of these things goes bang. Don't move too much in case they pick it up. They're looking for something electrical, and we may be the closest they get to it."

She scrambled beneath the sheets. He followed her, felt her scrabbling for his hand. He squeezed it once, bent over, kissed her roughly on the lips. "Not a good idea to touch anymore, Marion. Maybe we make more electricity that way."

The closest started to vibrate, and streaks of azure appeared inside its skin. "Under the sheet!" he yelled, and pulled what fabric there was over them. The thing was doubling in size, rippling blue and gold, swirling all the time. He took one last look, then pulled the pillow over his face. It took no more than a second. The thing imploded on itself with a deafening bellow and the room was filled with shattered flying glass. They could heart it arcing through the air above them, then impaling itself into anything it could find.

Marion screamed, and he felt sick as he realized she was cut. Then the pain came in his head too, and something warm began to drip down his scalp. She started to sob. Beneath the covers, he reached over, touched her hand, just briefly. It was warm and wet. Then he opened his eyes and pushed back the pillow from his head. The entire length of the window had been blown out in the blast. Water was pouring down from a shattered pipe in the ceiling. The street was open to them, twenty-three floors below. But you could see it. He liked that idea. There was no fire. This was something they could survive. He put a hand to his head: blood, but not so much you had to worry.

In the corner, hovering two feet off the drowning carpet, the third sphere was almost motionless, hissing with a thin, constant noise. It looked pale, less active than the first two. And a little smaller. But it was alive—if that was the right word. And it was moving, very slowly, toward the bed.

"Sam," Marion said from beneath the sheet. "I'm bleeding. Bad."

"Stick with it, love. And keep your head down." He looked at the sphere and wished he could hate the thing. But it wasn't really alive, he knew that. And there was a simple way to deal with it.

Sam Jenkinson climbed out of the bed and sat down in the chair close to the window. To his amazement, his drink was still on the tiny side table, half-full. Hand shaking, he reached over, picked it up, and took a sip. It tasted foul: warm and tainted somehow. The sphere had stopped moving toward the bed. It hovered between them indecisively.

"Now," he said, looking at the thing, going paler by the second a few feet away in front of the shattered window, "why don't you be a good little monster and go fuck off home?" It flickered, was almost white. For a fraction of a second he could see the side wall of the room through its glowing body.

"Sam?"

"Shut up, woman."

The ball rolled slowly toward him, hissing softly. He watched it stop a foot away and he really could see right through it. The thing was dying. Outside the day seemed to be returning to normal. It looked like a ghost. Or a thin reflection of the moon in water, he thought. The sphere stopped hissing. Then moved so quickly, he thought for a moment it had disappeared completely. Something pale and ghostly seemed to be crawling inside his mouth, up through his nostrils, even through his eyes, his ears, and it wasn't entirely unpleasant. It was warm, it sang, and when it was in the place it sought it was impossible to think of anything at all, impossible to feel anything except this strange, fevered thrum of energy that seemed to run inside and outside of his body.

The room went silent. Marion Jenkinson poked her head above the sheet, starting to feel weak, somewhat sick too. She looked across at him and went silent. He looked like one of those old pictures of a saint, with a halo that wasn't quite a halo, more a gentle ball of light that hung around his entire head. He was screaming, but she couldn't hear the noise. It seemed to get sucked from the room before it could get to her.

She closed her eyes and rocked gently, backward and forward, on the bed, until something hot and powerful picked her up with the sound of an exploding melon, threw her backward against the wall, left her slumped and bleeding, yelling at nothing, not opening her eyes, not wanting to see, clutching at the sheets, fists opening and closing, refusing to think about what was happening, what was flying in the room (warm and wet, making a sound like churning water) around her.

She didn't know how long she stayed like that. When she opened her eyes, she was cold. This wetness that covered her was cold too. She rolled over on the bed and looked up. The painted ceiling stared back at her, laughing, a sea of staring eyes. It was red with flesh, so much that it was contoured, seemed organic, physical. And one new feature too. Embedded in the staring, manic images was a piece of Sam Jenkinson, a single staring eyeball, around it a ragged corona of tissue and nerves.

She coughed into the sheets, retched dry bile, and tried to believe this was all a dream.

41

Holy Fire

An hour after the attack the smoke still hung over the city a couple of miles distant. It was an eerie sight. There was precious little consistency in any of the reports they had. In some places it had started fires. In others it had passed over buildings, even through buildings, people too, with no ill effects whatsoever. And sometimes the results had been simply devastating. The tower of the Stratosphere was now nothing but a burned-out shell. In the old downtown, the huge, block-long electronic visual display canopy that had brought visitors back to Fremont Street seemed to have attracted the full force of the attack. It had been torn apart in a rain of fire that the crowds underneath had thought was all part of the show, until the metal began to rain down in a molten flood on their heads and the street turned into a river of flame.

In some cases the floating spheres of energy had invaded people directly and then simply exploded. The casualty list was something the emergency services couldn't even begin to guess at. Every man and woman at Nellis had been brought in to help with the rescue operation. The storm had lasted more than an hour, and Helen Wagner watched every agonizing minute in horror from the airfield, which was entirely untouched. The range war with the Delta Force crew, who drove over from McCarran to make contact when it became apparent that radio comm was down, was soon forgotten. They teamed up with the Air Force people and tacitly acknowledged that if some lead on the Children were to emerge, then HRT would be the ones to follow up on it. There was too much work on the ground for them to think of anything else. She watched with quiet admiration the grim-faced, deliberate way they went about the job.

In a small office next to the main Nellis control tower Larry Wolfit was working away at the keyboard on his notebook computer. He wore a fresh checked shirt and jeans, big mountain boots sticking out from under the desk.

"You have a line out on that yet, Larry?" she asked. Barnside and Levine were somewhere else, outdoors, talking to the HRT people, she guessed. It felt more comfortable without them hanging around. Wolfit seemed to have spent the entire time since his arrival with his head deep inside the computer, hunting for clues.

"One just came through," Wolfit replied laconically. "Slow and very noisy but I can get something. After a fashion." Wolfit looked different outside the controlled, cloistered confines of S&T somehow. He was more at home out here, close to the wilderness.

"Good. So tell me what caused all this."

He screwed up his nose at the screen. "Ball lightning, probably."

"Which is?" She watched him struggle with the answer.

"Lot of arguments about that. Not conventional lightning, that's for sure. This is a real rarity in normal circumstances, though its existence is pretty well documented. The favored theory right now is some internally powered electromagnetic phenomenon. Maybe a microwave radiation field contained inside a spherical shell of plasma. Or very high density plasma exhibiting quantum mechanical properties."

She folded her arms and looked out the window. "You mean we don't know?"

"What ball lightning is? No. But at least people do generally accept it exists nowadays. Some think it could explain a couple of other awkward phenomena. Spontaneous combustion. Instant conflagration with no sign of the fire that caused it. Makes a lot of sense. Real Old Testament stuff too. This is holy fire. You could use it for a million explanations out there. The burning bush, who knows? The Children promised us a message from heaven. They surely delivered that."

"And the Shuttle?"

He shrugged. "They're still looking."

Military vehicles, coming and going. Ambulances carrying the dead and injured to hospitals where most of the electronic infrastructure was now burned to a frizzle. There was still power generation on the base, but the city's lines were down, and would remain so for days. There were already reports of how the heat, intense, dry, and devastating, was causing secondary problems among the survivors. It was 120 in the shade and rising, so fierce you felt exhausted just from a couple of minutes under the sun. She'd never liked Vegas, but there was something so foolhardy in the way the place was built up from the desert floor that you couldn't help but admire the spirit that had put it there. Now they had to begin all over again. And Lieberman was right: It was an island of electromagnetism in the middle of an empty wilderness. If Charley Pascal wanted somewhere to use, not just as a sign but as an experiment too, Vegas came custom-designed with the words "guinea pig" printed in bold on its calling card.

"So what's inside this ball you're talking about, Larry?"

He grinned wryly, an expression that said he was on shaky ground. "The best estimates say the temperature could be between fifteen and thirty thousand degrees Kelvin, with a pressure of ten to twenty atmospheres. That would explain the violence of the explosion if these things don't decay."

"You're not telling me what causes it."

He shook his head. "I can't. We don't know. This is at the edge of everything we understand."

"Sorry." She wished he didn't look so out of sorts. They needed every smart mind they could get. "I didn't mean to push you into a corner."

"That's okay. What we do know is that it's usually linked to thunderstorms. But not always. The biggest sightings we've had up until now were associated with electrified underwater volcanic dust vents. You get these off Japan. When they erupt, you get balls rising from deep on the ocean bed, through the water and eventually becoming airborne. There's an event recorded back in the thirties where one six meters across came on shore and lasted for two hours. Alternatively . . ."

He was looking up from the computer, waiting for her attention.

"I'm sorry," she said, wondering why she felt the need to talk to Lieberman right then. "I was somewhere else. Alternatively?"

"In 1957 a guy called Arabadzhi came up with a theory that what was really happening was the focusing of radioactive cosmic ray particles. Usually by the thunderstorm."

"Cosmic rays?" Her mouth was dry just thinking about this.

"Precisely."

"If you're right, the Children can skip the thunderstorm and the underwater volcanic vents altogether. What you get, when you focus it, is what we saw. One giant chunk of plasma that decays into the smaller spheres we saw coming out from underneath it."

She tried to remember the details of the plane crash. "Even when the solar storm was weaker, do you think this could have brought down Air Force One? And the other plane?"

"You bet. It was localized."

"And all the telecommunications failures?"

"No. That's different. We were getting that anyway, without Sundog, just on a smaller scale. That's straight electromagnetic bombardment and they make it worse by feeding some data into the white noise. What we saw here . . . I guess this is what happens when they turn the dial that's marked 'destruction' and focus it on one spot."

It was so small. But it was something solid. "We need to warn the people here about the radiation risk."

"You're not going to stop them from going in there just by telling them it's hot. Those guys won't quit until they've got everyone out of that hellhole. Besides, I suspect it's marginal. This thing seems to dissipate pretty quickly."

He was right about their determination. She knew that. Even if there were big yellow radiation signs posted all the way down the Strip they'd still be out there, combing the wrecked hotels and casinos, looking for survivors, not caring about tomorrow.

"All the same, Larry, we need to make people aware of what we think this is. And figure out some way of using that information."

He was still quietly tapping away, with a calm, clinical detachment that she thought she could begin to find annoying. Maybe Levine wasn't playing some deep game by passing over Wolfit for the acting directorship. There was a coolness in the man that was hardly inspirational.

"There's a theory," he said, "that the stuff gets repelled by dead electrical circuits and attracted by live ones, which is the opposite of normal lightning, of course. If that's right, maybe we could channel it. If she attacked cities, we could try to divert it away from key areas."

"You mean turn everything off?"

"Jesus. Not everything. If you did that the only faint electromagnetic current you'd get would be the one you found in living organisms. No, you need to think of ways of focusing it away by leaving some stuff on."

He didn't say it; he didn't have to. They both knew the reports. Of people exploding, being torn apart in thin air. A kind of spontaneous supercombustion. This phenomenon fitted more exactly the longer she thought about it.

"But we can do something. I need Lieberman in with us here. He's got the kind of mind that can get around all this. Get me through to him when you can. And I want to hear about this woman he's found. We're getting somewhere, you know."

"Yeah," he said laconically.

Maybe Wolfit just never got excited, she thought.

"If you want my honest opinion, we're pissing in the wind," he said. "Either the Shuttle knocks Sundog out or we just sit back and burn. Maybe we should be thinking about that second option a little more."

She wished she had the energy to be mad at him. "That's defeatist crap, Larry. You don't think that. I don't think that."

"Scientifically—"

"Let's leave the dialectic, Larry. We don't have time."

"That is a much-misused word," he bristled. "I am merely pointing out the facts. She told us to prepare. Maybe we ought to listen a little."

A quiet man, with an incisive, quick intelligence, she thought. And, in a way, he was right too. There was precious little contingency in the works. "Larry, we've gotten nowhere with the imaging efforts, the FBI is at a dead end with their investigation, and I'll be damned if I'm going to put every last hope we have on the Shuttle. Let's make the most of what we've got. There's got to be some research projects into this subject we can tap into. Get me some experts."

He shook his head. "Most of the research got killed in the cuts in the eighties. I mean, it's understandable. This is pretty peripheral stuff."

"But there is material out there. You're quoting it."

"Sure. And it's old. Like I said, that cosmic ray theory goes back to the fifties."

"There must be someone."

Wolfit nodded in a way she didn't quite understand. "Sort of. I was coming to that."

She sat down next to him and said, "Show me."

He hit the keys. "Back in the early nineties there was some postgrad work done at Berkeley. Basically one guy. Looks like good stuff too, what I can see of it. A lot of the files seem to be missing. We can check but I doubt we're going to pick up more."

"What he says . . . it backs the theory up?"

"Absolutely. A lot of it's pretty basic, but this guy claimed to have reproduced ball lightning in the lab. On demand. He knew the preconditions. He was able to create the stuff. Brave fellow."

She peered into the screen. It was a sea of text and flashing hot links. "This is the man we need, Larry. Get a phone number. Or better still, an address. We'll pull him in right away."

Wolfit peered at her. "No need. I can tell you where he is right now." Then he pulled up the personal Web page. It was old, last updated in April 1998 according to the date on the bottom, and there was precious little there except a few personal details—hobbies: Linux, Goth music, Nordic mythology, and beer—a brief academic résumé, and a photograph. Martin Chalk, looking a lot younger than the ID shot dispatched around the internal net, stared back at them from the screen, wide-eyed, gawky.

"The Children sure picked the right guy," Wolfit said. "Shame he's probably lying fried on some morgue slab out there instead of unraveling this baby for us."

"That's not the issue," she said quickly (sometimes, she thought, maybe she could get the hang of this Operations thing). "Not anymore."

"So what is?"

"He was here. Whether he walked or they pushed him, this guy must have been close to the Children very, very recently. Don't you see, Larry? We don't just know what they're throwing at us now. We know where from too."

42
The Farm

"I don't get it," Lieberman said. But when he listened to Mo's tale and watched the slow, relieved way it came out of her, he realized he did. They all did, he guessed.

They sat in a small private room in the mansion. Mo curled in a big armchair, Lieberman, Irwin, and Bevan around her in a semicircle. Not pushing her at all because they all knew there was no point. Extracting this slender strand inside her called the truth was a delicate operation. It would be so easy to snap the thing and lose it forever.

"No," she replied, and there was no easy way to explain. The past was still hazy to her sometimes. Fleeing a shattered marriage, finding refuge, when the money was about to run out, with the Children in San Diego. These events had a loose, filmy reality. What she remembered most was Daniel Sinclair, and the way his sweet, quiet face turned sour when Annie was born. And his fists. She still flinched when she thought of those. Even Bevan, Lieberman noticed, couldn't rouse the anger to turn on her. Every life had twists and turns. Mo had taken a wrong one, fallen into Charley's arms at some low ebb, when the Children just seemed to make sense. After that, it simply became hard to leave.

The news let her off the hook. The link from NASA was

screaming for attention. They had followed Schulz out to the
control room, sat watching the giant monitor, and felt some
huge wave of relief when Bill Ruffin's friendly face came up on
the screen, grinned at them, and said, "We're there. Apologies
for the delay but this is one big place to hide. Where are our
government friends?"

"Off-line," Schulz said. "We've got some major failure in the
system in Nevada for some reason. They'll be back when they
can, but we can handle this now."

"Suits me," Ruffin agreed, and cued up the external camera
from *Arcadia*. Now they could see Sundog in all her terrible
glory. The satellite sat above the earth like some giant insect.
The sun and the light from below outlined the black, sleek
form of the machine. Lieberman wondered at this collection of
antennae and scanning devices just visible on its underside,
tried to imagine how anyone could believe you could keep the
world at peace by placing this deadly, unstable collection of
toys in the sky above it. And then there was his personal con-
tribution. For years he'd dreamed of seeing the solar wings in
orbit. Now, when the moment finally arrived, it made him feel
ashamed. They looked like the black, equidistant blades of a
giant clover leaf, sucking the invisible energy from the cosmos
and turning it into something dark and deadly.

"How far have you got to run?" Schulz asked.

"Thirty kilometers," Ruffin replied. "We need to cut the engines real soon and drift on in there. If we time it right, we'll be
in EVA within ninety minutes or so, erecting your shade thirty
minutes after that, and taking that thing down within another
hour."

"That's a hell of a long time for an EVA," Lieberman said.
"You sure you can keep the Shuttle in range during that time
without using any power?"

He remembered reading about how the EVA was the most
dangerous part of any mission. There were so many things that
could go wrong: meteorite storms, equipment failure, harness
detachment. That was why you never, ever ventured out into
that big empty space without a solid line between you and the

ship. Once that was cut, you could float anywhere, be lost for good in a matter of minutes.

"Yeah," Ruffin said. "No problem."

Schulz beamed at the monitors. "Great news. What do you need?"

"Nothing right now." Ruffin had the look of a man who needed to get on with his work. "When we get to the EVA stage we'll take a floatcam with us. You can be a second set of eyes. I'd be grateful for that."

"You got it," Lieberman said.

"In the meantime maybe you people should just go and pray a little. No time for that here." Then he cut the call.

Schulz punched some keys, to no avail. "I wish we could get through to Helen. Damn network. Till then we just have to wait."

"We need to talk some more," Bevan said, looking at Mo, and she didn't object. They went into Bennett's vacant office, sat awkwardly at the table, Lieberman next to her, wishing there was something he could do.

"Ask away. I didn't betray you, Michael," she said. "I didn't betray anyone. Except myself. And Annie. Annie most of all."

She reached across the table, touched his hand. "Michael, I'm sorry if I offended you. What happened wasn't what you thought. Not directly anyway. I was scared. When I saw that woman today it was like opening a grave, lifting the lid on a coffin I thought was long buried. I couldn't shake that from my head."

"Yeah," he said, and squeezed her hand, then let it go. "But you see the problem?"

She stared at the table. Bevan had turned on a video recorder, taping all this for further analysis. Schulz looked miserable again; the news from the Shuttle had lost its potency. Outside, the night was alive with the buzz of insects, frantic in the close, humid air. And she was relieved, he thought. After the initial despair, the end of this deception gave her some kind of deliverance. Deceit and pretense didn't come naturally to her. Shedding this false skin was welcome, even if she knew that, in the end, it was bound to lead to some new kind of pain.

Schulz stared at the table, not wanting to look her in the face.

"You of all people, Mo. I trusted you. I thought we could make something permanent for you here."

"Me 'of all people,' " she said, smiling. "What sort of people do you think should get involved in things like Gaia? Crazy ones? Criminals?"

"Inadequate people," Bevan said quickly.

"Jeez, that sure opens things up a little. What do you think the waiting list is for that particular club?" Lieberman wondered aloud. "One million? Two? Get real."

She touched his hand. "Don't, Michael. It's okay. I don't mind. I don't expect you to understand. I don't want your condolences. I don't expect your forgiveness."

He poured himself a glass of water. Until Ruffin called them back into the game, there was nothing to do but wait. "Lots of marriages get broken, Mo. It's a long way from there to Charley."

"You need the context. Ask Irwin."

"Me?" Schulz answered, offended. "I don't know."

She shook her head. "But you do. You just didn't take that route. Back in the early nineties, Daniel started to live inside that damn computer. The Web was real to him, more real to him than me and Annie. I thought that I could rekindle if I joined him there. And it's so . . . enveloping."

"Yeah," he admitted. "Okay. I know."

"Is this some dweeb secret that gets to be shared among the rest of us?" Lieberman asked.

"Hey," Schulz said, "just take my—our—words on this, will you? If you grew up in the California geek community during the nineties you knew someone who lost it. This job we do, the way we do it, you can get eaten up by these things. It can swallow you."

Lieberman listened, eyes closed, feeling dog-tired, only half taking in the words. He was thinking about the day and this tangled jumble of images in his head: fire on the mountain, the sky ablaze. And Mo, naked, her limbs entwined with his, the hot, fevered focus between them, the way that kind of ecstasy could steal your very thoughts. He wanted to stop up his ears, he wanted to sleep. All the time he couldn't stop thinking about what was happening elsewhere. Sara leaving the hospital, going out into a world that was on the brink of chaos. This strange silence out of Vegas. Bill Ruffin and his crew floating in the emptiness of space, praying some jerry-built concoction of fabric and foam would save the day.

And somewhere, behind everything, Charley, no longer naive Charley, the genius with the appearance of some airhead bimbo. Charley with the crew cut, some cancer eating away inside her head, and this tragic, gnawing conviction that her own personal dissolution was somehow coupled, irrevocably, irretrievably, with that of the world.

"You spent two years with these people," he said. "Two years in which they went from being just a bunch of ecofreaks out onto the fringe to this . . . black place they are now. Why didn't you leave earlier?"

"Dumb question, Michael. I didn't leave Daniel. And he gave me nothing. No love. No affection. No respect. If I didn't leave him, why would I leave the Children, who gave me all those things? And more."

"But you must have known. . . ."

"Known what? I left there a year ago. They knew I was restless. They didn't like having Annie around after a while. She was the only kid in the place. And they told me to come here. Get a job in the project. Just stay below the parapet, talk to them when I wanted to. It was our chance to escape."

Schulz nodded. "And that's what you did. You did it, Mo."

"I came here. Yes. But I didn't know they had this in mind."

Lieberman looked at her and hoped for an honest answer. "And if you had known?"

She laughed. "I would have come anyway. Of course I would. Don't you understand what the power is in these things? Where the strength lies? It's in the closeness you have. That's all, and that's everything."

"Like a family," Lieberman said.

"Yes." She smiled, and she did look serene, she was beautiful that night. "Exactly like a family. But a real family. One that doesn't abandon you because it's too busy or finds something else to do. One that doesn't judge you because of who you are.

One that gives you love and support and understanding whatever the circumstances. How could you betray that? How could
you even think of it?"

"Yeah," Bevan grunted. "And so, when you found out we
had someone inside, you called them, E-mailed, or something,
and look what happened. That nice, kind family killed the one
person we had inside who could have led us to them."

"*No!*"

Bevan raised his eyebrows. "You expect me to believe that?"

"Believe what you like. All I can do is tell you what happened. I left San Diego a year ago. We traveled through Europe
first—they gave me some money and said there was no hurry—
and I got here in January. It didn't take long to persuade Irwin
to give me a job."

"No," Schulz confirmed. "Good Unix people aren't easy to
find here. I guess I should have latched on to the coincidence."

"And when you got here," Bevan continued, "you contacted
them when? How?"

"Once. Just after I arrived."

"You're kidding me."

"Once. By phone. To the house in San Diego, reverse
charge. Check it with the phone company. They wanted to
know who was working here. And if the project got into problems, that was when I was supposed to get in touch on a regular basis. I was meant to E-mail them, then they'd get back to
me with a phone number. Charley said she wanted me to be
their eyes and ears. She never said why. I never asked. I called
once and then forgot about them. Until this began."

"And we're supposed to believe that?" Bevan asked sourly.

She shook her head. "You still don't get it. Like I said, prox-
imity was everything. When I was there, I was a part of the
Children. When Annie and I were here, all that started to fade.
It seemed less important. There were other things in my life.
Annie. This idea of building something for us both, leaving all
that dreadful time behind. I thought . . ."

Lieberman wanted to be somewhere else, not watching this
performance. We all reach crossroads, he told himself. We all
take the wrong turning sometimes.

"I thought I'd never hear of Gaia again. I didn't want to. Just one call and they had no way of contacting me. They didn't want one; they said it would be unsafe. I forgot about them. I started to think about us. About how we moved on from all this."

Schulz's eyes lit up. "Hey! We got company." The lights were winking on the terminal. Out of nowhere the screen came alive. Helen Wagner gazed back at them. Lieberman thought she looked exhausted, a little battle-weary and crabby too.

"You had a rough time over there?" he asked. "We couldn't pick up anything through the network. You heard about the Shuttle?"

"It's bad here," she replied. "I'll tell you about that later, but I think we now know what Charley can throw at us. And yeah . . . I spoke to Bill Ruffin. That's the best news I've heard all day. It doesn't mean we let up anywhere else, though. The important thing right now is to close the net on these people. You're Mrs. Sinclair?"

Mo nodded.

"I'm Helen Wagner from the CIA. I know you think we're the enemy or something but you have to forget that right now. These people have just blitzed Las Vegas. We have a lot of casualties here and I want to make sure the Children don't have the chance to do this all over again. We need your help. We need your cooperation. Frankly, I'm beyond threats. I don't care what's happened in the past. If you throw your lot in with us now, I'll see if I can help you out. You just have to take my word on that."

"I'll do what I can."

"That's excellent. We require names."

"I can give you names. Joe Katayama. Anthony Tatton. Billy Jo Surtees—"

"Good. Bevan can get a list of those later. Most of all we need some clue of where they are now. Can you help us there?"

Mo shook her head. "I wish I could. They were in San Diego when I left."

"How were you supposed to get in touch with them?"

"Just on the standard E-mail address for their public Web site. Nothing secret. You must know what that is."

"We do," Helen sighed.

Mo Sinclair shook her head. "I'm sorry. Like I said, I thought I'd left all this behind, and once they stopped hearing from me I guessed—I hoped—they wouldn't contact me again."

"Mo," Lieberman said, reaching out, touching her hand. "Try. Didn't they even talk about moving somewhere else?"

She paused. "Sometimes. I don't really recall."

"Work on it. Did they talk about Nevada?"

She tried to remember. It was like opening the doors on a cabinet she'd forgotten: Everything inside was dusty and distant. "Perhaps."

One memory. "They said something about a farm. I remember that. Joe and Charley were talking about a farm that interested them and they thought about giving it a new name. They really wanted a farm. Isolation, I guess. And it was an odd name."

He held her hand. "Like what?"

Mo shook her head. "It was strange. Something like—I know this sounds stupid—Yogurt Farm."

"In America, Mo, that is *yo*gurt."

"I know. That's why it sounded odd."

"Yeah." Lieberman grinned. "Charley hated yogurt. But she had good taste in music. How about Yasgur's Farm?"

She smiled. "That sounds about right. But what is it?"

"Stop making me feel old. Woodstock, 1969."

Helen quoted on the screen, " 'We are stardust. We are golden. And we've got to get ourselves back to the garden.' "

"My, a lady from the CIA who knows Joni Mitchell too. Some week this is."

"It fits," Helen said. "So somewhere around here they have a place they've called Yasgur's Farm. And unless Bill Ruffin does his job, we've got under twelve hours to find it. You people think some more. I have to brief the President. He's on his way."

The screen went blank. No one wanted to speak.

"The President in Vegas . . ." Lieberman said finally. "It must be bad."

Schulz fiddled with the news channels now coming back

onto the monitor. "It is." Pictures of wrecked buildings, people in pain being rushed away on gurneys, panic, chaos.

"Is that what Charley really wanted, Mo?" Schulz asked. "Can you believe that?"

She looked at the pictures on the screen and shook her head. "Not the Charley I met. But I don't think that Charley is there anymore. This is a different person, and like I said, once you have that closeness, people just follow. All the way."

43

The Cambridge Mandate

Las Vegas, 2051 UTC

Tim Clarke insisted the Air Force provide him with supersonic transport to Vegas as soon as the severity of the attack became apparent. When he bawled enough, and looked as if he wouldn't stop bawling, they put him in the number two seat of an F15 and did as they were told. He was talking to people in the steaming heat of the emergency shelters set up on the city edge before Helen even knew he'd arrived. By the time she caught up with him, after an urgent, disturbing drive from Nellis through the deserted and wrecked Vegas streets, he'd left the camps of shocked, distressed people and gone to see the damage for himself.

Clarke was walking down the Strip, by the Flamingo and Caesar's, a bunch of Secret Service people following mutely in his wake, soaked in sweat, Graeme Burnley among them. Helen told the driver to stop and wait for her, then caught up with the gaggle walking behind Clarke.

Burnley stared at her when she arrived. He looked lost. "This is one hell of a bad idea. The guy insisted on it but I'm telling you now we shouldn't be here. God knows what the radiation level is. Whether we've still got crazies in these buildings. Or what good this is doing at all when we've got bigger decisions to make. Also"—his face was red and soaked in perspiration—"I wish to hell he'd remember that the rest of us don't fit the superman tag. You wouldn't catch me dead walking out here at this time of year, even when the weather was halfway normal. This is like marching through a furnace and it's as if he hardly notices."

She watched Clarke tread down the middle of the deserted road, taking in the devastation on both sides. Half the Mirage was burned out, some smoke still rising from the smoldering shell. Fire crews stood back, watching the giant building from a safe distance. It looked bad. All you could hope to do in this kind of situation, she guessed, was evacuate as many people as possible. And right along the Strip, stretching away into the distance, the story seemed the same: rising smoke, damaged buildings that stood like rotten teeth against the clear blue sky, and emergency services idling away in the deserted road.

"I wouldn't worry about radiation," she said. "We did some tests immediately. It's flash energy. If you get it, you know about it, but five minutes later it's pretty much gone, down to a near-acceptable level. At least with this attack it is."

"Great. That still doesn't explain why we're here. Jesus, we don't even have any film crew to get some mileage out of it."

She just looked at him.

"Okay, okay, I'm sorry. That was an awful thing to say. And pointless too. I think the idea we can news-manage this one into some nice, comfortable place is disappearing fast."

"I guess so," she said, and watched Clarke ambling slowly along, taking everything in. This was the second day of his presidency. She guessed someone in that position could only move in one of two ways: get bigger or get smaller. And she didn't have any doubts about which direction Clarke intended to take.

"Helen?" the President said, turning around to look at the little group behind him.

"Sir?"

"You're okay," he said, smiling. "That's good. Come and walk with me. And don't worry about the traffic."

Burnley shot her a caustic glance, and she strode up to Clarke. On his call they picked up the pace and put a little extra space between them and the followers.

"Hell of a place for a private conversation," the President said. "Walking down the middle of the Strip at four in the afternoon."

"If you want this to be private, sir."

He groaned. "Jesus. You people are so stiff it must make it hard getting up in the morning. So? What happened?"

"She turned up the controls. Focused it all somehow. We wondered what we'd get if she managed to pull everything together. Now we have the answer."

"But what caused this?"

"We're working on the fine detail, sir. Think of it as a combination of fire, a powerful burst of radiation, and some odd electromagnetic effects too. A cocktail, if you like."

"It looks like a bomb site, Helen."

"And it is, of a kind. Except that some of the injuries go beyond mere blast effects."

Clarke stared at her with that look she was coming to recognize, the one that said: *Tell me now, because we don't let up until you come clean.*

"It looks like we have some form of spontaneous combustion, sir. Of people. I'd like to leave it at that. For now."

"Jesus . . ."

"And while I'm dealing out the bad news, I should say that this is only a foretaste of what she'll have tomorrow. When we roll up to the zenith, the energy out there will be much greater than we have at the moment. This could be just a sideshow compared with what's to come. Today she burned a track a mile or so wide down the city. What she can throw at us when the cycle peaks will probably be four, five, even ten times that magnitude."

Treasure Island was coming up on the left. The two ships in the man-made lake outside were gutted, fire-eaten wrecks, half-sunk in the lagoon.

"And this was meant to be an instrument of deterrence?" Clarke wondered.

She shook her head. "No one seriously suggested that, sir. Not when you got into the SDI papers in any detail. We knew what we were building all along."

He kicked a stray Coke can with some force. "Bull. Some people knew. But you didn't. Your predecessor didn't."

"I guess not. I'm sorry, sir. If there's something you think I should be doing that I'm not . . ."

"Forget it. I'm just a grouchy old bastard sometimes. You ask anyone who was in the Gulf with me. Amazed the papers didn't pick up on that one when I became running mate. Maybe that was one way being black helped. I mean, what else did they have to say?"

"That's not fair. Or worthy of you. Sir."

"No," he said, dark eyes shining right into her. "And thank you for pointing that out."

"This meeting you've called . . ."

"Yeah. Thirty minutes to go. I know."

"What's the purpose of it? We have as much work under way as we can and the lines of reporting are in place. Also I think we are starting to get somewhere. From what I hear, you have everybody in attendance. The chiefs of staff, us, the Bureau, these federal emergency people Levine keeps talking about. More people from Washington than I ever knew existed."

He was staring at the shell of the big Treasure Island casino. "Did a fund-raiser there last year. Boy, was that fun. Those guys never expected to see me coming back as President. Or in circumstances like this."

"Sir. May I say something?"

"You don't sound like the kind of person who's easy to stop."

"You have to lose the race issue. It could cloud your judgment."

"My judgment."

"Yes."

He nodded, and she felt a little foolish. What was going through Clarke's mind just then was nothing that simple or visible. "Maybe you're right. And maybe not. Anyway, you asked a good question. Why are all these people coming here? You ever hear of the Cambridge Mandate?"

"No."

"Don't feel ashamed. I hadn't either, and it *is* supposed to be a secret. But I've been doing a lot of reading recently. Mainly because I don't like being surrounded by people who know a whole lot more about what's going on than me. The Cambridge Mandate goes back to the Kennedy administration. Bay of Pigs. All that nice part of our history when a lot of people in Washington suddenly got real scared that nuclear war was around the corner. Kennedy was in Cambridge at the time, which is where it got its name. What it did was pull together all the civil defense plans that had been put in place over the years and put them into a rounded whole. A neat, tidy set of executive orders that you can employ when the occasion arises and throw as tight a grip around this country as you can get. Martial law by any other name. And mark the timing of this. The Cambridge Mandate was designed to be used before the bombs started to fall. They were all Boy Scouts back then: *Be prepared*."

"Is this still around?"

"Oh yes. Updated and approved by every one of my predecessors, including Rollinson, not that I knew anything about it, of course. Bill always did think he was immortal."

She nodded. "You have to have something like that. Even with the Cold War over. I didn't realize it was quite so tightly organized, but I rather expected something would be in place."

"Sure, and that's what these guys are bringing down for me to sign. They don't want to wait to see what happens with the Shuttle. Their advice is we should put up the barricades now, take out the current Federal Defense Act, and tie the nation up nice and tightly this very minute."

"This bothers you?"

Clarke looked behind them, saw the distance they were keeping from the Secret Service people. It was a false security, he knew that. If they wanted, they could pick up the conversation anyway. "Of course it bothers me. Once that goes into place, this country is to all intents and purposes under a form of martial law. We take control of the telecommunications networks, install mandatory censorship in the news media. All existing forms of government are suspended and we work on the framework of the civil emergency network, which, in case you didn't know, is ostensibly answerable to local county officials and, in the end, state governors. Hell, I even have to hand over a whole piece of my powers to some new federal emergency council on the grounds that there's no other way to counterbalance the loss of democratic control elsewhere. This is a big thing. Every last detail is there, right down to the disposal of human remains. And it's open-ended. Think about that."

She tried to imagine what this world would be like. What the alternative might be. "In the short term, it might be a good thing. We don't need any distractions right now. We have to track those people down, not get pulled off-line by civil unrest issues."

"Yeah. I know. But what worries me is this: How often do you see people voluntarily handing power back these days? If the Children do get to cause us some damage, how long is it before we return to some kind of normalcy? And if they don't, what happens then? Do we all tear up the piece of paper and go back to what we were doing? As everyone keeps telling me, this Pascal woman is smart. Isn't it possible we're just playing into her hands? By treating this as the end of the world, maybe we prompt the sort of response she's trying to get."

"Sir, if you are going to impose some kind of order, you need to do it before the emergency if that's possible."

"Yeah. You're the millionth person to make that point to me today."

"It's a question of contingency, Mr. President."

"Really? You're right, up to a point. But think about it. In 1961 you could walk state troopers down the street and tell people to stay indoors and believe every word Walter Cronkite said on the one TV channel that was still broadcasting. You think that's a possibility now? Or is some guy going to come at you with a gun and decide to take advantage of the situation and do what he wanted to do all along? Or post some crap on the Net that scares the living shit out of everyone—and there's no way we can close that thing down entirely, believe me, not short of cutting off the power supply to the entire nation. Think of some of the right-wing crazies out there. You can imagine what they'd be saying. We've got a nigger in the White House who's taken our birthright away. We'd have so-called independent states springing up everywhere the moment they heard that Washington was taking over everything and running it through whoever we felt like. And like I keep asking, in a way, isn't that what these Gaia people want?"

They were at a big empty crossroads. No people. No cars. Just barren roads running off into the flat desert nowhere, and the husks of burned-out, shattered buildings. She shivered, even in the intense heat. What Clarke was talking about gave her pause for thought. "I don't know, sir. That's your call."

"Oh yeah, I'm aware of that. This is one big switch we're talking about throwing. So tell me. Is the Shuttle going to work? And if it doesn't, are we going to catch these people some other way?"

She thought about Yasgur's Farm and the woman in Mallorca, Martin Chalk and fireballs raining from the sky. And, more than anything, about three astronauts edging their way toward Sundog in orbit above them.

"You bet. The Shuttle can do it. If that fails for some reason, we'll get them ourselves. They're here. Everything points to that. This was as much a test site for them as a warning for the rest of us. They're watching. And we will track them down. I can't guarantee you this will blow over without some damage. Lieberman thinks we would probably be in line for that even without the Children. But we will find them. We will put a lid on this thing."

And nearly added: *Trust me.*

Clarke smiled at her and said, "Well, in that case, I think you've made up my mind."

Twenty minutes later, Helen Wagner followed mutely behind Graeme Burnley as they entered the conference room at Nellis. Clarke walked in, looked at the assembly of suits and uniforms, looked at the pile of executive orders awaiting his signature, and said, "Gentlemen, you can file these papers for another time. We're here to beat these people. Not give in to them."

He listened to the murmur run around the room, wondered who would be the first to object. Much to his surprise, it was

Graeme Burnley, who laid his pen on his notepad and sighed, like a man at the end of his tether.

"Mr. President. This is your decision. You're the chief of the Armed Forces. What you decide, we will do. But I have to warn you—"

"Warn me, Graeme?" Clarke replied, half-amazed. "Is that what I'm paying you for?"

"I'm paid to tell things how I see them. What you're suggesting, this wait-and-see idea, it runs counter to the advice of everyone. We have discussed this and there really is—"

"Mr. President," Ben Levine interrupted, "we're twelve hours away from what could be the worst global disaster imaginable. We need to act now. Not wait until the last minute."

Clarke watched the men in uniform nodding. "Really, Mr. Levine?"

"Yes, sir. This is plain practical preparation. And we're all of one mind on this."

"No we're not," Dan Fogerty interjected. "None of you even asked my mind. You just took it for granted I'd go along. The President's right. This is premature. We're accepting defeat before we've even given the game a good run."

"Twelve hours, Dan," Levine objected. "After that we could lose everything we've got to get the message over. TV. The phone system. Everything. You want to try putting some order into this country after that?"

Helen looked at Levine and knew, from the stony certainty on his face, that he wanted no interruptions.

"No, sir."

Every face in the room looked at her. She didn't even try to read Levine's. Some bridges needed burning. "That just isn't correct. Even if we don't manage to intervene before the zenith, we've still got some time. The best guess we have is that the zenith is close to midday UTC. That's six A.M. in Washington. It's not going to get hot enough or high enough to give the Children the potential for major damage in the U.S. until the sun's moved around a little, say four hours or so. We don't have to rush into anything right now."

"Thank you, Miss Wagner," Clarke said. "I hear what you all

say and I agree. My decision is we wait, gentleman. We wait and we work. Now, is somebody going to tell me how we find those people out there?"

Dan Fogerty raised his eyebrows at Levine, who was going red across the table, then shuffled the report in front of him, stood up, and began to speak.

DAY THREE
JUNE 21
SOLSTICE

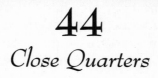

44
Close Quarters

Equatorial orbit, altitude 20315 kilometers above the Pacific, 0320 UTC

"Nice view," Bill Ruffin said. He and Mary Gallagher had just left the ship, attached to it by the long umbilical tethering line that snaked out in their wake. They had enough oxygen to last three hours, enough tools, as David Sampson had put it, to build a damn space station if they wanted. Sundog hung in front of them looking dead and still and gigantic. The earth sat below, radiant and blue. A few cloud systems drifted across the Pacific like stray feathers caught in a tantalizingly slow wind.

Ruffin had been in space enough to have gained an intimate feel for his position in relation to the land below. You couldn't measure locations in conventional terms here, you had to depend on technicalities like inclination and azimuth to define where you were. They found Sundog locked into an equatorial orbit that was just unpredictable enough to avoid easy detection. But to Ruffin there was an easier way to think of this place, and the analogy always came to him, on every EVA. If he reached into an imaginary pocket on his space suit and dropped an imaginary nickel, an imaginary gravity, unaffected by the very real atmosphere beneath him, would take it down in a dead straight line to hit the face of the earth. In this case around two hundred miles west and a touch north of the

Gilbert Islands. They had come across Sundog when the satellite was poised above the gigantic empty blue waters of the Pacific, and that was perfect. He didn't want Charley trying to mess with the thing while they got on with their work. That way the Children might spot some disruption in the power curve and start looking for a reason. This was the down time on the satellite's flight around the world. There was no one to burn for an hour or two, until Tokyo came up on the horizon. They had room to get this right.

"Forget the view," Schulz said in Ruffin's earpiece. "We're getting real close to this thing now and I want you to make damn sure she doesn't hear us."

"No dissenting voices here," Mary Gallagher said. She peered at Ruffin. In space, buried deep within their bulky suits, they looked like awkward intruders, creatures out of their element. That part always scared her a little. The Shuttle was like flying, a rush of adrenaline at takeoff and landing, and a lot of routine in between. EVA was always tension, from the moment you stepped outside the ship to the point you got back and breathed its dank, stale air again. There was so much to go wrong in this empty, bleak place, and from what she'd seen this was likely to be the longest space walk in the brief history of the science. It felt deeply odd to be doing this under the command of people she didn't even know. NASA control at Houston was now in the back seat. Once the satellite was in their sights, they passed the entire command process over to La Finca and left it to them to take the thing down.

"You got this?" she said, and flicked the floatcam on. The three-foot-high round cylinder with the rotating lens moved gently in front of them.

"Yeah," Schulz replied.

"Good," Ruffin said, "you have control of the thing. We got enough junk to contend with."

The engineers had done a fine job with Lieberman's blueprint for the shades. Packed into four compact tubes was a tightly rolled web of rigging with gas pump canisters sewn inside. Expanded, they could cover the solar panel wings of the satellite with room to spare. Compressed, they looked like a set of business equipment being hauled along for an exhibition. The canisters followed in his wake as Ruffin floated gently toward the satellite, propelled by nothing more than the momentum of his departure from the Shuttle hull. The ground crew had ruled out the use of any small impetus devices to let them navigate the gap between the ship and Sundog. Something like that could have triggered the defense mechanism. So instead he and Gallagher had just taken aim, pushed themselves gently off into space, and waited as they floated the four hundred meters or so toward the big black sails. It was hit or miss, but there really was no choice. And it looked as if they were going to get it right the first time around, which was good news, even though everyone had factored in three attempts. Ruffin was glad they weren't going to have to reel themselves in along the line for a second go. He shared Mary Gallagher's enthusiasm for bringing the EVA to a rapid close.

"Remind me about the superstructure of this thing," he said. They were midway between the Shuttle and the satellite and, in his estimation, would probably be able to touch the thing in under two minutes. He thought he knew this by heart anyway, but some reassurance wouldn't go amiss. "What can I touch? What can't I touch?"

"Okay," Schulz's voice said. "There are no alarm systems on the exterior. We assumed that the only physical visitors we were likely to get were friendly ones. So, in theory, you can touch what you like."

"In theory," Mary Gallagher echoed.

"Precisely," Schulz said. "What will trigger a response is if you fire up anything with much of a power surge. The Shuttle's down to standby, right?"

"Affirmative," Sampson said at the helm of *Arcadia*.

"We can confirm that too," the NASA controller added.

"Nice to know you're still there," Ruffin said to the team back home. "When do we go back onto your work schedule?"

"When that thing's dead, Bill," the familiar voice said. "Then we get you three out of there real quick and back home for a few beers."

"Done," Ruffin said. "So I can touch any part of this thing I want when we get close to it?"

"Provided you stay away from the earth side," Schulz confirmed.

Ruffin peered at the approaching hunk of metal. Close up it looked positively threatening, a big black mass of aluminum and silicon. They were now aimed almost dead center at its heart. If they continued on their present course, he ought to be able to reach out and grab one of the giant wings, steady himself and Gallagher too, get back in line with the satellite, and move on to their next task, assembling the shades.

"Don't touch the panels themselves," Lieberman added quickly.

"Hey, Professor. Why might that be?"

"They're fragile. If you hold too hard, the silicon could break, and that will surely do something to the power flow. Maybe it could notice."

"Understood," Ruffin confirmed, and rolled the floatcam in front of him. "You see where we're headed?" Sundog was closing fast and soon he would have to make a decision about which piece of it was going to stop their movement, prevent them floating right through and over to the earth side of the system and, for sure, triggering a response. "You guys see the support strut for the panel closest to me?"

"Got it," Schulz and Lieberman said simultaneously.

"Unless you indicate otherwise, I intend to make a grab for that. Once I have it, Gallagher here can slow herself down by grabbing hold of me. Then we get on with erecting this sunshade."

There was a pause on the line. "Looks good," Schulz said quietly.

"Here we go," Ruffin announced to no one in particular. The floatcam was probably broadcasting this, he guessed. Somewhere down on the earth they were watching these two unwieldy figures in oversized white suits floundering around in space, trying to hook themselves onto a hunk of metal that held a black butterfly wing pointing back at the sun. The fingers of his big glove closed around the aluminum strut and Bill Ruffin was amazed to discover that, for one short moment afterward, his eyes had closed of their own accord.

"Sir?" Schulz's voice said out of nowhere.

"We're here," Ruffin announced, and knew they'd be hollering and clapping in those distant places just then. He fastened a temporary line to the structure of the satellite, then looked across at Mary Gallagher. She had grabbed hold of his sleeve, steadied herself, and was already working on the canisters.

"Point the floatcam at the base of the satellite," Schulz ordered. "The central section facing out towards you."

Ruffin peered at the flat end of Sundog, like the bottom of some gigantic beer can, and moved the camera around so that it was in view. "What am I looking for?"

"One big single LED. It should look green."

Ruffin peered at the metallic plate. The light was there, all right. And it was green too. "Got it."

"We see it too," Schulz said. "Green means Sundog is primed and active. When the system goes to standby, that light should go to orange. Don't go anywhere near the damn thing then. Wait till it's red. That's total shutdown. It's dead bar a couple of backup circuits."

"Understood," Ruffin replied.

"Also," Schulz added, "if you trigger some kind of response mechanism, all the defensive weaponry is behind that plate. It has to retract before it can deploy. We built it like that so no one could see what was in there. If you see something moving, we got problems."

"Right," Ruffin said dryly. "We'll know when to run and hide."

It was a two-person job to erect each shade, and they'd been through this as much as they could down on the ground. The panels were made of fine, silver-colored fabric, tightly packed into the container. On each side of the wing there was a ribbed, airtight tube with a small pressurized canister of oxygen built into the base. The idea was to point the device away from Sundog, back to the Shuttle, hit the activate button on each canister simultaneously, and watch the shade unravel slowly. When each was erected, it was attached to the aluminum centerpiece and drawn into position.

Ruffin checked on the position of the floatcam and watched Gallagher finish the final portion of the central strut. "You people down below got a good view from there?"

"Yeah," Lieberman's voice said.

"Here we go. . . ." He and Gallagher nodded at each other, hit the button on their side of the canister, and watched the shade unfurl slowly in space, like the wing of a silver butterfly that had just emerged from the chrysalis. When it reached its full length, the two ribbed channels that fed the gas along the edge of the wing met on the semicircular end. The final result, Ruffin suddenly realized, was going to look like one of those old-fashioned ceiling fans that were now back in fashion in fancy hotels hunting for some period appeal. Slowly, not missing a single detail, they fastened the wing to one spoke of the circular centerpiece.

"Perfect," Ruffin muttered, and looked at the Shuttle. It was getting farther away than he'd expected. The long lifeline linking them to the exterior was now a low ellipsis. Sampson had done his best to make the drifting spacecraft match the progress of Sundog, but the limitations imposed on them made it hard. The two were just slightly out of kilter, drifting apart. Ruffin pushed the thought to the back of his head and got back to work on the other panels. Gallagher was ahead of him already and he could guess what was going on in her head. She'd seen the line paying out too.

It took thirty minutes to erect all four wings of the shade system and attach them to the centerpiece. By that stage the thing looked so much like a giant fan from some Mexican flophouse that Ruffin thought he could taste cold margarita at the back of his throat. The ground people had kept commendably quiet throughout. There was, he guessed, nothing you could say.

He admired the big shape floating out between them and *Arcadia* now, and knew it would only take a few more minutes to maneuver into position, then wait patiently for Sundog to cool down and lapse into silence before starting the final part of the job. The line back to the ship was close to taut, had a slowly diminishing sag to its length.

"We're ready to put this thing in place," Ruffin announced to everyone who cared to listen. "But before we do, we need to break the link with the ship. This thing's drifting too strong for us."

He nodded at Mary Gallagher and, in unison, they unhooked the clasps on the slim white nylon cord from their suits and let the line float away from them, out into the empty blackness of space, severing their one possible point of contact with a piece of the planet they called home.

Bill Ruffin took one last look at the blue emptiness of the Pacific beneath them and said, "Let's get this done."

45
Strategy

Three hours earlier Larry Wolfit had been playing with the imaging system in the makeshift headquarters of McCarran when there was a commotion at the door and a bunch of people walked in, Tim Clarke at their head.

Wolfit gulped audibly, stood up, and said, "Mr. President."

"Yeah, yeah," Clarke replied, waving his hand at the team of people in the room. This was both Bureau and Agency now, trying to work alongside each other, and if the breakthrough was going to come anywhere, he guessed this was where it would be. "Let's cut straight to the quick, shall we? None of us can rely on the Shuttle alone, and even if that bet does come off we still need these people reined in. That job seems to have fallen to you. All I want is the short demo, a picture of where we are."

Wolfit looked at Helen Wagner, who stood behind the President, with Dan Fogerty, Dave Barnside, and Ben Levine making up the rear. She nodded.

"This is a Bureau operation, Mr. President," he said cautiously. "I don't want to tread on anyone's toes."

"Larry," Fogerty said, "this is your toy, and it's your people back in Langley who are pushing the buttons. You kick off, okay?"

"Sure," Wolfit replied, and sat down, swiveled the chair back to the screen. Clarke walked over, stood at his back, and stared at the digitized aerial photography on the monitor. "Where's this?"

"Northeast Nevada, sir, close to the Utah state line. The town you can see there"—Wolfit reached forward and pointed to a cluster of light on the monochrome picture—"is Wendover, smack on the border. If I pull out a little we'll see Wells to the west. That's I-80 joining them. You see the continuous line?"

"Sure," Clarke said. "When I said demo I didn't exactly mean the real basic stuff."

Helen intervened. "What the President is trying to ask, Larry, is how are we doing?"

"Not so good. You understand anything about how this works, sir?"

"No."

"Well, what we have here is a whole set of digitized aerial photographs of the area. We got these from the Army, which has this kit too, but since we wrote the software it made sense for us to run the job. These are satellite pictures, good for a pretty sharp image of anything down to about six feet or so in size. The resolution is amazing, but that makes it all a little harder, of course, since there's so much data to process before you can find what you want."

"That I do understand," Clarke said.

"Right. So the way we try to shortcut things is we produce a digital profile of what we're looking for. You choose the item, then the computer goes off to see if it can find a match. Nothing's that precise, of course. So we have to have some control of the tolerance. I'll show you."

He worked at the keyboard. The map changed in contrast, a little hourglass came up on the screen, and four newly painted circles appeared. "This is what we get if we just run a straight match against the system. That"—he pointed at a circle outside the town of Wendover—"is an electricity substation. As luck would not have it, Nevada Power and Light favors a substation design that kicks off our dome algorithm pretty neatly. The same goes of this hit beneath it. The other two we can rule out too. One is a rodeo ring at a dude ranch—we can see that just by drilling down into the image from a standard daylight view. The other is a water tower—been there for years. We can cross-reference this into the local planning database pretty easily and see if there's a listing for the object. So when we rule those out, we need to degrade the match. Then see what happens."

Wolfit pressed a single key. A rash of new circles appeared on the screen. "That's just a one percent degradation. Gives us no fewer than nineteen new objects to investigate. And bear in mind we're looking at a mere hundred square miles or so of the target area here. We've been told to look at a square running five hundred miles on each side. That's a quarter of a million square miles, all told. So imagine replicating just this one percent degradation there. Then look what happens when we go to two. . . ."

He hit the keyboard again. The screen was covered in circles. "Then three." It was now virtually impossible to see the underlying geographical features of the image. Overlapping circles ran everywhere.

"If I move a couple of percents beyond that, we're going to lock up the system. We don't have the byte power to crunch those numbers. And even if we did, we don't possess the manpower to analyze the number of hits. I've got every last person I can find working on this back at Langley, plus we've co-opted the imaging departments of the Air Force and the Army too. But it's still a long process. Where we are now is that we've eliminated just about every one of the initial hits in around three-quarters of the target area—and most of them are those damn power substations or some preexisting water installation that comes through on the planning records. If we hit lucky, we just haven't got there yet and she's sitting somewhere in the unsifted area. If we don't, then in thirty minutes or so I push that one percent button and we start to pray."

Clarke looked at Ben Levine. "This is clever stuff, but it's not going to get us there."

"No, Mr. President. That was one reason why we put those papers in front of you, sir."

"Forget the damn papers, Levine. You heard what I said on that subject and that's that. If you don't find these people using this nice billion-dollar toy of yours, how do you propose to do it?"

Fogerty stepped in. "That's a Bureau issue, sir. I thought I'd make that point before Ben here did. We're running checks on everything we can think of. Existing databases, local police records, credit card companies, hotel bookings, anything where someone might have kept details of an address."

"And?"

"This isn't rocket science," Larry Wolfit said. "I can show you just as easily as any of the other guys. See . . ."

A new image came up on his screen. "This is a central database of all property records listed in the state of Nevada. We put in a keyword search for 'Yasgur's Farm'—and we do have fuzzy logic built in here so it would come up if they'd changed the spelling slightly—and what do we get? Nothing. Same goes for Arizona and Utah. We got the power companies, the phone companies, the water companies, Internet service providers, rental car firms . . . there's scarcely anyone who doesn't sell or monitor something that we can't tap into. Nothing. Not a single close match. Maybe they do use this Yasgur's Farm term themselves, but my guess is it's some kind of code word, not a real name. Geeks love that sort of stuff. And it doesn't help us a bit."

"What about the people?" Fogerty asked. "Are we still getting a blank there?"

"Afraid so. These must be decent, clean-living folk. No parking tickets, no speeding fines. Nothing that's put their record into any database we can find since they left San Diego with not a forwarding address in sight."

"Shit," Clarke said quietly.

Levine's voice broke the silence. "Sir?"

"Yes?"

"We can still go back on those orders. I don't like the idea any more than you, but if all we have is the Shuttle, we're cutting this fine."

Clarke's eyes gleamed in the half-light of the room. "If you push me once more on that subject, mister, I'll relieve you of your post here and now. Understood?"

Levine nodded and said nothing. Helen stared at Barnside, wondering if this was crazy, wondering if she really was the only one who could see this. Clarke turned to go.

"There is one other possibility," she said.

The President looked at her, some sourness in his eyes. "Well?"

"We know this has to be a remote location, right?"

"For sure," Larry Wolfit said, watching the screen, playing with the imaging application again.

"Well, in that case it wouldn't have an official name, not in the sense that it was one that went down on credit cards or in the property records. More than likely it's a post office box number that's the official address."

Barnside was watching her, smiling as if he enjoyed seeing her try to guess through something so out of her field. "Even if you're right," he asked, "where does that get us? We still have nothing to go on."

"Really?"

When she thought about it she could still feel the harsh, clean cut of the Atlantic air against her skin. And some pain behind it all as well. Childhood and pain went together.

"For a while, when I was a kid, we lived in Maine, somewhere really remote. That was a box number too—had to be, the mail people said. But no one lives in a number. We had a name for the place. Haven Cottage. And that's what we called it."

"Nice memory," Barnside said, unsmiling, "but I still don't see where it gets us."

"The point is that after a very short while we started getting mail, from people we knew. They would put the name we used for the place alongside the PO box number. Pretty soon, we'd get mail that dropped the number altogether, just read Haven Cottage, the area, and a zip code. And that still got through. Every time. When you're remote, that happens. You could just put someone's name on it if you felt like it, because—"

"—the mailman knew," Clarke said, staring at her. "Jesus, here are you guys punching away at computers and the answer we need is probably sitting inside the head of some mail depot manager right now, ready for the taking."

Barnside was shaking his head, grinning all over his face. "Can't be that many of them. These are remote, low-population-density areas. And these people must get mail. Just print out the contact names for the depot managers, Larry. The Agency guys can take it from there."

In the corner of the room, a printer started to whir. Pretty soon names were spewing from it and Fogerty had his men dispatching them as they came, carving out the different territories. Helen watched them pawing through the sheets of paper, Barnside silent at her side, and waited until everyone had moved away from them, to stand behind Wolfit and watch the progress on the screen.

"Say it, Dave."

"Say what?"

"That I am muscling in on something I don't understand."

"Oh that."

She wished he'd cut the stupid grin. "Hey. You're right, of course. You're right a lot, Helen. It must be hard being you."

"Thanks."

He was struggling with something, wondering whether he really wanted to say it. "You're trying to justify yourself, I guess."

"Bull . . . " she groaned.

"No, it's true."

She glowered at him. The man could be so infuriating. "Why do I need to justify anything?"

"That cottage. It was where he killed himself, wasn't it?"

She didn't bother to reply.

"No problem," Barnside said. "I understand. And that drove you here, drove you into the Agency, kept you fighting to keep your head up all the way. As if that proved something."

"I don't," she spat, "have to prove a damn thing."

"No?"

He wasn't smiling anymore. He was downright uncomfortable. "You know what I'd think in your position, Helen? I'd think I'd get in there, I'd show these people who destroyed him, who ruined this innocent man. Except I wouldn't have the guts now, not me. Believe that."

She watched them racing through the pages coming out of the printer, and she couldn't think of a thing to say.

"And something else too, Helen. Once you get there, once you know the kind of world we live in, suddenly everything doesn't look so black and white anymore, does it?"

She tried to stop listening. She wished she could move away. "Meaning?"

"Meaning that once you know what life's like in this place, you get to wondering whether everything is as nice and simple as that. Whether any of us is as innocent as we seem. And maybe whether your old man really was innocent."

She wished she hadn't given up smoking. She wished she had a drink. "You talk too much."

He shook his head and put a big hand, like a bear's paw, gently on her shoulder. "If it's worth anything, I read the files. Years ago. I know what your family was doing in Maine. That was where you ran? When they were closing in on him. In Boston. You just upped roots and got out of town for a while, thinking this would all blow over."

"That's irrelevant," she said, catching her breath in the stifling, overcrowded room.

"No. It is absolutely relevant. This is where he ran. And this is where he killed himself when he knew the game was up. Is it right you were the one who found him? That must be hard to live with."

Speaking very slowly, she said, "Will you get off my fucking back—"

"No. I won't. Because you're letting something personal get in the way of the job. And you're too smart, too damn good for that."

"You're an a-a-asshole, Dave," she said.

"An a-a-asshole?" he said, eyes twinkling. "Hey, I never knew you had a stutter lurking beneath the surface there, Helen. Listen. I read the files. All the files. Not just the ones that went to the Senate committee and got them off the hook.

Your old man was clean. As clean as any of us. You got to believe that and let this thing go before it eats you right up."

She could see the little cottage in her mind's eye. If she tried, she guessed she could smell the salt air coming through the window, mingling with the cold, harsh aroma of spilled blood.

"I didn't enjoy saying that," Barnside added. "But it needed saying."

She looked at Barnside and knew that, in his own odd way, he was trying to help. "Well, now you've said it. So can we get on with the job?"

46

Calling the Postman

Las Vegas, 0331 UTC

As the Nevada night fell and Bill Ruffin worked with Mary Gallagher to erect a flimsy, opaque clover leaf in space above the sun-drenched Pacific, FBI agent Bernard Mason phoned the U.S. Postal Service sorting office in Alamo, north of Vegas, out on the long drab line of 93 running through the desert. He got a mouthful of abuse for his pains.

Mason held the phone away from his ear, waited for the cursing to subside, then said, "Sir, I know it's the busy time for you."

And wondered to himself: How many busy times do you get in a one-horse town like this? On a day when the world, by official order, has put a closed sign on its door and the entire phone system has been down until only an hour ago?

"Then call back later," said the old, sour voice on the end.

"Sir," Mason continued, "this is the FBI. And this is important. What's more, you don't have a delivery tomorrow, what with the emergency and everything."

"You're so clever, smart-ass, how come you even knew I was here?"

"I phoned your home. Your wife told me."

There was a pause on the line. "She told you that?"

"Yeah."

"Bitch. I told her I was going drinking. How'd she know I just came in to catch up on some paperwork?"

"I guess some of us are just wedded to the job. They notice, you know. Mine does."

"Yeah," the voice said, a touch of empathy there. "Well. What do you want?" And listened.

"New York State," the man said at the end.

"Excuse me?"

"Yasgur's Farm. Woodstock, New York State. Don't you people know history?"

"Yeah," Mason said. "We know that one. But this is someplace named after it. In Nevada. Maybe."

"Maybe?"

"I'm just asking. I thought you guys just liked to get stuff through, even if it had the wrong address, no zip code, that kind of thing . . . just like the Mounties, always get your man."

"Hey, you want to hear about no zip code? We get stuff here with no goddamn name on it sometimes, and they still expect it in their mailbox the next morning."

"Precisely, sir. So I was wondering. If something came your way with 'Yasgur's Farm' on the front of the envelope, would you people know what to do with it?"

"Don't ask me. I'm just the manager. But if you wait a moment I'll ask a man who might know."

The line went dead. Mason shuffled through the sheaf of numbers in front of him. Nevada was a big place. It seemed to have an awful lot of post offices. Ash Springs was next.

"You still there, Mr. FBI?"

"Oh yes, sir."

"I spoke to Ronnie Wilson who, surprise, surprise, is taking the opportunity of this unexpected holiday to prop up the bar at Joe's. He's our field operative." The man chuckled. "You get that?"

"I am trying to contain my merriment, sir. And?"

"He says there's someplace out at Cabin Springs, the old dry lake, out on the back road through the wildlife refuge. Couple of times recently he's had to make some special deliveries out there. Says they had zip codes, a PO box number, and 'Yasgur's

Farm' on the label. You believe that? These people. Either they give you too little information or it's too much."

Bernard Mason blinked, felt his heart make a little jump, and reached for the pen. "He's sure about that."

"Oh no. He's just making the whole damn thing up. You people have lives to go to or what?"

"Okay," Mason said, "give me the details."

Thirty seconds later he pushed a piece of paper in front of Fogerty and said, "We got a hit. Remote farmhouse out on a back road that runs out from 95 all the way through the wildlife refuge straight into 93 just short of Alamo. Close to the 93 end."

"Map," Fogerty said, and watched Larry Wolfit mangle the keyboard. The zip code pulled up an area map from the Postal Service. This provided an overlay for the digital security image.

"Jesus Christ," someone said behind Fogerty. An officer in Air Force uniform was following the screen.

"You know this?" Fogerty asked.

"That's on the edge of the Nellis restricted area. We let people through because of the refuge and there's a couple of homes, mainly for weekenders. We're taking practice bombing runs up to ten miles short of Cabin Springs. They're right under our nose. This is going to be easy."

"Really," Fogerty said quietly, and went back to the screen. "Have you found this place yet?"

Wolfit had the refuge up on the map. There was precious little detail at this altitude, just the thin line of the desert track and an outline, like an ink spot, of the lake itself.

"There." He pointed at a speck of light the size of a pinhead, then zoomed in, took up the resolution, and drilled down through the layers until the picture was clear. Yasgur's Farm, from above, looked like a sizable modern ranch house, probably extended over the years from a single rectangular shack. Now it was large, four distinct sections tacked onto each other, probably giving a good three thousand square feet of space if the place was single-story, more if they had any second-floor extensions.

"It's big enough," Helen said.

"But where's the dome?" Fogerty asked.

"Property records," she demanded, and watched as Larry Wolfit pulled up the database.

"According to the state file, this property's real name is Buena Vista Farm," he said. "Dates back to the fifties. Property changed hands in March. New owner a corporation registered in Switzerland. No more details."

"Yeah. Great," Barnside said. "But like the man said, where the hell is the dome?"

Wolfit zoomed out again, hit the degradation button on the filter, and saw a single bright circle appear a quarter of a mile away from the house, along what looked like a ridge.

"Water tower," said the man in the next seat. "It's down there on the map. Mentioned in the state filing too, planning permission back in 1989."

"Sure," Helen said, and watched as Wolfit zoomed in on the thing. "But if you wanted to really hide something, what would you do? You'd find some preexisting feature and replace it. Remember what Lieberman said? These people are clever. We've been looking for something new. Maybe that's what they wanted us to look for."

"Good." Fogerty nodded, watching the image come up in size on the monitor. Wolfit ran it up all the way. No one was impressed. The image was so indistinct, it could have been anything. The dome. A rodeo ring. Even a water tower.

"We've got Nighthawks in that area," the Air Force man said. "I can get one there in five minutes."

"Will the folks in the farm know?" Fogerty asked. "We need some element of surprise."

"Not a chance. These are helicopters with silent flight capability. We can be over there at six hundred feet and they won't hear a thing. And you could put the movie they get on HBO if you want."

"Do it," Fogerty said. "And while we're waiting, get the HRT people in the briefing center, work on the assumption we have a hit here."

The room suddenly became less crowded.

"I have to go with them," Helen said. Fogerty stared at her, eyes wide behind the big owl glasses, and then at Barnside, who had moved next to her.

"You still feel that way, Miss Wagner?" Fogerty asked. "You could run it from here if you wanted."

"No," she said quickly. "I have to be there. The whole purpose of this mission is to capture their system intact and working. I need to be there with my team. I need to be on-line to La Finca all the way. And once you've secured the target, I want you people out of my hair."

Barnside shrugged. Fogerty gazed at her in silence.

"Here she comes," Larry Wolfit said. "We've got a live feed from the chopper."

The monitor was now occupied by a blue-tinged video screen, the image distinct and sharp, but eerie, like the picture from an early moon shot. The desert floor looked like the surface of the moon too. Then a lone coyote wandered across the screen, there was the outline, hard and straight, of the road, and a scattering of scrubby brush.

"Where are they going?" Fogerty asked.

"The house," the Air Force officer said.

"Kill that," Fogerty demanded. "I want to see this dome first. Without that, we've got nothing."

Someone barked orders at the back of the control room. They could see the direction of the chopper change on screen. Some low scree came into view, more scrub, and then a shape, circular but indistinct.

"Go in closer," Fogerty said.

"It's at max resolution already."

"Then fly lower."

The man in uniform hesitated and said, "But what if they hear—"

"Just do it," Fogerty said. "We don't have room for guesswork."

"Sir."

It was, Helen thought, just like the film of an Apollo mission, the sort of stuff you watched when you were a child, wondering what all the fuss was about. The gray, bare landscape rose up to greet you, looking airless, inhospitable. Someone gasped. "Hold it there," she ordered.

A mosaic of polygons covered the surface of the flashing image, and around the exterior ran what looked like a perfect circle.

"They skinned it," she said. "They've put an exterior skin right around the whole damn thing to make it look like a water tower from the ground, and then just left the top open hoping we wouldn't see."

Fogerty stared at the screen. "All this gets recorded, is that correct?"

"Yes sir," Wolfit replied.

"Good. Well, let's get this helicopter back to altitude and over to the house. We have plans to make."

Helen waited, looked at him.

"Well?" Fogerty asked.

"I'm still awaiting your decision, sir."

His face gave nothing away. "This is a Bureau exercise, Miss Wagner."

"Sir—"

"But I take your point. Be there for the briefing."

Levine gave out a sardonic smile. "Sure, that's okay with me too, Dan."

"Good."

"You should take Barnside along too," Levine said. "He could come in useful."

Fogerty looked at the big man. "I guess you people are happier in twos. Sure thing."

Barnside grinned at her and she didn't know what to make of it. "Hey, Helen," he said. "We'll make a team yet."

47

Connect

Equatorial orbit, altitude 20315 kilometers above the Pacific, 0405 UTC

At this height above the earth the satellite's velocity was 3.86 kilometers per second and the period required to complete a single orbit 723.37 minutes, almost exactly twelve hours. Charley had positioned Sundog to sit squat in the center of the earth day, wherever it was over the globe. That way she could make the most of the storm that was building in space behind it. She could adjust the speed across the globe at any time by firing up the satellite and adjusting the orbit: higher meant slower. Lieberman had worked out the forecast for the present track. She had it right on course for Western Europe when the zenith rose up to greet them, and well in line for North America over the following twelve hours. Perfect timing, Lieberman guessed, a natural Charley attribute.

He didn't mention any of this as they watched the astronauts on the big screen at La Finca. He'd done his best to show them how to shut his part of Sundog down. Now it was just a question of letting the crew get on with its job.

Bill Ruffin and Mary Gallagher sweated inside their suits, watching the four wings of the giant oversized shade hang over Sundog, casting a vast, deep shadow over the solar panels, and beyond to the satellite itself. The two astronauts felt at home in space, knew how to handle zero gravity, how carefully and slowly they had to maneuver, to feel the objects they were trying to work with. It was a mistake to rush a single thing. If one vital part went missing, received an accidental knock, the impetus would send it flying, with a balletic slowness, out of their reach forever. Ruffin and Gallagher would have no second chances, and that thought stayed with them during this interminable period of waiting.

The LED on the base plate seemed to have been stuck on orange for years. Then Ruffin slowly closed his eyes, dreamed of home, a warm Florida beach, cold beer, a nice quiet raw bar with country music floating out of the speakers.

Lieberman's voice broke through the silence of their helmets. "We saw the light change. My part's over. You're in Irwin's capable hands now."

"Thanks, Professor. You can have a job at the Cape any day."

Ruffin looked at the light. It was red, no mistakes there. Mary Gallagher was already reaching into her tool kit, waiting to be told. He took a deep breath and, without thinking, scanned the black horizon for the Shuttle. It was a long way off now, a kilometer at least, looking like a kid's model in white plastic. They still had plenty of air left. Plenty of time too. All that was needed was to bring the satellite off-line, then call up Dave Sampson, get him to bring the ship back up, maneuver around once more, pick them up, and head off home.

Home. Such a small, insignificant word for a concept so huge it could occupy your entire life.

"Bill?" Mary asked. They were in the shade cast by the clover leaf, and the satellite shielded her from the bright reflecting surface of the earth just then. He could imagine her smart, sparky eyes staring at him through the visor, behind the deep reflected image of the glowing living globe that sat there now.

"Nothing," Ruffin replied, and wished his mouth didn't feel so dry. "Let's get on with it."

The two of them removed the clasps of their lines from the struts, worked their way down the aluminum arms of the panel structure, and reattached the cords, this time to the exterior of the satellite itself. Ruffin stared at the red light, shining like a little beacon. Sundog looked dead. "This thing is down now, Irwin. Why can't we just leave it at that? If she's got no power, she's no threat."

"The power won't stay off," Schulz replied. "At some stage Michael's wings are going to move out of alignment, and then she wakes up, Charley's back in business. The only way we can be sure that thing's dead for good is for you to get behind the panel and key in a final shutdown sequence. But you get a good window from the shade trick. As long as the power's down from there, we're okay to open her up."

Ruffin looked at the giant sunshade. It cast an enormous shadow right over the entire solar panel clover leaf and part of the satellite too. It was rigid in space, kept in place by the tiny, immutable forces of momentum that were shared by these strange mechanisms performing an odd little distanced dance, an unconscionable height above the surface of the earth.

"I get it," he sighed, and thought: "It would be too easy just to throw a shade over the thing and go home." He looked at *Arcadia* and asked, "You can see us okay from there, Dave?"

The radio crackled. "Not too well. I'm some way off now and the angle's bad. But don't you worry. Once you take this thing down I'll be around and scooping you up in no time."

"That sounds good." Ruffin jerked on the cord of the float-cam, which was still static behind them, back with the solar structure. "You're going to take us through this, Irwin, step by step. I know we practiced in training but I like all the eyes I can get."

"Sure," the voice from the ground said. The cylindrical camera came up to Ruffin. He steadied it with one hand, then pointed the lens at the body of the satellite. It was, as luck would have it, cast in darkness by the huge parasol they had erected. Ruffin had half expected this: Murphy's Law applied in space too. He and Gallagher took out two powerful flashlights, attached them to an external antenna, turned them on, and illuminated the entire area.

"You got that?"

Somewhere on earth, Ruffin knew, they would be looking at

the matte-black exterior of this thing, seeing much the same view he did now. There was an access panel on the outer skin of the satellite. It had a smartcard slot on the side, and enough warning signs by it to put off any curious intruder who didn't hold the key. The panel was positioned, sensibly, close to the base of the unit, so anyone trying to work on Sundog could see the status light at the same time.

"They can't reprogram the access code," Schulz's voice said. "If that worries you."

"Hadn't even occurred to me until that moment," Ruffin said, then took one final look at Mary to make sure she was on top of this, pulled the card out of the tool kit, and pushed it into the slot. Nothing happened.

"We live to fight another day," he muttered, and waited. The line was silent. "Anyone there?"

"Damn," Schulz whispered. "The door panel is on a hydraulic mechanism. It should have popped open when you inserted the card."

Ruffin looked at the thing. It was about three feet wide and two feet deep, a flat, plain lump of metal, with what looked like rubber hermetic seals around the edge.

"Suggestions?" he asked.

"It's stuck," Schulz said immediately. "If it had rejected the card we wouldn't be having this conversation right now. There's a small explosive device built to guard against unauthorized access, and that will work even on power down."

"Thanks again for the welcome information," Ruffin said calmly. He looked more closely at the panel. Something was visibly amiss. He pulled the floatcam farther in. "Take a close look at the seal. It looks warped down one side to me. Does that mean anything?"

The line went quiet, then Schulz replied, "I agree. It looks as if the material is compromised in some way. It's pressurized from the inside. I guess if it's loose maybe the servo doesn't have enough power to break the seal."

"So all we need do is rupture this manually, and then the panel will depressurize? We should be able to pry it off if need be?"

That long silence again.

"We need decisions here," Ruffin said, and noted the anxiety in his own voice.

"I just want to be sure. I was looking at the actual plan of that section. And you're right. There's no reason why you can't pry the panel off completely now. The backup system has accepted the ID card. It's going to stay quiet."

"That's nice." Ruffin looked at Mary. "You got something like a screwdriver in there? This is going to be like prying off the lid of a jar of jam, I guess." She pulled out a long, flat-handled lever and handed it to him.

"Just get underneath the seal, loosen it, use as much force as you need," Schulz said. "The pressure should do the rest."

"I'm with you there." Ruffin thrust the blade gingerly into the crevice around the near edge of the panel. "I'm getting right—"

It happened in an instant. He felt the lever go loose in his hand, then the panel door shot up violently toward him, collided with the front of his suit with an impact he could feel through the thick material and the pressurized interior. The force was astonishing. It sent him bucking backward, rolling head over heels out toward the panels, out toward the blackness of space. He could hear people screaming in his headset. His mind was a blur. Then the safety line attached to the satellite cut in, jerked him to a painful stop, and the pictures gradually stopped spinning in his head.

Someone, a familiar voice from NASA, was yelling in his ear, "Check suit integrity, Bill. Goddamn check it!"

Ruffin took a deep breath, closed his eyes, found himself thinking once again of home, that beautiful beach, gulls squawking lazily overhead, then looked at the gauges on his sleeve panel. "Looks good here. You people getting any readings down there that suggest otherwise?"

A pause, then the NASA voice said, "No. Guess we were lucky."

"Yeah." He pulled gently on the line and floated back down to the satellite. Gallagher watched him all the way, and he guessed her eyes were wide open and worried behind the glass.

"Hey." He reached over, touched her with his big glove, a

ridiculous gesture and he knew it. "There was nothing you could do. It's okay."

"Sorry," Schulz said over the line. "I guess there must have been more pressure inside that thing than I appreciated."

"No problem. Like the man said, we're all making this up as we go along." The panel door was gone now, long gone, floating off somewhere into the void. The opening revealed precious little: another covering panel, this time held by tamperproof screws around the edge.

"Teamwork time," Ruffin said. Gallagher passed him an electronic, torqueless screwdriver, and took out an identical device herself. Then they turned the tools on and set to work on the screws, three down each vertical side, the same number on the horizontal. It took ten minutes, but this time there was no pressurization problem. The plate just came away in their hands. It revealed a dark, deep hole that wasn't reached by the lighting they had originally jerry-built. Ruffin motioned to Gallagher and she unhooked one of the flashlights, held it in her hand, and pointed it down the hole. Ruffin smiled. This was what he had been praying to see ever since the Shuttle had lifted off from Canaveral: a small LCD screen with sixteen places for digits on it, each blank, and beneath a numeric keypad. He pulled the floatcam in farther and listened to Schulz's purr of relief.

"Sixteen numbers and we're there," Schulz said.

"Know them by heart."

"I'll read them off all the same."

Ruffin punched the first one in and couldn't believe it. His hand really was shaking, deep inside the cumbersome glove. It took a couple of tries to get it right. Then he hit the green enter button, watched the number come up in its little window, and moved on to the next.

He was on the seventh when Schulz said somewhat nervously in Ruffin's ear, "What happened to the sunlight?"

Ruffin fumbled the number again and swore mildly. "Sorry. You lost me. We're nearly there. Can't it wait?"

"No," Schulz said firmly. "We've got a wider view of the area than you from the floatcam. Pull your head out of that hole and take a look around you. The sunlight's changing."

Something stirred inside Ruffin's head, annoyingly out of reach. Reluctantly, with a sigh that was audible to everyone listening around the world, he pushed himself away from the control panel and blinked in the bright, piercing shaft of sunlight that was now falling on their backs.

"Shit. I jerked the damn satellite when I got thrown back like that. It's moved. It's out of sync with the shades."

"Bring the floatcam back," Schulz barked. "I want to see the wings."

"No need," Ruffin said grimly, but moved the camera unit anyway. Up above them he could see the two clover leafs, one attached to Sundog, the other floating free. When he got thrown back by the pressure of the door, his line had shifted the entire satellite out of kilter with the shade above. Ordinarily, he guessed, some adjuster rocket would have fired in and straightened the thing up. But Sundog was down. Just then, anyway.

"No problem," Schulz yelled, in a voice that said just the opposite. "I can't risk trying to key in the rest of the sequence. We just need to get you back out of range of the thing, back where you were, then put the shades in place again."

Ruffin looked at the flimsy silver apparatus they had erected. The four identical wings had now moved close to thirty degrees out of alignment with the satellite. The solar panels had to be getting almost their full entitlement of the sun, and what Schulz had said rang in his ears: This thing stayed down as long as the power was off.

"How soon?" he asked, unhooking his line from the satellite, watching Gallagher do the same, slowly, certainly, making sure she got it right the first time.

"Don't know. Look at the LED."

Ruffin took hold of Gallagher's arm and pushed both of them away from the hull, back out toward the errant wings. They rounded the back of the satellite. He glanced at the base plate. The light was red. He took a deep breath, and then it was orange.

"She's waking up, Irwin," Ruffin said slowly. "Orange now."

"Get yourself out of there, nice and steady," Schulz yelled. "Get out of range. We go back to square one."

"Yeah." The light changed again. "It's green."

No one spoke. The two suited figures floated out into space, out toward the silver wings. They were ten meters or so from the base plate now, Ruffin guessed. The line was still silent. He watched the metal plate begin to retract, slowly, with a mindless, mechanical certainty, sliding open to reveal a deep, complex pit of equipment. What lay underneath was impossible to recognize, a tangle of spikes and antennae, sensors starting to move sluggishly, like some waking beast sniffing the air, trying to locate its prey.

"The door's open," Ruffin said. "It's connecting."

In the tinny speakers of his helmet someone said, "Oh my God . . ."

They were clear of the thing now. Far enough away to have been safe, if Sundog had failed to pick up their presence during their slow flight back from its perimeter. Beneath them, radiant blue and gold, the earth lay like some precious, distant jewel. Bill Ruffin reached out and held Mary Gallagher's hand, and still the picture of the damn beach wouldn't leave his head. The gulls circling, the smell of salt water, the taste of that drink, these things were real.

"Our Father," he said quietly, "who art in Heaven, hallowed—"

It looked like something from a kid's game or a prop from a movie set. The thin red beam just came right out of the guts of the beast straight at them, a waving wand of energy slicing through space, slicing through their suits, their bodies, making this last moment seem so strange, so unreal, a writhing, agonizing dance in the airless black vacuum they'd dared to brave, so big, so endless it could swallow them up forever and never leave a trace.

In Bill Ruffin's helmet, now floating through space attached to a dead torso severed in half by a waving wand of light, there was a cacophony of voices, yelling and screaming, all on top of each other, none making sense.

Eighteen hundred meters away, in the cabin of the Shuttle, Dave Sampson, mind reeling, still trying to believe this was happening, listened to the babble of sound, tried to pick out what he recognized, what was foreign. Someone he knew, a NASA voice, not calm now, but still familiar, was yelling at him to get out of there, and damn fast, screaming so loud it covered up completely Schulz yelling the exact opposite. Idly, without thinking, he reached down and flicked the buttons on the start-up sequence, heard the giant machine start to come to life.

There was a sound, familiar and encouraging. Servos coming to life, pumps energizing, the slow rumble of power feeding into the system, electricity running the complex length of the spacecraft. And something else, from way behind. When Dave Sampson looked up from the winking lights of the panel and stared over his shoulder, there was nothing there now except fire, a vast, all-consuming fire, that rolled toward him like some ancient, fearsome weapon from an old and angry god.

48
In the Waking World

La Finca, 0511 UTC

"Not your fault," Lieberman said gently to Schulz, who looked pale as death. "It's not anybody's fault."

Schulz looked devastated. "I should have thought about it. When he got kicked back and held by the line. I should have realized that would move the satellite out of sync."

"And so should I. Those guys knew the risks. They wouldn't blame you, any of us. They were bigger than that."

"Yeah." Schulz sighed miserably.

"So let's get on with the job. This game's not over yet."

And it wasn't, even though Charley clearly thought otherwise. Schulz guessed she must have known something was wrong when Sundog went off-line. That had to show up on the Children's system. She didn't need to activate the defense mechanisms and blow the Shuttle team out of the sky. The satellite was perfectly capable of doing that for itself. But she could take some kind of revenge. Fifteen minutes after they lost the ship a curt E-mail came through from her, copied to La Finca, the CIA, the Agency, and the main international news wires. It gave a brief, deliberately inaccurate account of the destruction of *Arcadia*. The last word Charley wrote was: *Prepare*.

Schulz had closed his eyes and asked Mo Sinclair to watch the wires, the Net sites, any source of information she could find, and try to monitor what Charley might be up to as the solar storm began to rise to its peak. Lieberman watched her working, saw the shock in her face, then sat down by her side, began to help, at one point touched her hand, felt good that she returned the pressure. And like this they turned these facts, figures, and pictures into a running report that chilled the blood, and brought home the true nature of the event that was shaping around them.

This was a global catastrophe, by its nature not a contiguous sequence of discrete occurrences. It moved over the earth slowly, at the speed of the dawn, and breathed its poisonous fire in no particular order, to no discernible pattern. To Mo Sinclair it felt like being trapped in the path of an oncoming hurricane, unable to take your eye off this monstrous thing that was blotting out more and more of the horizon as it approached, and unable to move too. You might as well hope to dodge the footsteps of some fairy-tale giant who was stumbling drunkenly toward you. There was as much chance of salvation in standing where you were as trying to second-guess the program of this crazed, all-powerful leviathan.

There were such reports on the news wires. The storm had broken the precious digital thread that bound together the modern world, tied newspaper to radio station, TV network to the World Wide Web. Suddenly the conduit of information that had been taken for granted was leaking and flaky, and with this went the notion of currency, of validity. This was the digital world at its best and worst. Where the pipes held, the major channels came through with reports that were occasionally flimsy but at least held the promise of some grain of truth inside them. In the absence of fact, rumor raced in to fill the vacuum, and the Net was alive with dubious stories, half-baked theories, tales, and hearsay, multiplying around the world like some feverish digital bacteria. She found herself hating this junk, wishing it would go away. She didn't want to think about some of the crazier theories out there, the ones that said this was the end of everything, that Judgment Day was on us, and it was time for the earth to start cracking, the skeletons to start walking out of the ground.

What the storm did for some people, she realized, was strip
away a layer from the outer part of themselves and let the baser,
animal side that lay beneath come to the surface, grin insanely
at the sky, and get on with the job of being "free." Chaos and
freedom were close bedfellows and when that veneer of polite-
ness, of community, of sensibility was destroyed, it was difficult
to tell one from the other.

What she saw coming in from the sources she could rely on,
the sporadic reports from CNN and the BBC running through
the Web TV sites, only served to prove this. When the storm
struck, people didn't stay inside. There was looting, there were
riots. When the human animal was cornered, put into the tight,
confined, inescapable space of the city and had the burning
light of the sun in its face, not everyone wanted to curl up in a
corner and dream of the good times. To some this catastrophe
was welcome. It tore down the old world and put something
wild and anarchic and new in its place. Which maybe was what
Charley had wanted all along. And beneath this newness was
something that, when Mo thought about it, was more terrifying
than the prospect of cataclysm, of political upheaval, or of
wide-scale fatality. Stripped of humanity, out in the open, beneath the feverish fire of the sun, people became something
different, something that laughed at the very idea of an organized, decent, caring world. This rolling, teeming wave of fire
didn't destroy the planet. What it unmade was the simple, accepted notion of society, and put cruel bedlam and the mindless, heated rage of pandemonium in its place.

The reliable information they could garner confirmed the
scale of the devastation, and how ineffectual the measures
taken to secure against it had proved. And these, she couldn't
help thinking, were just the early reports. There could be
much worse to come. According to both BBC and CNN a series of tsunamis that devastated the northern coasts of Japan
had stirred some kind of millennial movement, led by local
cults. Tokyo's subway had been occupied by sullen, terrified
crowds, the red light district of Osaka destroyed by a machete-
wielding mob. Secondary earthquakes devastated much of
modern Kyoto but left the ancient temples standing, and it was

here that the population congregated, scared, angry, vengeful. Martial law was put in place, as it was in most cities that lay in the path of the storm, but it was hard to persuade soldiers and the police to go on the streets to enforce it. These cities remained on a knife edge, even when the sky returned to normalcy. Once the storm was over, the streets became a little calmer. Some kind of amnesty for the rioting was being promised. Still, it was impossible to say when a semblance of normalcy might return.

From the main networks, they were able to gauge the amount of damage in the capitals from Japan through to Eastern Europe. It varied from minor—Moscow seemed to be untouched, if the reports were to be believed—to shocking. The ancient quarters of Tashkent and Samarkand were in flames, destroyed by sporadic fires and local earthquakes. The two remaining active nuclear reactors at Chernobyl seemed to have imploded upon themselves and dispatched into the clear golden sky a cloud of radioactive dust that threatened both Belarus and the Ukraine.

Telecommunications were a mess everywhere now, the chaos extending beyond the path of the storm. The TV people said that most Western governments planned to keep the markets shut until they could invent some way of reopening them without a massive, disastrous collapse of confidence. Stock prices had fallen so deeply that several major financial institutions and multinational corporations were technically bankrupt at the point of suspension.

Beneath the facts lay a churning ocean of rumor and misinformation, and she couldn't turn her face from it, however hard she tried. It was like driving past an accident on the freeway. The rumors ran unchecked and multiplied around the unofficial Web sites set up to monitor the storm. There was no way of verifying them. All she could do was read the snatched, illiterate dispatches, a chill going down the back of her spine, and wonder at the state of the world.

In Islamabad a solar observatory was torched by a chanting crowd of hysterical worshipers from a city mosque, and every one of the staff inside burned to death, some pushed back into

the flames when they tried to escape. A mob in a remote village in Armenia destroyed its local church, built a pyre on the
bare hillside, and burned everything that could be stripped
from the ruin. Afterward, they crowned a seven-year-old girl
with a diadem made from metal foil, paraded her around on
their shoulders from sunrise to midday. By then she was covered in burns, her skin peeling, and they ceremonially mur-
dered the child in the village square. The local chief of police
wielded the knife that was used to kill her. In Istanbul, the last
song played by Bosphorus Rock 101 before the power failed
was by U2. Bono sang, in a low, melancholy voice, "I'm not the
only one, who's staring at the sun." Then the airwave disappeared in a sea of white noise.

With Lieberman working alongside her, Mo patiently stored
this rising flood of venom and promised herself that one day
the world would recover enough of its senses to sort the wheat
from the chaff, tell her how much of this really happened, and
how much lived inside the head of the mob.

Finally, some small voice inside chastising her for the order
of things, she turned to the academic Net. Here they sifted
through what data was still trickling through on the monitoring
network that should, in another world, in another time, have
leisurely recorded the course of events from apex to apogee,
waited a few years, then produced some learned papers.

There was a consistent, unbroken line of reporting from only
a single point in the chain, Learmonth, in Australia. Everywhere else was down, either through a direct storm effect or
because somewhere in the chain of digital command that ran
through to La Finca the line had snapped. Did it matter? Probably not. Just now, Learmonth was all they had. And the data
was incredible, outside the bounds of anything anyone had
ever seen.

Learmonth recorded the temperature of the photosphere,
the sun's outer layer, at 7,000 degrees centigrade, a thousand
degrees higher than its previous record. The fire at the core
was constant at a steady 22 million degrees, 2 million above its
historical peak, and a temperature which, she guessed, a physi-

cist might believe theoretically impossible, if theories made sense anymore.

You didn't need to rely on the observatories in any case. Those who were rash enough to wander out into the day could, with the naked eye and a suitable filter, see most of the disk of the sun obscured by a single giant blemish. Soaring flares were visible without a telescope, like a halo around the burning core, and on the earth there was a stream of reports about freak atmospheric conditions involving sundogs, false coronas, and strange lights in the sky that were so bright they blotted out even the sun itself.

Schulz walked over and interrupted their frantic keying. "We need to give them the news," he said, and the sound of his voice made both of them jump. The power of what they had seen on the screen was so magnetic nothing else seemed to matter.

"We're ready," Lieberman said with a nod. In La Finca, three heads appeared in a video window at the top of the screen: Helen Wagner, Dan Fogerty, and the dark, complex face of Tim Clarke.

"We were following your reports," Helen said quietly. "That's excellent work, and I know it must be harrowing too."

Mo and Lieberman had painstakingly painted the major incidents on the screen, recording every confirmed event that came in over the wires, marking it with a little electronic flag colored for the seriousness of the effect: pale yellow for minor, bright yellow for substantial, red for an emergency-level disaster. The markers ran in a curve, following the true circle route across the northern hemisphere, rising in the Pacific east of Japan, then moving slowly with the rising sun, through the eastern provinces of Russia, through China and Mongolia, on, relentlessly into the Kazakhstan and the Urals. The yellow flags disappeared long before the sweep of the storm reached the Caspian. From then on there was only red, sporadic, and they all knew why. When the effects grew more serious, it was harder to report them. They could only stare at these blank spaces on the map and wonder what was going on there, guess-

ing how long it would take to cross into Western Europe, which
sat in the path of the maelstrom.

"What's the worst we know of?" Clarke asked. "What's
this?" He pointed to a red marker near Sapporo in northern
Japan.

"There's been a rapid trigger of earthquake activity in the region," Lieberman said. "Most of it offshore, fortunately, but
that's led to tidal wave activity. There's hundred-foot tsunamis
reported, major damage, serious casualty figures. We've also
got seismic readings from several stations around the world that
indicate quakes around Beijing and some activity in central
Asia, close to Samarkand."

"Communications?" Helen asked.

"Patchy. We're getting a surprising amount out of Japan and
the Far East. Maybe that's because a lot there is based on cel-
lular technology already. They never got around to building
physical wired systems, so there's less infrastructure to be
knocked out. I don't know. It's just a guess. The way things
stand now, I guess we're looking at a national emergency that
beats anything we've seen in Japan in living memory, certainly
the Kobe quakes back in '95. The rest of it, we just don't know.
The TV news is also running stories about political uncertainties in some of the central Asian states, even Moscow too. You
must have something through diplomatic channels."

"Not that you can rely on," Clarke replied. The President
looked hard at the map.

"This is all really northern. Yesterday you people said we
were getting reports of hits way down to the equator, in the
southern hemisphere even. Now they seem safe."

"It's what you'd expect," Lieberman said. "Yesterday the
storm was more diffuse. It was weaker and it covered a greater
area. Today the alignment is more effective. So everything is
more focused. More powerful. And confined to a smaller area."

"I didn't realize that would happen," Clarke said. "It's a
blessing of a kind, I guess."

"Not really," Helen added. She looked at Lieberman and
knew he was thinking the same. "We can't be fooled into
thinking the effects are confined to the vicinity of the storm.

Tsunamis can have a wavelength of several hundred miles. We haven't seen any volcanos triggered yet but if that happens the collateral damage can be huge, a really long way away."

"Yeah," Lieberman added. "And these earthquakes? You know what kind they are yet?"

"From what we've seen they're all strike-slip faults," she replied quietly. "That seems to be the type that is more likely to be triggered by the storm."

He closed his eyes for a moment. "Don't tell me. Let me guess. The San Andreas. This is a strike-slip?"

"Yes. We are going to put out a full-blown quake alert from north of San Francisco to south of San Diego, the length of the fault, pretty soon."

"Jesus." He hated the very idea of an earthquake—that something you took for granted, something that lived beneath you, the rock you walked upon, should suddenly give up the ghost, shrug its shoulders, and collapse into chaos.

"Well," Clarke said finally, watching them all, "is someone going to try to answer the big question?"

The La Finca team was silent.

"Professor Bennett," Helen said, "you're the expert here. How much of this is Gaia? And how much would we be getting anyway? What will we gain by taking Sundog off-line when we find them?"

Bennett shook his head. "I can't answer that precisely. We have no way of knowing. Without Gaia, these would be extraordinary circumstances. This bad? It's hard to believe. They're orchestrating this, even if they don't understand the detail any better than we can."

Clarke nodded grimly at the team around him. "This information stays with us for now. Understood? I don't want those people out there shoving those damn papers at me all over again."

"Sir." Fogerty nodded. "But they will be back."

"Then get inside that damn farmhouse and make sure they got no reason."

"Right," Fogerty said. "The earliest we can hope to secure this is two-thirty A.M."

"What?" Lieberman's face stared at them from the screen, contorted with disbelief.

"You heard," Fogerty snapped.

"That's more than two hours from now. That's like ninety minutes or so from the zenith."

Fogerty looked exasperated. "We have the one chance here. I don't want it to go wrong."

"Michael," Schulz said. "If we get back control even fifteen minutes before zenith, that's enough. We can switch off whatever input the Children have."

"Great. One chance. And this may decide whether we wake up tomorrow with a world we recognize or not."

"Correct," Tim Clarke said. "Do you have any other suggestions?"

Lieberman fell silent. He hated the way people in authority had this effect on you. "Yeah," he said, just as he felt someone was starting to reach for the off switch. "Why don't we use our brains instead of racing around chasing our asses?"

"Meaning what, Michael?" Helen asked.

He looked at her face on the screen and was shocked by the impatience, the momentum in her face. "Mo," Lieberman said, taking her hand. They both stared into the monitor. "You see this woman, Mr. President? They sent her here to help them. She didn't. She's getting treated now like she's some kind of pariah. Like she's your old man, Helen. And you know what? Even though she didn't help them, and they know that, these people still seem to be running rings around us. You get that? You understand why we always seem to be one step behind?"

Tim Clarke glanced at his watch. "No, mister. Do you?"

Lieberman said nothing.

"We know where they are, Michael," Helen said slowly. "We can get in there, take back control, and put an end to this thing. We're not done."

And he understood that. He just couldn't work out why it gave him no comfort.

49
HRT

Nellis Air Force Base, 0531 UTC

John Collins, the head of the FBI's Hostage Rescue Team, had assembled Helen Wagner, Larry Wolfit, the two other people in the Langley S&T team, and Dave Barnside for a short, personal briefing before the main meeting. At the end, Helen asked, "So you mean we stay out of your way until you think it's all secure?"

Collins was a big man, six feet tall, a fit-looking fifty or so, with gray, close-cropped hair, and bright, piercing eyes. He stared at her and nodded. "Guess that about sums it up. Once we have that place under our thumb, you can do what you like. My job's over. But until it is, I don't want my folks tripping over you, understand?"

Helen nodded. "The odds are these people won't return fire or anything like that."

"Probably not," Dave Barnside said. "Nothing that neat or clean. More likely the place is wired with Semtex, just like it was in San Francisco and Spain. You got anything to keep us clear of that? I don't want my ass blown all over Nevada."

Collins's expression stayed deadpan. "We've got equipment that can detect the obvious signs of explosives. It's a trade-off, really. You people are short of time, and a complete scan of that site would take a day or more."

"You've got fifteen minutes," Helen said. "Any longer than that and we might as well not be there."

"Right. In that time we can clear the obvious signs. We got sniffers that will detect common explosives, triggers, trip wires, pressure plates, that kind of thing. And, while I hear what you say—these people haven't used guns before—I'm not taking any risks. We go in there on the basis that this is a hostage rescue and the equipment that interests you—in the farmhouse, in the dome—they're the hostages. We immobilize anything that threatens that objective."

"Don't get too excited," Helen warned. "We may need those people in there to help us get things moving again."

Collins shrugged his big shoulders. "Point taken. We'll do what we can."

They walked out and watched him take up his place in front of the overhead projector in the Nellis briefing room. The air-conditioning made a loud, continuous noise, but it still couldn't dispel the close, enervating heat of the night.

The walls were plastered with aerial photographs and local charts. There were no more than twenty HRT agents there, plus some Marine helicopter crew members who would ferry them into the area using big twin-rotor Sea Knight helicopters.

Collins rose at the front of the room and started to talk. "We can keep this short, folks. I want you people in the air at ten to the hour. The target is forty miles almost straight due north from here. We've got five Sea Knights handling the transportation. That means you should be hitting ground around two-fifteen A.M. local just under a quarter of a mile from the target. I want the farmhouse and the dome secured in twenty minutes maximum. Then we hand over to the specialist guys, though the team leaders may be required for some local interrogation. We work in four teams, five in each. What information we can glean from intelligence suggests there may be up to thirty people in this building. Currently the light output is modest. My guess is a good number of them are taking a nap. Even if they're all awake, the likelihood is that few if any of them are carrying handguns. We can't take that as read, so use all the usual precautions and act with discretion. But the brief here is to treat this like a hostage situation. We want control and we want this situation stabilized, with minimum damage, as quickly and efficiently as possible. Bill?"

A tall black man with a lean, ascetic face rose and faced them. "The template for this is one of those nonnegotiable, low-damage situations we know so well. We practiced this long and hard. Now's the time to make it work. We got one main room in this building, some smaller ones off it, down a long corridor . . ."

He pointed to the plan on the wall. Yasgur's Farm was a sizable place, Helen thought. There could easily be thirty people or more in there.

". . . plus bedrooms, of course. Now remember: low damage. And that goes for equipment as much as people. We want to pass this property on to the folks who need it in much the same condition it is now. You're all familiar with these."

He held up a small metal canister and a pair of goggles. "Flash grenades are the key here. We divide into four teams, one for each door. Each team has a delegated member for grenade duty. On the signal, you pop a single one through the window and the rest of us go through. You know the drill. These things are pure light. Anyone who's awake inside that room won't be able to see straight for two minutes once the cycle ends, and then won't regain full sight for another hour or more. And remember too that you get four flashes over thirty seconds, and just now and again we get a rogue one that misses its timing and fires up later than that. The rules matter here. Your goggles stay on for two minutes after that last pop, just in case."

John Collins, arms folded at the podium, stared down at them. "I go with the first team. Now, isn't that a surprise?"

A line of laughter ran through the team. She liked Collins's timing. It punctured the nervousness they all felt.

"Once we're through, if this thing goes right, they'll be sitting on the floor, immobilized, before they even get their eyesight back. If you see weapons, respond, and warn the rest of us. When every last man and woman of them is out of action, we hand over to the technical people. Okay?"

Bill was handing out sheets of paper. It was the floor plan of the farmhouse, with delegated areas for each team to control.

"Sir?"

Collins peered at Helen. "Miss Wagner?"

"The dome. How do we handle that?"

"Okay," he said, and turned to the aerial photographs, pointing at them with a laser wand. "The dome is on a rocky incline to the northwest of the property. We can't land any closer to it than we can to the farmhouse itself. What's more, if you look here"—he pointed to a series of marks on the image, moving in a straight line from the farmhouse to the dome—"you can see what we interpret to be some kind of control system, probably microwave. We'll have to reach the dome on foot and the only way to do it is to cross the microwave system on the way. Our guess is that they have, in all probability, wired this up with some line-of-sight detection system. Hell, you can buy the stuff you need down at Radio Shack for twenty dollars. They'd be crazy not to. But what that means is we don't want to be running up this track until we have secured the building. That could give them undue warning, and, if there are any devices in the way, it would prevent us from dealing with them."

"So?" Helen asked.

"So," Collins replied, letting them all see his eyes roll upward a little, "once we are in control, four Cobra support choppers come up with the lighting rigs from a U2 concert strapped to their asses. When they switch that on, the desert floor will be as bright as it looks at midday. We get to see anyone trying to sneak out of the area. We get to see every inch of the way from the building up to the dome. My men clear it first. You and your team follow. We know the time situation, believe me. We will do this as quickly as is humanly possible. But until we give you the nod, I'd be grateful if you'd stay clear of the area. Understood?"

"Sir?"

Collins looked at Barnside. He'd had enough questions already. "Mr. Barnside?"

"I'm Operations. I should be with you in the farmhouse."

"I know your job, Mr. Barnside. You can come along behind with the support team if you like. But the same rule applies.

You stay out of our hair until we invite you through the door. Plain manners."

"Hey"—Barnside grinned—"I'd come just for the pleasure of watching you guys perform."

They laughed at that. Just good old male camaraderie, Helen guessed, and exchanged knowing glances with Larry Wolfit, who was busy scribbling notes on his pad. Wolfit leaned over and whispered in her ear, "Look. If these people want to play soldiers, I'd rather Barnside was with them than us. We let the other two guys go on ahead, and we just stay back, wait until it's clear. Okay?"

"Yes," she said. Then John Collins clapped his hands and the room began to empty.

Ten minutes later they approached the huge, dark shadows of the Sea Knights, like giant crows beached on some faintly lit shoreline. The rotors began to cut through the hot, black air, winding up until they made a noise so deafening it was impossible to talk, impossible, even, to think beyond this brief, urgent slice of time that lay ahead of them, hidden in the vast, all-enveloping folds of the night.

50
Doubts

Joe Katayama made a spire with his hands. Long, thin fingers, powerful, all-encompassing. Charley Pascal smiled at him and said, "Be patient, Joe. We have to wait."

They sat alone at a desk at the end of the big control room, now half-empty. The Children were leaving as planned, climbing into the collection of old cars they'd acquired, slowly heading off down the dry dusty road that linked them to the outside world. She felt happy. Something so large, so cosmic was starting to fill her head. It felt warm, familiar. Full of love and some odd kind of recognition.

The whir of the big network server was just audible, like the distant sound of an army of tiny night insects. There were enough people still left to do what was necessary. Soon they could be safely down to just three—herself, Joe, and young Eve, who knew the system so well now, and would stay right up to the final sequence before she too left to find some new life in a world that would be rebuilt around her.

Eve. Just the thought of the name filled her with joy. This was a rebirth that didn't even need Adam. By the time of the zenith, Charley would be the only one left on the farm. The danger of the group remaining intact was too great to contemplate. There would be some kind of revenge, and it was inevitable that, at some stage, the authorities would find their lair. If that was soon, she would be occupying it alone, with her drugs and her needles, safe in the knowledge of what she had achieved. And the rest of them could, when the time came, spread the word, about Gaia, about the need to nurture the precious planet, preserve it for everything that lived, not just the human species. Not that the world needed it. Charley had faith in her god. What would pass, would pass.

The team had departed according to the roster Katayama had drawn up. There were only eight of them left now, with four more climbing quietly into a car outside. This was a kind of death, she thought. Their absence stole some degree of life from her. Like a string vibrating in sympathy, her own private poison had risen on cue. She could no longer feel her lower limbs. Her hands shook from time to time, and there was a distinct neural tic down the left side of her face, like some tiny stroke.

This was not the work of a god in the conventional, human sense. Not an entity as such at all. Yet Charley Pascal felt sure that her own journey into the long, dark, thoughtless sleep ahead would be timed to perfection. A few hours after the zenith, when it would finally be safe to allow the cycle of the satellite to carry on its work, she could close her eyes, listen to this system dying into nothingness around her, and then let perpetual night engulf her.

Katayama asked, "What happens if we lose the feed?"

The flat, crass question made her jump, almost annoyed her. "We won't lose the feed."

He stopped messing with his hands, placed them flat on the plain yellow pine of the desk. "But what if? They got the Shuttle damn close to us. We were lucky to get away with that."

"Luck had nothing to do with it," she said coldly. "You still don't understand, do you?"

"I understand you're pushing this right to the end, Charley. We could just program the thing now, destroy the uplink, and then have done with it. There'd be nothing they could do, even if they found us."

"They won't find us in time. How could they?"

His eyes never really opened, she thought. There was something so masculine in this.

"They're not smart enough, Joe."

"Maybe not," he grunted. "All the same, it's a question that's worth asking. Does the risk balance out the reward? Does what we get by waiting really make it worthwhile?"

Charley Pascal sighed. It had been a long time since anyone had truly questioned her authority, and now that it had happened, she felt affronted. "That's my call, Joe. You're important to us. What you've done, sorting out the equipment, sorting out our security, that's vital. But you're not an astronomer or a physicist. And I am. So believe me when I say we have to do it like this."

"Even with the risk they might get here first?"

"Sundog isn't bulletproof," she replied testily. "We can wind it up just so much and after that it breaks. Sometime after the zenith, the amount of pure energy that we'll be pushing through that system defies analysis. Even I'd be hard-pressed to put a figure on that. We've got to use it wisely or the whole thing will blow. To do that I need the best, most recent guess we have on how the storm's changing after the zenith, when we can use it to most effect. And I need to see how it responds when we do open up the gates all the way. I've got to do it like that, Joe. Otherwise we could be sending fireballs into the middle of the Atlantic, or making people sweat in Boston when we might be razing Chicago to the ground."

"Yeah," he said, shifting restlessly in his seat.

She didn't want an argument just now. "Look. We've got the best information on the trend of the cycle there is. No one could supply us anything more timely."

"I know." A shadow of a smile. It was as close as Katayama could get, she thought, and realized, with a twinge of guilt, that she was glad this forced, close relationship now had so little time to run. "I just get impatient."

"Men do. And besides, isn't there something else you're forgetting?"

He stared at her with those heavy-lidded eyes, not understanding.

"We're not alone in this, Joe. We are part of the engine. We are agents of something bigger. If we weren't here helping the cycle along, somebody would be in our place. We can't lose. It's unthinkable."

"Right."

Sometimes he could be so impenetrable, so difficult to read. "I want to see the cycle report," she said curtly.

"Okay." He got up, went behind the wheelchair, pushed her over to the terminal. Eve was sweating over the incoming data. She looked little more than eighteen: a thin, flat-chested kid with long dark hair that kept falling in front of her face as she typed. She wore an I LOVE LINUX T-shirt and cutoff blue jeans. A scrolling window of text and graphics swam across the screen.

"In a nutshell," Charley said.

"Big," Eve replied in a flat English accent. "There was a lull for a while a couple of hours ago, and then it started to build. You can look through the reports. Major seismic events in Asia. A lot of telecom links down too. Confined to the northern hemisphere. There's nothing that seems able to touch anyplace below the equator directly. They'll still get hit by aftereffects, of course."

"How much of this is us?"

Eve shook her head. "Not a lot. I'm putting in some extra background feed, a big broad wash, nothing focused like we did in Vegas. Is that right?"

Charley nodded. "I don't want this pushed too hard until we have a real target. We could have done something with Tokyo, I guess, but that could have jeopardized what we have later."

Eve looked at her. This was not some game. She wanted to get this right. Everything else seemed unimportant. "You think we could break Sundog, Charley?"

"I know we could. The power in the storm is unimaginable. If we use it too quickly, or at the wrong time, it could blow everything. And if the cycle comes up really high, that may not be at the peak. We could be wasting what we have then. Why turn it on New York if there's enough heat there already?"

Eve glanced down the corridor. "You still want me to go last?" she said, no emotion in her voice. (Eve had no emotions,

Charley thought; this life, for her, was just a passing stream of events.)

"Joe's last. You go before him."

"That means I have to make my own way out there, alone," Eve said, the long dark hair flicking in front of her eyes.

"No. None of us is alone. You can't even think that."

"No." Eve's face was blank. Charley watched her reactions and glanced at Katayama. There was no room for changes at this stage.

"I don't know what I'll do," Eve said.

"You'll find out, Eve. Don't worry."

"I know. . . ."

"Eve," Joe said, that same thin smile on his face, "this is the only way."

"Think of what they would do if they found us here together," Charley added.

"And what they'd do to us," Katayama said. "In the end, we get to be heroes. In the beginning—"

"They crucified Jesus," Charley said, and immediately regretted the analogy. This was a superficial one. They deserved better than that and it seemed to scare the girl.

"I guess we'd be in big trouble. But watching everybody go—it's as if the fewer of us there are here, the weaker the whole thing feels. I start to ask questions."

Charley touched her arm, felt the warm young skin. "No. We're all one in this. You'll come to feel that, Eve."

"I guess so." She looked so young. Pale complexion, tired eyes.

"I'm taking a rest now," Charley said, and signaled for Katayama to push the chair. "You keep at it. You come and wake me if you need to talk."

"Sure."

Katayama pushed the wheelchair into the bedroom, lifted her body carefully out onto the bed. She winced, almost felt like screaming. The pain was beginning to work its way into new parts of her body, creeping slowly with each minute, running like a gentle, sluggish fire. She pointed out the needle and the morphine on the bedside cabinet and said, "Watch her, Joe. We can't change things now."

"She's scared, Charley. She's just human."

"Exactly." Her face was screwed up with the pain. Then she closed her eyes and tried to dream the sky into her head.

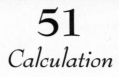

51
Calculation

La Finca, 0803 UTC

After they finished talking to the people in Vegas, something went out of the atmosphere of the room. Bevan, much to Lieberman's surprise and near-admiration, had come over, looked Mo in the eye, and said, "Hey. What's done is done. The big guy's right. Let's just focus on the job."

And then the rest of them, leaving Lieberman and Mo to fill it with some vast, empty silence. She broke it. "Michael . . ."

"No," he said, putting a finger to her lips. "You don't need to say anything. Really."

"I do." She was dog-tired but there was still some sense of serenity about her. Talking about her pained, fractured past had lanced some wound.

"Maybe. But not now. We'll have plenty of time when this is over, Mo. If you like. And that's your choice."

She came close to him, kissed him gently on the cheek. Then Annie was through the door, watching them silently, not knowing what to make of this.

"You look bright and sparky," he said. "Unlike the rest of us. You got some sleep?"

"Yes. Mom?"

Mo was over, stroking her hair. "What's wrong, Annie?"

The girl blinked, big wide eyes that said, *Scared, scared, scared*. Mo held her to her waist, eyes closed, face screwed up in agony again, and Lieberman thought: This is one pretty picture Charley has given the world.

"Hey," he said, striding over, some bustle in him he didn't even begin to recognize. "Will you two snap out of this, please?"

His arms were around both of them, feeling this warmth there, feeling the comfort of their physical presence. Annie stared up at him, wide-eyed, looking for something.

He reached down, held her chin. "This will be okay, kid. Trust me. We can see this through. All three of us."

"I heard Irwin talking." Her voice was soft and damaged. "They know."

Mo groaned.

"Know what?" he asked. "That you two got a bum deal from life? Met some weird people along the way? So what, Annie? You didn't do anything. You just found some odd company. Big deal. One day, you two can come to San Francisco with me. If you like. You want weird people? I can show you ones you wouldn't believe."

"Michael . . ." Mo said.

"It's an invitation. That's all. Think about it at your leisure."

Annie stared at him. "They won't take me away?"

Lieberman bent down, gazed into her pale, serious face. "No. Why? And anyway, they wouldn't dare. We'll see this through. The three of us. And when we get out on the other side, I don't know what happens. But it gets better. For all of us. That's a promise."

"A promise," Mo repeated, her head buried deep in his shoulder, so deep he couldn't begin to see her face. Michael Lieberman closed his eyes and wondered at this moment, its intimate closeness, the power of emotion that lived like an electric charge between them. Family, he thought. This, he guessed, summed it up. Sharing the pain, the ecstasy together. He really didn't need to wonder why Mo took to the Children when the floor disappeared from underneath them. Open arms didn't demand questions.

"So," he said, breaking the hot, labored silence. "Do we get to go outside now? Take a breath of fresh air? There's drinks on the terrace, from the sound of it."

They unclasped themselves from each other and walked out into the scorching day. The rest were seated on the veranda, underneath the shade of a gigantic palm, jugs of fresh orange juice on the table. Annie ran ahead and sat on the edge of the pond, watching the golden shapes of the fish come up to the surface now and then, throwing pebbles into the gray-green viscous water, following the circles they made. He and Mo pulled up chairs and helped themselves to the drinks. He felt edgy. Everyone just wanted to do nothing but wait, he thought, and wouldn't Charley be so happy with that.

"Tell me about this satellite again, Irwin," he asked. "What did you do to my original design? What did you add?"

He watched the surface of the old stone fish pond, Annie perched on the edge. Feeling helpless. Feeling exhausted and grateful for the shade of the palm that cut the power out of the gleaming day.

"I thought we'd been through this, Michael," Schulz replied, a distinct, sharp note of annoyance in his voice. "We're all a little tired here."

"Let's wait and see, you mean?"

"Look, we've done what we can. When they get that system back on-line, we're all ready to go. Till then, let's just relax, huh? There's no point in running 'round and 'round in circles over nothing. We may need all the energy we've got later."

"Yeah. No point."

They didn't even think the cycle reports were that important anymore. Everything had come to focus around this place outside Vegas, walking in there, guns blazing, stealing back what someone else had stolen from them.

"We're tired," Mo said.

"Me too. But doesn't something bug you about all of this?"

"Such as what?" Bennett asked.

"How, ever since it started, we never really got around to doing any thinking for ourselves, because someone else was always feeding a chunk of information that shaped what we did anyway. Like this Vegas thing. Like taking out the domes. And there's a curious thing too."

"What?" Schulz asked.

"How come everyone else in this loop—Spooksville in Langley, most every European capital we can think of, Tokyo, Vegas, San Francisco, they're all looking up at the sky and see all manner of crap coming down on them. And we just sit here watching most everything work? Do you ever think about that? Aside from the explosion of the dome, we haven't had a single serious outage. It's all happened elsewhere."

"No reason for it to happen here," Schulz said. "We're way away from any major financial centers. Why should she target us when she's blown up the dome anyway?"

"Well, correct me if I'm wrong, but I thought we were supposed to be in charge of the whole thing."

" 'Were,' " Schulz said.

"Point taken. Still . . ."

"Still what, Michael?"

He rolled the dregs of his orange juice around in the glass and watched Annie playing by the thick green water of the pond. She had a little paper yacht folded from a used sheet out of the laser printer. He could still see the text on it: numbers, formulas, graphs, all the mechanical things you used to describe what happened in this wonderful place called science. "Still, I think we're being dumb, somehow."

Bennett, who looked dead to the world, said, very slowly, "I don't think any of us would argue with that."

"No. So Sundog. Remind me, Irwin. You took my design and added all that ugly Star Wars stuff on the bottom."

Schulz sounded offended. "Michael, how can you call it ugly? You only saw it on the damn model."

"Okay, I know, I know. Ugly is as ugly does. And my name's Forrest—"

"*Michael!*" It was Mo this time, and she looked close to annoyed.

"Sorry. I babble creatively. Einstein did it too but no one snitched." He watched Annie pushing the little boat across the pond. Sundog was something like this, only with the extra dimension of space added in. This was science too. Somewhere there was a bunch of numbers that could add up the satellite's present position. Somewhere a little line of buzzing electrons ran back from Sundog right to Charley, directly to her lair, talking in some two-way conversation only they understood. It irked him no end that a chunk of equipment he'd initially designed was being used in this way. And something else too.

"You're wrong, Irwin," he muttered.

"About anything in particular?"

"About all that ugly stuff you tacked onto the butt of my beautiful machine. I didn't just see it on the model." The image was still there in his head and he knew why it had stayed hidden. There was just too much pain in those last moments of the Shuttle crew. He'd liked Bill Ruffin, felt touched by the dogged, dutiful enthusiasm of the crew.

"Maybe you weren't watching, but after your nice machine killed those people, that floatcam of theirs got jerked around by something itself—I'd rather not guess at just what. It moved around from the dark side of Sundog out into the light. The business end, I guess you'd call it."

Schulz took a big gulp of his drink. "I guess I wasn't looking right then."

"No. I don't blame you. But I don't think I was hallucinating. It made it there, for a few seconds anyway. And then the line went dead."

"The satellite would have fried the thing, Michael," Schulz explained. "That's what it's supposed to do."

"I guess so." He did see it, he was sure of that. A bristling array of dishes, antennae, and assorted chunks of military metal. He was right. It was ugly. "We still got that video on the system, Irwin?"

"It's on the system."

"How do I find it?"

"I can do that for you," Mo said, looking interested. "Any particular reason?"

"No." He wished he could think of one. "I guess I'm just feeling restless." He looked at his watch. It was nine-fifteen local. If Helen and her people got lucky in Nevada, the satellite might be back under their wing within two hours. That gave them a little under an hour before zenith to take the thing down.

He got up, and Mo Sinclair followed him. They went back into the control room, and he didn't know why but there was some low buzz of interior excitement hanging around his head, like a cloud of flies. "You find me that video, Mo. I got a call to make."

He watched her bring the PC alive and dialed Helen's number. "I'm waiting," he said to the screen on the desk. But there was nothing there except blackness.

Then he turned back to the video. It was there, as he remembered it. The antenna on the satellite did move, like a dog cocking its ear to the call of its master, and he couldn't, for the life of him, work out why this bugged him.

"Is that important?" Mo asked, watching the brief flicker of the film before the floatcam was blown to pieces.

"I don't know," he muttered. "Or rather, yes. But I don't understand how."

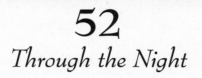

52
Through the Night

Nellis Air Force Base, 0923 UTC

"Hi. Jeff Green."

The FBI agent stuck out his hand and grinned. In the bright, artificial light of the Nellis pad he looked small and insignificant. No more than twenty-five, Helen thought. Short cropped hair, a friendly, open face.

"Green," Barnside said, and took his hand. The contrast between the two men could hardly have been greater: Barnside big, older, darker. And Green just starting out, bright-eyed and optimistic. Larry Wolfit, by Helen's side, just coughed. This wasn't some nice, cool detached wildlife project in the Rockies. He really didn't like getting this close to the action.

"Mr. Wolfit, one of our science guys," Barnside explained. "A touch shy. Most of them are. But not all. You're here to look after us?"

Green laughed. "No, sir. You're capable of doing that for yourselves. But they said I should stick with you all the same. Like the man said, it's important you stay out of their way when they're going in. They're playing with some neat stuff out there." He took a small metal canister out of his night combat suit. "These flash grenades, for example. They make our job a lot easier. But you get one of those in the face without goggles on and you'll know it."

"That's understood," Helen said. "The key thing for us is to get in as quickly as possible once you've secured the area."

"Agreed. There's five of you in all?"

"Yes. The other two are already on their way with their gear. I heard what Collins said about clearing the farm first. I still want them in place as close to the dome as possible so we can get in there when it's free."

"Sure. And you three guys?"

"I'm just going to amble on up front with the support people," Barnside said. "I could spend my whole life watching other people work. I guess the science people hang around talking formulas or something. That right?"

Helen did her best to smile graciously. "We can wait our turn. Can we go now?"

"In our slot," Green said. "The other four machines go ahead of us. In formation. We make up a lone rear. That's the way it is, not my decision. We get down a minute or so after they land. They got half a mile to walk before they can enter. We can just follow along slow. We all got maps?"

They stared at the charts in their hands. Green was starting to take on the manner of a tour guide. "Good. If you look at our landing position, you can see there's a track leads sideways from the site. That takes you to the foot of the ridge. Mr. Barnside, you'll be able to follow in the footsteps of our guys who go ahead. I suggest we wait at the ridge itself. If you want fast access to the dome, once we can allow that, I suggest the rest of your people start to make their way there pronto. If everything goes according to plan, we'll be inside that place in a matter of minutes."

"Understood," Helen said.

"You mind me asking something?" Green really did look young when he came up with the questions.

"Fire away."

"Just five of you? Is that enough?"

"Five or fifty," she answered, "it wouldn't make much difference. All we're trying to do is connect that system up to the network and check if it's still working. Most ten-year-old kids with a PC could do that, if you want the honest reply. We hook it up, and then someone else works out how to control it."

"Which," Barnside interjected, "is why I don't understand your need to be there, Helen. If this is admin, you'd have more resources back here."

"We've been through that. The conversation's over."

He shrugged and looked at Wolfit. "Have it your way. I think Larry here would be happy to stay put. That right?"

Wolfit gave a humorless grin in the half-light.

"You guys going to kiss and make up or something?" Green asked.

"No need, Green," Barnside said. "We're professionals. We get on with it."

She watched the activity on the airfield. Farther up the pad the turbines were getting loud, making the kind of noise that preceded takeoff. She looked up at the cockpit of their own machine and saw the copilot of their own helicopter staring back at her. The opaque night-vision mask he wore made him look like some giant insect. He stuck out a thumb, motioned to the inside of the craft. A crewman was waiting at the door, holding out a hand. Struggling up the little ladder, with his help, they climbed in, and when everyone was seated he slid shut the door. She was amazed. The sound of the outside world disappeared. The aircraft's interior was clean and shiny, with what looked like a telecom rig in the corner.

"Why's it so quiet?" she asked the crewman.

"This is an unusual ship. Command module. It means we have to rig it out with noise-canceling stuff, make sure we can carry out normal voice conversations in the air. That way you people can communicate without going through us, or having to wear cans."

She pulled out her pocket communicator, looked at the blank screen. "You think this thing works in here?"

The man shook his head. "No idea, lady. But if you want to make a video call, you can get through using the fixed comm center over there. Just key in your ID and it will route your calls straight through."

Somewhere ahead of them the noise level was rising. She peered through the small, high windows and saw one of the Sea

Knights climb into the sky, a giant black form, rising on what looked like a single feathery wing.

"What's the light going to be like?" she asked Green.

"Poor, probably," Green replied. "Don't let what you experienced on the field down there fool you. The sky is absolutely clear but we have almost no moon. As soon as we're airborne, the lights go out in the cabin. It takes an hour for the human eye to acclimatize to darkness, so we won't be getting out in perfect condition. But it will be a lot better than going from full light to full dark."

"You brought some goggles?" Barnside asked.

"Yeah. Probability is you won't need them."

He started to throw around pairs of simple, tinted goggles to each of them. "This isn't night-vision stuff," Barnside said gruffly.

"No, sir. We're not going to be needing that. By the time we're going anywhere serious, the Cobras will be behind us lighting up that place like a football stadium. These are just for the flash grenades. If, by any chance, they're still in use when we get close to the house then we put these on. You need to be within twenty feet or so for the effect to be bad, so this is just in case."

"Yeah," Barnside barked. The noise level was rising inside the machine. They were close to takeoff. "I'd really like some night goggles."

"Like I said," Green said, taking a small service flashlight out of his pocket. "We don't need them. There's a clear division of duties here, sir. I hope you can go along with that."

"Sure." And Barnside gave a sour grin at Larry Wolfit, who looked ready to throw up. Barnside's big head lurched backward and forward on his shoulders as the machine began to move. With a soft, rising roar, the helicopter rose into the night sky. Seated opposite the silent Wolfit, Helen watched the lights of Nellis recede beneath them. Off to the south was the city, a bizarre tangle of fire and artificial illumination. She didn't want to think what the night would be like there: no certainty, no order. Vegas wasn't a place to be alone just then.

The machine leveled out and they felt it tilt gently forward as it moved into a horizontal cruise. The interior lights dimmed. Larry Wolfit, visible from the faint illumination of the emergency exit sign, stared back at her looking drained. S&T was supposed to be available for operational duties, it was written right there in the contract. But that happened so rarely. To be plowing through the impenetrable night sky, heading for a rendezvous none of them could predict, wasn't really why you joined the club.

She sat next to Green, strapped into the bench seat, while Barnside, in the corner, stared mindlessly out the window, not saying a word. And she tried to clear her mind, tried to focus on the hours to come, to make sure every angle was covered. Then she dreamed. It was impossible not to dream, moving through the black velvet night in the belly of this giant machine, like some silent insect whirring toward its prey.

She was ready to nod off—so little sleep these last few days—when Barnside, his voice raising several decibels in volume, said, "Hey, I think you got a call."

She had, out of habit, rerouted her videophone onto the on-board comm screen by her seat as soon as she climbed in. Now it was flashing with an incoming signal. Green passed her the remote control, she pointed it at the screen, and Lieberman's face appeared, bright and animated in the gloomy, enclosed interior of the cabin.

"Good morning. Where the hell are you?"

"That's classified. You look . . . perky."

"Yeah. I was wondering . . . how's it going there?"

"What?" she said, and wished this conversation could be more private. Everyone could hear it in this small, enclosed interior of the helicopter.

"Just asking."

"Michael," she said testily, "we are in the middle of an operation. I really don't have time for small talk."

Lieberman looked worried, uncomfortable, and it was so obvious even on the lousy picture of the video screen. "No, it's just . . ."

She waited and it didn't come. "Just what?"

"I just want you to know we're not sitting on our butts. We're still working on some ideas too."

"Good ideas?" she asked, interested.

"Maybe. And anyway, you won't need them. You got Charley in your sights, right?"

She nodded. "It looks like it. And for the record, Michael, I never imagined you were sitting on your butts. Not for one moment." He seemed worried, and momentarily tongue-tied too. "Now can we go back to work?"

"Sure. But if you do need some extra help, come calling. I might just have something extra in my bag of tricks. Nothing to trouble you with now, and I don't think you'll need it. You just get on with the job and I'm sure it will all be just fine."

"We'll be in touch when we have news. These portable communicators ought to work on the ground. It's night here. She can't throw any of the storm at us."

"Maybe she can throw other stuff."

"Yes. We've thought of that. This is quite an operation. Maybe one day I get to break the rules and tell you all about it."

The pale, bearded face nodded. "That would be nice. Helen?"

She was looking at her watch. An annoying habit, one she hoped to lose. "We need to keep this short, Michael."

"I know. All I wanted to say was . . . be real careful out there. Charley just loves surprises."

"Thanks for your advice."

He winced. "Oh right. There goes the aging hippie academic telling Miss CIA what to do. Sorry."

"No. I appreciate it. I apologize if it sounded like I didn't."

"Right. I'm going back to my algorithms now. We'll talk on the other side of this thing."

The screen went dead, and as it did the note of the helicopter's engine changed, dwindled down several tones.

"Some guy, huh?" Barnside grunted. "What the hell was all that about?"

"He's just nervous, wanting to do something. Touching, in a way."

"I guess so. But he's got an idea about something. He's soft on you too. You get that?"

She shook her head and groaned. "You know, sometimes, Barnside, you start to remind me of the bad uncle I never had. The one who always embarrasses you at birthday parties."

He roared out a laugh. "Hey. I *like* that!" And even she couldn't stifle a stupid grin. Then the aircraft lurched. She held on to the passenger rail to steady herself and looked at Larry Wolfit. He was really close to throwing up.

Green pointed out the window. "We're going in. You can see the first four ships on the ground already."

"So," Barnside said, "I just go ahead of you people and follow the route marked on the chart?"

"Yeah, sir. There's a bluff right beneath the dome. You can wait there until they give you the all-clear to go into the farm. You ought to get a good view of the fireworks, provided they're not over by then. And we just work our way behind you, a little more leisurely, I think. I don't want to bump into those guys in the middle of the night. You should remember that too."

The helicopter was hovering now, descending slowly to the desert floor. It came to earth with a jolt. Green had been right. Outside it was pitch-black. From where they'd put the Sea Knight down, it was impossible to see even a single other aircraft, though the stench of Avgas that came through the door when the crewman threw it open suggested they couldn't be far away.

"Ride ends here, folks," the crewman said jovially. "We all booked you on return tickets, so you take care."

Then they were out in the night air, and Helen felt her breath disappear inside her. In the desert it was cold, a dull, sluggish cold that could sap her energy. And there was a smell too: of dry vegetation, something distantly rank in the air.

Barnside walked off into the darkness. The rest of the S&T crew headed toward the dome, a single grunted "Bye" as they disappeared into the night. Green switched on his flashlight, though they didn't need it yet; the downward-pointing landing lights of the helicopter saw to that.

"A half a mile?" Wolfit asked.

Green nodded. "All nice and straight and level. There's some rock cover between us and the farmhouse we can use to screen us. That dictated the landing site."

"How are you feeling, Larry?" Helen asked. He seemed happier to be out of the helicopter.

"I'll be okay," he said with a weak grin. "I just hate those damn things."

"Join the club." Green grinned.

"That call from Lieberman?" Wolfit asked.

"What about it?"

"You think he's on to something?"

"He's one smart guy. We won't need it, though."

"No," Wolfit sighed, and she wished he weren't so tense, so scared by what was ahead of them.

"What if the farm has lookouts or something?" Helen asked.

Green shook his head. "We'd have picked them up with the aerial scan. I guess everyone's in the house. That's nice. How it should be."

Wolfit coughed loudly. "Maybe we should be moving."

Green nodded. "Sure."

And they set off, the HRT man in the lead, flashlight casting a lone yellow beam into the night. He'd been right about their eyesight, she thought. Once they moved away from the dim presence of the helicopter, once there was nothing in the darkness except the puny beam of the flashlight, you really could see a little more. The desert made its living presence known to you. There was life there: the high-pitched rustling of insects, and farther off the long, low howl of something larger.

"You been in the Bureau long, Green?" Wolfit seemed eager to talk. Nervous, Helen guessed. She was happy just to listen and think about what lay ahead.

"Two years, sir."

They were out of sight of the helicopter now. It must have been a good four hundred yards behind. Ahead, looming larger in front of them, was the rock ridge he'd talked about, a small hogback that now stood solid black against the gray, starlit backdrop of the night sky. The team must have crossed it by now, she thought. Soon there ought to be some sign of the attack.

"Guess this must be the biggest thing they ever gave you?" Wolfit asked gloomily.

Green laughed. "Nice try, sir. You know I can't talk about operations or that kind of thing."

"Sure."

Wolfit walked a little faster, left Helen behind, caught up with Green, put an arm on his shoulder. "But we can talk in generalizations, now, can't we? This must be the biggest thing. It's the biggest I ever got, what with the President, our new President, breathing down our necks, huh?"

"I guess so, quite something, really."

She caught up and touched Wolfit lightly on the shoulder. "It's okay, Larry. We're just here to run up a network. Nothing dangerous."

"Sorry. Guess my mouth was running away with itself. And me the nature lover. I'm supposed to feel at home in this place."

Then he jumped as if he'd stood on a rattlesnake. The first flash had exploded on the other side of the ridge, and even partly blocked as it was by the solid mass of stone, it seemed incredibly bright, a veil of phosphorescence that put spots of color at the back of their eyes. And no sound. The silence was strange, unsettling.

"It begins," Green said, and laughed. The sky became alive with the dancing lights of the flash grenades, and Helen stared at the ground, trying to keep them out of her head, fumbling in her pocket for the goggles.

Green stopped walking. "I think we should stay here for a minute or two. Stay in the lee of the ridge, try not to look at the sky. You see what I mean about the brightness now? And we don't even get a direct view of those things. We just stay out of sight."

"I see," she said, and worked the goggles onto her head in any case. They made the night go black again. What little detail there was disappeared except for the flashes overhead, and that made you want to look at them even more. She snatched the things off after a few seconds.

Green watched her. "Yeah. They don't suit me either."

"Fucking technology," Wolfit yelled, loud enough to make both of them jump. "You believe the stuff they make us work with these days?"

"It's a little late to get into that conversation, Larry," she said, puzzled. "I think you could pick another occasion." And the thought came out of nowhere: Larry was really nervous.

There was a huge ripple of light in the sky, and noise now too, maybe gunshots, maybe just the popping of more grenades. It was impossible to tell.

"They give you Bureau guys all that stuff," Wolfit continued. She tried not to listen; he was starting to embarrass her. "Take those new P54s the Army is giving out. I mean, they sound real interesting." Green's silence was palpable.

"You going deaf or something?" Wolfit asked flatly. "I know guns. Sometimes when I'm out in Yellowstone they call on us to go shoot some wolf that breaches the area, kills some stupid cow. You believe that?"

"Sir, you can't expect me to talk about operational issues."

"Oh no. Oh no. It's called culling, Green. You know that term?"

"Larry . . ." Helen murmured. "Calm down. This is going to be okay."

"Hell," he rambled on, "I saw the damn thing in his suit when we were climbing onto the helicopter."

"Sir. It's supposed to be classified."

"I know *that*. I know exactly what it is too. The P54. Manufactured by Armstrong in Philadelphia. First workable handgun made entirely of composite material. Half the weight of a service-issue unit. Built-in silencer. Massive firepower at close quarters. A piece of shit if you want to hit anyone more than thirty yards away too. That's what I hear."

"Okay," Green said, a nervous edge to his voice. "You know what you know. That fair enough? One more minute and I think we should be going."

"That's not comradely," Wolfit grunted.

"Enough!" She could hear how shrill she sounded. The desert scared her. The job scared her. Wolfit was starting to scare her too. She didn't need someone out of control right then.

"No," he said, voice rising. "It's not enough. All these damn secrets. All these damn people think they know everything there is to know. And the truth is they know nothing. *Nothing.* You going to show me that thing?"

"Can't do that, sir. Can't—"

And almost choked as Wolfit was on him, a single sharp punch in the stomach taking out his breath, hands running all over his night suit.

"Larry," she yelled, walking over to the fight. "What the hell are you doing? I am reporting this, you believe it. Even if the kid's too scared to."

"Yeah?" She couldn't see his face properly in the darkness. He was hidden in the shadow of the ridge. "Well, you go ahead and report me. Who gives a shit?"

Larry Wolfit felt the P54 in his hand and wished he weren't sweating so much. It was light, so light he could hardly believe it. A little big for most ordinary duties. And long too. The integral silencer seemed responsible for that. He lifted it up and down with his right hand a few times.

"This the kind of thing you like, Green? The kind of thing you approve of? Guess there's a little work to do on the size, but they'll get there. Thank you." He turned the weapon around, held it by the long barrel, held the handgrip outward.

"I just wanted to look," he said apologetically. "Sitting around on the edge of things like this just makes me uneasy."

"Sure thing," Green mumbled. "I think we should be going now." Then he reached out for the gun. Larry Wolfit flipped it over in his hand, slipped his finger into the trigger guard, pointed it at the sky.

"Trick or treat?" he said. "You should never fall for that one. Don't they teach you that in the Bureau?"

"Yeah," Green said. "But not with fellow agents."

"Pity," Wolfit grunted, and fired a single round. It made a noise like a balloon exploding underneath a pillow. Jeff Green was lifted off his feet, flew backward noiselessly, fell to the ground in a silent heap.

Then Larry Wolfit turned around to face Helen. He was out of the shadow now and he looked half-crazy. The dark shape of the gun was in his hand. "Wasn't meant to be like this," he said. "Wasn't meant to be like this at all."

53
Entry

Cabin Springs, 1003 UTC

There were only a couple of lights on inside the farmhouse, and they threw little illumination onto the scene. "Millfield?" John Collins said quietly into his voice mike, half-listening for the distant circling of the surveillance helicopter overhead. When they were in place, Collins could floodlight the scene. But they were late. An entry in half-darkness seemed inevitable. "You read anything?"

"Negative," the far-off voice squawked into his single earpiece. "We got no sound, no heat indications since we started this thing, John. Either these people are gone, sleeping, or just plain dead."

"Yeah," he said. His team was stationed to the left of the front door, just out of range of the obvious infrared security trigger that had been fastened, like an amateur-hour burglar alarm, to the nearest stanchion in the frame. The farmhouse was wood, with a big open veranda, and stood in a flat patch of rocky ground. Behind it were a couple of agricultural buildings, a horse ring, and a yard with three or four cars in it.

What looked like a newly made path led off to the adjoining ridge. Somewhere on the top, no more than four hundred yards away, he guessed, was the dome. He could just make out the dark shapes of his men working their way into position. It had all been so easy, and that made him feel uncomfortable. Some snags were inevitable. It was best to get them out of the way as soon as you could.

"Initial plan," Collins said. "Flash goggles on. Team one goes in first, the rest of you in order. Keep your heads, in there; I'd like to come out of this with no casualties on either side. And good luck, folks."

Then he pushed the goggles back down onto his cheeks and nodded to the team. One of them walked up to the small downstairs window, sidestepping the infrared beam, and threw a flash grenade through the pane. There was a low tinkling of broken glass. Collins looked away at the ground, waiting for the first flash. It came like a brief bolt of lightning, with a soft puff of air behind it, and he led the team in a steady, fixed walk to the door. Then five more (counting, he kept counting, and listening for the yells, the screaming, but none came), and he was nodding at them, watching the one with the sledgehammer pull it back and start to thunder away at the big wooden slab. It fell in two, and they were through, screaming like crazy, hearing the sound of explosions and crashing glass from elsewhere in the building.

"Team One entered, control not established," Collins said, and paused while one of the flash grenades let off a late rogue blast that painted the entire room a harsh, stony white, drew everything out like some kind of bas relief that wasn't quite real, more a piece of strange modern art than a picture of something physical around them.

"Team Two entered, no contact," said a voice in his ear.

"Team Three entered, no contact."

"Team Four entered. Ditto."

The last commander paused. "What the hell is going on here, John?"

"Maintain vigilance." Collins watched the room come back into normal focus. It was full of cheap desks, cheap furniture, a whole line of PCs still glinting and alive, the twirling picture of some screensavers rolling around their monitors. Somewhere in the corner one of the team was throwing up, a repetitive, physical noise that sounded as if it might never end. Fear made its presence known in the oddest of ways.

"Keep those goggles on, man," Collins barked. "And don't think this is over. Millfield? Have you seen anyone leave this building since we entered?"

"Negative, John. You guys went in, no one went out."

"Right." Collins walked through into the hall, met two of the other teams wandering in to meet each other.

"This place is empty, John," someone said, invisible behind the flash goggles. "Hell, it smells empty."

"Yeah," he said. "I know."

"There's food in the kitchen, dirty plates," the Team Two commander said. "But no clothes, no suitcases. They made it out of here."

"Still rooms to go," the Team Three man said. "We'll take upstairs, constant vigilance, usual drill. Use the flash grenades. Don't take anything for granted."

The four men in black ascended the narrow wooden staircase, machine pistols in their hands, and Collins could hear the popping of grenades up there, see the bright phosphorescent light chasing down the plain white corridors of the farmhouse. You didn't prosper in this business on your instincts, but just then John Collins knew his were right: There was nothing to be found upstairs.

"Fred," Collins said to the Team Four commander. "Get your guys seeing if there's any subterranean rooms on this place. A cellar or something."

"But John, it's built on solid rock. What'd they use? Mining equipment or something?"

"Just do it, will you?" Collins snapped, and wished there weren't so much crankiness in his voice. "And while you're at it, bring in some of the explosives guys. I want this place cleaned internally. Make sure we don't have any surprises waiting for us. We got a little extra time to spare. No reason why we shouldn't use it to make sure everything's safe here before going up that hill to the dome."

"Okay." The man shrugged.

"So where'd they go?" the Team Three man asked. "They made it out of here already? And left us the keys to the safe?"

"I don't know," Collins replied. Then called up the Cobra team and diverted them from the lighting detail to sweeping the area, looking for vehicles snaking their way out into the outside world. "Get that S&T woman for me. Maybe they set this thing on automatic and ran."

"Damn," the Team Three man said, and ripped off his goggles.

"Keep those fucking goggles on!" Collins yelled.

"Sir," the man mumbled, and struggled with the eyepiece.

The radio buzzed in Collins's ear. "We got some traffic thirty miles distant, couple of cars," the helicopter captain said. "Could be anybody, that far away."

"Pick them up."

Team Two came back from upstairs. The leader stripped off his goggles and said, "Nothing—"

"Put those fucking gogg—" John Collins heard his own voice rattling around inside his head. It sounded shrill and stupid. "Never mind."

"What the hell's going on?" the man asked grimly.

"This well sure looks dry," Collins muttered, and shook his head. He walked over to the nearest terminal. The monitor was flicking over on the screensaver: mindless geometric patterns repeating over and over again. He punched the space key. "You believe that?"

The screen cleared and Gaia's Web site sat there. "I think these people have got some kind of live Net connection here. A T1 line or something. Those Agency people are going to be jumping up and down with glee."

"John," the Team Four leader said. "We got the okay from the explosives people. This place looks clean. They're running through the path to the dome too, but it's slow work. They wired up some IR burglar alarms on the way. They feed into an audible warning system. No signs of explosive anywhere so far."

"That's good. These guys really did think they'd pulled this one off, huh? Or maybe they didn't want to hang around to see the consequences."

"Guess so," the Team Four leader answered.

"It is so. Pretty soon I'm going to sign this one off to those Agency people. Let them get the geeks in and see if they can bring this thing on-line."

"We got the dome team kicking their heels already," the Team Four man said.

"Well, tell them to wait. They need the go-ahead from their own boss first. So?" John Collins ripped off his flash goggles and glared at them.

"Sir?" someone said.

"So where the hell is she?"

54
In the Desert

Cabin Springs, 1029 UTC

The night was more visible now. Helen could see Larry Wolfit clearly, a tall, slim shape, his outline blurred by the shadow of the rock ridge. He waved the gun a couple of times in front of her face. Then, too quickly for her to anticipate it, he stepped right up and punched her hard with his free hand. She fell back onto the hard, dusty ground, clutching at her cheek, trying to think, to make sense of this. Wolfit stank of sweat and fear but for some reason she felt more puzzled, affronted even, then scared.

"J-Jesus, Helen," he stammered. "This wasn't supposed to happen. None of it. Why the hell did you take the job? Why the hell do you keep working at it like this?"

Scrabbling in the dust, all she could think about was Belinda Churton. What she would do, would be thinking in a situation like this. And why even her reactions, in the end, were just not good enough.

"Get up now, will you?" he snarled. "It's pathetic watching you squirm on the ground like that."

She rolled over, curled into a ball, waited for the next blow. Then, slowly, so he understood this was her decision, not his, she got to her feet.

"There," he said. "Now, that's better." She felt the side of her head again. It was tender, beginning to swell.

"Decision time, my dear," Wolfit said miserably. "Decision time." He pulled back his fist again. She flinched. Then he dropped it. "Hey, just testing reactions." And was on her in an instant, had hold of her hair, pulled it hard, yanked her face into his, his mouth a vicious, taut line in the half-light.

"Why did they choose you, Helen? You going to tell me that? It was supposed to be me. To save us all this trouble."

He wrenched her ear; she screamed. "Shut up!" he shouted.

"You're hurting me."

Wolfit let go, pushed her viciously, kicked out with his feet, took her legs from under her. Back on the ground, she thought, and still nothing working quite right in the head.

"You just overreached yourself, you know," he said, a little calmer now. "We spent too much time on this thing to have it go to waste now. What with you and your friend in Spain thinking you just might bust this all up, you just might have a good idea. You got no ideas. You understand me? None at all."

She thought of Belinda, dying in a roar of homemade explosives. And Wolfit, always quiet, always watchful. He was waving the strange, overlong gun as if it had some kind of special power.

"Go on," she said, not looking at him, not even thinking about anything except how strange this was, how odd a way to leave this existence. "Get this over with, Larry. One more for your list."

"Your fault, Helen. Your fault entirely."

"Sure. That's what all you people get to think. If Charley told you to walk over a cliff I guess you'd do that too, and blame me on the way down."

He was standing over her. The tiny crescent of the moon hung above his head, a curtain of bright, shining stars around it (and she wanted to think about the stars, not about him, not him at all).

"You scared? I guess I'd be."

"Oh my." She almost wanted to laugh.

"This funny or something? You asked that kid over there to join in the laughter?"

"You're pathetic, Larry. Even with that big gun hanging out of your hand like a limp dick. Pathetic."

"Really? Maybe you should ask Belinda fucking Churton about that when you see her again."

And then she did laugh. "You should hear yourself. Is that what the new tomorrow sounds like?"

"Stupid, stupid. You don't understand a thing. This is all about bigger issues than you can ever understand. You got to burn sometimes. You got to cull."

There had to be people, she thought. People at the helicopter. People at the farmhouse. If this went on long enough, they'd come, they'd be looking. If they knew where to find her. If they got there in time.

"So tell me," she said, reaching down, rubbing her aching leg, feeling, through the thin fabric of the combat suit, the thin, slow trickle of blood starting to dampen the material. "Make me understand. Tell me what Charley told you."

"Nothing I didn't know already, except I didn't want to face it. You got to unmanage things. That's the point. Turn back the clock, just put in the status quo as close as you can get it. And don't close your eyes when the tough decisions come."

She waited, wishing she could hear something.

"This can't go on," he said, and there was some nervousness there, some pressure for time, she could sense it. "We're just fucking up the planet, fucking up everything."

"So what's new?"

"What's new is the chance to start over."

"Won't happen. However bad it gets, Larry. You're smart enough to know that."

"That's bullshit. We figured it out."

"Tell me about the 'we,' Larry. Tell me about the Children, and how the hell they got to someone like you."

Wolfit's shoulder chucked up and down but she didn't hear him laugh. "Two kinds of people. Those who get it. Those who don't. You just spent your whole life walking in darkness. Just like everyone else in Washington. You think I never saw things while I was working in that place? All the cruelty? All the cynicism?"

"You're talking about cruelty? Larry . . . did you take a look at Vegas?"

"People die in wars. You got to see the big picture."

"You sound like Hitler."

He laughed then. "Like I said. You either get it or you don't. And now it's just too late for me to throw a little light on the matter. There's things moving out there, and I can't let you have even the faintest chance of stopping it."

The gun rose, made a dark shape against the backdrop of stars. "If you'd been a little less nosy, if you'd done as you were told, maybe you'd have lived to find out. We gave you every chance to back out. But no. . . ."

Something moved, close to them, back near the ridge. She checked her breathing, shuffled slowly, as noiselessly as she could, into a pool of darkness cast by the higher rocks.

"Damn me," he muttered. "Damn me if that kid isn't still alive. Two pops from this thing and he's still grunting." He flicked the switch on the flashlight, swept the narrow yellow beam over toward the ridge. She had to watch. There was no choice. Jeff Green was curled up in a ball by a single hulking rock, a big dark pool of blood growing around his stomach. His eyes glittered in the torchlight, wide open, scared, like those of an animal. He was doing something with his hands, and some small inner voice told her not to stare too hard. It looked like he was trying to push his spilled guts back inside his body.

Wolfit, crazy now, she didn't doubt it, put on a phony southern accent, like Foghorn Leghorn worked up on speed, all this nervousness bubbling over inside him. "Boy. I say *boy*. You need some help over there?"

Green opened his mouth. Something liquid came out, ran down over his chin, dark and viscous, and no human sound, nothing but a low, physical gushing, rhythmic, fading slowly away.

"One more pop and then you can say night-night," Wolfit murmured. The kid said something unintelligible. His hand moved again, and something small, something silver, glinting in the moonlight, rolled across the rocky ground toward them.

"Night-night," Wolfit said, not seeing this. The gun jumped in his hand, making that sickening popping sound again, and

Helen Wagner saw Green's head explode like a pumpkin, felt something hot and sticky rain in droplets on her face.

"Hey," Wolfit said clinically. "That's what it looks like. You think we can play that game now, Helen?"

And what Belinda Churton told you to do was think, Helen reminded herself. More than anything. Think. Of what they discussed in the helicopter, of the little silver cartridge rolling across the rock floor of the desert, winking in the moonlight. Something hissing, fizzing beneath the curtain of winking stars.

Flash.

This hurt. She was scrabbling over onto her side, mind racing, just realizing what the dying Green had rolled toward them when the grenade ignited. Her body blocked most of the brightness, but enough got through to throw her, fire some bright, white curtain across the back of her mind and make her, in an instant, blind, insensate, helpless. Somewhere behind her—yards away or just feet? these distances meant nothing in this white, dreamlike world—Larry Wolfit screamed in pain, an animal noise, of agony and loss.

Blind people can still kill you, she thought. Then rolled, hard and fast, across the ground, not minding the sharp rocks digging into her body, eyes screwed shut against the agony.

Flash.

Even with her eyes shut and her arm set against her head, the light came through, a livid red-tinged orange, the color of flesh, the color of blood.

"Fuck you!" Wolfit screamed. And somewhere to her left there was the low, soft whisper of the gun and a sharp explosion in the ground. Dust and rock flew up and battered the back of her head. Two more to go. She reached into the pocket of her suit, grabbing for the goggles, found the cheap plastic lenses in her hand, heard Wolfit's lumbering footsteps once more, rolled again, then carefully, slowly, so as to make no noise, pulled them over her head.

Flash.

She knew what Wolfit must be doing now. Standing there, the gun in one hand, his free arm covering his face, waiting for the grenade to run out of steam. She opened her eyes. And saw nothing. The world was pale white, no detail, no movement. This brightness was so strong it wiped out the senses for a time, like staring at the sun, and there was no telling how long it would be before they returned. Then something stirred in the whiteness, a shape moved, there was the sound of those big mountain boots crunching the desert gravel.

"I can see you," Wolfit said, and she thought: Lying, he's lying again, he always lies, this dishonesty seeps out of his pores like sweat. And she stayed still, stayed silent. The dim white shape moved, a ghostly arm extended away from her. It jerked; the gun made a sound. Somewhere close by the ground exploded.

She almost had to bite her tongue to stay quiet. And that was what he wanted. To make her taunt him. Hear her voice, then turn, grinning. Eyes screwed shut tight once more, then she opened them, gingerly. More detail. Less light. Her eyesight was slowly getting back to something close to normality, the complex structure of the eye recovering from the shock of the first flare.

There are four, she thought. And tried to remember how many were already gone.

His outline revolved, arm extended; the gun jerked again. Wolfit was guessing. His sight was gone completely, she thought, and now he was just trying to listen, maybe even work methodically around himself in an arc, hoping to catch her.

Flash.

So near she could hear the sound of the phosphor fizzing in the air. And it hurt again, even through the goggles. She closed her eyes and wanted to scream. No, a voice (Belinda Churton's distant, ghostly) said. Correction, Helen. You did scream.

We heard you.

We all heard you.

And in that instant she became aware of the noise she was making: the loud, labored sound of her breathing, the sobbing gasps that welled up in her throat, the constant, rushing roar of the blood through her veins. She forced her eyes open. Pain. His presence was overwhelming. She could feel him there, a huge black figure in front of her, see the shape of his legs no more than two feet away, and didn't dare look up, knowing what was there (long and dark and deadly).

"Women," Larry Wolfit said slowly. "Just can't keep quiet, can you?"

"What the hell are you?" she yelled, hearing the words trip out of her mouth automatically, not caring anymore how they betrayed her.

Wolfit sounded as if he were offended by the question, as if she ought to have known the answer already. "Me, Helen? I'm just a little piece of the mechanism, a little cog in the celestial machine. Nighty-night, now."

And it was like the sound of a rapier moving through the air, so sudden, so full of force. She heard this rush of energy, heard too Wolfit groaning, then screaming, became aware of his presence diminishing, blinked, blinked again, found some vision returning, fought with her eyes, searching for some control.

He was gone. Something lifted him up, bulk and all, and threw him a good five feet away. Larry Wolfit lay, a crumpled heap, unmoving, on the hard desert floor. The sound of footsteps. A hand came down and fell gently upon her shoulder.

"Don't touch me, you bastard!"

Not her voice, this was not her voice at all.

"Okay. Okay."

Something familiar. Memories flooding back into her head.

"Helen. It's me," Barnside said. "It's okay now. You're safe."

"Safe?"

She heard herself laugh, and still the voice sounded as if it belonged to someone else. Slowly, with no small degree of pain, her sight was coming back. The dry, dead desert floor, Wolfit's slumped body, all these were becoming real to her now.

"I don't know what the hell's been going on here," Barnside said (sympathy, some kindness in his voice; she could recognize the presence of these things in the world). "But he's gone. I'm telling you now. And we got work to do. It looks good in the farmhouse there. We need you."

Kneeling on the desert floor, a dead man's blood drying on her face, full of pain, her vision a blur, Helen Wagner held up her right arm, rigid, fixed, the muscles taut like steel wire, and said, "Help me up. I can't see yet."

"Yeah," he said.

She took his hand, then pulled herself to her feet, clinging briefly to his big frame. "Wolfit's dead?"

"Oh yes."

"Damn," Helen Wagner said, and lumbered down the track.

55
The Nevada Dome

"You can send your dome people in soon," Collins said. "We're pretty sure it's clear up there."

"No." Her eyes still hurt, but her vision was just about back to normal. "I want you to check the exterior again. We were warned against these people. If they were smart enough to turn someone inside the Agency at Wolfit's level, they're smart enough to play other tricks too."

"That's true," Barnside said, and she couldn't escape the look in his eyes.

"Thanks, Dave. I forgot to say that."

Barnside looked flattered. "You don't need to thank me. It's my job. But I still don't get it. I just whacked one of your most senior guys in order to stop him whacking you. What was some-one like Wolfit doing hooked up with these people? Didn't you guys have a clue what was going on there? Someone at a level like that?"

"I said thanks. Can we start moving now, please?"

"Agreed," Collins intervened. Then barked into the radio.

"And I want to be there when they open the door. Tell them that."

"Sure. I looked at the PCs. They all seem to be working. We

could have done this for you. There's a generator out back, chock-full of gas, could run for another day or so."

"Really." She walked over to one of the computers, pushed the mouse, watched the screen come to life. "And there's no one here?"

"No," Collins replied. "We've picked up some people on the road out. They look promising."

"Charley?"

Collins shook his head.

"So where the hell is she?" Barnside grunted.

"Search me. She seems long gone. And the Katayama guy too."

She pushed this to the back of her head. There was so much fighting for attention just then: Wolfit and the Children, Charley Pascal and Sundog. You couldn't fit it all in. You had to work on some priorities. She flipped open the videophone and placed it on the desk. The little LCD screen sparked, the speaker buzzed. Irwin Schulz looked back at her from the control room in La Finca, Lieberman by his side. Schulz seemed happy, confident. "How you people doing?"

"We've got the base. We'll check the dome in a moment. It all looks good. Everything seems to be intact, not that I've got a link through to the dome yet. But there's nothing wrong with the network here. I can get you on-line to that soon enough."

"That's great!" Schulz beamed.

"How's Charley?" Lieberman asked nervously.

"Gone."

"Oh. In that case—"

"Not now, Michael. Let's take this one step at a time."

She double-clicked the Net access icon on the screen. "These people have got a fixed IP address, believe it or not. Can you come in on top of that?"

"You bet."

The screen cleared to show the home page of Gaia. She reeled off a string of numbers. "Got it," Schulz said.

After about ten seconds image of the Gaia page disappeared from the monitor and was replaced by Schulz's face in a video window.

"You can see me?" he asked.

"Yes. Is that all you need?"

"Absolutely." He turned to look at someone off screen. "Mo? Can you take this over now? Helen?"

"Yes?"

"This will, to all intents and purposes, be our network in a minute or so. If you can reestablish the link with the dome, we can run it from here, straight through your connection."

"You can't see the dome on the network either? I hoped it was just me."

"No. But I can see the command application. Charley must have just ripped off ours down to the last byte. Which is interesting, since we didn't complete that until she was long gone from the project."

"I may be able to fill you in on that later," she said. "But let me get this straight. All you need now is the physical link reestablished to the dome?"

"Correct. From the aerial pictures we've seen, it must be through microwave dishes. If it's been deactivated, the likelihood is that you need to switch it back on physically, inside the dome itself."

"Right?" She looked at John Collins. "Your people up there are okay on this?"

He nodded. "We can't find any reason not to go in. It all looks clean."

She looked at her watch. "Seventy minutes to zenith, Irwin. That give you time?"

"Oh yes. We're working on the program already. All we need is for you to throw the switch."

She looked at Barnside. "I'm going to the dome now. Contact Fogerty at Nellis. Tell him where we are. Tell him we were compromised in some way by Wolfit. He needs to assess that."

"Done," Barnside replied, and started to hit the numbers. She got up from the desk. Her leg hurt. She'd managed to wash some of the gore off her face but she still felt dirty, wounded, and soiled.

"We ought to check you over," Collins said.

"Later."

"Eglin. Hargrave," Collins barked. Two of the HRT team nodded. "You come with me and Miss Wagner up the ridge to the dome. We've had one scare tonight. I don't want any more. The Cobras are out looking for the Children. We don't have the lighting quite how I'd prefer it."

"I don't think that's necessary," she said.

"Well, I do. And security here is my job."

She tried to smile. The man was like a rock. He walked to the door, held it open, and she was glad to be out of the place, out in the cold desert air, underneath the gray curtain, the stars winking. And somewhere out in space the planets queuing up for this celestial dance, standing in line with the high point of the sun.

"Damn," Barnside said as she tripped over a rock, grazed her knee. He helped her to her feet, for the second time that night. "I spoke to Fogerty. He's looking into it. You know, this would be a sight faster if these guys carried you. Or does your dignity preclude that?"

"To hell with dignity, mister," she answered, and heard Belinda Churton's voice behind the words. Eglin and Hargrave came up on either side, strong arms reaching down, lifting her in a cradle movement. Collins shone a big bright flashlight beam up the path, and then the group began to trot up toward the great round specter of the dome that stood against the night sky. The path leveled out at the top. The S&T team was outside the dome on a large, flat plateau, talking to the Bureau team. Her two carriers put her lightly down on the ground.

"Ouch," she said softly. The leg was hurting more now. Collins was right. It needed looking at.

"Boss? You okay?" Jim Sellers, one of the S&T people, peered at her, concerned. "Where's Larry?"

"Later," she said. "I'll be fine. The computer network is ours. We're all on course to get this thing done, Jim. We just need this end fixed. So let's get on with it, shall we?"

"We handle the entrance," Collins said. "No chances."

She walked up to the dome with him. It was bigger than she expected. The Children had thrown a fifteen-foot-high skin around it so that, from the road, a passerby might think it was some kind of water tower. But now that they were level with it the real shape was apparent. The geodesic rose above the fake paneling. It looked natural in the desert somehow, like a pattern on rock, or the skin of a lizard.

"We got the door," one of the Bureau men said. "One big plain padlock on it. You give the word, John, it's off."

"Do it. And nothing personal, Miss Wagner, but while they're at this, we stay clear." He took her arm gently and they walked back to the perimeter of the plateau and stood with Barnside. She glimpsed down. It was a good hundred feet to the farmhouse, the drop almost sheer from this angle. Her vision was back, all the way. The night was clear now, almost magical. It was hard to believe that there was so much pain, so much death enclosed in its soft, dark folds.

One of the Bureau men came up with a huge pair of cutters, attacked the metal fastening on the plain metal double door. It came away in an instant.

"Check for sensors," Collins said. Two men raced to the door, flashlights weaving, instruments in their hands. "Clear," one said.

She pulled out the videophone and turned it on. "Irwin?"

His face came up bright and pale on the screen. "You've done it?"

"We're going in now. We'll need your help understanding this thing."

"No problem. It's just like firing up a generator or something."

"I hope so." Collins had left her, was by the door.

"Wait," she yelled, and walked, half-shambled over to his side. "I want to see."

"Well, who am I to argue? Ben. Those double doors run outwards. You just open them up for us, huh? And then leave it at that. We take a good look inside before we take a step in there."

"Sir."

It was like opening Pandora's box, she thought. Like closing your eyes and waiting for someone to drop some present—good or bad—straight into your hands. The doors came back, groaning wildly in protest, a shrill noise in the night, and a small bell rang in her head: No oil?

The interior was black, opaque, impenetrable. "Lights," Collins said. Barnside walked up with a big field lamp, the sort they'd used around the farmhouse.

"Let me," she said, and took it, parked it straight in front of the door, then hit the switch. She put the videophone on the floor, pointed the little camera on the top straight into the dome. "You're getting this, Irwin?"

"What?" said a small, tinny voice from the speaker on the ground.

"*This.*"

Schulz's voice rang out uncertainly in the Nevada gloom. "I can't see a damn thing, Helen."

"No," she said, staring at the vast, empty exterior. "There isn't a damn thing. Nothing."

No sound came from the little videophone. She picked it up, looked at the white, shocked face there. "It's empty, Irwin. One desk with a PC on it. No transmission equipment. No scan system. No network. Nothing."

John Collins swore quietly under his breath, saw what she was doing, saw she was moving too quickly for them. "Hey. Don't go in there. Not yet."

But she was through the door, staring at this complex structure from the inside, looking at this vast, vacant space, so perfect, so symmetrical. When she was three feet into the dome, the big flashlight behind her casting a giant shadow onto the crystalline pattern of the inner skin, the PC in the corner flashed once, came alive, the screen began to move.

"This whole thing," she said to no one in particular, "was just a blind. Martin Chalk and Vegas. They set us all up. The farm. Everything. Charley's not here. She never was here. It was all just a joke."

With the sky about to fall down on the world, she realized.

The PC beeped and an image of the sun appeared at its center. "So where . . . ?" she wondered, and the words wouldn't form in her head.

"Sensor triggered," one of Collins's team said. "We're sniffing something here, John. Maybe Semtex."

"Shit," Barnside said, and followed her into the dome, peering frantically around, scanning. It was at the apex. The place you looked last. A big brown suitcase suspended from the polygon at the peak of the dome.

"We're out of here," Barnside yelled. "Evacuate down the ridge. As fast as you can." Collins was with him, inside the dome, tugging at Helen's arm. "I'll deal with this," Barnside said, and in one swift movement heaved her over his shoulder, turned, and started to run.

There was nothing in this outside world, she thought, nothing but the bobbing stars, the sound of frantic breathing, and this scrabbling, tumbling descent. Then the night turned to thunder, fire and smoke filled the air, and they were on the ground, coughing, choking, trying to clear the dust from their lungs.

Pain.

Something broken. Someone shouting. Barnside screaming, a long, loud animal howl. Then the sound of rotor blades in the sky, the bright, broad constant light falling from their underbellies.

Barnside's big, strong face came in front of her, looking concerned. "I think I maybe broke your arm. When we fell."

She tried to work out where she was, which way was up. "It'll mend," she mumbled automatically.

The physical world could stop you from thinking if you let it, she guessed. And thinking was really all that was left now. With her one good arm, she pulled the videophone out of her suit pocket, propped it up on the ground. "Give me Lieberman," she said swiftly, as Schulz came to the screen. In an instant he was there, looking troubled, older somehow.

"Michael," she yelled. "You knew this was going to happen."

"I did?"

"Don't fuck me around!"

He looked lost, desolate. "I'm sorry, I just told you what I knew—she's smart, smarter than us, in all probability." Then he went quiet, let her get her head back. When he judged she was ready, he continued. "I got around to some calculations on the receptor dish, based on the video we got from the satellite. I tried to figure out some position for the ground station from the way the dish was moving, where it was pointing. These are really rough, bear that in mind. But she can't be in Nevada. It has to be east of there. Way east, from what I could calculate of the angle of the dish."

"Damn. You didn't tell us?"

He looked miserable, ashamed. "I tried. But then I decided there's precious little point in standing in front of a charging elephant yelling at it to stop. Do you think it would have worked?"

She didn't speak.

"And," he added, "I could have been wrong. I was praying I was wrong, if you want to know."

Finally, she said, "Where is she? Where's Charley?"

"I don't know, Helen," he said slowly. "Really, I just don't know, and I can't calculate that with any degree of accuracy from the data we have. All I know is that it is a long way east of you, and probably somewhat north too. Maybe this side of the Atlantic even."

"Then I guess she just won," she sighed. "We're an hour away from this thing going critical. I guess I just call the President now and tell him we're done here."

"If you feel that's the right thing to do."

"Give me an alternative."

He was struggling with himself, she could see that. "Yeah. I've been pushing an alternative at you all along. Why don't we stop looking where she tells us? And start thinking for ourselves?"

"Fine," she said, and, for the first time, there was some sourness, some defeat in her voice. "I'll tell that to the President."

"Don't bother," Lieberman said. "I'll tell him myself, if you like."

56
Choices

Which he did. They set up a video conference on the system: Clarke at Nellis, Helen in pain on the ground at Cabin Springs, and Lieberman, Schulz, and Bennett, with Bevan watching over their shoulders and Mo Sinclair working the computer, at La Finca.

"Thanks, but I got people breathing down my neck trying to get me to sign executive orders on this one," Clarke said grimly. "If we really have no hope of stopping these people, I don't have much choice. From what I've seen of the damage before this thing peaks, maybe I ought to be doing that anyway, whether or not you people do have any luck."

"We're missing something here, sir," Lieberman said quietly. "If we can just see it, I think we can get back in the game."

Helen kept her peace.

"I'm not hearing the famed science people from the CIA," the President grumbled. "You care to enlighten me on your position right now, Miss Wagner?"

She tried to think straight through the pain in her arm. It wasn't broken, as Barnside had feared, but it damn well hurt. "We have less than an hour before the cycle starts, sir. We also have clear evidence that our operation was compromised.

They're worried, for sure. I guess that's why Wolfit attacked me. But I can't offer any hope that we can get back in the game."

Jim Sellers was punching furiously away at a portable terminal a few yards away.

"We're running the scanning checks as thoroughly as we can," she continued. "But now we're told it could be a long way east of there. I can't get anything out of that. It's too big. We already know there's precious little chance of finding it through digital tracking alone. I can't—"

"Jesus," Lieberman found himself yelling, "do we all just give in that easily?"

"No," Clarke replied. "We've worked damn hard on this one, Mr. Lieberman. People have got hurt. People have got killed, for chrissake. We don't give in at all. But sometimes we just have to cut our losses. If we really have no option except to wait and see what they can throw at us, then I ought to be signing these papers now. God knows, there's parts of the U.S. that could use martial law at this very moment."

"So what's new?"

"I don't have time for the smart-ass remarks, Lieberman."

"I wasn't aware I made one. Sir."

"Hell, get off the line, will you?" Clarke bellowed. "We need people here solving problems, not making them."

"No. You can hear me out. We've all fouled up on this one, me included. And you know why that was? We just didn't think. We treated these people like they were some crazy cult, not equals."

Helen closed her eyes and listened, trying to still the pain in her head. "I don't see where that gets us, Michael."

"It gets us back to where we should have been all along. They've been putting up targets, we've been popping at them. Instead of asking questions, trying to think straight. I mean, what is the proposition Charley's put before us now?"

No one spoke.

"Okay, let me bury myself a little deeper," he continued. "First we tracked these people from San Francisco to San Diego. Then, after a lot of work, we tracked them through Vegas to this place we thought was Yasgur's Farm. Except we got it wrong. This whole thing was just a put-up job to lead us off the track if, by some chance, we got smart enough to detect a track in the first place. It looks like they were doing some Gaia work there, maybe erecting the Web site or something. But the real people, Charley in particular, they were elsewhere, just running some nice little virtual conspiracy across the Net."

"You're not taking us anywhere," Clarke said.

"No? So I ask again: What is the proposition we're being asked to believe now? What is it that Charley hopes we're thinking?"

Helen hugged her bad arm and tried to jog her brain into action. "That somewhere else they have an identical setup to this one, except that it has a working dome. And if we could find that, we'd be back on track."

"Right. And the big question has to be: Is that true? Can that be true? Is it really possible?"

Clarke watched them, waiting for someone to break the silence. "Well?"

"It's a hell of a job," Schulz admitted. "I mean, to be honest, putting together one control room and a single dome, even one with nothing inside it, that must have been tough in the time they had. Putting two together . . . it's possible, of course. But it wouldn't be easy."

"Right," Lieberman continued. "So let's ask some practical questions. Did she buy enough material to build two domes?"

Helen shook her head. "Not that we know of. The company we traced had just the one order. No other company dealing in dome material had anything that could count as a second one."

Lieberman almost smiled. She could see something there. He detected a spark. "Fine. So did she have the equipment to put inside it?"

Schulz made a pained face. "We went through that one before, Michael. This is fairly standard telecommunications, satellite broadcasting kit. If you had the money and the know-how, you could put it together without having to breach any government guidelines or anything."

"Yeah, I know. But this isn't stuff you buy off the shelf of Radio Shack. It's big and expensive. Someone must have kept a record somewhere. So. Did they?"

Helen shook her head. "We have no trace of any equipment purchases in the U.S. or Europe which could match that order. That doesn't mean she didn't get it somewhere else, maybe piecemeal to deceive us—"

"No," he interrupted. "But it does mean she probably never bothered."

"Michael," Schulz said, his voice rising to a whine, "she had to buy it. What alternative is there?"

"You're looking at it the way she wants you to. 'What's the alternative?' That's where she kills us. We know the alternative; we're just not considering it. She doesn't need a second dome. She doesn't need the equipment."

"Not possible," Schulz said flatly.

"It has to be. I don't know how. But that's what we have to figure out."

"If I follow you," Clarke said, a flicker of curiosity in his face, "what you're proposing is that she has some way of tapping into an existing system and running Sundog through that?"

"Yeah. I guess that is what I'm saying."

"Well, can someone tell me how?"

"Not possible," Schulz said emphatically. "No one can talk to Sundog except through the networks we created. Charley could copy that herself; she couldn't just impose it on someone else, not without them knowing, not without us knowing either. It's just not possible."

Lieberman didn't let go. "So, what is the answer?"

"Michael," Schulz said, close to screaming, "there isn't one. There were, as far as we know, only three domes in the world capable of controlling Sundog. No one else has that complete mix of technology, not even Charley herself, if we follow you. And those three domes are down. She did it herself. They're useless. End of conversation. End of story. Roll on the apocalypse, because I'm damned if I know how we can stop it."

Clarke watched the two teams on the monitor. He knew despair when he saw it. They really had run out of options, out of ideas. "I think you made my mind up, folks. You've tried your damnedest but I can't let this go on any longer."

"They're wrong. You're all wrong." Mo Sinclair blushed when she spoke, as if this weren't her place.

"Excuse me?" Clarke asked impatiently.

"She didn't take out all three domes," Mo said. "She took out the one in Kyoto and the one in California. But what she blew up here was the control center, and that's a long way from the dome itself. We were there, Michael. Don't you remember? I don't recall seeing any explosions at the dome at all."

Flames and noise, the helicopter bucking beneath them. He did remember. There was one image that stood out in his memory: the low, flat concrete control center disintegrating in front of his eyes, and a sea of smoke and dust rising up toward the summit of Puig Roig. And somewhere inside that shroud, still golden, still intact, the dome, a good five hundred feet above the destruction.

"Shit," Schulz said, eyes wide open. "We assumed that bringing down the command center took out the dome too. And it does for us. But if she could get a line in there . . . Are you sure?"

Lieberman wanted to hug her. "Yeah. We're sure. We were there."

The President glowered at them all. "Someone want to tell me what that means?"

Schulz said quickly, "If the dome here is still in one piece, all she needs is a microwave run up the ridge and they're in business. She's got the software. She's got the know-how. You don't need to build a damn thing else."

Lieberman closed his eyes and thought of all the activity of the previous day, and the way the soldiers had been stood down, sent home with a shrug of the shoulders as if to say: Game over, go back to base, practice the crowd control. "She's here," he said. "She's been here all along. And we just sent our men away, trailing their guns behind them."

"You're guessing," Bevan said defensively. "This whole thing is just a wild guess."

"Maybe," Clarke said. "But you got less than sixty minutes to find out, one way or another. After that I sign those papers. And God help us all."

57
Zenith

La Finca, 1134 UTC

"I'll go," Schulz said.

"You can't do that," Helen said down the line. "We have to have someone at La Finca who knows this thing inside out, Irwin. We can't spare you."

Mo listened to the conversation and shrugged. "You just need the network brought back on-line, Irwin. I can do it."

"No, absolutely not."

"Irwin," she insisted, "I want to go."

"Mo," Lieberman said, and he knew this battle was lost from the beginning. "You have nothing to prove. Nothing to feel guilty about."

"That's easily said." She picked up a copy of the Unix handbook from the desk drawer, packed a pen down the spiral spine. "I want Annie with me. They know her. She can't stay here on her own, and she may be able to help too."

"These people—if they are there, and that I doubt—could be dangerous," Bevan said. "I don't want a kid around. We're cutting this fine as it is."

"We go together or I don't go at all. They won't harm us. They're not like that."

"But—" Lieberman said, pleading.

"No." Annie walked over, sat on her mother's lap, stared mutely at them all.

Bob Davis, the wiry helicopter pilot, came into the room, glanced at Lieberman, and said, "I've looked and I've looked and this is all we have. One machine pistol. One nice and lady-like little Beretta. You"—he held one of the weapons out to Bevan—"can take the machine pistol, I'll stick with the kid's stuff. I make this decision on the grounds that you are a better shot than me. I hope I'm not wrong."

Annie stared at the gun, eyes wide.

"We won't need that crap," Lieberman said.

"Really," Bevan answered. "I'm trying to regroup some forces from Palma but it's going to take an hour or so. If we do find something, we relay the position and wait for them."

"We can't wait, Bevan. You know that."

Davis looked at them. "The girl's coming? You're kidding me."

"Yes," Mo said. "Anyone else here speak Unix?"

"Oh wonderful," Davis groaned.

He took a set of keys out of his pocket. "Let's talk on the way. This is one old helicopter we're using here and I want it warming up a good two minutes before we attempt to levitate. Ready?"

Lieberman picked up the videophone, got ready to fold out the screen. Helen's face stared back at him. She looked hurt. It was hard to imagine her in pain, in darkness in the Nevada desert.

"Good luck, Michael," she said, halfway across the world. "It's my turn to say that now."

"Yeah," Schulz agreed, toying with the keyboard. "You stay in touch. The moment you get an IP address, you let me in there. We can do this, I believe that."

"I know." He wished he could get rid of the image of Charley's face, wished he didn't feel such foreboding about just the chance of meeting her again. They went out to the dry flat ground of the helipad, climbed inside the purple-covered Squirrel that sat there, alone now.

"Three in the back, one in the front. And you"—the pilot

pointed at Lieberman—"are the front man. I need you to be my eyes. It's hard trying to fly this thing and scour the ground at the same time."

Lieberman climbed into the left-hand seat feeling his guts start to churn already, thinking, all the time, how much he hated these things. Davis played with the controls, the engine whined, and slowly the rotors started to turn. Davis motioned for him to pick up the headset and put it on.

"Only two sets of cans in here, I'm afraid. So the people in the back will just have to lose their hearing for a little while." The machine began to lift beneath them, rise and steady in the hot, unstable air.

Lieberman hit the talk button. "Irwin? You hearing me?"

"Yeah," said a distant tinny voice.

"And Helen?"

"Yes." It sounded as if they were the same distance away, both trapped in some remote digital universe. "So what am I looking for? Dishes?"

"Absolutely," Schulz said. "Maybe just one. Maybe several. It depends where they're based and what the terrain is like between them and the dome. This is line-of-sight. And they don't need to be big either."

"Right."

Helicopters and computers. These were, he was fast beginning to realize, his two least favorite things in the world. "Irwin? You think they've been piggybacking off our network for some time?"

"Makes sense, if they tapped into the link. Even when we had control, we only used the network when we needed it. They could have used dead time, then locked us out when they decided to take control. Could have been messing with it for weeks."

Lieberman shook his head. "I still can't believe you wouldn't notice someone building an alternative microwave link up to your dome."

Schulz sounded touchy. "Really. Well think of it this way: If they have the protocols, and Charley seems to have taken them with her, all they need to get through is a dish the size of a satellite TV antenna. You tell me how easy that is to spot up there. And you're looking for it. Which we never were."

"Point taken." Lieberman watched the big mountain rise up in front of them. The dome was hidden from this angle. On the seaward side of the range, pine forest ran green and uninterrupted all the way to the water's edge, not a building, not even a track in sight. Davis passed him a large-scale map of the island. "You work it out," he said. "Where are these people supposed to be based? In a building? In a cave? Or what?"

Lieberman pressed the transmit button. "Irwin, what do they need to run a control center like this? Power, obviously, but lots of space too?"

"Just what you saw here at La Finca. What they had in that place in Nevada too. We built that big command center on the mountain underneath the dome because that was handling traffic from Kyoto and Lone Wolf on top of everything local and we did some R&D there too. That was like the server for the whole system. But if they're just dialing in, all they need is room for ten or so workstations and a line-of-sight microwave setup."

He still couldn't picture it. "I'm trying to think of the kind of place we're looking for."

"Michael, you're looking for Yasgur's Farm, surely. Only the real one this time."

And then it came to him. He could almost see it. Schulz was right. Creating this simulacrum in the desert of their real home was just the sort of joke Charley would like.

"Fly to the top of the peak," Lieberman said, letting go of the talk button. "Let's check our base assumption first."

The machine rose sluggishly in the hot, thin air. The day was bright and cloudless, the sun relentless. No interference. No shocks. More proof, if you needed it, Lieberman thought. Charley kept the island clear of attacks for practical reasons. If she blasted La Finca, she could be blasting herself. The helicopter cleared a low col, spiraled upward, and, with a sudden lurch that left his stomach in midair, they crested the mountain. He looked down on the dome, and beyond to the blackened hulk of the command center. He nodded at Mo in the back, then hit the talk button. "The dome's perfect. Not so much as a crack in the skin."

"I guess we were stupid," Schulz said. "Look for someplace within range where they could site a dish, Michael. The angle on the receptor at the dome is fairly shallow. My guess is they must have the last antenna at three thousand feet or more. Which means they probably have a line of dishes running back to their control center. No one's going to find a place to build a base at that altitude without us knowing."

Lieberman scanned the horizon through a pair of binoculars and glanced at the chart. The seaward side of the range had to be out. There was no obvious place for a base, and the forest was too thick. But on the landward side, the terrain ran away into a complex formation of sharp, dramatic valleys and long, bare headlands, tumbling all the way down to a plateau at around a thousand feet.

"Think about it," Davis said, holding the helicopter in hover. "We know they're not on the seaward side. We know they can't be on the island plain—that would be too public and the distance would probably be too great."

"So they're somewhere in that mess," Lieberman said, looking at the rolling, tumbling landscape in front of them. The machine dropped suddenly, lurching to one side. Davis struggled with the controls, brought it back to straight and level.

"Sorry. Turbulence."

"My." Lieberman stifled a gastric burp. Then he put the glasses to his eyes once more and surveyed a rocky spur that stood a good eight hundred feet beneath the summit of Puig Roig. "Close in on that."

The helicopter moved forward, starting to descend. "Got it," Davis said, and Lieberman found himself envying the pilot's eyesight. Even with the glasses, it still looked like a gray blur to him.

The machine moved swiftly to close the gap, then Davis put it into hover thirty feet away from the rock face. The dish had been disguised, a little halfheartedly, with some brushwood. Lieberman pulled out the videophone, pointed the lens out of the front of the helicopter.

"This look right, Irwin?"

"Yeah," the remote voice replied. "Where is it?"

"About half a mile southwest of the dome."

"Got to be more in the line, Michael. There's nowhere to run a base close to there. Look for the receptor antenna. It's like a smaller dish, with a rectangular box in it. Where that's fixed on the thing, that's lining up with the next link in the chain."

"There," Davis said instantly. It was to one side of the main antenna, pointing down, back into a narrow valley. The helicopter turned away from the mountain and began to descend through the huge cleft in the rock.

"You know where we're going?"

"Just like a treasure hunt, old man." Davis grinned. "One clue leads on to the next."

They watched the dark, narrow valley come up to greet them. The shadows embraced the little metal machine as it fell. Abruptly, the interior of the aircraft felt cold. Lieberman turned around, watched Bevan mutely hugging the weapon, Mo holding Annie in her arms.

"You two okay?" he said. They nodded.

"Don't throw up, Michael," Annie said.

"Hadn't even occurred to me."

"There!" Davis was pointing to another dish, half-hidden in a small clump of scrubby pine.

"We're still nowhere near something that looks like a base," Lieberman said. The helicopter bounced up to the rock face, stopped ten feet from the dish, Davis peering at the thing, looking for a pointer.

"Like I said." Davis smiled. "It's a treasure hunt."

And then the Squirrel dived again.

"WHY NOT?" Joe Katayama wouldn't let this one go. He was annoying her, there was no escaping the fact.

"Because I said so."

"Eve just left. Everyone else is gone now. It's just you and me. If something goes wrong, if they do find us, they could turn this around."

"Joe, Joe." The dope was in her head, she could feel it, but that didn't make her weak or crazy. If anything, it strengthened her, made her sense what was happening more effectively than ever. "Have you forgotten why we're doing this? Not to harm people. Not to harm the world. For Gaia. And she's with us. You can't feel that, I know. But you have to believe me. It's so."

"I believe we risk jeopardizing everything by leaving this system open. Give me the code, Charley. Let me set the program in stone, then destroy the dish link. That way no one can touch it."

"And no one gets to see this through, correct any errors along the way."

He made a sour face, sat down next to her wheelchair, and folded his arms. "Charley, if this is about being scared. . . ."

She closed her eyes and let out a long, pained sigh. "Scared? Joe. I am the woman who's turning the world on its head. I don't know how much blood is on my hands. Do you think this is because I'm scared?"

"I need the code. Please. Give me the code."

"It's time for you to leave," she said icily. "I don't need you anymore, Joe. Go. With my love. With my respect. Don't push this any further. I wouldn't want those things put in jeopardy."

And you don't know how to do it without me, Joe, do you? she added silently.

It was suddenly plain to her. For all his skill, for all the work he put into setting up the fake dome, getting hot-wired into the real one, Joe was lost on the network. Without her, he could only watch.

"No. You're not a god, Charley. You're not always right. There's something happened in your head that means you don't see straight anymore, and I can't allow that. We have to go through with this, all the way, and we have to make sure no one stops us."

"You have no faith. You have strength, Joe. You have a terrible strength, like men do. But you have no faith. And in the end you're as stupid as the rest of them. You should go now.

You don't understand those figures coming in about the storm. It's erratic. It's changing. I can't just leave it alone."

His cold Asian eyes watched her. He was quiet, and in this silence Charley Pascal tried to remember: Where did Joe appear from? And failed. Her head was running down into oblivion, like a clock unwinding, like a child's toy with a failing battery.

"Yeah," he said unpleasantly. "Stupid." Then got up and walked for the door.

"It's your time, Joe!" she yelled.

Katayama walked over to the corner of the room. "What the hell are you doing?" Charley screamed.

"Something you can't, Charley."

Rage, red rage.

"Fuck you, fuck every last part of you!"

He stopped, looked back at her over his shoulder, and for a brief moment she felt afraid. "You crazy bitch," he said quietly. "Just stay there, dying. If you want a shit from now on, crawl to the can on your own. I don't carry you anymore. Understand?"

"Joe?" The old Charley, good Charley, scared Charley, watching the last person she would ever see in this world walk out of the room, a fog of seething anger around his head. "Touch that fucking system, Joe, and I'll see you in hell, I promise that. You leave those things alone."

"Yeah," he grunted, going out the door. "You come make me." And was gone.

Charley Pascal wanted to scream, wanted to curse this iron frame that trapped her. But her thoughts felt messed up, the world wouldn't stay upright. Her head began to spin.

Somewhere overhead, soft and repetitive, was the beating of rotor blades, getting louder, getting nearer, falling from the clear blue sky like ghostly rain.

It looked like a miniature version of La Finca. When they got to the end of the line of dishes, down in the heart of the val-

ley, still a good fifteen hundred feet above sea level, they found
Yasgur's Farm—the real one, Lieberman knew that immediately. It was accessible only through a single dirt track and
stood in a meadow of parched yellow grass, the odd poppy waving blood-red out of the soil. Golden stone, a four-square barn
of a house, with a few farm buildings at its periphery. And no
sign of life. No sign it was anything but deserted.

Davis peered at him.

He stared at the pilot and said, "It has to be." Then turned
to Schulz and Helen on the video screen. "We think we've
found the place. We're going down."

"Michael," she said, "take care. We can't get in support for a
good twenty minutes or so."

"Yeah." He tried to smile. Then the Squirrel bobbed and
wheeled, descended to the ground in a cloud of dust, and, with
a solidity Lieberman adored, found its feet on the dry grass in
front of the house. He pulled the cans off his ears, turned to
Mo. "You and Annie stay behind us. We don't know what we'll
find here. We don't want you in the way until we need you.
And when we do need you, it has to happen fast. You have to
establish a network link straight through to Irwin, and he can
take it from there. Right, Bevan?"

"Right." He looked younger now, less confident. Maybe he
was scared, just like the rest of them. Lieberman popped open
the door and jumped down into the dry, thin air, took a couple
of deep breaths, praying for his head to clear. The light was too
strong, the day too hot. It felt like they had landed in an oven.
Davis and the others joined him, staring at the house.

"Company," Davis said. And they watched the tall, lean figure of Joe Katayama walk toward them, then come to a halt six
feet away, between them and the house. He stood still, arms
folded, staring with cold, quizzical eyes. Lieberman looked at
every inch of this big, powerful man and thought: He's un-
armed. Davis stood, tensely playing with his weapon, and
Bevan watched this small drama unraveling, nervous too.

"Joe," Mo Sinclair said behind them, and Lieberman could
hear Annie let out a low, quiet whimper of fear.

"Hey, listen to me. We're going in," he said to the imposing, still figure. "This thing has to end now."

"No." When his big head moved slowly from side to side like that he looked wooden, like a statue, not quite human. "You're too late. The zenith's nearly here. And we burned the link after we set the program. It's all gone now. You've got no pathway up there. You've got no hope. Like the woman said: *Prepare.* Now, why don't you go tell your bosses that?"

"Right. Well, that sounds nice and sensible. But you don't mind if we check for ourselves, now, do you? And me and Charley, we go back some—it would be a shame to come all this way without saying hello."

"No, you can—"

"Mummy!" Annie's shriek brought Lieberman's head back down to earth, back from this image of the sky, dancing, wheeling, aligning, that filled it right then. A shadow passed in front of him, something following it. Mo was walking toward Katayama, her back to them, her hands out from her sides, fingers stretching, saying, "No, Joe, it's okay, Joe. . . ."

And Annie, screaming, ran behind, catching up fast.

"Hey." Lieberman touched Mo's hair briefly. "Let's all stay cool. Okay?" And didn't feel cool at all (this is some form of redemption, the inner voice said, this is Mo paying herself back).

"Joe," she said, so close to him, a hand reaching up touching his cheek (a cold cheek, Lieberman thought, seeing, in his head, the picture of the girl with the snapped neck on the Web, and registering these big strong hands). "We were wrong. Wrong. Can't you understand that? All of us. And when you get out of this place you'll understand that, you'll see it was just our closeness that made us crazy like this. We lost perspective."

"Perspective," he said, and in one swift movement reached forward, pushed Mo aside, snatched Annie by the hair, twisted her around with a single violent blow, and from somewhere there was a gun at her throat, the barrel glinting silver in the dazzling sunlight.

"No . . ." Mo said, scrabbling on the ground, close to sobbing (tears of rage, Lieberman thought, tears of fury).

"Shut up," Katayama said calmly. "You fucking people. You

get back in that machine. You get out of here. Leave us alone. You understand that? And when this is over, when we see what's done, then you come back for her. If you can."

Annie was tight in his grip, not struggling, eyes wide open. Flesh on flesh, flesh on metal, and the sky bore down on them all, like a heavy golden weight on their shoulders.

Screaming (no words, nothing you could understand), Mo Sinclair rose from the ground, took hold of his giant, muscled hand, and then tore at it with her fingers, tore at the tendon (the shield goes down, Lieberman thought, this is the way this big, cold man is thinking just now), her body was pulling him away from Annie, the silver shape moving, Annie ducking, getting free from his grasp, and behind the animal gasp of Davis's labored breathing.

Then Lieberman was pushed aside by the small, frantic figure, gun rising, these figures moving so slowly in the hot, meager air, like puppets dancing on strings, limbs jerking, mouths agape, all fear and fury. A sound, like the cracking of a whip. Then a second, different in timbre, from another direction. He looked at Katayama, who was exposed now, his shield had escaped, and slowly, with the agonized motion of broken film running wild through the mechanism of some ancient projector, a small red dot appeared in his cheek, grew, became a livid, pumping rose, the color of blood, the color of flesh, then opened, like a window into his head.

Someone screaming, Annie, racing back, not caring, not minding. And Mo Sinclair, slumped to the ground (two shots, he thought, two different sounds), a dark, intense stain spreading across her cheap white T-shirt, bubbles of blood appearing at her mouth.

Look.

You look, Charley. This is your doing. Not mine.

Look.

He ran over, was by her side, not knowing what to say. Annie was weeping, shaking uncontrollably. The red stain covered most of Mo's chest now, and it was alive, something pumped strength into it from inside her, stealing away her vitality by the second.

Her eyes rolled, so white, so open. "Annie . . ." Her mouth was filled with blood, dark and pulsing. Hands trembling, Lieberman shook the videophone free, flipped it open, yelled for backup, yelled for a doctor, and didn't even wait to hear the answer. Bob Davis knelt by him, touched Mo lightly, touched her wrist, tried to hold the girl off.

"Be careful, Annie," Davis said. "She's hurt. You mustn't make it worse."

"Where the hell did he get the gun?" Lieberman yelled, his mind racing. Ellis Bevan stood behind them, ashen-faced, looking scared. Lieberman joined Annie, kneeling by her side. "Hey," he said, holding her hand. "You just keep calm, now. We can get help in here. We can call someone on the radio."

"No time," Mo said (the blood bubbling, boiling over her tongue, her teeth, her voice thick with the viscous blackness there). "Michael, go. . . ."

"We can carry you," he mumbled, astonished at the flatness of his own voice.

"No," Davis said, looking gingerly at the wound. "We can't move her. It's too dangerous. She has to wait here for the doctor. It's the only way."

"Michael, I'm cold. . . ." Her eyes were losing their light, her skin seemed paler, thinner, and Annie howled, screamed and howled (in this place, Lieberman knew, you go mad, everything disappears, gets stripped from your soul). Mo's thin arm, the walnut tan already looking lifeless, came up slowly; a hand, a single finger, went to Annie's face.

Michael Lieberman closed his eyes, wished himself out of this nightmare, wished himself anywhere else in the world. Then felt her fingers close on his.

"Annie," Mo said (voice so thick, Lieberman had to work to follow her now). "You have to help Michael now. You have to leave me, go with him."

"Mom," Annie whispered, her face long and ashen, and they could feel her grip weakening, the life draining out of her.

He watched all this from some distanced, remote part of himself, and knew then that your mind goes crazy watching someone die. You go to some space, some part of the world where nothing is real, where a voice inside you screams: *Take me, take me.* But there was no way to change places, one life for another, even if he thought it the cheapest deal in the world to make. He watched Annie in her agony, watched Mo slipping away into the dark, his consciousness dwindling into this single, searing focal point of suffering. It was like kneeling in a golden, roaring ocean of heat and light screaming silently around them all.

"Michael," Davis said (his voice coming from outside this world they had entered). *"Michael?"*

He opened his eyes, looked at Mo Sinclair's prone frame, her colorless face, eyes closed, chest scarcely moving.

"I can't handle this on my own," Davis said. "The medics are on their way. There's nothing we can do here."

"Annie," he mumbled. She held her mother's hand, eyes closed, softly weeping. "Annie. She's right." He scarcely recognized his own voice. "We've got to do this. You've got to help me try."

The girl said nothing. He felt like a jerk. Ellis Bevan was over by Joe Katayama's body, searching through the pockets.

"Did you find anything?" Bob Davis asked him.

"No," Bevan replied, scanning the horizon. "There could be more of them. We should bear that in mind."

"I don't think so," Lieberman said. You could feel, from Katayama's presence, what kind of role he had in this place: one of strength, one of enforcement. "They're gone. If we're going to do this now, we've just one more person to see."

Annie watched Davis place his jacket over her mother, watched the small movement of her chest, wiped the tears from her eyes with her arm, not sobbing anymore, not trying to avoid this sight. She looked at Michael Lieberman and took his hand.

"I can do it," she said.

CHARLEY PASCAL SAT IN THE WHEELCHAIR, eyes unfocused, drugged maybe, Lieberman thought, and said, "I'm sorry about your mother, Annie. We're creatures of the dark. We all live in agony. You get to know that as you grow older, you get to understand its taste in your mouth."

Annie tapped away at the keyboard, pausing now and again to wipe her eyes.

"Spare us this, Charley," Lieberman said. "You've done enough."

Davis stood by the door, not letting go of his gun. Bevan was beside Charley, watching her like a hawk. And how much damage can a crippled woman do? Lieberman wondered. Ask someone in Kyoto. Ask those people struggling for life as this wall of heat and poison sweeps across the world with the sun. Ask Annie and Mo.

He propped the videophone on the desk by the side of the monitor, watched Annie typing away, and prayed for the thing to work. Slowly, hesitantly, the system made some contact with the outside. Schulz appeared, a little indistinct, Helen, even more shaky, in an adjoining window.

"Annie?" Schulz said, puzzled. "Where's Mo?"

Lieberman pushed himself in front of the camera. "We don't have time, Irwin. Mo's been shot. They're calling for the medics now."

Schulz looked as pale as a sheet of paper. "Oh my God—"

"Irwin," Lieberman said, close to barking. "We're here. This is your play now. You try and get in through the front door."

"Sure. I'm sorry. All I need is the IP address. Do you know what that is, Annie? How to get it?"

"I think so," she said quietly, moving at the keyboard, watching the screen.

"What happened, Michael?" Helen's flickering image asked, the concern obvious on her face, even through this less than perfect picture.

"Later. We're behind. Let's just work on this, okay?"

"You look—"

"*Later!*"

She was silent.

"Try it now," Annie said.

Schulz seemed preoccupied for a moment, then beamed back at them. "I think you did it, Annie." They could hear the sound of the keyboard clacking down the line. "Right. We're there. Well done. In a moment, the network's ours."

Lieberman watched as the girl buried her face in her hands. Then the big monitor cleared, lines of geek commands scrolled up and down too quickly to read, and Schulz and Helen came up again, in separate windows, looking a little less flaky this time.

"What next?" Lieberman asked.

"The key," Schulz said. "She's put her own password on it, probably just an ordinary word, except it's encrypted so we can't read it directly from the system. Just give it to us, Charley. We can get it anyway. Save some time here."

She sat in the wheelchair, not worried about this, Lieberman thought, just waiting for the celestial dance to do its stuff.

"Don't be ridiculous, Irwin," Charley said. "Why should I do that?"

"Because we need it," Lieberman said. "Can't you separate what's going on inside your head from what's happening out here? This isn't some dream; these aren't shadows of your imagination. These are real people. This is a real world."

"I know that," she said sourly. "I worked that out a long time ago."

He shook his head. She looked a little scared, he thought. Maybe there was a chink of light somewhere inside still. "No you didn't, Charley. You just saw what was happening inside yourself and thought this was some kind of mirror image of what the rest of us deserved. Well, you're wrong, and if you thought about it you'd know."

"Still letting them fool you, Michael. Such a waste."

"This isn't Berkeley circa 1971, Charley," he said. "Quit dreaming."

"Go to hell."

"I'm there already, I don't need directions. Also, I don't need you. Helen?"

Her head nodded on the screen. "He's right. This is a standard Unix-based password. With the technology we have in

Langley, and you're hooked right through to that now, we can blast our way through every one of those in a little under forty-five minutes. So you see we will get it. You won't stop us."

"Go ahead," Charley said.

Lieberman looked at Helen on the screen and didn't say a word.

"Why do you fight this, Michael?" Charley asked. "If it wasn't us, it would have been someone else. This is Gaia working. It has to happen. We can't carry on like this."

He stopped staring at the computer and wondered if it was worth pleading with her. But there was craziness in her eyes, a dead, fanatic certainty. This illness, and whatever else it brought, put her beyond that kind of appeal.

"Michael," she said, "this is crazy. You should be thinking about rebuilding this world after the storm blows over. You could lead them."

"Jesus," he yelled. "Where did you get this from? Peace and love and corpses? Are you really still stuck in that vision? What do you think comes after this? Eden?"

"If that's what we want."

"Bullshit! Bob? Where the hell is that medical team?"

Davis was going through the door already. "I'll chase it."

Lieberman looked at Bevan. All Bevan's confidence had disappeared. He was shocked, and scared. "You too, Ellis. See what you can do for Mo. I can handle this."

"Sure," Bevan said lamely, and was gone.

Lieberman shook his head. There were too many images there. Mo's agonized face. The world winding down, like numbers flicking through the code program on the screen, so quickly you couldn't even recognize them. As this celestial ballet began in the sky, he felt drained and dead.

"We will get that code, Charley. But you could give it to us. You could do that for yourself, as much as anyone else in the world."

"Just wait . . ." she said (and closed her eyes, saw the planets wheeling in space, felt this force moving within her).

"No. You're wrong. Sure, you can push those buttons, burn the earth badly right now. But what we all wake up to tomor-

row isn't some new age of enlightenment. It's just human beings getting hurt, getting scared. You're worse than the people
you hate, Charley. You're the dinosaur. Not us."

Helen was staring at him from the screen and he didn't need
words to understand the message. The monitor wasn't sparking
with hits the way it should. Something was wrong.

"You can feel things, Charley. Things the rest of us can only
guess at. Don't tell me you can't feel that too." She wasn't listening, he guessed. She was holding tight on to the arms of her
wheelchair, eyes closed, face taut with pain.

"I need my medication. They're on the desk."

"Right." He nodded. "What kind of pills might they be?"

She stared at him. "You'll give it to me? Is that meant to be
some kind of a deal?"

He shrugged. "No. You know me. I hate deals." Then he
walked over to the desk.

"Michael?" Helen said, a taut note of concern in her voice.

"You heard. She needs her pills." He handed her the bottle
without looking at it. She took it, opened the cap with shaking
hands, poured several capsules into the palm of her hand.

"Thanks. You always were a good guy, Michael. That's why
people take advantage of you." She looked at the pile of capsules, took a deep breath, put them in her mouth, then swallowed hard. He watched her struggling, took a bottle of mineral
water from a desk nearby, gave it to her to drink.

"Michael," Helen said, voice rising from the monitor.

"Thanks." Charley was looking at him, her face full of pain,
so much older than he remembered. "You can't get it, you
know."

"What's that?"

"The password. I'm not so stupid that I'd leave it open to
some dumb number-juggling app like that. You're wasting your
time. That's why she's squawking at you. Don't you know
that?"

"Hey"—he shrugged—"I kind of guessed. It was worth a try,
though. We're desperate, Charley. What do you expect me to
do?"

"I told you. Think about what comes after."

"Sorry. That's the kind of crap that got us here in the first place. 'Catch a falling star . . .' "

"And put it in your pocket . . ." Charley said, a lazy, drunken smile on her face.

"Annie?" She looked at Lieberman with old, tired eyes.

"You did well but I don't need you anymore. Take Irwin off-line, will you?"

"You mean," she asked, puzzled, "cut them off?"

"Yeah. Just from the line to the satellite. I still want them to be able to talk to us."

"Okay," Annie replied, and hit the keyboard.

"Michael!" Helen's voice sounded shrill and piercing from the tinny speaker.

"Don't fret," he said, and sat down next to Annie at the adjoining PC.

"What's going on?" Schulz asked nervously.

Lieberman looked at their pale, exhausted faces. "Are you having any luck?"

"I don't think so," Helen admitted.

"I thought not. Annie?" She was calm, but he knew what she wanted.

"Your mom will be proud of you. You go to her now."

It had been a long time since he'd punched these particular keys in anger. He kept getting things wrong. And it was years since he'd designed those big solar wings now hanging over the world.

"What are you doing?" Charley asked, her voice a blurred smear.

"Remember. Lone Wolf around 1982. You were there. You recall that too?"

"No," she drawled, a line of taut anxiety behind the slurred voice.

"But you do. And you know something? Maybe there is some kind of god around. Because yesterday, and I didn't even know it at the time, something came back from that time, and I didn't even know it until right now."

Sitting by the sea at Half Moon Bay, on a warm July afternoon, the two of them happy (this was when they were just friends, colleagues), full of the confidence and optimism of youth. Shading their eyes and looking up at the sun, thinking how they could help everyone by putting a piece of silicon and metal in the sky to leech a little of its power and make the world whole.

"What do you recall of that time?" he asked absentmindedly, working at the keys.

"Naïveté. Dumbness," she said.

"Yeah," he muttered. In his mind's eye he was back with their old selves then; he could see them, bright-eyed and full of enthusiasm, arguing about the right lock to put on the system, the mot juste that would keep it safe from prying eyes.

He turned and looked at Charley. "You remember."

"I don't know what you're talking about," she answered, some dim form of fury behind the statement.

He looked at the screen and it was like peering at a past picture from his life. All Schulz's stuff was state-of-the-art visuals, like a video game made for the military. But back in the eighties, when he and Charley had been putting the satellite together, the original one, it was just command-line material, string upon string of impenetrable, inconvenient codes that brought forth impenetrable, inconvenient responses. It amazed him the way they still lived inside his head.

"What are you doing?" Charley said icily.

"The right thing," he said, and watched the screen clear, throw up one single question: PASSWORD?

It was a playful argument on the beach that day, one that amused them at the time, trying to find a lock for the bold, brash scheme that would give mankind a nice little push into space. And they both came up with the answer, kept it secret between the two of them, knowing that there was nothing more apposite under the circumstances.

He typed in the word: PHAETON. And closed his eyes.

Dumb kid, hapless kid, stupid kid, he thought. But, hey. The moron was a trier.

Charley had used something to lock this new system up, and even though the situation wasn't the same, was full of black poisonous toys they had never envisaged back then, it was still appropriate.

"It heard you," Schulz squeaked out of the monitor, sounding like a teenager. "I saw the screen. Dammit, Michael. It heard you!"

"Yeah," he answered softly, and wondered why there was something like shame hanging around the back of his head just then. Some of the old Charley was still there, he guessed. It made her lock this new, bright, fiery Sundog with the same key they used on the old one, the good one, as if it were some kind of incantation, full of a deep, mysterious power.

"I can take it from here," Schulz said. "Just plug me back in."

"I know that." Lieberman wasn't looking at anything but the screen. "But this is my baby, Irwin. Mine to play with." He was typing furiously now, astonished by how much came back to him.

"Michael," Helen said very firmly, "what are you doing?"

"I remembered, yesterday. Out of nowhere. Or maybe out of somewhere. I wouldn't care to guess. What do you think, Charley?" He turned to look at her and it was like staring at someone on the point of death. Her face was gray and lifeless; her eyes had lost that bright Charley spark.

"Don't, Michael."

Lights started to move on the monitor. Familiar windows began to appear.

"We can take it from here," Schulz repeated.

"I heard you the first time. Like I said: This is my baby. You just get that damn helicopter here."

He looked at Charley. Her head was in her hands. "Correction. Our baby."

Schulz watched what was happening on the screen and said, "Michael, no. . . ."

From somewhere, Helen was yelling, loud, angry, and more than a little scared.

In under thirty seconds it was done. He watched the confirmation codes come through. Then he walked behind the desk, found the power cables, ripped them out of the wall, relished the dying hum of the hard drives spinning down into stillness, the silence that was descending on the room.

"You didn't listen," Charley said, her eyes almost closed now. "The god's not out there. It's inside us. Inside everything. The earth most of all."

"Didn't I?"

"No," she said drowsily, eyes half-closed, some softness in her voice that reminded him of the old Charley. "And no devils, Michael, you never did understand that. There are no devils. Only the ones we make ourselves. We make our own crosses. We hammer in the nails."

"Yeah," he muttered, looking at the distant shape of Annie, who was now out in the yard with the pilot, both of them crouched over the still, small figure on the ground. "I wouldn't argue with that."

"I don't want to see this," Charley Pascal said. She grabbed the wheels of the chair, tried to push, and lacked the strength.

"Where to?"

"Over there. My bedroom."

He pushed her slowly toward the door, and recognized the white, plain room and the part it had played in the deadly little drama he'd watched in horror on the Web. She wheeled herself inside, turned around, and watched him reach for the door. Charley's face was bloodless. Her eyes were wet.

"Don't hate me," she said.

Lieberman looked at her, then turned around without speaking.

The monitor was dead and gray. The job was done. Somewhere high above them in space those giant wings were wheeling into a new position, opening their eyes to stare the sun straight in the eye without blinking. And whether it worked or not was really beyond him. This was the final act. Time and the storm growing in the sky had taken everything else away from them.

He left Yasgur's Farm, strode out into the burning sun. The day was like a furnace, no wind, no oxygen in the air. You could be on another planet, he told himself. You could be in hell.

He walked over to Mo Sinclair, a still form in the blazing heat, the red on her chest drying to a dust-caked ocher that moved almost imperceptibly with each faint breath.

"We need the medics right now," Davis said, and looked at the sky. It was the color of gold and empty. Bevan was scanning the horizon desperately. "We can't just wait out here like this. I think we ought to get her out of this heat."

Annie touched her mother's hand. It was dry and cold. Lieberman bent down, picked up Mo's body in his arms, lifted her off the ground, and began to walk, slowly, carefully across the dusty ground, letting the thoughts run out of his head like water overflowing from a pail. Davis and Bevan watched and stood beneath the sun, waiting for the sound of blades to cut through the day.

In the darkness of the barn, the air hot and swimming with flies, he laid her on a bed of straw, not looking anywhere except her face (which is where the soul resides, a stubborn memory told him that; the rest of you, the blood, the physical mechanics of your body were all, somehow, irrelevant).

They sat down next to her on the soft, brittle straw, watched the world outside through the stone doorway, a rectangle of burning light, getting brighter, more intense by the minute. Annie touched his hands, held both of them together, in a shape that was so close to prayer. The air grew thin; the buzzing of the insects gave it a febrile, relentless power.

Zenith.

An odd word, he thought. Like an incantation from some occult rite, or the secret name of God. Too small, too weak to describe this celestial alignment that stood above the head of the world, bore down on it with all the dead, heavy weight of the stars. There were no words for this, only the relentless, surging beat of the universe, pumping through your blood, hammering on the walls of your skull.

In silence, clutching each other for comfort, they watched the day turn to fire.

TWO MONTHS LATER . . .

58
The City

Lieberman remembered so clearly the last time he walked into the St. Francis Hotel. It was for the small, uncomfortable reception after the wedding, with relatives and people from Lone Wolf standing around, sipping warm wine, looking at each other, and saying, without speaking, "This won't last, this won't last." And he had gazed at Sara, so happy, not letting this thought get anywhere near her head, knowing they were right.

It sat on Union Square, like a beached ocean liner, the shoppers and the tourists mingling around outside, blocking the sidewalk, tripping over each other. Except that this time there weren't so many. He walked across the square unobstructed. The change in the economy that followed the storm had rolled through into everything. There weren't so many buskers, playing bad jazz and blues, waiting outside the Gold Coast Bar for the spare dollars of people wondering whether to brave the queue for Planet Hollywood.

Recovering.

That was the word of the moment. It popped into his head the first time he went to see Sara, still in bed at home, taking longer to mend than anyone had expected, looking as if her color was returning, slowly. In a month or so, she'd be back at work, trying to put this strange event behind her, trying to forget the occasional pains, the memories (trapped inside a falling shell that looked like a giant insect's eye, and that bright searing light, gold and fire, that seemed to accompany everything to do with Sundog).

People are good at forgetting, he thought. They have to be. No one can walk through life feeling the scars of existence—of death and personal loss, the constant round of interior agony— every day. We all need somewhere to put this legacy of grief out of sight, not quite forgotten, just hidden, for the times when it's needed as a reminder of just how fragile this daydream really is.

Recovery wasn't just an idea for Sara. The world was adjusting to the notion too. The solstice had scarred the earth and its people, not in the way Charley Pascal had hoped, but there was pain and there was injury all the same. The sky had ceased to be something anyone could trust. A fissure had opened beneath the solid rock of certainty that underpinned the human state.

The damage had been real and unmistakable. The most dramatic part had been in Asia, before the storm rose to its full height. Thanks to the odd team that had assembled at La Finca, the livid power of the syzygy had been leached by the time the zenith rose in earnest, somewhere past the Prime Meridian. It had been spiraling downward when it reached the East Coast of America with the break of dawn, and dwindled almost to the level of a bad solar storm when it reached California. There had been serious damage to telecom networks. The financial system had stayed in disarray for weeks. People saw their pride dented, found it hard to accept that the world wasn't as firm and certain and controllable as they had hoped.

But there had been no more ball lightning after Vegas—this was truly Charley's creation, and, he guessed, she'd been saving it for America all along. The casualty toll ran to tens of thousands, but few were in nations where the native language was CNN, and Lieberman knew (in that old, cynical part of him that he tried to keep quiet these days) what this meant. It all lost some of its importance. Before long, some statistician was wheeling out the numbers from the last flood in Bangladesh, the last earthquake in China, and saying, *Hey, in the great swing of things it doesn't add up to much at all.* There weren't many dead in West Kensington or Gramercy Park, Nob Hill didn't catch fire, there was no earthquake in the seventeenth arrondissement. They'd even reopened part of Vegas and started to promise the new Strip would be so much better than the old one. *What's the problem?*

He went up to the twenty-first floor using the old elevators at the front of the building, stepped out almost straight into the arms of a big man who looked as if he were made of rock. Gray suit, gray face, the earphone of a walkie-talkie shoved in his ear, a bulge in his jacket pocket. And peering into Lieberman's face with a curious look that could almost have passed for jealousy. "Professor Lieberman?"

"Yeah." He felt out of place in his jeans and faded denim shirt. It had been cool outside, a touch of rain. That was nice. He'd walked through the rain all the way from his apartment, almost twenty-five minutes, and was conscious of looking a mite bedraggled. He didn't care. It felt good to be damp from that delicious rain.

"Miss Wagner is waiting for you."

They went down the corridor, the plush red carpet giving way beneath their feet like the pelt of some dead animal, then walked into a suite. She sat on her own at a big table in the center of the room, shuffling through some papers. When he came in she stood up, smiling wanly, and he knew right away what both of them were thinking.

"You want me here?" the big man asked.

"I can handle this, Dave," she replied, in a voice that sounded somewhat strange. It had lost its harshness, the edge of anxiety he'd come to know.

He watched the giant shape disappear out the door and said, "You get your own bulldog with this job too?"

"Dave's quite a guy. Saved my life. And a lot more besides. Took me a while to realize how much."

He felt uncomfortable with the way she was looking at him. "Hey, I know. We don't look the same now that we're not postage-stamp pictures on some damn computer monitor."

She nodded. He was right. He looked stronger, fitter than she had expected. She extended a long-fingered hand.

"Straight to the point, Michael. I imagine I should have expected no less of you."

"I guess not."

"Do you want a drink?" she said, looking at the cabinet in the corner. Bright, smart eyes, watching him all the time. Women like this could be hard to be around after a while.

"No thanks."

"I'm going to have a Scotch. It's after six and it's been a long day. Are you sure you won't join me?"

He shook his head. "Thanks, but no. I'm taking a break right now. I did some drinking on credit before. I got a couple of free years before I have to go back and do it all again."

"Ah." An expression he recognized, and it typified this woman: quiet, polite, noncommittal, standing back, taking a good look before leaping in. Not the Lieberman style at all.

She walked over to the drinks cabinet and poured herself a sizable glass of Glenfiddich, then dropped a couple of ice cubes into it. "You may need it."

"Really? No, I don't think so." He joined her back at the table, trying to convince himself this wasn't some kind of contest. "You summoned me."

"Did it sound like that?"

"Yes. Exactly like that."

"I'm sorry. I was curious to see you. Didn't you have the same feelings?"

"I've a lot on my mind, Helen. Finding work. Rebuilding some kind of career beyond freelance academic assignments. I learned my lesson there. That life is too damn dangerous for me."

"I gather Sara's fine."

"You checked?" They never really got out of your life. He should have known that.

"Yes. I went to see her. Didn't she tell you?"

"No."

"She seems to be making a good recovery. In a while she'll be back to normal."

"'Normal,'" he repeated. "Now, there's a word."

"She also understands our position."

"I guess that's why she never mentioned your visit." He tried to mask his disappointment, and knew he should have expected no more. When you got down to it, this was the CIA.

"Michael . . ."

"Let me guess. Now it's my turn too."

"It's important for us to make sure we have control over what is and isn't known about Sundog. A lot's in the public domain already."

"A lot?" he asked, wide-eyed. "I have been looking, you know. It's all just crazy conspiracy theories. *X-Files* stuff. No one's close to what really happened."

"I know. We originated a lot of what you call '*X-Files* stuff.' It suits us."

"Nice job. Nice business."

"No," she said quietly. "It's not nice. Some things aren't nice at all. But they are necessary. They have to be done. You thought that too, didn't you?"

Lieberman shuffled in his chair. He guessed he knew this moment had to come. "Meaning?"

"Meaning thanks to you we don't have that thing in the sky anymore. Whatever you did with those solar panels made sure of that. The government is several billion dollars the poorer. You mind telling me how?"

He shifted on the chair and tried to smile. "It's dangerous playing with fire, you know. Turn this mirror a few points too far, open up those delicate little panels, and"—he snapped his fingers—"kaboom."

She let out a thin laugh. "An expensive kaboom."

"I made it, Helen. It was mine to unmake. If you like, I can try and pay it back in installments. Once I get a job."

She took a sip from the glass. "You scared the life out of me. I wondered what the hell you were doing."

"Thinking. Remembering."

"Thank God someone was. They can build it again, you know. All those pieces in space don't mean a thing. It will be bigger, it will be better, and it won't have some secret little password you and Charley dreamed up all those years ago. Why the hell did she use that?"

He could still remember Half Moon Bay. And how that old, old story popped into his head over a beer on a bright, burning day in Mallorca. "Because it was appropriate. Deep down the old Charley was still there. I know you don't like that idea, but it's true."

No, he told himself, she doesn't like that idea at all. "We were lucky, Michael, damn lucky."

Luck. An odd word under the circumstances. He wasn't sure he believed in the concept of luck at all anymore. "They will build it again someday, I know. We don't learn. It's our big failing. You know what makes me hate this most of all? There's a part of me says Charley was right. This is a big, screwed-up world, and we're the ones who are screwing it up. And maybe it won't end, ever. Maybe we just carry on with this agony for as long as we hold the keys to this place."

"That part of you is mistaken."

"Really? You know, it seems like years ago that I looked at you and pointed out that it was maybe some similar syzygy that wound up wiping out the dinosaurs. Do you ever get to wondering whether maybe we just replaced one set of dinosaurs with another or something?"

He looked at her glass. It was almost empty. "You're in danger of drinking too much."

"I'm over twenty-one." One more sip before she said what she had to say. "I'm sorry we couldn't have got the medics there sooner, Michael. They had all sorts of problems to contend with."

"Yeah, I know." Mo's dying face still came to him sometimes, but he couldn't blame anyone except Charley for that. He ranted and he raved on the dry, dead ground, screaming at the sky, staring into the golden nothingness as if he could pull something out of it that would make Mo Sinclair live again. But he'd known all along that this was futile, some dim, dark ceremony he had to endure. "It wouldn't have made any difference. There was nothing any of us could do."

"She was a hell of a brave woman."

He didn't want to talk about this. There was nothing useful to say.

"And the girl? Annie? I know you brought her back here."

"You do keep tabs, don't you?" he grumbled. "She's in good hands. A nice local babysitter for the evening."

There was a noise from behind him. "Wrong there," said a big, booming voice.

He turned and saw Tim Clarke standing, smiling, by the connecting door to the adjoining room. Behind, in what looked like an enormous suite, was a bunch of busy people mingling around PCs and fax machines.

He looked at the President and said, "Excuse me?"

"Hell." Clarke beamed, walked over, took Lieberman by the hand, pumping his arm up and down vigorously. "Come here." They walked over to the adjoining suite. In the corner of the next room, head bent to a PC, Annie was watching a small black kid play some kind of adventure game. "She's just having some fun with Benny," the President said. "It's good for him. A kid doesn't get much fun in the White House, particularly an only child. And good for her too."

"Isn't that kidnapping or something?" Lieberman asked quietly. There was something here he didn't like. Clarke was looking him up and down. The man, in the flesh, seemed more intense, more human than he did on the box.

"I thought it might make sense for you two to have a chat afterwards. On the way home."

"So why am I really here, Mr. President?"

"You don't like small talk, do you?"

"Not in situations like this."

"Good. I can approve of that. Helen?"

She closed the door on the adjoining office and picked nervously at her hair.

"You ought to congratulate her," Clarke said. "You've got the next director of the CIA standing next to you. Fired the present incumbent today and I'm ashamed to say I enjoyed it. Time to ring some changes around here. Sundog told me that at least. Subject to approval, of course, not that it will be a problem— I'm popular in Washington right now for some strange reason. A woman running the CIA, a black man in the White House.

This is turning out to be an interesting century, don't you think?"

Lieberman's head was reeling. "Hey, I'm a scientist. Don't expect me to understand this stuff. Helen here is the boss?"

"Sure," she said. "And Barnside—the bulldog, as you saw fit to describe him—is going to be my deputy."

"Wow. Nice cop, tough cop act, huh? You've convinced me already."

"If you like." She nodded. "And you're wrong on one point. You do understand what's going on very well. Without you, we'd have been lost. You were fast, you were incisive, and you had a good broad spread of the issues and the subjects we had to face."

"Yeah. I'm a repository of half-baked information."

"More than that," the President objected. "You're straight too, Michael. And that matters. That we can use."

He wondered about that drink and then rejected the idea. "I've been used enough for one lifetime, thanks. I don't want to sound ungrateful but I'd like to take Annie home now. It's getting late."

Clarke put a huge hand on his shoulder. "Hell, she's helping Benny zap aliens. And boy, does that kid need help. A little while longer, huh?"

"Right. So, Mr. President, again: What do you really want?"

"You. I don't care where you put your office. In Langley. Next to me. You can be attached to my staff or Helen's. We got in this mess because we're inventing stuff without even stopping to think where it leads, and you can make sure that doesn't happen again."

Helen put down the empty glass. It now looked like a prop in some play he was only just beginning to fathom. "You said it yourself, Michael. How could Sundog have got that far without someone realizing the implications? Why didn't we see the syzygy issue earlier?"

"Yeah. But that's me. I criticize everything."

"Fine," Clarke said. "Play the devil's advocate for us. Come to Washington. We'll fix up accommodation, schooling for Annie. The pay's good too."

"This is my city. I love it here."

"Sometimes you have to move on," she said. "I think this would be a good time. For both of you."

He wished she weren't looking at him like this. As if it mattered in more ways than one. She could turn on the vulnerability in a flash, and he didn't know whether to believe it or not.

Clarke was not ready to let go. "We need to learn. Science is great. Science is good for us. But all of a sudden it's just so big, and no one tries to get the whole picture. Why the hell didn't we build your solar satellite? I don't know. Maybe there were good reasons. Maybe not. But if we don't start learning along the way, one day all this clever stuff will bite us. Almost did this time. These things we invent right now are so huge we can't afford to screw up. We don't have anywhere else to go. Good or bad, this is the one planet we have."

"I think," Lieberman said slowly, "the Children would have agreed with you there."

"Sure. And why not? I don't mind saying it. In some ways they were right. Not in the solution they proposed, naturally. But the analysis, parts of that are just plain common sense. It's a delicate balance and we've been managing it badly."

"No, no, no." Lieberman shook his head and wished he were out of the room. "This isn't me."

Helen opened her briefcase, took out a pile of neatly stacked reports, and pushed them over the table. "Sundog isn't the only case we have on our hands that is a little, shall I say, problematic. Read the files, Michael. Just do that for me. Then think about it. Talk to Annie. We have the President's plane leaving in the morning. You could be on it. Both of you."

He looked at the documents, saw the seal, the red classified warning. "If I read these, I don't have a choice, now, do I?"

"Yes," Clarke said immediately. "You can pull out and you'll never hear from us again."

He stared at the papers and tried to wash away his curiosity. "Thanks."

"No," Tim Clarke said, extending his arm. "Thank you."

It was like shaking hands with a bear. Then the President got up, headed back for the adjoining suite, Helen following him.

"Michael," he said at the door.

"Mr. President?"

"If you read that stuff, then just go home to bed and shrug it off, we really have got nothing to talk about. Understand me?"

59
Decisions

"He beat you, huh?"

Annie's eyebrows popped up her wrinkling forehead. That look of indignation and outrage could have come straight from her mother. "He didn't beat me," she said, loudly enough to attract the attention of the three diners in the Fog City Café, watching the clock pass through midnight, toying with their food. "I let him win. There is a difference."

"Well, the kid does live at the White House. I guess you've got to cut him some slack."

She looked at him—fondly, he thought. They never spoke about what had happened, never even talked about the future. Maybe it was for fear of destroying this small piece of calm and sanity that sat in their lives like a fragile toy, ready to break if it got too much attention.

And yet . . . time was ticking away between them already, and the toy never became any less fragile. Annie didn't worry, not on the surface anyway. He had come to understand that. Instead she replaced anxiety with some still, mute form of acceptance. As if she were made for the world to mess around with as it liked.

"I think they offered me a job," he said, and marveled at the way the contents of those damn files kept reeling through his head. Helen certainly knew how to get his attention. Annie shrugged as if she knew this already. Her mother again. Always seeing through things.

"Are you going to take it?"

A little circumspection wouldn't go amiss in the Sinclair family genes, he thought. "It's not a simple decision, Annie."

"No?"

This was crazy. There was some central tenet inside his life, he guessed, that made him want to treat everyone he met as an adult. It was a matter of courtesy, and it was ridiculous too. Annie was a kid, and much as he hated the idea, kids didn't prosper in a democracy. You needed to teach them. You needed to show them the way.

"Annie, we have to talk about this sometime. We've been running from what happened, and that was right then. But not now. We've got to think about the future. You're a kid. You need things I know nothing about. Like a school. A home. A family."

Her face lost years, became defenseless, impossibly young. Back to a child again, right away. And it was just the idea of thinking things through that did this. "It'll be fine. In the end."

Annie flashed her eyes at him, Mo in there somewhere. "And besides. I never really knew a family."

Except the Children, he nearly added for her. And no one would be putting them forward for the good parenting award.

"I can go to school, can't I?"

He sighed. "That's not the point, Annie. It's a question of suitability. What kind of a parent would I make? And your mom still has her parents in Scotland. Maybe—"

"Scotland!"

Here come the tears, he thought. He could see the heads turning in the restaurant, out there at the periphery of his vision. But she wasn't crying. She was just pale and stone-faced. She got used to rejection after a while and he recognized that process. After a while it all became just a low, familiar pain, like a toothache.

One big silence, so big you could pour the universe into it if you felt like it.

"If that's what you want," Annie said eventually, staring at the tablecloth.

"What I want?"

He put his hand on hers, looked into her young eyes. "Of

course it's not what I want, kid. It's a case of what's best. You've got a life ahead of you. What the hell do I know about preparing you for that?"

"As much as my mom did."

"No!"

She didn't back down, just glowered back at him over the half-eaten food. "What happened to your mom was awful, Annie. I don't just mean the end. Everything. She got the roughest deal of all, and I doubt anyone could have coped with it better. For most people—me included—it would have been a whole lot worse."

She blinked and there was a tear or two there. "Do you mean that?"

"Of course I do. I'm not in the habit of lying, in case you hadn't noticed. It gets me into trouble all the time."

Annie brushed something away from her face with her arm, half-grinned at him crookedly. "She said that about you. On the first day, I remember. She liked you, Michael."

"You don't need to sound so amazed."

"That's okay."

"For what it's worth, I liked her too. She was something special. To go through all that and keep such strength, such closeness to you. That was quite an achievement."

A question hovered in her head, and Lieberman remembered the way Mo would pry this from her, so gently.

"You want to ask something, Annie?"

"What would have happened?" she asked hesitantly. "If she was still alive? Would you and her . . . you know?"

"For a while. Then I would've got scared and run away. And left you both feeling miserable and full of hate. There. I told you I made a bad liar."

Her eyes looked liquid again. "Why?"

"Because that's what's inside me. It's big and black and empty, and whenever something comes close that could fill it, I get scared. She scared me that way."

"Oh." She toyed with some food on her plate, not eating it, just wondering whether she could pluck up the courage. "And I scare you too? That's why you want me to go?"

"Annie . . ."

The voice was a touch too loud, he knew that, heads were beginning to turn, and he didn't give a damn. "You want the truth? The truth is there's some crazy voice inside me saying we ought to stay together. Try to make this work. Like some kind of family."

"That feels bad?"

"No! I like it. It makes me feel grown-up. It makes me want to face up to things. And that's the problem. It clouds my judgment too. Is this the right thing to do? I don't know. All the selfish stuff crops up, muddies the waters. And sometimes I get to thinking . . ."

You had to say it, he told himself. Being a family is about sharing these feelings.

"I start to think we could heal each other in some way. And we both need healing. We don't talk about that. It's like a taboo subject. But that's the truth."

"I know." Annie had never mourned, never cried, really. They'd just gone into this silence together, found this escape route, which, he kidded himself, was about practicalities like money and dealing with the immigration people. It wasn't. They were just running from the memories.

"And these are just dreams, Annie. Just dreams. Things in your head."

"What's wrong with things in your head?"

"They don't come true."

"Never?"

It could have been Mo talking, Mo puncturing his vain little certainties. He laughed, felt foolish, closed his eyes, and let this small moment of epiphany settle down, like a film of sparkling dust, upon his consciousness.

Somehow, out of nowhere, he'd thought of Phaeton that day, sitting in the little Spanish café, his head full of stuff that wouldn't go away. If he'd been Charley, maybe he'd have thought this did come from somewhere else. This was Gaia, saying things had gone a little far the other way, with Semtex Charley and the Death Ray from the Sky. That maybe there was still the chance to set a little balance into the equation.

Dreams did come true, but not on their own, not like something out of a fairy tale. They needed sweat and pain and people committed to them. Sometimes there was a terrible cost along the way. And just knowing that punctured the uniform, measured world he'd come to take for granted these past forty-three years. All the linearity and logic that ran through it, all the staid, accepted common sense that said the dead stayed dead, these things were an illusion, a flimsy fabric over some inner reality that evaded you, skipped away from your sight, like a shy deer fleeing the hunter, like the ghost of an image, half-seen at the corner of your eye.

This rigid set of beliefs inside him were all part of one vast lie. Or maybe a smaller part of one greater truth. Either way, in the end, this was a dumb, rigid straitjacket of literalness that strangled you, told you just to wait in the corner, sighing in the dark, until the last day. Until there was no breath left inside you.

"'More things in heaven and earth, Horatio . . .'" he muttered.

Annie blinked. "Excuse me?"

"Shakespeare. God, you need an education. I'll take you to the theater sometime. You'll like it."

He shook his head, searched for some money to pay the waitress, who was hovering a few feet away wearing that "Are you leaving soon, sir?" look. "They want me to go and work for them in Washington. Some kind of job, a big job. A house stuck out in the Virginia woods somewhere. A school for you. Jeez, I'd need an au pair or something."

"A what?"

"Someone to look after you. When I'm not there."

She made a little smile. "That could work."

"Yeah? You don't know me. If she was ugly I'd get offended. If she was beautiful I'd make a pass. Either way we wind up in agony."

She gave him a look that bordered on condescension, and he knew he deserved it. "Michael, I don't mind being looked after by someone else. I sort of expect it. I am growing up."

"And there's a thought."

"Maybe you should try it too," she said, blushing at her boldness.

"God, your mother has a legacy. You don't have a choice. I'm an adult. I do. That's what the word 'adult' means."

The waitress came back with change and an expression that almost held open the door. "Yeah," he said gruffly, "we're going."

Annie smiled at her. "He's nice, really. Just a bit grouchy at times."

"You're telling me, honey," the woman muttered, and started to clear the table, looking in disbelief at the miserly tip.

Outside, the night was getting chilly, fog was creeping in from the bay. The air stood damp and salty, not moving anywhere in a hurry. Annie linked her arm through his, just listening, wondering.

"And what's more," he yelled at nothing in particular, down the length of the street, down the switchback hill, with its cable-car track and the solitary drunks and lovers of the morning stumbling along the sidewalk, "I like this place. It's my home."

They walked back toward the apartment, and she didn't listen after a while, just let him ramble on about the city and his life, and how this was so, so difficult. Then, when they got there, Annie said, "What's it like? Virginia?"

"Green. Full of trees. Mile upon mile. You can't walk anywhere without stepping in raccoon shit."

"Michael!"

"Sorry. I apologize."

She stopped on the doorstep, looked up to the third-floor window of the tiny rented apartment. "Does it rain there, Michael?"

"Incessantly. They don't have roads, they have canals. Third-generation locals get born with webbed feet. It's horrendous."

Annie smiled at him. "I've never lived anywhere that rained a lot. Have you?"

"Not that much. Hell, no." Rain, Lieberman thought. Now,

there was a thing. Feeling the dampness seep through your scalp, watching it make the grass green, make the world alive.

"Interesting," she said.

He peered at her, and felt a little drunk, even though there wasn't so much as a beer inside his system. "Annie. Do you think all that stuff's true? About me growing up?"

She mulled it over. "It's up to you."

He made a little smile. "Yeah. Your mom would've said something similar."

"I guess it can't be that bad, then."

"No." A thought. It lit up his face with an enthusiasm that made her want to laugh. "Hey. They got this new plane for the President. A new Air Force One."

"So?"

"He said, if we were ready, we could fly back with them to Washington. Right now. Today."

Annie's eyes grew wide. "Wow. In Air Force One?"

"Yeah. Well . . . ?"

"You're the grown-up."

"No, but I'm working on it." He put his key in the door, felt it turn, and was satisfied. He did have a choice. Of a kind. "Here's the deal," he said, stepping into the narrow, gloomy hall, thinking this place wasn't so great after all, he wouldn't even miss it. "You pack. I'll make the phone call."

"Yeah!" She raced for the stairs.

Too fast for him already. He knew that, just watching her take the steps two at a time. She'd be going to college when he was pushing his mid-fifties. He might not live to see her kids. Life was so cruel, so complex and unforgiving. Sometimes it just made you want to curl up and lie on the ground, wondering at the dead weight of the generations that surrounded you, going back, going forward. All of them expecting something, all of them asking: *What about us?*

He hesitated in the gray, empty ground-floor hall, and wondered at the pictures, the memories, running through his mind. Helen Wagner and the Pandora's box of files she'd passed over the table. The big, complex, friendly figure of Tim Clarke, vast hand extended, ready to jerk you out into the great wide world the moment you touched it. And, bigger than all of them, the sky on fire, casting its fierce, burning light on Mo's face, still with death, in the shadowy interior of an ancient, run-down barn. This was an image carved deep inside his head, omnipresent, always waiting for some kind of an answer.

"Michael?"

He couldn't miss the thrill, the anticipation inside Annie's distant voice as it echoed around the bare, soulless interior of the apartment block.

"Coming," he said, then took a deep breath and began to climb the stairs.